BOOKS IN THE DRAGON THIEF SERIES

SEASON ONE
Dragon Thief
The Chicago Job
The Poisons Book Job
The Vault Job
The Femme Fatale Job
The Scavenger Job

SEASON TWO
The Crown of Kingship Job
The Green Scroll Job

THE DRAGON THIEF
SEASON ONE
OMNIBUS EDITION

DRAGON THIEF

KAT SIMONS

T&D PUBLISHING

The Dragon Thief
Season One

Contents

As always, for my family.

The Dragon Thief Series

Dragon
Thief

Bestselling author of the Cary Redmond Series
Kat Simons

DRAGON THIEF
BOOK ONE

***One magic thief, one dragon shifter,
and a whole lot of deadly mayhem…***

Myra has made many mistakes in her life. Breaking into a dragon king's hoard… Not one of her most successful mistakes. As a thief with a touch of magic, though, she adores a good challenge. Unfortunately, the dragon king adores a good repayment for damages done. Not that she even stole anything! They caught her before she could.

But no one argues with a dragon king. Do the job for him, or suffer the consequences.

The job in question… Steal back the dragon king's son.

Myra never suspects when she reluctantly agrees to the king's terms that the youngling she's sent to rescue will turn out to be a sexy hunk of a dragon shifter whose deep voice and outstanding height push all her buttons. Or that her night will turn out so… interesting. Or that escaping his kidnappers will toss them into a deadly race against time.

But Myra loves a good challenge. Especially an interesting one.

CHAPTER ONE

Who steals a dragon?

Myra had stolen a lot of things in her life. Jewels. Magic objects. Money. But a dragon?

Even she wasn't that brazen.

Yet, here she was, breaking into a high security building the middle of downtown Manhattan because someone else had the stupid idea to *steal* a dragon shifter. Just... Myra wasn't even sure what to call it. Hutzpah. But that felt too complimentary. Gall felt too weak. Idiocy maybe? Idiocy seemed like a good word.

She felt like a bit of an idiot, too, for allowing herself to get roped into this.

But she supposed this was what you got when you messed with a dragon king.

She crept silently from the closet where she'd used an untraceable, and disposable, laptop to hack into the building's security system and disable the motion sensors along the routes she needed. She'd also set the security cameras on a loop so they wouldn't record her activity. The guards outside her destination were going to be a little trickier, but according to the schedule she'd found in the security records, they'd be changing in less than ten minutes which gave her a tiny window of opportunity.

She just had to get into the locked room. She'd be getting back out again through a route that bypassed those guards.

If all went to plan, she'd get in, get the dragon king's son, and get out again without anyone being the wiser. His kidnappers would walk in to discover an empty room, and it would take them a week to figure out how it had all happened.

But that was if all went to plan.

Unfortunately, in Myra's experience, things rarely went to plan.

She waited in a corridor where she could see the guards outside her destination, but hear the changing guard coming in. There would be a moment, when they stood outside the antechamber exchanging codes and information. Not long. Forty-five seconds maybe. But that should give her enough time to pick the lock and get inside.

The sounds of the approaching guards had her gut tightening and a small smile played across her mouth. She did love her job. Even the anxiety was a rush.

Using a little touch of magic to disguise herself—hiding her scent and any visual cues that might give her away to people used to working with shapeshifters—she waited for the guards inside the antechamber to step out and speak with the incoming guards. All of them were large, three men, one woman, every single one dressed in a pants suit, except one of the men who wore a kilt. She admired the fashion sense in what would otherwise be a pretty matched set of individuals.

She snuck across the hall behind them, relying on her magical screening spell to keep herself hidden, then paused just inside the antechamber and listened. No alerts. No one had heard her.

So far so good.

Hurrying to the locked door, she pulled her lockpicks out from inside her multi-pocket vest and knelt down. It wasn't a complicated lock. Mostly there for show. What they had inside couldn't be contained with an ordinary door lock.

She finessed it in fourteen seconds, without even having to use a magical push, and slid inside, quietly closing the door behind her. She relocked the door from inside, just in case someone thought to test it. Then she held perfectly still, her ear to the door, listening as the new guards settled into place with a minimum of conversation.

When no one sounded an alarm, she took a deep breath and turned to face the room. Smiling. One step down. Now the important part.

The room was a large, bare, concrete box. The floor, the walls, even the ceiling just bare concrete. No paint or decoration. No rugs or carpets. No wood. Nothing that would easily burn. There were no windows either, even though the room was located on an outside corner of the high-rise.

The door she'd come through was "wood" on the outside, but inside it was obviously solid steel. From this side, it looked like a vault door. A vault door with a shitty and useless lock, but still pretty solid.

It wasn't the lock that was keeping the occupant inside the bare concrete room, though.

No. That was the chains.

Because the lights in the room were very low, barely above nightlight for visibility purposes, she heard the chains before she saw them. The dragon king had warned her those would be there. She came prepared. Still, hearing the chink chink against the concrete floor gave her a little shiver. Poor kid.

She didn't dare speak until she got closer, because while the guards looked like ordinary humans who relied on more mundane forms of security, they were guards used to working with shifters and might well be shifters themselves. She didn't dare tempt their hearing. She was only confident they wouldn't pick up her scent because she'd disguised that to open the door.

They weren't the only ones used to working around shifters.

She wasn't one herself. Just a garden variety thief. With the right kind of magic to make that job infinitely more fun. But when you went in to steal a certain grade of collectibles, it did put you in the way of shifters as well as other members of the magical community.

Myra didn't mind. She liked the challenge.

Though, as she crept closer to the hunched form opposite the door, huddled under what looked like a thick blanket, she decided dealing with dragons who could breathe fire and crisp her in under a second was not the kind of challenge she wanted to repeat in the future if she could at all help it.

She stared at that hunched form under the blanket as she approached carefully, wondering if the kid was okay since he wasn't moving. She had no idea what to expect from the dragon king's son. She hadn't even been shown a picture. Something something, no pictures of royal family taken, something something. Hadn't made sense to her, but whatever. The dragons could do as they liked. She was just told the stolen shifter was the king's son. And he wasn't being held for ransom or anything normal like that. Apparently, there was some other nefarious plot afoot. Which the king had also not seen fit to explain to her.

And that was fine, too. She didn't need to know what the kidnappers had in mind for the king's son. She just needed to know where he was so she could get him out. Steal him back, so to speak. Then she got the dragon king off her back for their little misunderstanding, and all would be right in Myra's world. She could go back to stealing what she wanted to steal.

The hunched form remained motionless as she neared. She was

pretty sure the little guy would know she was here by now, because even though her spell to confuse shifter senses was still in place, she suspected a dragon shifter, even a young one, would just *feel* someone in the room with them.

Not taking that into account was what had gotten her into trouble with the dragon king.

But the closer she got to the king's son, the more she worried. Was he okay? The king said he was young, but hadn't said how young, and her imagination conjured images of a shivering, shaking, terrified child trying not to show just how scared he was as he huddled underneath the blanket.

When she was close enough to whisper without being easily overheard by the guards, she murmured, "Hey, it's okay. I'm here to get you out. You don't have to be scared of me. I'm a friend of your dad's. I'll have you out of here and back to him soon."

The hunched form finally moved a little, so Myra stilled, giving the boy time to adjust to her. She didn't want him to accidentally fry her with a blast of fire he couldn't control because of fear.

But as she watched, the hunched form got larger and larger. And now she worried he was trying to shift inside this concrete room on the fortieth floor of a high-rise building.

That would be really really bad.

"Listen, don't shift. Okay. There's not enough room." There were innocent people in this building as well as the thieves. She did not want the place brought down by a youngling dragon shifting and destroying half the building in the process.

The form unhunched completely as a very deep voice said, "I'm not an idiot and neither are they. I can't shift, even if I was stupid enough to do it."

Myra blinked a few times. That voice sounded very...adult for a kid.

She blinked a few more times as the hunched form tossed off the blanket that had been covering him.

Uh.

That was no youngling kid.

Chapter Two

The fully grown adult man sitting on the concrete floor was a revelation to Myra, having been under the impression she was here to rescue a child. And wasn't that the last time she took a dragon king's phrasing at face value.

"Youngling my ass," she muttered as she approached the man. "Do not fry me. Your father did send me."

"Why you?"

"Because I'm an excellent thief," she murmured as she got close enough to inspect the chains.

And close enough to get a good look at the king's son.

He wasn't what she might call ordinarily handsome. The messy dark hair and blue eyes were pretty conventionally attractive, she supposed. But his features were too broad, and heavy, and maybe a little too sharp. There was a scar across his jaw, under beard scruff. And another across his forehead.

He looked a little worse for wear, and not just because his button-down shirt and dress pants were rumpled. He looked like he'd been going a few rounds in the shifter fight club.

No, not conventionally handsome, like his kingly father. Definitely not pretty.

But all of it together—his broad face and messy hair and scars—really…worked for him. He didn't need ordinary handsome. He had something more, something compelling that was…

Frankly, a little distracting.

She couldn't afford to be distracted right now. Breaking magic binding chains took a very special sort of concentration. And they only had a small window of time to make this work.

"I've had my fill of thieves over the last few days," the dragon muttered. There was a rawness to his voice, like he hadn't had anything to drink recently.

"You'll be rid of me soon enough," she said. She pulled a bottle of water from one of the myriad pockets in her vest and handed it to him.

He stared at the bottle for a long moment.

She waved it at him and held his gaze. "Just water. No spells. I'm a thief, not a wizard. My magic doesn't do poison or anything like that."

"What does your magic do?" he asked as he took the bottle.

She smiled a little as she looked down at the cuffs on his ankles and the one on his wrist. "Makes locks into puzzle toys," she murmured.

The cuffs keeping a fully grown dragon shifter captive weren't things to be taken lightly, of course. These were made from some of the best quality steel she'd ever seen, infused with a copper alloy that held the magic, which raced over the surface of the cuffs in a swirl of purplish-blue light. The cuffs were attached to chains with links as thick as her forearms, and those were bolted to the floor by more thick, fused metal with lines of magic swirling through it.

So, not easy. But also, not outside her skill set.

A little rush of adrenaline-fueled excitement moved through her as she pulled out her lockpick case again.

"Why can't I smell you?" the man asked.

"Spell. Lot of shifters around." She had most of her attention on the cuffs, but his voice sounded less raw so she assumed he was drinking the water she'd given him.

"But you're not a wizard?"

"No wizard magic. Just thief magic." She grinned at him. "Don't worry. I'm a good thief."

"Is that why my father sent you?"

She winced inwardly. "Mostly."

"What does mostly mean?"

"Shh. I have to concentrate." She returned her attention to the cuffs, and her leather lockpick satchel as she selected her tools.

"No one shushes me."

"Maybe they should. You're not very good at it." She pulled out two long, thin picks, then set her fingers against the ankle cuff. Shook her head. Replaced the two picks and pulled out another two. Yes, those would do.

"I'm a king's son and a dragon shifter. No one shushes me."

She let out a deep, impatient breath and met his gaze again. "Listen, do you want out of here or not?"

"I want out of here."

"Then hush. I have to focus. And we only have so much time."

His eyes narrowed, but he didn't speak again.

"Finally," she muttered. Then she set to work on the locks.

Not her best time. The ankle cuffs took a little more finessing than she'd hoped and there was a moment there when she actually worried a little. But still, in under ten minutes she had him completely free and was setting the magic infused cuffs gently aside.

"Don't burn anything, and don't shift," she said as the man stretched his legs out and gave his body a big shake.

"I'm not an idiot," he said, glaring at her.

"Just have to make sure. Dragons…" She waved her hand in the air and hoped that explained everything.

From the way his gaze narrowed further, she assumed it hadn't. Or he was just unhappy with the explanation.

Either way, they didn't have time for her to sort through his grumpy facial expression. "Can you stand? Do you need help?"

She had no idea how long he'd been chained in place, and the chains weren't long enough to have allowed for a wide range of movement. He'd been taken a week ago. If he'd been chained in this spot for all that time, he would probably be pretty sore and stiff.

"I can stand," he said, giving her a condescending look.

She snorted and shook her head. "Lot of smugness for someone who went and got themselves stolen."

She stood back while he climbed to his feet, using the wall behind him to push upward. She collected his empty water bottle from the floor so he wouldn't have to bend down again, and slid the crumpled plastic into one of her inner pockets for later recycling.

His full height was something to behold. She wasn't what one might call tall. In fact, she had to stretch to reach medium. He, on the other hand, was… Well, tall was an understatement.

And that was going to complicate things.

She scowled. Glanced back at the door. No one seemed to have noticed them yet, which was good. But her escape plan had just taken a hit.

"Your dad should have warned me you weren't a kid," she muttered under her breath.

"He implied I was a child?"

"He called you a youngling." She faced him again, moving close enough to make sure they could speak quietly. He wasn't as stinky as she'd have expected after being held captive for a week in a concrete room. Little ripe, but not the sort of pungent sweat and fear stench she'd have expected. "Failed to give me your name, too. Lot of 'my son' but not a lot of name usage. What's your name?"

His expression was hard to read when he stood so much taller than her. How had he hunched in on himself enough to look like a kid when she'd walked in? Must be a lighting thing. And no that wasn't a flutter in her stomach because she adored tall men. That was…nerves. Just nerves.

"Christopher," he said, his voice deep.

Did he sound irritated? She thought he sounded irritated. But she didn't have time to deal with his irritation. "Listen, Chris—"

"Christopher. I don't like Chris."

"Fine. Christopher. My plan for getting out of here was predicated on the fact that you were…well, small. And since you are not small, things are going to get a little cramped. Are you claustrophobic?"

He shook his head. "But if you're thinking we can exit through the air ducts, they have motion sensors and alarms in those. It's not a viable option."

"Are you the thief here? No. I'm the thief. Trust me. I have that part covered." Questioning her bona fides. How rude. "And we only need the air ducts for a short section. Can you squish yourself up enough to do this? I don't have a plan for going back through that door without it bringing all the security in the building down on us. And that would be bad."

More than bad. It would be suicidal. The kidnappers knew how to contain a dragon or they wouldn't have gotten Christopher here. They'd know how to stop him trying to escape in an obvious way. The whole reason *she* was here was to sneak him out without anyone knowing until it was too late. So front door with the handy guards who would raise an alarm was not an option.

"I can manage." He didn't sound particularly confident, but he wasn't arguing with her either.

Good. She hated when the loot argued with her.

"You good to go now?" she asked. "All the blood returned to all the various body parts?" For reasons she refused to acknowledge, mentioning his body parts and blood flow made her stomach flutter again. Weird.

"I'm fine. I can manage."

"Groovy. Let's go."

If he'd been the child she was expecting, she'd have taken his hand. But since he wasn't a child and there was all this stomach fluttering stuff going on—nerves, just nerves about the plan getting complicated—she motioned him to follow her instead.

And tried to ignore the feel of all that muscle and heat just at her back.

Chapter Three

The air duct was located high on the wall, near the ceiling. And of course, the screen wasn't just a simple, easily removable screen. It was thicker metal than the usual vents, and it was locked into place. But it hadn't been massively reinforced with complicated locks and stuff either. After all, there were supposed to be motion sensors in the ducts. Why waste too much energy on an impenetrable screen?

The duct's location was a little tricky since Myra couldn't bring a regular ladder with her. The room had high ceilings, not outrageously high, but high enough she couldn't just jump up and touch the screen.

Because she'd assumed she was stealing back someone child-sized who wouldn't be able to just reach up and boost themselves into the vent, she had brought a foldable ladder she could hook into the duct once she had the screen off. She glanced at Christopher. Her ladder would not take his weight. But since he was tall enough —and she presumed strong enough by the looks of him—to boost himself up to the air duct, she figured they were still okay.

For her part, she just needed some wall climbing sticky pods. Like the kinds of thing used at rock climbing centers to simulate hand and foot holds along climbing walls, her pods did a similar thing, giving her hand and foot holds for scaling sheer surfaces. Her pods weren't bolted into anything of course, she just slapped them onto the wall. But since they were reinforced with a little magic, she didn't need the bolts.

The first pods went onto the wall just above her head level with one for a toe hold at her waist. She set an additional three pods as she needed them while she climbed, pulling them from another convenient vest pocket. She loved her vest pockets. There were so many of them. And they held so much. She wasn't sure how she'd managed to do stealing before she'd gotten this vest.

Once she reached the screen, she had it removed in short order, a few handy twists of her lockpicks to deal with the basic lock. With one hand holding a sticky pod, she hefted the heavy screen down the wall with her other hand.

"Take this," she grunted. "Gentle on the floor."

Christopher didn't argue with her or comment, just took the screen like it was a piece of paper and set it against the wall a foot away. She supposed that was better than if he'd been a kid. If he'd been a kid, she'd have had to climb back down the wall one handed to set the screen aside. It wasn't a long climb of course—the room wasn't that tall—but this did save a step.

"Can you climb using the hand and toe holds?" she asked. "Or can you just boost yourself up?" He didn't really have to stretch much to reach the air duct. His height really was pretty impressive.

"I'll follow," he said.

From this angle, looking more down at him than up, she could sort of see him better but that didn't help her read his expression any easier. Heavy eyebrows pulled down over his blue eyes, which were pretty arresting when she got a good look at them. His mouth was set in a line. His muscles were tight. And he kept glancing at the door.

But whether he was scared, irritated, bored, or angry, she couldn't tell.

And she supposed it didn't matter so long as he followed her instructions so they could get out of here.

"Follow as quietly as you can," she said. "You'll have to lay flat on your stomach and push using your feet and hands, but try to be as gentle on the duct as possible so we don't make much noise."

He grunted. She assumed that was a yes and shimmied into the duct. She had some wiggle room, enough she could turn back to make sure he was behind her. But he filled out the entire rectangular space, his shoulders brushing the metal walls.

Good thing he wasn't claustrophobic. She had a twinge of it just looking at how little space he had in here.

She led the way, slowly and carefully to keep from drawing attention to movement in the duct should anyone happen to be paying attention. She doubted anyone would be since they assumed their motion sensors were still working. But she was a careful thief, if not an entirely cautious one. If she'd been cautious, she wouldn't have gotten into this mess to begin with.

Fortunately, they only had to shimmy through about twenty meters of duct before they reached their destination. From the very quiet grunt behind her, she assumed the journey was not a comfortable one for Christopher.

At their exit air vent, she paused to study the room below. A storage room for electronic equipment and old filing cabinets. There were some tall metal shelves lining the walls. And a few giant photocopy machines currently taking up the center of the room.

Removing the vent from this angle was a little trickier. It was screwed into the wall from the outside rather than the inside. But no actual locks in here. No motion sensors. No cameras.

Just a very handy window.

She bent some of the metal on the screen, giving herself enough room to reach her hand through, and went to work on the screws with her little screw driver, pulled from yet another pocket. She glanced back at Christopher as she worked. He was frowning at her.

"How many pockets does that vest have?" he murmured.

"So many pockets," she said with happy sigh. "So. Many. Pockets."

When she got the screws undone, she angled the screen around to bring it back inside the duct and set it to one side. Then she poked her head out of the open vent to get a better look at the room. All good. Empty. No sounds from any direction to indicate someone had figured out their prize dragon shifter had been stolen.

Yay, her.

The vent opened over one of the metal shelves, which made climbing down both easier, and potentially noisier. So she took a moment to set up a sound dampening spell before crawling out of the vent feet first and easing down the shelves like a ladder.

By the time she reached the ground and turned around to gesture Christopher down, he was already out. He jumped down from a higher shelf than she would have risked and landed next to her in a crouch. They both held still, listening. And when no alarms sounded, he rose to his full height.

Which felt like it took a long time.

"You afraid of heights?" she asked, still keeping her voice low.

"I can fly. I'd make a piss poor dragon if I was afraid of heights."

She snorted a laugh. "Didn't answer my question, though, did you?"

"I'm not afraid of heights."

"Good. How about scaling buildings along thin ledges? That bother you?"

"You were going to do that with a kid?"

"No. I had a different plan. But that won't work with you." She gestured at him. "You're too big."

She couldn't read the expression that crossed his face—a scowl or a repressed smile or just confusion—so she didn't try.

"This is an adjustment to the original escape plan," she said. "My original plan involved more air ducts and a convenient elevator shaft."

"You were going to take a youngling into an elevator shaft?"

Ah, now she could read his expression. That was definitely a scowl of anger. "I wouldn't have let a youngling get hurt," she said. "The elevator was the easiest way down. But the section of air duct we would have had to go through is too narrow for you. So we're making some adjustments."

"Where does the thin ledge outside the building lead?"

"So many questions." She shook her head. "It leads to a room that we can't access through the air vents, but which is in a part of the building not controlled by the group who stole you, and so is an easier room from which to sneak out to a stairwell." She raised a hand. "Before you say it, I've taken care of the cameras and everything inside the stairwell as well. This isn't my first rodeo. But we can't reach the stairwell easily without moving outside the building for a bit."

"Why did you fix the cameras inside the stairwell when you intended on taking the elevator shaft?"

"Because I'm a careful thief who plans for multiple contingencies," she said, hands on her hips. "Are you finished and can we go now? They will notice you're missing sooner rather than later. And that is a complication I'd rather not deal with."

"Have you planned for it?" He sounded smug, like he'd issued a gotcha.

"Of course, I have." She shrugged. "It's just...not a great plan.

Better not to have to use it." Also, she'd planned on discovery while moving a child through the building. The fact that Christopher was not, in fact, a child, had really limited her alternative options. "Let's go."

She stalked to the window, trying to ignore the very large dragon shifter at her back. She supposed once she opened the window, he might be able to just shift and fly home. Except they were in the middle of New York City and someone was bound to notice the flying dragon before he could cloak his presence. The dragons weren't exactly a secret, but one flying through the New York skyline would be noticed. And might alert the kidnappers to his absence too soon. The king had wanted his son freed without the kidnappers realizing he was gone.

Also she wasn't sure how fast a dragon shifter could shift. If it wasn't instantaneous, he might just hit the ground before he achieved flight.

That idea gave her a shiver.

"You okay?" Christopher asked.

The question surprised her. "Yes. Why?"

"You shivered. Are you afraid of heights?"

He'd been paying enough attention to notice her shiver. She wasn't sure what to make of that. "I'm not afraid of heights." She grinned. "Actually, I love heights." And tall men. But that wasn't the point. "Scaling heights is second nature to me."

Which was true. She'd been climbing around where she shouldn't have climbed since she was a kid. The magic that made her so good at thieving also seemed to have given her a slight adrenaline addiction.

She studied the window. It wasn't one of the usual sealed ones most high-rise office buildings had these days. This was one of the old school ones that pushed up and could be tipped inside for cleaning. There was a screen over it. And it was locked shut. But neither the screen, nor the lock, were much of a deterrent to her.

Pushing the window up without making noise was actually the hardest part. She used a little "grease" magic to quiet the initial squeak, though that initial sound made her wince and Christopher hiss.

The hiss was an interesting sound. A sound that was very *not* human. And reminded her of his father's court. There'd been a lot of very quiet hissing. Only a handful of dragon shifters had been there, so it wasn't like she'd been surrounded by hundreds of them. Less than half a dozen. But when they're dragon shifters, that's enough.

One is enough.

The one at her back waiting on her to inspect the ledge outside the window was more than enough.

She pulled back inside. "Big enough for me. You'll fit but I hope you have cat-like balance." She asked that last as much as stated it.

He grunted.

A real non-answer answer. Have to do. They didn't have time to argue.

"We're going to the left. We're walking around a corner. And then there will be another window like this one." She didn't mention the other window was a more traditional high-rise window that didn't open. She had that covered and they didn't have time for his questions. "Ready?"

Another grunt.

"Alrighty."

She slid out the window.

Chapter Four

Myra mostly ignored the drop and the view as she moved out onto the ledge outside the high-rise window. She liked adrenaline, but she also knew how to measure it out so she didn't get shaky. Staring down at the street when she was sneaking out someone who's skills in ledge-walking were in question was a good way to overjump her adrenaline with fear. Wouldn't help anybody with that sort of spike.

If she was alone, she might have enjoyed the view up here. The streets of Manhattan below. The closely packed collection of high-rises. All glass and steel and stone and mostly dark windows rising around her as shadows against the nighttime. The glow of soft pink streetlamps far below. The star-like pattern of occasional window lights scattered over the horizon. The clouds overhead brightened to near orange by the city lights.

This part of Manhattan was mainly business buildings with only the occasional residential place. So at two in the morning, it was quieter than some might think for a supposedly twenty-four-seven city. There was still the occasional bump of cars below, and the releasing air of a bus stopping and opening its door. The cold burn of metal, cement, and tar from a nearby construction sight lingered in the breeze that cooled her cheeks. And a heady punch of salty Hudson River stench caught the very edges of the night air.

Yeah, if she wasn't worried about the very large dragon shifter stepping out onto the very thin ledge next to her, she'd have really enjoyed this view.

Fortunately for them both, this building was one of the old ones with beautiful stone architecture and lovely designs that included things like ledges and decorative carved stone accents. Across the street was one of those smooth steel buildings with nothing but windows and a slick drop to the streets below to recommend it.

She secretly hated the new constructions but not because they made breaking and entering from outside the building harder—she didn't mind that. She had her ways of dealing with that, and she liked the challenge. She just didn't like the aesthetics as much as the stonework and uniqueness of these older buildings.

She inched along the ledge, sliding her feet to ensure she pushed away any potential obstacles that could trip them up, keeping her gaze on their path and destination.

"You doing okay?" she asked, without looking back at him. She took his slightly louder grunt as an "okay."

Adult shifter, used to flying, she reminded herself. This wasn't sending him into a panic. She hoped it wasn't. Fact he was still behind her was a good sign. She hoped.

Going around the building corner was a bit tricky because of one of those decorative stone curlicues she loved so much sticking out just a little far. She showed him what to do by turning so she gripped the stone, her stomach to the decorative swish, and inched around it while holding onto it. She risked a look at him long enough to see he was following her lead. On the other side, she was able to turn again so her back was to the large gray bricks once more. She waited to make sure he managed the maneuver, and when he did without issue, she let out a long breath.

Yeah, she hadn't needed to worry. Apparently, dragons did have cat-like balance.

The window that was their target was two more down. When she reached it, she used the lip over the top of the window for balance as she pulled out yet another tool from her vest pockets. This one a cutting tool. But not just any cutting tool. This one had a little magic in it so the cutting was easy, silent, and the glass wouldn't break.

She stuck the central part of the tool to the window by a suction cup, then stretched out the wire with the cutting tip at the edge and slid the sharp blade around the dark tinted glass. She cut a bigger circle than she normally would to accommodate the large man with her, then slipped the circular chunk now attacked to her cutting tool through the window, setting it down gently on the carpet inside. She slid the rest of the way through the hole, going head first and rolling to get back to her feet. Before Christopher could slip through, she scurried back to move the circle of glass out of his way. She needed that to fix the window and she didn't want the piece cracked.

Christopher came through the hole head first, too. Slithering inside, rather than rolling over his head and back to his feet, as she had. He just crawled inside, down the uncut part of the window and onto the ground like crawling around on all fours was natural. He stood as gracefully as he'd slipped inside, rising to his full height like he did this kind of thing all the time.

Okay. She was impressed.

"Good job," she murmured.

He scowled.

Fair enough. "Sorry for the slight condescension. Wasn't intended."

Another grunt.

"Not a big talker, are you?" she said as she lifted the circle of tinted glass, using the suction cup stuck to the center as a handle. Carefully, she settled the circle back into the hole she'd created, and keeping it in place with one hand on the suction cup, she used her other hand, which she no longer needed for balance on the window sill, to slide the cutting tool at the end of the wire backward over the cut, sealing it this time with some handy magic.

When she stepped back and detached the suction cup, winding the tool back into a small ball she could return to a vest pocket, she admired her handy work. No visible signs of the cut. Even the tinting had smoothed back together without leaving any telltale lines.

"I'm impressed," Christopher said, sounding surprised.

"He speaks!"

She ignored his scowl to examine their surroundings.

There was a large conference table in the middle of the room, with three rectangular shaped gadgets in the center used for, she assumed, audio-visual presentations or whatnot. The table was surrounded by tall-backed swivel chairs. One wall had a screen pulled down. And there was a small cart against the wall, the purpose of which she had no idea, though the faint stale coffee smell made her think a place for setting up coffee service during meetings. Fortunately, this wasn't one of those conference rooms with an entire wall made of glass. And the door was closed.

This was part of a law firm, one of the few other businesses on this floor, and as far as Myra had been able to tell, the firm had no connections with the group that had kidnapped Christopher. Though, the group who'd had the hutzpah to steal a dragon could have hidden their links to the law firm, she supposed. She'd managed to dig pretty deep into the law firm's computer files, though, and there didn't seem to be any ties.

She motioned toward the closed door. "There's a short hallway beyond that and a door just to the left that leads to a set of stairs. There's an alarm on the door. Do not open it. Let me do that." She lowered her chin to give him a look.

His expression never changed.

She assumed that meant he'd listen to her and continued. "We're only going down six flights. Then we'll come back out into the building and take another set of stairs."

"In case they follow our scent?"

"Your scent. Yes." Hers was still disguised by her handy spell.

"Why not go up?"

"Because this is a high-rise, and I don't have a handy way to get us to the next building for an escape."

"I have wings."

"Yes. I'm aware." When he continued to just stare at her, she shook her head and said, "No flying. Too much chance of being spotted. The point is to get out without being spotted. Your dad prefers knowledge of this whole mess doesn't get out of immediate dragon circles."

She reached for the doorknob, but stopped, hand on the knob, her instincts making the hair on the back of her neck stand up.

She lifted her free hand for silence, but Christopher had gone still the minute she did. They both stared at the door. Then she set her ear to the wood. She didn't have shapeshifter hearing or anything. But she did have a little eavesdropping spell. Which she used on the door.

Inside the office, not at the door yet, but still… Someone inside the law firm. Moving around, pushing things that bumped over carpeted floors. A whispered curse.

"Check all the closed rooms," someone said.

She met Christopher's gaze. "Change of plan," she mouthed.

She sent a locking spell through the doorknob. Then scanned the conference room again. Another air duct.

This one was smaller.

She hurried to the side of the room under the duct and whispered, "Boost me up."

She didn't have time to mess around with wall climbing pods or ladders or even the rolling conference room chairs—though that's what she'd have used if she was alone or had an actual child with her. Instead, she had a very large dragon. Strong enough to give her a lift.

The ceiling here wasn't nearly as high as it had been in the room where the kidnappers had kept Christopher. He lifted her—with an ease she'd have to ponder later—and set her up onto his shoulders, which put her at eye level with the duct screen.

No alarms here—she touched the screen to make sure—so she simply had to unscrew the bolts. There was room for her, but barely enough room for him to squeeze in.

Gonna be tight. "Set me down. You first. If you can't fit, we'll have to go back out the window."

Which she didn't want to do because hanging out on a thin ledge when people were looking out windows for you was a lot more precarious than hiding in a vent. Vents had other exits. The only place to run on a building ledge was…off.

Again, with a shocking ease, he lifted her off his shoulders and set her on the ground. Then he boosted himself up to the vent, his arm muscles flexing under his much-damaged shirt. And wasn't that just rude since they didn't have time for her to admire all those lovely muscles at the moment.

To her surprise, he slipped through the opening easier than she would have assumed. Great. So he fit. Now she just had to get up there. But with the lower ceiling, jumping up and grabbing the edge of the duct was within her skill set. She lifted herself into the vent, head first, her feet finding purchase against the smooth wall as she clambered inside.

The vent wasn't large enough for him to turn and face her, so she was looking at his bare feet and his just-barely-angled head so he could see her. She could move enough to get the screen back in place, but she had to use a little magic to hold it up since bolting it back into the wall wasn't an option in such a small, cramped area.

Once she had their trail covered, she motioned him to move. He slid forward on this stomach, pushing against the steel duct with his feet, and managed to move through the narrow space a lot easier and faster than she would have expected. She scrambled after him, going over her mental layout of the building, looking for a good escape option.

They were about to turn a corner in the vent system when she heard a sound from the conference room behind them. She set her hand to Christopher's ankle to stop him. He froze. She did too, her ears straining to hear more than murmurs.

"…telling you they took the stairs."

"Got the cameras back up in there. No one's…"

"…past the alarms. Can get…"

"Shhh."

"He breathes fire, man. This was a bad idea."

Well, Myra thought, at least someone recognized that. Stealing a dragon was a piss poor idea, no matter what they had intended.

She was going to conveniently ignore the fact that she was *also* stealing a dragon. This was entirely different. The dragon in question was cooperating with her theft.

Knowing they'd figured out her hacks and gotten the security systems turned back on was irritating. How the hell did they find those so fast? Also meant they not only knew Christopher was missing already, they'd have the entire building monitored and maybe even locked down while they hunted for him.

She didn't *think* they could lock down the entire building. Too many other people here. Other businesses. Even if it was two in the morning. But the kidnappers could make getting out without being spotted impossible.

Damn it. So much for getting Christopher away before they knew he was missing.

She wasn't sure how they'd managed it, but she was mightily annoyed they had.

CHAPTER FIVE

yra held still as she listened to the people in the conference room moving around and shoving at things and then the room grew silent. She held perfectly still for another five minutes. Making sure they hadn't just gone quiet to listen for noise. Even the most patient of people eventually gave in and made sound when they were listening out for a possible thief. So she'd just learned how to outlast most people.

Though, she also had not always been this patient.

Fortunately, Christopher didn't make any sound either and he didn't try to rush her. He was so still that if her hand hadn't been on his ankle, she might have thought he'd slithered on ahead in the narrow air duct.

As she grew more certain the people searching for them had left the conference room, she became increasingly more aware that she was still gripping Christopher's leg. His skin wasn't as hot as she'd have expected from a dragon shifter, but warm enough to feel good. She removed her hand from his ankle.

He met her gaze and she nodded, motioning him to move

forward around the curve in the duct. The darkness closed around them, then, making it impossible for her to see, but she'd memorized the layout of these ducts and could tell where they were heading—maybe a little of her magic helped with that, too.

This direction led them to a section of wider vents, but also brought them back in the direction of his captors and that wasn't the direction she wanted to go. The stairwell was no longer an option. And the way she'd gotten in—through a service elevator, after taking care of security sensors accessible from outside the building, and then carefully sneaking through gaps in the guards' routine until she was in a position to disable the rest of the security system from the inside—was not an option now since she had Christopher with her and he was a lot harder to *sneak* around with given his size.

Her disguise magic was good. She might have been able to slip a child-sized person past the guards and into an elevator. Maybe. A child-sized person she could hold close enough to encompass them with the magic that kept her hidden. But a person as large as Christopher, even held close, was…

Yeah, that wasn't going to work.

When they reached an intersection of vents going in a few different directions, she stopped Christopher with a hand on his ankle again. She was sure no one would see the tell-tale light now, as they were deep enough in the ducts it shouldn't travel, so she cracked one of the thin light tubes she had in an inner pocket of her vest and wrapped it through a fabric tab near her collar. The green glow was enough to allow them to finally see, but not enough to attract attention. The bigger ducts meant they now had enough room they could move around to face each other better, too.

They needed to talk.

"Okay, so," she said, keeping her voice at a whisper. "We need to decide what we do next."

She leaned close enough she was speaking into his ear. Sound carried in vents, farther than light, and she wanted to minimize that. But leaning in so close to him, she was way too aware of his warmth, which was really nice, and also maybe a little too aware of the fact that he hadn't showered in a few days. He still didn't stink as much as she would have expected. He didn't actually *stink* at all. Which was weird. Or maybe she just didn't mind the sweaty smell of him? That was even weirder. She'd write it off to him being a shifter and leave it at that. No reason to investigate why she might sort of half like the smell of him all sweaty.

She blinked hard a few times and said against his ear, "They've blocked the next two options I had for getting us out. Stairwell security is back on. And if that's on, then their elevator security is back on."

"How did you get in?" he asked, also moving so he was speaking against her ear to keep his voice low.

His breath was very warm, too. "Service elevator, disabled security for that from outside. If they found the internal hacking, they found the external hacking."

"So the air ducts?" He looked around, his scowl fierce.

That expression should probably have scared her. He could breathe fire and he looked really really pissed. She wasn't particularly scared. That was probably a character flaw of some kind. Chalk up another one.

"Probably back to being monitored closer to their section of the floor," she said. "They didn't have the entire story rigged, though. Too hard to do with the other businesses. But if we keep going that way—" she nodded to one of the branching ducts, "—we'll crawl right back into their motion sensors. We go that way—" another nod toward a different branching duct, "—we go in a little circle that dead ends back at the law offices and the conference room."

The fact that the people after them had gotten into one of the other businesses to look for them was…worrying. She'd been relying on them not wanting to draw attention by breaking and entering on those other businesses.

"There's a vertical duct that way—" she motioned with her hand down the third directional option they had, "—one that connects multiple floors and runs alongside the elevator bank."

"But?"

"It's made of sheer, slick metal walls and a forty story drop to the ground floor."

"No ladders?"

"No ladders."

"Don't suppose you have something handy for forty stories of climbing in that vest of yours?"

She smiled. "I actually do have something in my vest that can help with a vertical climb."

"That vest is…impressive."

"So is the person who packed the pockets," she said, waggling her eyebrows.

"Yes," he said, a very faint smile cracking his scowl. "Very impressive."

She snorted, and turned away so he wouldn't see how much she wanted to preen under that compliment. "So the problem is," she said when she felt she could whisper in his ear without getting weird about it, "while we won't have to worry about motion sensors in the vertical vent—old building, no one thought about installing them yet—we do have to worry about sound carrying. That shaft connects to the vents on each floor and the way sound carries, we might attract some attention. Any attention risks attracting the attention of the people after you."

"So…we just don't talk?"

She rolled her eyes. "Can you climb down forty stories using rubber hand holds like rock climbing and not grunt or make noise? That's what I'm asking you."

"Yes."

"Good. Because you're going to have to do that."

"This wasn't an option if I was an actual youngling, was it?"

"No."

It had been on her contingency plan, of course. Which was why she knew it was an option at all. But she had really really not wanted to have to use this option with a kid. First time all night she was more grateful than irritated that Christopher wasn't a kid.

Progress or not? She wasn't sure.

Because they didn't have time to fart around, she motioned him down the direction to the vertical air shaft. She conveniently didn't mention that she only had enough of her handy climbing pods for the distance of a few floors, so she'd have to remove them and place them as they went. She didn't want him to worry unnecessarily.

They'd have time for that when they reached the shaft.

CHAPTER SIX

Myra looked down the length of the dark, smooth metal shaft, letting the movement of air cool her face. Sound seemed larger and more echoey here, even without her and Christopher making any noise. The space felt open after the ducts, but also…deep. Very very deep.

Deep enough the bottom was shroud in the darkness.

She wasn't afraid of the height, or the climb down. She'd done this a lot—not air shaft climbing, though she had done that, but rock climbing up and down very large, flat mountain faces because it kept her in good shape and kept her climbing skills sharp for just such an occasion. So she wasn't afraid to go down this shaft.

On her own.

Having the son of the dragon king with her, on the other hand…

"Sure you can do this?" she murmured near his ear as she cracked another light tube and tied it to her vest so they'd have a way to see as they climbed down the dark shaft. The old one had faded to a barely-there green glow.

Christopher nodded. "Dragons can climb, you know?"

"I did not know that. Why would a being that can fly need to learn how to climb?"

"Wings are big and get in the way in some spaces. We don't use them all the time." He glanced at her, and his usual scowl softened into something *almost* like a smile. "How much do you know about dragon shifters?"

"Lot less than I thought I did," she said without hesitation.

Like that fact that even having gone without a shower for at least a week, his sweat still didn't smell horrible. After being close to him this long, she was kind of used to it, and might even not mind it.

When she started wondering what he'd smell like after a shower —or maybe in a shower—she blinked hard a few times and said, "Let's go."

She pulled out some of her climbing pods and leaned into the air shaft to place the first few on the wall. She startled a little when she felt Christopher catch hold of the back of her vest, holding it as she leaned farther down.

She grinned up at him over her shoulder. "'Fraid I'll fall and leave you stranded?" she mostly mouthed since she didn't want to make much sound.

He grunted a reply. Which was just as well. Silence right. They wanted silence.

But it was hard to ignore the little flutter in her stomach. She was supposed to be here getting him out, and here he was making sure she didn't plummet to her death. To be fair, his actions were probably more pragmatic than altruistic or even gallant since she had the vest with all the good stuff in the pockets. Still, it was nice to know he didn't want her to fall and die.

With his hold securing her, she stretched even farther into the shaft and placed an extra few climbing grips to give them a little more room. Then she pushed back inside the vent, or rather she started to push back into the vent and then Christopher just lifted her with an easy, one-handed tug.

Impressive. Little scary. Also a little sexy.

She silently cleared her throat. Then next to his ear, said, "I'm going first, so I can place the pods as I go down. The ones above you that you no longer need? I'm going to have to…call those down to me. I only have enough for about thirty feet."

"You need me to remove them and hand them to you as we go?" he asked, also against her ear.

She enjoyed the warm brush of his breath, which did not smell like sulfur and that was probably very good because they didn't need him breathing fire right now. Though she almost laughed as an image came to mind of a scene from the movie *Die Hard* of fire roaring up an elevator shaft. If there'd been a dragon behind that fire instead of a C4 explosion, she and Christopher could reproduce that scene.

Not that they had time for that.

"Not necessary," she said, answering his question. She wiggled her fingers. "Magic. I've got this. But don't panic when you start seeing the way back up the shaft disappearing? And remember, absolute silence. Grunt in your head."

When she pulled away from him to look him in the eyes, he was back to frowning. But he did nod. So she assumed he'd be good with all this and swung her legs out into the shaft. Smiling a little when he blinked suddenly and reached for her, only checking himself with his hand almost on her vest.

Decent reaction time. Not as good as hers. But decent. And she'd just learned her reaction time could beat a dragon shifter's. That was handy. Especially when she returned to his father's lair and had to deal with him again.

She started down the shaft, falling into the rhythm of climbing easily. She paused far enough down to give him room, then looked up to watch him move out of the shaft and take his first tentative step onto one of the climbing grips. She wanted to tell him not to worry, they'd take his weight—even his substantial weight—because magic. But since they weren't even supposed to be grunting now, she kept her mouth closed and waited.

After his first few, testing steps onto the climbing pods, when they held his weight, he moved fully down into the shaft, climbing a lot easier than she'd feared. She let out a long, silent breath and started climbing again.

She paused when she needed to, to place more grips. And when she got low on the ones in her vest, she stopped long enough to mouth a return spell. The grips above vanished and reappeared in her pocket.

The first time she did this, Christopher looked down at her with his brows raised and eyes wide. It was the first time she noticed his pupils were huge, almost encompassing his irises and making his blue eyes look black. She'd bet cash money he could see in the dark shaft better than she could. Lucky. The green glow from her light tube only traveled so far. The bottom of the shaft was cloaked in darkness and still felt very far beneath them.

It occurred to her that dragons probably did need good night vision, given so many of them liked caves. Even the shifters liked having a "cave" somewhere to hoard things. And dragons of all shapes and sizes were super protective of their hoards, which she'd learned the hard way. So she probably shouldn't have been even a little surprised by good night vision.

She really didn't know nearly as much about dragon shifters as she probably should have before getting on his father's bad side.

Live and learn.

As they passed another air duct feeding back into the building three floors below where they'd entered the shaft, she started to breathe easier. The farther down they went, the closer to escape.

Even if they had to leave the shaft before reaching the ground level, it would be a lot easier to escape the building from one of the lower floors without anyone noticing.

So long as their escape plan wasn't discovered *this* time, they were home free.

Cockiness. Her Achille's heel.

When the first flash of blue lightning zipped past her, she cursed that cockiness.

She should have known better.

Chapter Seven

Another sizzle of blue lightning flashed into the dark shaft as Myra flattened herself against the wall, trying to make less of a target. She looked up, in the direction the magic shots were coming from, but couldn't see around Christopher.

"Who?" she hissed.

"The kidnappers."

"Shooting magic?"

"Have a wizard with them."

Great.

The dragon king hadn't mentioned a wizard. The possibility of there being shifters among the kidnappers, yes—though he hadn't specified what kind of shifter—but he had absolutely not mentioned a magic wielding wizard. And he really should have mentioned a magic wielding wizard!

No wonder they'd found her security hacks so quickly.

Another zing of electricity arrowed down the shaft, making a mockery of her little green tube light. She squinted against the glare, and said, "Down. Next duct."

They were still ten feet above the duct beneath them, but going back up to a closer duct seemed like a bad idea when that was the direction the dangerous magic was coming from. So down it was.

She heard some shouting and a howl, which was interesting, and there was a lot of cursing—some of which came from her. She set and called the climbing grips as fast as she could while still moving downward as fast as she could go. Blue magic ricocheted off the smooth metal walls inside the shaft. Her heartbeat pounded hard.

A grunt from just above her.

She looked up in time to see Christopher leaning awkwardly back, his hands slipping from the climbing grip.

"No!"

She grabbed his hand on the way past, clutching his forearm as he wrapped his fingers around hers. His skin was slick with sweat, and he weighed a ton. Not good for her hold. She squeezed tight to his hand and held her body against the wall to aid her grip on the climbing pod. And because she needed it, she added a little magic to keep her own fingers from slipping.

"Let me go," Christopher said. "I'm too heavy. You'll fall."

"Shut. Up. Let me concentrate."

She glanced up again. Now she could see the wizard leaning out of the air vent three floors up. His features were hard to see from this distance, though she suspected if she'd been a shifter of some kind, she would have made out more than the dark hair and vaguely pale skin. Even the *he* part of her assessment might be wrong. Didn't matter. The wizard fired more blue lightning down into the shaft, this time aiming at the wall opposite, angling the shot like a ball on a pool table, trying to hit them on the ricochet.

"That's cheating!" she shouted up at the wizard.

There were more howls behind him and then another head poked out of the vent.

"Thirty-fourth floor," the head said. "Go. Get them."

"Let me go," Christopher said again.

She was straining to hold him and not lose her grip, hard enough when he was holding onto her. When she felt his hand loosening, she cursed. "Stop that! I'm not letting you fall."

But she couldn't climb like this. And the duct opening was still too far below. And they were going to have company there soon.

"I'm placing more grips. Get ready." She hated doing this purely with magic because she couldn't ensure they were secure setting them this way. But beggars couldn't be choosers.

She narrowed her eyes to concentrate and focused on moving the climbing pods around, sending all the ones left above her to a ragged ladder like line below her.

"Take hold of one." She grunted when she felt Christopher gain purchase, easing some of his weight from her. "Make sure it holds before you let go of me."

"Got it," he said, releasing her arm.

She looked down and let out a breath, seeing him once again holding onto the grips. "Down to the vent," she ordered, then looked up again.

In time to see a blue sizzle of lightning arrowing right for her. "Shit." She flattened against the wall, moving as far to one side as she could while still holding the pods.

Wasn't far enough. The magic shot hit her arm, sending a shockwave of electrical pain through her limb.

Her body jolted. Her fingers loosened. Her vision darkened.

She let out a pissed off gasp when her body didn't respond. Her stomach tumbled, but even that felt distant and out of her control. She couldn't scramble to regain her hold. She couldn't even curse. She couldn't do anything.

But fall down the nearly forty story air shaft.

The last thing she saw before the darkness swallowed her was Christopher, hand outstretched, reaching for her.

Chapter Eight

Myra snapped awake, suddenly, but held herself perfectly still as she scrambled to remember why she'd been unconscious. Cold wind hit her face before she even had her eyes open. Looking down, she blinked. The cityscape of high-rise buildings rolling past *below* her was…unexpected.

Without looking away from those passing buildings, she murmured, "This is going to require some explanation."

"Soon," Christopher said from above her.

The feel of arms around her back and under her legs, the air so cold and wind so sharp it made her eyes water, the heat pumping off the body she was cradled against. A lot of disorienting sensations hitting her all at once. Including the height. She wasn't afraid of heights. Normally. But usually, she had some sort of control on just how high she was.

She forced herself to look up. Christopher's face, still in human form above her, his gaze out over the city, his eyes glowing a little in the darkness. The very large wings sprouting from his back and shoulders were new.

He'd had a shirt on when she'd broken him out of his cell. The shirt was gone now. Not even scraps to show for it. And his bare skin was a good deal warmer than it had been earlier in the night. That heat kept her from shivering with the cold at this altitude. There was a sweep of purple and yellow scales over his skin now. The color of the scales blended into the wings, which had strong bone ridges with a thin purple membrane between bones. They reminded her of a bat's wings. Except the wing span was easily… twenty, thirty feet. Hard to tell from her angle dangling in his arms under him. Like a fish in a hawk's talons. Except this hawk was a lot bigger. And his talons were holding her in a warm, comfortable cocoon.

And she was pretty sure Christopher didn't intend on devouring her. In the bad way.

"I'm not splat at the bottom of an air shaft," she said. And though her voice seemed to whip away from her on the cold air, he apparently heard her just fine because he answered.

"No."

"You can do partial shifts?"

"I can do partial shifts."

Handy. "The wizard and the others?"

She'd swear he winced. But it was hard to tell at this angle and with the overall fact that they were flying and he was concentrating on that.

"I might have left some…crisped shifters and a very crisped wizard in the air ducts after I saved you."

She nodded. Skipping right past the part where he'd saved her—she was probably going to need solid ground under her for that one—she said, "That's going to stink up the place. Imagine the maintenance crew are going to be a little surprised when they discover what's causing the smell."

His mouth ticked up in an almost-smile. It was a nice almost-smile.

She was very tempted to kiss that mouth, and that almost-smile. But she didn't want to distract or startle him while he was flying.

He dipped his wings to one side, picking up a new air current, and banked to the left toward one of the tallest buildings around. Fascinated as she was by the sight of him, she turned away to assess where they were. Everything looked different from this angle, of course, but she was pretty sure they were somewhere in Midtown, higher end, getting close to the Park. Since it was the middle of the night and the park would be empty but for the unsavory types, she wondered if that's where they were heading. What did a dragon shifter care about unsavory human types, right?

But no, the tall building seemed to be his target.

Another of the older buildings, with excellent stonework, a mix of red brick and white stone balconies and accents. This one had a flat roof, with the usual old water tower, lines of air vents, and a raised building where a stairwell would be. The edge around the roof was about waist high with lovely carved crenellated details. Landing on that roof in the arms of a dragon when those kinds of details reminded her of castles was as interesting as waking up high in the air with the city racing past below.

Interesting seemed to be her go-to word tonight.

She was trying to decide if she liked interesting or not when Christopher touched down on the roof. She normally did like interesting. Usually interesting meant fun. Glancing up at Christopher as he continued to hold her in his arms and stare down at her, she thought this might just be fun. She also thought his expression was fascinating. And she was very tempted to touch his jaw and see how he reacted.

Then she frowned. "How old are you, really? In dragon terms."

She raised her eyebrows. "Like, if I were to kiss you, would that be some sort of…child molestation?" The idea horrified her.

His expression turned into a scowl. "No. Of course not. I'm not *that* young." His scowl softened, but his frown didn't go away. "You really don't know much about dragon shifters, do you?"

"Nope." She shrugged and started to pat his chest so he'd set her down, but the feel of warm muscles and solid shoulders momentarily distracted her. So she let her hands linger on his scale-covered skin, the texture smooth and warm. And because she was watching, she saw his eyes whirl from nearly black with a golden glow over them to something with a more purple glow. None of it like his blue eyes from earlier that night, but fascinating to watch.

"So…" she murmured. "Age-wise for a dragon?"

"Old enough," he said, his voice deeper now and his gaze more intent.

Her stomach tingled and tightened at that, a little tremor of excitement running through her. And again she thought the word *interesting.*

With a great deal of reluctance, she patted his shoulders and said, "Better set me down before you get tired."

Not that he showed any signs of that. He seemed to hold her like she weighed little and could do this all night. Which was a thought one step farther than her brain could handle at that moment.

He did slowly release her legs so she dropped to the ground, but he kept an arm around her as she got her balance. For which she was grateful, because the wobbly feeling she got standing on her own caught her off guard.

"So, what happened?" She vaguely remembered getting hit by the wizard bolt, and the sensation of helplessly falling would stick with her for years. But then the blackness and… And that was it.

"The wizard was tossing around magic designed to render us unconscious, and they didn't care if you fell and died."

"Would you have died if you fell?" she asked.

"Not died. Just been wounded."

Still. "Glad none of that happened." She nodded to his wings. "You shifted in the air shaft?" His wings actually looked too big for the space they'd been in, so… "How did that work?"

"I can adjust the size of my wings," he said.

That earned him an eyebrow raise. "Wow. Might have been useful to know that earlier in the night."

"You didn't want me to shift."

She gave him a look.

"How did you end up working for my father if you know so little about dragon shifters?"

She waved a hand in the air. "Lost a stupid bet. Long story."

"We have time now."

She sighed. This was embarrassing. "The short explanation is that I assumed when I broke into your father's hoard, I'd just steal the least valuable thing there was. No one would miss it. I'd get out and win my bet. No harm no foul. Except, I sort of underestimated how pissed your dad would be just by me getting into the hoard."

"Because no one should have gotten anywhere near his hoard," Christopher said, sounding both aghast and, she thought, maybe a little impressed. "Were you supposed to steal something in particular? Who hired you?"

His sudden intensity on those last two questions had her raising her hands, a defensive gesture. "First, no one hires me. Most of the time. I steal for myself. Not for other people. And I don't steal from people who would miss what I took. In fact, most of the people I steal from have so much stuff, they've forgotten most of it exists. Do you know how much *stuff* people collect?"

"I'm a dragon. I have an idea."

She both winced and smiled at that. "Your dad's hoard was pretty impressive." At his look, she said, "I wasn't there for anything in particular. Just a trinket to prove I'd managed to get in. It was a bet. A dare with financial backing, if you will. Old rival. We're always testing each other. I figured this one was easy money." She shrugged. "Who knew?"

"Anyone who knows anything about dragon shifters would have known."

"We've already established I don't know nearly as much as I should have." And really, she needed to rectify that situation. Or never deal with dragon shifters again. Either way.

Except, as she looked up at Christopher, with his magnificent wings folded against his back, and that very interesting purple glow in his eyes, and his warm, solid shoulders, she knew she didn't want to stop dealing with *all* dragon shifters.

He crossed his arms, a gesture that emphasized his shoulders and chest muscles. She narrowed her eyes. Had he done that on purpose? He'd done that on purpose.

Then he spoke and she changed her mind about his motivation for crossing his arms.

"The shifters and wizard who kidnapped me? They wanted something from my father's hoard."

Shit. "I…didn't know that. Was that why your father was so pissed?"

"My father would always be pissed about someone breaking into his hoard. It's supposed to be impossible."

"Compliment? No? Okay, so… What did the shifters and wizard want? And what kind of shifters were these? Your father failed to mention the species." And the wizard. But she wasn't going to get into that part now.

Christopher skipped over the species question, too. "My father has a magical artifact in his hoard that could turn shifters into indestructible monsters."

"That sounds bad."

"Which is why my father keeps it secured in his hoard where it's supposed to be safe from thieves."

"Oops?" She wasn't sure what to say to that. Breaking into the hoard had been challenging, but not impossible. At least not for someone like her. And frankly, she was a little proud of that. Even if it had gotten her into some trouble.

"The shifters couldn't find anyone to break in, no one capable of it anyway. They hired the wizard to help. He failed."

She wanted to wince again, but also wanted to preen.

"Did this rival of yours ask you to bring out something specific?"

"Nope. Nothing. Just something to prove I'd been there." But she was starting to see why this all looked very suspicious. "Why did your father send me to steal you back rather than kill me? He had to think I was part of all this."

"You weren't?"

"Of course not." She put her hands on her hips and glared at him. "I told you already, I wasn't going to steal anything of value or even anything specific. A coin or something would have done."

"But it could have just been a test run. Your rival setting you up to steal something larger for them later?"

She let her arms drop as she considered that. Damn it. "Possible. He's a real asshole. That wouldn't be beyond his machinations." Made her feel stupid for falling for the trick, though. She was going to have to repay that asshole. "Except I'm not a hired thief. I only steal for myself." She shrugged. "Mostly for the challenge. And because I'm good at it." At his look, she said, "What? It's fun."

"Could he have 'bet' you that you couldn't steal something like the artifact? Would you have tried then?"

"No idea." At his scowl, she said, "If I didn't know what the artifact was, how valuable it was, or what it could do, I wouldn't agree until I'd done some research. Does that help?"

"And when you discovered what it could do?"

"You mean when I learned it could magically turn shifters into unkillable monsters, would I still steal it and hand it over to an asshole rival? No. Of course not."

She wanted to be offended that he'd asked. But to be fair, they'd known each other a few hours, and she was here because she'd broken into his father's hoard, and really, she didn't have a lot of moral ground to stand on when it came to thieving. Still. She wasn't the kind of thief to want indestructible shifters loosed on the world. That would be bad for everyone. Thieves included.

Christopher stared at her for a long moment, his arms still crossed, before he finally said, "My father must have seen that strange thread of honesty in you."

"Strange?"

"For a thief."

Okay. She'd give him that.

"Or he wouldn't have sent you to break in and free me."

"I am good at stealing things. Even things that have already been stolen." Which reminded her. "How on earth did they manage to steal you? Being as how you're…" She gestured at him, the sweep of her hands taking in the wings and vaguely referring back to the fact that he'd turned the shifters and wizard in those air ducts into burnt husks.

"Why do you keep referring to what happened to me as me being stolen and not me being kidnapped?"

"I don't deal with kidnappers. I'm a thief. I deal in stolen things."

"Semantics."

"But it works for me. So how did they manage to get to you?"

The faint color on his cheeks, high on those already cut cheekbones, was probably the most charming thing she'd ever seen.

"I was...tricked," he said, turning his head enough he was no longer meeting her gaze.

"Tricked?"

"They set a trap for me." His jaw locked tight on that.

She raised her brows. "Trap?"

"I might have a problem with..."

"With?" Her instincts rose and she stilled. What the hell did a dragon shifter have a problem with that it made him so nervous? Couldn't be anything good.

"I... I can't abide a..." He muttered the last few words so she couldn't hear them.

"A what?" She leaned in closer to hear him better.

"A damsel in distress," he barked out, without meeting her gaze.

She nodded, staring up at him for a long minute. "A dragon. Who worries about...damsels in distress? That's..."

"Interesting?"

"I was thinking more along the lines of ironic and funny, but we can go with interesting here." She felt a smile tugging at her lips and pressed them together so she didn't laugh out loud. "Spotted a woman in trouble. Swooped in to save the day. She was part of a trap. You got clobbered by the wizard's anti-dragon magic."

"Something like that."

"Oh, I have to hear this."

He huffed out a breath and she'd swear there was steam on the huff. He seemed to be radiating a little more heat, too. But it was really the rosy color in his cheeks she found most delightful.

"Mostly...it was like you guessed. She was a shifter, a lion shifter. Not in any danger in the end. And the wizard... They had the containment collar on me before I knew what was happening. Knocked me out. I woke up in the cell."

She nodded, her lips pursed, waiting for him to meet her gaze. He didn't. So she nudged his chin with her fingers. His skin was scorching hot, but it felt weirdly good and that was something she'd think about at some point in the future.

When he finally met her gaze, she said, "That's the sweetest way I've ever heard for someone to get trapped. No reason to be embarrassed."

"It's…not something my dragon brethren understand."

"I imagine. What with eating virgins and all that."

He scowled again and it wiped away some of the mortification in his expression. "That's real dragons. Not dragon shifters. And even real dragons don't always do that. And haven't done that in centuries."

"Told you I don't know much about dragons." She shrugged.

"You don't…" He let out a breath. "You don't think it's a weakness?"

"Not even a little."

"Got me captured by people who wanted to blackmail my father and steal an artifact to create monsters."

"Shit happens."

His charming smile cracked through his scowl. She returned it with a big grin. Bumping his shoulder, which was still really warm, she wandered closer to the edge of the roof, so she could take in the view.

"Pretty risky, you shifting, even partially, to rescue me. You could have let me fall."

"You did just hear what I said about damsels in distress, right?"

She chuckled. "Fine." She eyed the wings on his back, folded tightly over his spine, but the tops rising several feet above his already impressive height. "Still, pretty risking. Flying out over the city like that. Don't care how late it is, someone probably saw you. Your father wanted to keep this all quiet."

"I cloaked—yes, I can do that—but most people wouldn't be expecting to see a partially shifted dragon at this time of night over the city, so even if they did see me, they wouldn't believe what they were seeing?"

"Probably think you were Batman or someone."

"You think my wings look like bat's wings?" He spread them out, puffing up in a way that was supposed to be impressive and succeeded spectacularly.

"Is that insulting to a dragon? I feel like you found that insulting." She laughed and said, "I like your wings."

"Hmm." He gave them a little flutter before folding them in tight to his back again.

She looked out over the dark cityscape, at the surrounding high-rises with their occasional lit windows, the dark shadow of Central Park a few blocks away, the lines of car lights running up and down the square Midtown blocks. The wind was a lot less cold when they weren't flying, but it was still crisp and chilly on the rooftop. A sharp contrast to the heat pumping off the man next to her.

Not just man. Dragon.

So much she didn't know about dragons.

She gave him a look from the side of her eye. "Do you have a hoard? Like your father's."

"If I do, would you steal from it?"

"Nothing you'd miss," she said with a shrug.

His mouth twitched. Then more seriously, "What do you do with the things you steal?"

"If I need the money, I sell my take through a very cooperative auction house that likes the caliber of items I bring them. They don't ask too many questions of me or the purchasers, no one is really stuck on provenance, and we're all happy with the financial outcome of the exchange. If I don't need the money…" Shrug again. "I usually return whatever I stole the next night, or the next week."

He blinked down at her. "You return stuff you've stolen?"

"Sometimes. Depends. Why?"

"That's…"

She smiled. "Interesting?"

"That's a good word for it."

She nodded, her gaze skimming the skyscrapers, and the spectacular view of Manhattan from this height. "It is my go-to word tonight. Interesting."

"Speaking of." He moved just a little closer, his gaze moving over the view like hers. "I seem to recall you saying something about kissing me."

"I did, didn't I?" She swallowed.

"You never did, though. Kiss me, I mean. Even though I'm old enough."

Her cheeks heated at the reminder of her worry. "I never did. I wasn't sure… I thought you might object."

"I wouldn't object."

She glanced up at him just as he glanced down at her. "Interesting," she murmured.

He smiled. A smile that sent a lot of trembly sparks through her body. A smile she could really get used to.

They leaned in at the same time. Meeting in the middle. Her going up on her toes. Him leaning over, a hand on the low wall circling the roof. His lips were incredibly soft. The kiss was very gentle. And her insides danced in such anticipation, she melted closer.

"Interesting," he murmured when he pulled back.

"Mmm." Yeah. The kind of interesting she'd like to indulge in more.

This close to him, she realized his scent was…different now.

The flight or maybe the partial shift must have worked like a shower because there was no longer that low-level stress sweat smell. Now he almost smelled like…

"Why do you smell like sugar cookies now?" she asked.

He raised his brows. "Do you like sugar cookies?"

"Love them. But I've never smelled a person who smelled like sugar cookies." It was one of those sweet vanilla scents that made her want to get closer and draw more of it in. Subtle. Not overpowering. But there. Teasing her and making her a little hungry.

His smile did something more to that hunger. A hunger that had nothing to do with food.

"You should probably start to learn more about dragon shifters," he said.

Sounded like a threat and a promise at the same time.

Like a dare.

She was a sucker for a dare.

"Maybe I should." Her gaze dropped to his mouth. To that smile. Then she met his gaze. The purple glow over his blue eyes drew her like a lure. "We should probably let your father know you're out now."

"Probably." He glanced out over the skyline. "Want to fly there?"

She grinned and looked out over the skyline as well. "Sounds…" She gave him a look. "Interesting."

He laughed, the sound making her heart do that fluttery pounding thing. Then he swept her up into his arms so fast she gasped. She wrapped her arms around his neck. Feeling surprisingly secure like this.

"Hold tight," he murmured next to her car. Then he bent his knees and launched into the sky, his wings snapping open and taking two powerful downbeats before he caught an air current that brought them higher.

Myra laughed even as her stomach dropped to her toes and a thin edge of fear sent adrenaline into her blood. She loved that feeling.

She glanced up at Christopher, just as he smiled down at her.

Yeah. She definitely needed to learn more about dragon shifters.

She had a feeling she was going to be spending a lot more time with one of them.

The Dragon Thief Series
The
Chicago
Job
Bestselling author of the Cary Redmond Series
Kat Simons

THE CHICAGO JOB
BOOK TWO

Saving a dragon can complicate a thief's life…

One job for the dragon king. Myra had been obliged to do just one job to make up for the teeny, tiny mistake of breaking into the king's hoard. Rescue his son. Restitution satisfied. Myra, clear and clean from one of the bigger mistakes of her life.

And since the son in question turned out to be a sexy dragon shifter named Christopher—not Chris—a shifter she wouldn't mind getting to know better. The job… Not a total wash.

But still, just one job.

The dragon king has other ideas.

Myra doesn't normally work for other people. She steals what she wants, when she wants, because she wants to. Her favorite marks…rich people who don't even know their stuff is missing. But when a dragon king wants to hire you, and pay you a small fortune, to retrieve an old relic, what's a thief to do? Having Christopher along for the ride, doesn't hurt. Spending more time with him is almost worth the irritation of working for his father again.

Complicates things too, though. Myra likes interesting. Complicated worries her.

And her feelings for Christopher are getting complicated.

CHAPTER ONE

Taking a stupid bet and breaking into the dragon king's hoard had been Myra's first mistake.

Thinking she'd be able to get away with doing just one job to make up for that lapse in judgement had been her second.

She was still deciding if kissing the dragon king's son had been the third mistake. Jury was still out. Depended on how this current confrontation went.

Standing in the middle of the dragon king's court, in an elaborate mansion some people might have called a castle, amidst a compound of other buildings, circled by a fortified wall, built among the hills and hard gray rock in the far upper west end of Manhattan, Myra had assumed she'd hand Christopher over to his father, bid them both farewell, and that would be her done with the dragons. At least with the king. With Christopher…

Again, jury still out.

But the dragon king had decided to throw all those assumptions into the trash and make Myra rethink all her life choices. Or at least the one, very bad choice that had put pride before common sense when she took that bet.

She suspected the reason the king wasn't done with her yet was because she'd *succeeded* in breeching his hoard more than the fact that she'd attempted it. Lots of thieves eventually attempted to break into a dragon hoard. Hard to resist all that gold and jewelry and cash and bonds and…well, the wealth. The sheer wealth. Who could resist that?

But most thieves couldn't get around the security of a dragon hoard. Especially not a dragon king's hoard. They usually got caught somewhere along that process, still a long way from actually reaching the treasure.

Myra had gotten caught standing in the middle of the hoard admiring some of the crown jewels.

Fortunately for her, those skills were more valuable to the dragon king than killing her as an example would have been. And also fortunately—maybe?—she'd broken in just after the king's son had gotten stolen. Yes, yes, technically Christopher insisted he'd been kidnapped, not stolen. But she was a thief. She stole things. She thought in terms of theft. Not kidnapping. Returning a stolen item was within her purview.

And that's what she'd done. Retrieved Christopher from the shapeshifters and wizard who'd stolen him, and then returned him to the king unharmed. Mostly.

True, she'd assumed she'd been sent in to rescue a kid—because the king kept calling his son a youngling—and her plan to get back out of the high-rise building had needed to be changed at the last minute. She was good at improvisation, though. And she'd had backup plans. Multiple backup plans.

Those plans just hadn't accounted for the near seven-foot-tall wall of muscle and adult male physique standing next to her.

Still, they'd gotten out alive and unsinged. Only the kidnappers had gotten burned. Myra considered that a job well done.

The king had decided that her completing this excellent bit of work was not quite enough.

"Father, you've asked enough of her. Let it go." Christopher shifted his position to stand just a little in front of her as they faced his father, which was nice because standing before a dragon king was intimidating as hell even if the king was in human and not dragon form at that moment.

Sitting on an elaborate throne made of bones and gold with some winking jewelry in between. She'd eyed that throne the first time she'd seen it, wondering how hard it would be to remove, say, that little diamond near the base without anyone noticing.

She had not been left alone for long enough to find out.

Like his son, the dragon king was a huge man, standing well over six and a half feet tall in human form, with dark black curly hair cut neatly, and light eyes that switched from blue to green depending on the light. His skin tone was pale in this form. She'd never personally seen him in dragon form, but the rumor was his scales were bronze colored, with a bit of red. She had no idea how old he was because dragon shifters aged different to humans, but he'd been around and been king for a long time, so she assumed he was old. There were silver threads in his dark hair, but it was hard to tell if those were natural or an affectation to give himself gravitas. With the king, you just couldn't be sure.

Unlike his son, the king was what one would call classically handsome. The bones on his face and jaw were strong, his features perfectly symmetrical, his forehead high under his crown, his lips thin but suited his facial structure. Had he wanted to, the king could have made a killing as a leading man in Hollywood. Probably wouldn't have even mattered if he could act. Because even outside of the good looks, he was compelling. There was a sort of aura to him that made people notice him. An inner power that took up space and commanded rooms.

He and Christopher shared that trait even if they didn't share much in the way of looks.

Probably helped they could both shift into dragons the size of low-rise buildings.

"She is not done with repaying me for my magnanimous decision not to kill her," the king said in answer to his son, his voice deep, rolling through the high ceiling room like thunder.

"She showed you exactly where your security systems were weak and vulnerable before anyone with real nefarious intent got in," Christopher said. "And she assisted me in breaking out of the tower so you couldn't be forced to do something…difficult to take back."

The shifters and wizard had been trying to get a relic the king kept in his hoard that, according to Christopher, turned shifters into unkillable monsters. That would have been bad. She'd been delighted not to have been the one committing that fuck up and handing the relic over. No one had even mentioned a relic to her. She'd taken a bet from an old rival, to prove she could get into the hoard. And all she'd intended on taking out was a trinket to prove she'd been there.

But, after hearing what Christopher had to say about his kidnappers, she realized she'd been the guinea pig, the one they'd sent in to see if it was even possible to get into the king's hoard. Her rival might have even been working with the shifters, though she'd have to question him to find out. Even if he hadn't, even if he'd been tricked into issuing her the bet, the end result had been her getting into the king's hoard, only to get caught.

Kidnapping Christopher was their insurance plan if the break in hadn't succeeded. Stealing the relic, or blackmailing the king with one of his son's lives…either way would get the job done.

No one expected the king to hire a thief to get Christopher back.

"One more job," the king said. "Nothing that isn't within your realm of expertise." He spoke directly to Myra, ignoring his son's comment. "And we will consider ourselves even."

"My debt was paid when I got Christopher back," she said. "You want me to do a job for you now, that'll require payment. Up front. And details before I accept."

She was bluffing. Big time.

First, she never worked for other people. No one hired her to steal things. She stole because she wanted to. What she wanted to. When she wanted to.

But in reality, if the dragon king told you to do a job for him, there wasn't an awful lot someone like her could do about it. Except turn it down and then die. She didn't want to die, so she'd accept the job. So long as it didn't involve doing something she didn't do. Like kill people.

The king's expression tightened but that was his only show of tension. A blink and he smiled at her. It was not a comforting smile. There were a lot of teeth involved. Reminding her that in his other form, the king could swallow her whole.

"There's a relic that has long eluded me. But it would be infinitely safer inside my hoard rather than loose for any…any unscrupulous individual to access."

"What's this relic do?" She'd been left in the dark about the monster creating relic last time. She didn't want to make that same mistake.

"Nothing humans need worry about."

She came within a microsecond of snort-laughing at that comment. With all the dragons around Manhattan, a human with any sense in their head always worried about the things those dragons did or were interested in. Just common sense in this world. The dragons might go out of their way not to appear as dragons very often. And they usually cloaked when flying around for the comfort and peace of mind of humans. But that didn't keep humans from worrying about what the dragons did.

Instead of laughing, she gave the king a very level look. She couldn't completely ignore the unfortunate tingle of curiosity that moved through her blood, though.

"What's the relic?" she said.

She wasn't saying she'd actually take the job. But she wasn't saying she wouldn't either. In fact, even though working for the dragon king was a bad idea and she didn't consider she owed him anything else anymore—she *had* just brought him back his son alive and well—her own curiosity did tend to get the better of her.

Between her curiosity and her professional pride lay the seeds of her own destruction.

But what could a thief do.

Chapter Two

The king considered Myra from his bejeweled bone and gold throne. The chill in the high-ceilinged throne room seemed to get momentarily chillier. The scent of dragon —a mix of reptile and sulfur but with a hint of leather—got a bit stronger.

Myra ignored the faint warning signals and waited him out. If he wanted her to do a job for him, she did have to know what she was going to be stealing.

A moment passed in that chilly silence. A beat. And then, "The relic is a chalice. A goblet." The king smiled.

Or really it was a stretching of his mouth into the semblance of a smile. This was another place where he and his son diverged. She found Christopher's smile charming. The king's was terrifying.

"Chalice? A cup. Is it made of precious stones and gold?" Because that would encourage her to take this job. She liked precious stones and gold.

"No."

Too bad.

"It's made of something more valuable."

"Something more valuable than precious stones and gold?" She shook her head. "Platinum?"

This made the king chuckle. "It's made of the skin and bones of a dragon."

"That sounds…kinda gross." A cup made of skin and bone? Not. Good. "Cursed, is it?"

It had to be a curse, right. No one made things from skin and bone that didn't have magic and curses involved, and she was not a magic and curses kind of person.

Well, that wasn't entirely true. She was a magic person. Her magic just ran toward skills that made breaking and entering easy, like an ability to hide her scent and some magic lock-picking skills. And she liked stealing a certain caliber of magical item because they brought a good price. She drew the line, though, at magically cursed things that required skin and bone to make them.

"Not so much cursed as bespelled with power that is too deadly to be loose in the world."

"Then why is it loose in the world? Out of curiosity."

"This isn't something a human should be sent to retrieve," Christopher said before the king could answer.

"Didn't say I was going to go get it yet," she pointed out to him.

He didn't glance down at her. Which was annoying. And maybe stung a little. If she allowed herself to notice the sensation.

The king kept his assessing gaze on her, though. Not glancing at his son. If the king's gaze wasn't so damned intimidating, that might have given her an ounce of smugness. *Someone* wasn't afraid to look at her in front of his relatives.

"I think, given what our Myra is capable of, she is the perfect one to retrieve the chalice."

Our Myra?

"I'm not a dragon," she said. "Not a subject of your majesty's."

That had to be very clear right here and now or she was a little afraid she'd somehow end up a subject of the king's without noticing. Something about him and the way he wielded power... implied that.

"But we both know you'll do this for me," the king said.

"Oh? Do we?"

"I pay well."

"That would help. Except I don't normally work for others."

"For this amount of money, I'm sure you'll make an exception."

"I don't just work for the money, either."

And that was true. It was also what got her into trouble more often than the money. The money was good. But not the real challenge. The real challenge was *could she get away with it*. Could she do the thing that no one else could do. That was the fun part.

"The chalice is kept in a vault. It shouldn't be an issue for you."

"Then why would I bother?"

"Because getting *to* the vault is impossible."

"Nothing's impossible." Just very difficult. Unfortunately, though, the king had her now. He'd hit his mark with that shot. She loved very difficult. Still, wouldn't do to let him know too soon how interested she was. "Describe impossible, just so we're clear."

"The vault itself is inside a building owned by a wizard. A multi-story complex with several subterranean levels. It fronts as a business bank and financial institution, but no one enters or leaves without permission. The building is bespelled so that only invited guests can get past the entryway. Anyone else who tries... dissolves."

"Fun."

"Father," Christopher barked. "She's not taking this job."

"I can speak for myself." Myra didn't take her gaze off the king to glance at Christopher this time. "Go on."

"If, and that's a rare if, someone manages to get past the initial security spell, the entire compound is rigged with traps—both physical and magical—that change on a regular basis. The elevators, maintenance shafts, even some of the floors are all set with traps."

"What level is the vault on?"

"In the very center of the building, on the second subterranean level. There are two more levels beneath the vault floor. Both are also bespelled with traps."

"Of course they are. And obviously no window access to the level with the vault."

"Or tunnel access. The ground beneath the building is also bespelled. As are the walls that make up the building."

"In the city?"

"In *a* city," the king said.

"Where?"

"Father," Christopher said again. "No."

Both Myra and the king ignored Christopher's growl. "Chicago," the king said.

Ah. There was the rub. "Chicago is inside another dragon's kingdom. Is that why you haven't gone after the chalice?"

"There are…treaties."

"So no dragons can go after this cup?"

"Not officially. No." His gaze danced to his son and away so fast she might have missed the gesture if she hadn't been watching him so closely. And wasn't that glance interesting.

"Why's it not just as safe in the wizard's vault as it would be inside your hoard. Sounds impossible to get at." For some people. "Why not just leave it there if it's been there for a while already not causing any mischief?"

"It is not safer with the wizard," the king said, his expression going cold and stoney. "It belongs with the dragons."

"Then why doesn't the Chicago king go after it? It's in his territory."

"He is too busy attempting to quell a rebellion among his dragons to deal with the situation. I would, in fact, be doing him a favor by retrieving the relic."

"Sure." That's what the king would be doing. Right. "This rebellion… That going to cause any issues with the heist. *If* I agree to go after this chalice," she added just to be clear.

"Shouldn't."

The king was lying to her. But he'd also presented her with an impossible job, something she had a very hard time resisting. "What else don't I know? If I touch the chalice, will I die? Turn into a dragon? A monster?"

"Touching it… No. Drinking from it would be bad, though."

"Good to know." Shouldn't be too hard to avoid drinking from a skin and bone cup. The very idea made her own skin crawl.

"You can't send her into enemy territory like this," Christopher said. "She's not a dragon."

The king flicked a glance at his son this time, his smile deepening. A disturbing smile, that. "No. She's not. Which is why I can send her in without risking a war."

"She can't go alone."

Now the king directed his full attention on Christopher. "Are you volunteering?"

Her turn to look up at Christopher. Was he volunteering?

"She can't go alone. The territory, and the relic, are too dangerous."

"I work alone just fine," she said.

"I'll go." This said to his father, ignoring her comment.

That wasn't something she'd tolerate for long, sexy shoulders and impressive height be damned.

"The son of the king can't be caught," the king said. "This time."

Oh. That was a dig. And not a very nice one either. She saw the comment hit home, but only in the way Christopher's jaw tightened slightly before returning to its normal state of rock hard and intractable.

"I'm going," Christopher said. "We'll stay below the radar."

"I haven't agreed to the job yet," she pointed out.

"But you're going to," the king said. "It's a challenge."

Bastard. "What are you paying me?" If he was going to have her number, she was going to get paid well for it.

He named enough money—cash and gold—to set her up for the next few years. Not that she wasn't already sufficiently set up. But the amount of money on offer was obscene. Easily four times what she normally made on a job.

If he was willing to offer that much in payment, it meant the relic was worth easily five times that amount. If not more. Might even be a priceless artifact.

She'd only swiped a few priceless things in her life. Okay, maybe a few more than a few, but still. Not as many priceless things as things with very definitive prices.

She nodded slowly at the king. "Money in my account before I start."

"How do I know you'll complete the task and not just run off with my money?"

She lowered her chin and gave him a look. "I'm a thief. Not a liar. I have my reputation to protect."

"An impressive reputation at that."

"Consider it a good faith gesture," she said.

"You broke into my hoard. I don't have *good* faith in you."

She grinned. "But you have faith in my skills or we wouldn't be talking."

"You will take my son. He will ensure you live. Or if you don't, that I can get my money back after you die."

Christopher growled, a sound so quiet it was hard for her human ears to even pick up. But she was certain his father heard. And there was an odd sort of hissing in that growl. A combination of sounds a human couldn't make.

"Fair," she said to the king. "I usually work alone. But with dragon politics a possible issue, I'll allow it. This time."

Except the son of one king getting caught in another king's territory during a time of rebellion would create *more* of a political problem than just her sneaking in.

She wasn't entirely sure why she was agreeing to take Christopher with her on this job. Why she was agreeing to the *job.* The Christopher part... That probably had something to do with the kiss. And whether or not it had been a mistake.

The job...

Well. She never could resist a challenge.

She glanced up at Christopher and smiled, wagging her brows. "This could be fun."

CHAPTER THREE

"This is a damsel in distress thing, isn't it?" Myra asked Christopher as they stepped out onto the roof of the mansion that looked more like a castle.

No exiting through the front door like a normal human for the dragon shifters. Even if she hadn't come with Christopher flying her in, she'd have had to have been flown in by some other dragon to be allowed entrance to the mansion.

Not that there wasn't a main door entrance, but anyone who came there got greeted by one of the king's staff and never got farther. You wanted an audience with the king, you flew in. And it helped if you had an appointment.

If you didn't want to see the king, and were just looking to break into the king's hoard, you took a different route all together and avoided the front door and the roof at all costs.

The king had done up the roof, a long flat space that spanned the length of the huge house, lining the low wall encircling the building with dragon statues and carpeting one half of the stone roof with grass—real grass somehow—so the younglings had a softer landing. The other half was covered in smooth red sandstone that matched the rest of the building. There were two actual, honest-to-god guard towers at either end of the mansion—which was one of the elements that made it looked like a castle—from which dragon sentries ensured those approaching were welcome.

Myra hadn't directly seen how those guards dealt with unauthorized approaches on the mansion, but the rumors said it involved streams of fire and charred remains and really that was all she needed to know.

Thick woods covered the rocky hill on which the mansion and the surrounding compound sat, and beyond those, a long road met up with the main streets of Manhattan. From up here, she could see the lights and sparkle of the city spreading out below, and far off on the horizon to the east, a pink line across the sky signaled the approaching sunrise.

She'd basically been up all night, first rescuing Christopher, then returning him here. But the buzz of the evening still sang in her blood, leaving her more restless than tired. She'd be tired in an hour when the adrenaline from the last few minutes wore off.

Christopher, also staring out over the city in the distance, didn't respond to her dig, so she bumped his bare arm with her shoulder and got him to look down at her. He'd taken a brief minute to change after they'd arrived, before they had the audience with his father, but he hadn't changed much. He still had no shirt on, only a new set of clean, unripped, black dress pants. He'd also remained barefoot. Barefoot looked very cold on the stone roof.

The autumn was progressing. The trees spreading out below them were a multi-colored patchwork of oranges, reds, yellows mixed with evergreens. But that beauty would fade soon. Winter wasn't that far off.

When Christopher—not Chris, she'd learned last night—met her gaze, she grinned. "This isn't me being a damsel in distress," she assured him. "You don't have to come with me to steal back the chalice."

"I'm coming with you." His voice was still deep and his mood was hard to read. "It's not a damsel in distress thing," he finished, looking a little uncomfortable.

And entirely too sexy and adorable. That was his soft spot, apparently. Damsels in distress. She loved that about him. It had gotten him into trouble, at least once that she knew of. The other dragons saw it as a weakness. But she thought it was sweet.

She nodded and looked out over the city again, feeling his wings spread out behind her. He could shift just that much of him, opening wings while the rest of his body stayed in human form. She'd had no idea dragon shifters could do that before last night. Turned out she knew very little about the dragons. Just that she mostly tried to avoid them.

At present, she was doing a piss-poor job of avoiding them.

"I need to sleep and do a little planning before we leave," she said as she turned and jumped up into his arms, delighted when he caught her without comment or hesitation. A little tingling started low in her stomach. He was very warm. Almost hot. The scales over his shoulders and chest soft and pliant under her sensitive fingertips. Last night, she'd sworn he smelled like sugar cookies. A funny sort of scent for a dragon shifter. This morning, she picked up more of the leather and musk smell of dragons she'd gotten from inside the mansion.

"Drop me off somewhere close to a subway station," she said, trying not to run her fingers over his shoulders.

He scowled. "I should take you home."

"Is that a proposition?" she asked, waggling her eyebrows.

His scowl deepened, but something hot and knowing moved through his gaze, increasing those tingles in her stomach. His arms flexed against her, where one curled around her back and the other under her knees. Like this, she was almost nose to nose with him, which made watching the changing emotions in his expression very easy, and super fascinating.

"I meant, I would feel better not just leaving you on a city street."

"I'll be fine, big guy. I'm capable of getting myself home. I'm capable of getting myself almost anywhere." Which was what had gotten her into all this in the first place.

"Fine. Where and when will we meet later."

"Tomorrow—" He opened his mouth and she held up a hand. "I need time to plan and research." That was her excuse anyway. She already had most of a plan. She just needed to work out the details. "The chalice isn't going anywhere and if it does, I'll learn about it during my research. Plus, I need sleep. Remember?"

He grunted, snapped his wings out to the side, and stepped up onto the low wall circling the roof. She looked down to the heavily tree-filled ground far below. Lot of hard rocks down there. She met Christopher's gaze. He met hers. Then he stepped off the side of the building.

Her stomach tumbled in the moments of freefall before the first downbeat of his wings caught an air current and dragged them back upward again.

She grinned. "That's fun."

His answering grunt made her chuckle.

He circled back toward the city, taking them beyond his father's estate and out over the edges of neighborhood houses and low-rise buildings, farther into the city than she'd expected him to take her. Moving over higher apartment complexes and neighborhood parks, streets lined with restaurants and bodegas just opening their doors to welcome the morning commuters. Her stomach growled at the thought of a bagel and coffee, which earned her a raised brow from Christopher.

She shrugged. "Been an adventurous night. I need to eat."

"So do I," he admitted.

Myra hadn't expected such a simple comment to be so full of innuendo but there it was. Hanging in the air around them. Making those tingles in her stomach start up again. She ignored them because, for the moment, they had to work together and the implications of that earlier kiss were going to have to wait.

"You'll be free of me soon and can get yourself fed. Don't go rescuing any distressed damsels before tomorrow, though. I can't be rescuing you every day."

That earned her another grumpier sounding grunt.

He landed lightly at the edge of the Colombia University campus, touching down on the sidewalk and folding his wings back in the same move. He didn't immediately set her down, but searched their surroundings first, as if looking out for danger.

Myra had to press her lips together not to grin again. He was ridiculously gallant.

She gave his chest a pat and he set her back on her feet, dropping his hold under her knees first and keeping a hand at her back until she was on the sidewalk. Even then, it took him one longer beat than necessary before he dropped his hold.

More stomach tingles. "I'm good from here. Meet me tomorrow at noon at Penn."

"I can fly us to Chicago."

"First, too cold." Dragon flight through the city was cold enough. He was so warm, his skin pumping off heat like a furnace, he kept her from freezing while they flew, but still. "Second, too obvious. Even if you cloak. We're going into a rival king's territory. No point in alerting them to us ahead of time. And third, I like the train."

"We're taking a train?"

He sounded so horrified, she grinned. "Can't take a commercial airline. Too much security to get through, and I'm going to need a few things I'd rather not have to check."

"That's a twenty-four-hour train ride," he said.

"Yup." She gave him another pat on his bare chest, which was unnecessary to their upcoming job but was good for her mood. "Pack light. We won't be able to hang out in Chicago long."

Mores the pity. She liked Chicago and hadn't been there in a few years. Be nice to see more of the place. Wouldn't hurt her feelings to take in the city with the handsome man beside her either. Although, handsome wasn't quite the right word for Christopher. Not like his father. Christopher was…compelling. Hard not to look at—she imagined even with a shirt on he'd be hard to ignore. Something about the arrangement of features, his piercing blue eyes, the hard line of his jaw. Taken individually, his features shouldn't have worked together, but his did, and the overall effect was magnetic.

"I could just fly us there," he repeated, his brows raised.

"Too cold," she also repeated. "Too long a flight." Unless dragon shifters could rearrange space-time during long flights? She had no idea.

She really really had to learn more about dragon shifters. She knew the bare minimum, like everyone else. Just enough to know to avoid them and to stay on their good sides if encountering them. She probably needed to ask Christopher more questions about what he could and couldn't do.

Which was another good reason for the long train ride.

"I could keep you warm while in flight," he said, his voice deepening.

And the innuendo there made her head spin. Yeah he could.

Wait, that wasn't what they were supposed to be talking about. "I'm still not up for a multi-hour dragon flight."

Although, maybe one day. Because actually, dragon flight was pretty fun. When you got over the fact that you were looking at the city from a very unique angle. She wasn't afraid of heights, but even she'd had to take a moment to adjust to that new view.

"We're going by train," she said, firmly, to put an end to the discussion. Because anymore innuendo would derail her intention to get some research on the chalice done before they left. "We're going into territory where you shouldn't be. That means going in in a way that won't be obvious. Dragon flight is obvious. People tend to notice the wings."

"You'd be surprised what people *don't* notice."

Actually, she often was. "My point is still valid. Just in case, we go in the way humans would, and we try to ensure no one notices one of the dragon king's sons is in another dragon king's territory until after we're well gone. It'll be enough having to deal with another wizard."

While she had magical skills herself—all aligned with her occupation as thief—she didn't spend a lot of time around other magical people. And she avoided wizards when she could. Bastards were a pain in the ass. Her latest encounter with one, just last night, had nearly gotten her killed. Having to deal with another one so soon had her especially cautious. Which was a new feeling for her. Caution wasn't usually her strong suit.

"Tomorrow at noon," she said. "Penn Station. Main Amtrak hall."

"It's a big station. We need a more specific location."

She looked him over. "Christopher. You are hard to miss." She was tempted to pat his bare arm, but she thought better of it. Too distracting. "Don't worry. I'll spot you. Just be there on time. I don't want to miss the train."

"How do you already know what time the train to Chicago leaves?"

She grinned. "Go get some shoes on. You're making me cold looking at you."

He held her gaze for a long moment, like he intended on continuing the argument over the train. Or maybe exploring the innuendo a little more. That thought had those tingles in her stomach dancing again. Actually, she was pretty sure they'd never stopped.

Her gaze dropped to his mouth as she waited for him to speak. And the memory of what his lips had felt like against hers had her breathing a little unsteady.

But after a beat, a moment filled with all kinds of potential, he simply said, "Get home safe so I don't have to come rescue you again."

"I rescued you."

"And then I had to rescue you."

"So we're even then."

He chuckled. It was a very sexy chuckle.

"See you tomorrow, your highness," she said, and enjoyed his scowl. "Get some rest. You've had a rough week."

"And you? You'll rest?"

She didn't need rest. She had a heist to plan.

Chapter Four

Myra didn't answer any of Christopher's questions until they were settled onto the train in their sleeper car. She'd arranged the private bedroom suite, using some of the money the dragon king had given her upfront to pay for the job. Had she been traveling alone, she'd have booked a roomette, or maybe even a coach seat and just slept sitting up. She could afford the sleeper car. She just preferred the ability to keep an eye on her surroundings that a coach seat afforded.

Plus, never knew when an opportunity might arise from an overheard conversation or chance meeting. Couldn't have those lucky bits of serendipity as easily from inside a private room.

But she and Christopher were going to need privacy to talk about the upcoming job. And honestly, he was so hard to miss in a crowd, being as he stood a foot taller than the average human, it was better to have him tucked away in a private space where he drew less attention. They were attempting to reach Chicago inconspicuously.

She'd splurged on the suite rather than gotten them separate rooms because the dragon king was paying and because it would make talking easier. But even in the relative luxury of having individual room spaces separated by individual, tiny bathrooms and a narrow corridor, the suite was still pretty small. Especially when her roommate was so large. When standing, Christopher had to duck to keep from bashing his head on the ceiling. And she wasn't entirely sure the fold down beds were going to hold him. He'd definitely have a hard time stretching out. Wasn't much she could do about that. There was only so much room on a train.

The tight confines were going to test her professionalism, though.

He settled on the long couch, that would eventually turn into a bed. She sat in one of the fold-down chairs that gave her a good view out the window and put as much space between her and Christopher as the room allowed. Still, bumping knees was entirely too easy as the train jerked into motion.

"So what did you learn?" he asked, his gaze darting out the window to the platform as the train moved out of the station, slowly chunking along the tracks.

"I learned that your father is a terrible liar," she said.

His brows rose, but that was the extent of his reaction.

"The rebellion in the Chicago king's territory is more significant and much more likely to cause us issues since some of the rebellious dragons are working with the wizard holding this chalice I'm supposed to steal."

Christopher's brows lowered dangerously. "I was not made aware of that part."

"Didn't think you were or you would have mentioned it."

She wasn't sure why she thought he would be honest with her where his father hadn't been. She barely knew the man. But there was a sense of honor there that spoke to his honesty. A degree of chivalry she rarely encountered these days, chivalry that wouldn't allow him to lie to her about potential dangers.

Plus, he was only coming along on this caper because he assumed she needed help and he couldn't resist helping a damsel in distress. Not that she was particularly distressed about anything she'd learned. Most of it just upped the challenge of this job.

"But I was pretty sure the way your father tried to downplay the rebellion that it was going to cause us trouble. And I was right. We'll have to go around both dragon shifters *and* the wizard's spells to get through the building."

"And how do you intend on doing that?"

She grinned. "Remember when we met and you couldn't pick up my scent?"

He grunted, a reply she took as a yes.

"I've got a spell for that." She waggled her fingers at him. "That'll take care of the dragons' ability to smell us. All you shifters rely on your heightened senses too much. It's a weakness."

Another eyebrow raise. This one sardonic.

"As for the ever-changing spells inside the building, that's a little trickier."

"Do you have a spell for that?"

"Don't need one. I double checked your father's information, because he's an untrustworthy source, but it turns out he was right about the level of magical difficulty involved. Spells all over the building, popping up in random places, designed to kill or liquify or cause any manner of disgusting damage. There's no predictable pattern to the spells or where they'll show up. They are constantly cycling around the entire building, including in the usual thief places like air ducts and elevator shafts."

His half smile got those tingles in her stomach going again. That was going to be very distracting. She should probably ask him to stop smiling like that at her.

"I remember your fondness for air ducts and elevator shafts. Also climbing along ledges outside buildings," he said.

"It's a cat burglar thing." She shrugged. "At any rate, the randomness and severity of the spells ensures no one who doesn't belong can move through the building without risking a horrible, painful death."

"As my father said."

"Ah, but see, here's the thing. There are people who *belong* in the building. People work there and have to move around despite all the spells scattered everywhere. And you can't have your employees and henchmen getting themselves killed regularly because of all the spells popping on and off around the place, changing constantly, now can you?"

He frowned, leaning forward slightly. That closed the space between them in the tight cabin, which did nothing for those tingles in her stomach. "So there must be something that keeps the people allowed in the building from being affected by the spells."

"Exactly."

"Another spell? A preventative shield?"

"An employee ID card."

He blinked. "An ID card? An ordinary ID card?"

"Okay, a bespelled ID card. But yeah, a card."

"How does that work?"

"The ID card is…tagged, I guess you'd call it. There's a magical microchip inside that the death spells recognize. If you've got one of these cards on you, the spells recognize you as someone who belongs in the building, and they don't explode you. Without an ID card, you die."

"You talk about dying very casually."

"Oh, I'm not casual about my own death. I have no intention of getting liquified by a wizard spell. Just relaying facts about the situation here."

He leaned back again. "But if all it takes is someone *carrying* a physical object like a card around in their pocket, can't an employee just…hand their own ID to another person and give them access to the building? Or couldn't a thief like you just steal one? Is that your plan?"

"Wouldn't that be entirely too easy. No. And I'm insulted you'd think I'd do a job that was as simple as picking a pocket."

He pressed his lips together, leaving her wondering if he was annoyed or trying not to laugh. Based on the look in his eyes, she was going to go with laugh.

"No, each ID is coded to an individual's DNA. The DNA signature is linked with the magical microchips spell. The card can't actually be handled by another person without the card melting."

"So…someone's spouse moving the card to dust would be bad?"

"Very, if said someone wants to remain employed at the wizard's place. Motivates everyone to take very very good care of their ID cards, as well. No randomly forgetting your card in the bathroom or dropping it on the 'L', right?"

"Probably saves a lot of money having to replace lost cards," he said.

"Definitely." She glanced out the window as they moved above ground, chugging along the west side of Manhattan, with spectacular views out the left side of the train of the Hudson River. If they could see out of the right side of the train, she suspected they'd be able to see the dragon king's mansion, or at least some of it in passing. But their suite's view looked across the river to New Jersey instead. She didn't mind. The river view was soothing.

"So you can't just steal someone's ID card?" Christopher said, bringing her back to their conversation. "How do these cards help us get into the building?"

"Actually, you're going to be more complicated to get in than I will be. Seems the dragons that work with the wizard need very specific cards. Dragon DNA being a different animal, so to speak, from human DNA. There aren't very many of those. The wizard only lets so many dragons into his stronghold."

"Smart. Too many dragons and it'll become a dragon stronghold instead of the wizard's."

She had no doubt. "I'm still working out how to get you into the building. But I've got a card for myself already."

His brows snapped down and his mouth dropped open and it was the most satisfying thing she'd ever experienced, being able to shock the son of the dragon king. Well, maybe not *the* most satisfying experience. But it ranked right up there.

"How?" he demanded.

"Cleaning staff. Have to get around too. They were hiring."

"You got a job on the cleaning staff in less than twenty-four hours applying from New York?"

"I didn't say I applied and got hired. At least not in the technical sense." But she had hacked into the hiring agency's computer and inserted herself as a new hire. "I'll need to stop at HR to get my ID card coded to my DNA, but once that's done, I'm in. You will be another issue. I can't pass a dragon shifter off as cleaning crew. Especially because we have to worry about the dragons inside recognizing you as one of the New York king's sons."

He grunted at that reality. "I'm not letting you go in alone. We need to find me an ID card."

"Working on it as we speak."

"How?"

"Secret thief magic."

He dropped his chin and gave her a look.

She laughed. "Fine. My hacking skills are only so good, but good enough to run a scan of the dragon IDs on record. I'm looking for a match for your general physical appearance. Once I've got a candidate, we'll just need to arrange for his card to melt and you can step into HR to get a new one. They'll be using your DNA to the new card, so you'll be free to move around. So long as you avoid the other dragons who will know you are not who you claim to be."

"What if the dragon I'm pretending to be gets to HR before we do? Or they discover the mistake while we're still inside."

"Got a plan for that, too. But it's still a little ephemeral. I'll get it worked out before we arrive."

"You'll get it worked out?"

"Yes. I will. Don't worry."

"Would it hurt your feelings if I said I was worried?"

"My professional pride, yes."

"Then I won't say it."

She tried not to get too soft inside over the fact that he didn't want to hurt her feelings, because he *had* insulted her professional skills. But since he didn't know how good she was at what she did, she'd forgive him this time.

"Don't worry," she repeated. "I've got it all worked out."

"Including where the chalice is inside the building?"

"Including that. Getting to it…"

Well, that, of course, was trickier.

Chapter Five

Dinner in the dining car was pleasant enough, and gave Myra a chance to study some of her fellow passengers. As she'd worried and suspected, though, Christopher drew an inordinate amount of attention.

He was hard not to look at, even though he was dressed casually in jeans and a long-sleeved dress shirt. He even wore shoes, which she appreciated—she was starting to notice he didn't like having shoes on all that much. His hair needed a cut, but he'd combed it. And nothing about his appearance superficially should have drawn attention. At least when he was sitting down.

But a man nearly seven-foot-tall walking through a train car just drew attention. And it only took one look at his piercing blue eyes to startle the unwary. She was wary and his eyes sometimes still startled her.

She was also very aware of the whispers surrounding them. Her hearing wasn't as good as his, but that didn't keep her from picking up the spreading rumors, first as they'd entered the dining car and then after they'd been seated. The speculations started with wondering if he was a professional basketball player or a shapeshifter. No one could find pictures of him, so everyone in the dining card was convinced he was a shapeshifter.

And that was getting a little too close to home.

"It's probably not good that people are suspicious of you being a shifter," she whispered, leaning over, resting her forearms on the wood and Formica-covered table.

She raised her brows when she realized his ears moved, just a slight shift forward, but still. Human ears didn't move on the skull like that.

"It's only a few of them," he said, keeping his voice low too. "And most aren't assuming dragon."

"But a few are," she said.

He shrugged. "They've almost rejected the idea, though. Why would a dragon be on a train and not flying, or even on a private jet?"

"Do you have a private jet?"

He lowered his chin and gave her a look. "Why would I need one?"

"I don't know... Fly your lovers around the world? Rescue damsels in distress in foreign countries? Take human associates partying? I have no idea what you do when you're not being kidnapped or helping me swipe a dangerous chalice."

And, she realized, she'd like to know more. She *wanted* to know what he did when he wasn't rescuing damsels. Her personal curiosity needed to wait until they weren't be watched by curious train passengers, but it didn't stop the questions nudging at her.

"I don't have a private jet," he said, after considering her for a silent moment. "Bad for the environment."

Her mouth twitched. She lost the battled not to chuckle. Then shook her head. "Environmentally conscious and likes to rescue damsels? What sort of dragon prince are you?" This last she said very quietly so no one else would hear them over the sounds of the train. She wasn't even sure he would until he answered her.

"The good kind."

Yeah. She sort of thought he was. Even if she didn't know what he spent his time doing most days.

They were served a remarkably yummy meal of steak and roasted vegetables. She indulged in the chocolate mousse dessert, which Christopher waved away.

"No chocolate?"

"I'm not crazy about chocolate."

She blinked. "Your first real flaw."

He gave her that raised eyebrow look that made her grin.

"More chocolate for me, then." She loved the stuff.

When they left the dining car, a few more whispers followed them. She listened close to pick up what she could, but once they were back in their sleeper car, she asked Christopher what he'd overheard with his superior hearing.

"I thought we shifters relied on our heightened senses too much," he said.

"You do. Doesn't mean I won't call on those heightened senses if we need them. What was everyone saying?"

"Most of it just gossip and nonsense. A few of the people who thought I might be a dragon shifter came back to that idea. Others were whispering that maybe I was famous and you were my… current relationship."

"Very careful about the way you said that." The whisperers had not been so discrete with their word choice.

That they didn't know who Christopher was, but were assuming he was *someone*, was a little difficult. She was very used to flying under the radar, so to speak, pun intended. Standing out in a crowd when she wasn't trying to was not a very comfortable feeling.

"The ones suspicious that you were a dragon shifter… What did they say specifically?"

He shrugged. "They were wondering if some of the stories about dragon shifters they'd read in the gossip rags might be about me. Someone suggested I looked familiar."

She'd heard that part. "Did you recognize them?"

"No. And there are no pictures of me online or in the press. They're confusing me with another dragon."

"So, the Hells Kitchen party…?" She kept her lips tight together so she wouldn't grin.

Even she'd heard about that party, which had turned into the social event of the year. And had devolved into absolute chaos. She didn't know Christopher very well. Maybe he was a party animal in his off time. But if he was, he did a good job of hiding that character trait. If he'd been involved in the Hells Kitchen event, it would be a very interesting insight into his character.

"Wasn't there," he said, his expression neutral. "Someone else was responsible for that."

"And the European prince?" She knew for a fact that rumor was about another, much more public facing dragon who performed on Broadway and didn't look anything like Christopher, but she was enjoying teasing Christopher.

"Never happened."

His deadpan response broke her grin free. "Not into princes? Just princesses?"

"There might have been the occasional prince in my past. Just not that one."

She chuckled, delighted with him and a little embarrassed by how charmed she was. "So none of the whispered rumors were about you?"

"None of those, no. Don't worry, most humans don't know who I am."

But they were getting a little too close to the truth. She was glad she'd gotten them a private suite now. The less they walked around among the other passengers, the better.

The fact that so many people knew all those rumors about various dragon shifters was a revelation, though. She'd spent most of her career avoiding dragon shifters and anything to do with them. Until the ill-fated bet and sneaking into the dragon king's hoard, she'd never attempted to steal from dragon shifters because she'd felt like that was courting trouble she didn't need. There were plenty of other people to steal from. Lots of wealthy people that didn't even miss their possessions. Didn't even know what they had because they had so much! She hadn't needed to tread on dragon toes to keep herself occupied over the years.

Obviously, that had given her a blind spot. A more serious one than she'd suspected.

"I really need to learn more about dragon shifters," she murmured, half to herself.

"Yes," Christopher said, his voice deep. "You do."

Something in his expression left her breathless, her pulse suddenly pounding in her throat. And those butterflies in her stomach were back. The shift in the air in the small room made her very aware once more of the fact that, although they had two different rooms and that little corridor and those two tiny bathrooms between where they'd be sleeping, the short distance wasn't much of a barrier.

A memory of their brief kiss the night she'd rescued him—and he'd rescued her in turn—made her lips tingle. It had been a very good kiss. She'd like to revisit that kiss.

But did she dare while they were supposed to be on a job?

The way Christopher's gaze dropped to her mouth she had a

feeling he was thinking along similar lines. Neither of them moved for a long moment. Tension and anticipation danced along her nerves. They did have a whole night ahead of them.

But at the end, when the train reached Chicago, they had a job to do. One that was already dangerous. And he already had trouble resisting a woman in danger. If something happened between them tonight, would that make it harder for him to concentrate during the job?

Would it make it harder for *her* to concentrate?

Possible. Very possible.

They'd have time after the job. She hoped. She did want to explore these tingles more. And really wanted to revisit that kiss.

But maybe it was better if they didn't tonight.

"We need to sleep," she said, appalled to hear how disappointed she sounded. Not obvious at all, Myra. She rolled her eyes and huffed out a breath. Which made Christopher smile. The smile did not help.

"You gonna be able to sleep in that bunk?" she asked, nodding to the fold down couch and, above it, the fold down bed.

"I can sleep anywhere," he said.

"Hey, me too." Well. They at least had something in common. Even if he didn't like chocolate.

She shuffled to her side of the suite and pulled down the top bunk.

"Not sleeping on the bottom?" Christopher said. His voice traveling across the small corridor that wasn't much of a corridor sounded intimate in the small space.

"I like the high ground," she said, glancing back. He'd pulled down the top bunk too, leaving the bottom as a couch.

"Me too," he said with a shrug.

He toed off his shoes, which she was a bit surprised he hadn't done the moment they walked into the room, and then disappeared into the tiny cubicle that was his bathroom. She shook her head. His shoulders would be bumping the wall in there, but they hadn't had a lot of choices.

She pulled off her own soft-soled black tennis shoes, leaving on her socks, and set her shoes near the door. They were slip-ons, easy to get into in the dark in an instant if needs be. The rest of her clothes—black leggings and a black cotton tunic—she kept on. The tunic looked nice enough to wear to dinner with a dragon prince but was comfortable enough to sleep in and conveniently meant she remained dressed overnight. She hung her multi-pocketed vest next to the door on a little coat latch, so she could grab that if she had to leave the room in a hurry. She'd packed the vest specifically for this trip, and all her good tools were hidden away in various pockets, including her best set of lockpicks. Because a woman never knew what she might need.

When Christopher came out of his tiny cubicle bathroom, she went into hers. Her nose twitched. The cubicle was very clean, and smelled strongly of the cleaning agent. She was grateful she didn't have a shifter sense of smell, though she wondered if the strong chemically scent bothered Christopher. By the time she came out, she half expected him to be up in his bunk already, but he was standing at the window, looking at the dark countryside. Not much to see, at least for her human eyes. Mostly darkness and trees, going by too fast to be more than a blur.

"You okay?" she asked, standing in the tiny space that passed for a corridor between their halves of the suite.

He didn't turn, but she could see him looking at her in the reflection on the dark window glass. "I'd be better if my father hadn't asked you to do this."

"You do realize I wouldn't be doing this if I didn't want to, right?"

"Because he's paying you."

"Because it's fun."

He turned around then. "The chalice is in a vault in the very center of a wizard's complex, that requires getting through locks, motion sensors, and biosensors. And if you get any one part of that wrong, the security spells on the vault will liquify you before you have a chance to gasp. All of that is after we've made our way through the ever-changing spells in the rest of the building that will kill us if our ID cards stop working for some reason."

"Like I said. Fun."

"How are you still alive?"

She chuckled. "The fact that I am should tell you something."

He huffed out a groan and glanced away, before giving her a once over. "You're sleeping in your clothes?"

"You are, too." She nodded to his jeans. He even still had his shirt on. Which was a pity. But probably good for keeping her on her side of the suite.

"Just in case."

She nodded. "Same."

His gaze swept the length of her again, and his blue eyes darkened, a faint purple glow coloring the blue. "Shame."

Oh. Wow, did that start the tingles in her stomach again. And those tingles were moving lower. "Definitely a shame." But necessary. At least for tonight.

She slipped back to her side of the suite and pulled herself up onto the narrow top bunk without bothering with the ladder. She glanced back to see Christopher watching her from his side of the room, his expression impossible to read, his arms crossed over his chest. His sleeves were pushed up. He had very nice forearms.

She sat on the edge of the bed, her legs dangling down, her body folded forward to accommodate the low ceiling, bracing her hands on the edge of the bed, waiting for Christopher to speak. When he didn't say anything after a few moments, she raised her brows in question.

His expression went through a series of subtle shifts, none of which she could read, until he finally shook his head and turned back to his own bunk. Leaving her hanging. So to speak. Rude.

He hopped up onto the top bunk without much effort, and with no help from the little pull-down ladder either.

"Show off," she said.

"Just keeping up with you." The bed groaned under his weight.

She winced. "Hope that holds you. Maybe you should sleep on the lower bed."

"I'll be fine." He adjusted himself so he was laying on his side and could look down the narrow corridor at her.

That put his head toward the door, which made her twitchy. "You can sleep with your head pointing the other way if that makes you more comfortable." She gestured at the door.

"I prefer this. If someone comes through the door, I can reach their head better." He reached his hand out and made a sort of cupping gesture to mimic grabbing someone by the head just in front of the door.

She blinked. Huh. Having a dragon shifter guarding the door was a new experience. Little scary. Little thrilling.

"Whatever makes you comfortable, then." She rolled onto her own bunk, her back against the wall, her body curled up tight and angled so she could see the door but her head wasn't near it. She didn't have Christopher's grip.

Her position meant she couldn't see him anymore, with the bathrooms in the way, but if she listened quietly, she could still hear him breathing.

A few moments passed in silence. Then, "You can sleep, Myra. I'll make sure no one gets in."

She grinned up at the dark ceiling. "You need sleep, too."

"Not as much as you."

"Never had a dragon shifter bodyguard before."

His response was very quiet, so she wasn't sure if she was supposed to hear it. "Get used to it."

Her smile softened. A dragon prince bodyguard would probably cause a whole lot of trouble. But it didn't sound too awful. So long as the dragon prince in question was Christopher.

CHAPTER SIX

Myra snoozed a little, waiting until it was the early hours of the night—or morning depending on your perspective—before she slipped from the bunk, slid into her shoes, and snuck out of the sleeper car. She was pretty sure the person she was looking for was in coach, but she had a few cars to check.

She'd only gotten a glimpse of him during dinner. Long enough to know she and Christopher were being followed. Whoever he was, he was pretty good. Stayed to finish his meal after she and Christopher stood to leave. Didn't show her and Christopher a lot of attention.

Unfortunately for him, that had been the giveaway.

With so many other people in that dining car staring at Christopher, whispering about Christopher throughout the meal, the fact that that one lone diner never even once turned to see what all the fuss was about. Never glanced their way. Never looked at them on the way out of the dining car, even when they passed…

Well, that had been too obvious to go unnoticed.

Myra did wonder if Christopher had spotted the tail. Or maybe even sniffed him out. He didn't seem like the type to miss that sort of thing. But he was also the type who got himself kidnapped by enemies because he'd tried to save a woman he thought was in trouble and walked—or in his case, flown—into a trap. Given that he did have a blind spot like that, she couldn't be sure he'd realized the issue.

And she hadn't mentioned it because, in all honesty, she wanted to talk to this tail on her own, without the rather intimidating presence of the dragon king's son looming over her.

She moved through the coach cars on silent feet, passengers on either side of the aisle stretched out in their individual seats, tucked up under blankets, sleeping. The occasional insomniac or night owl or just someone who couldn't sleep sitting up, with their faces in their laptops or phones, the light casting weird multicolored shadows across their features in the otherwise dark train car. Outside the train, the countryside flashed past, the occasional clump of lights on the horizon to mark distant towns.

There wasn't a lot of warning before she came upon their tail. He was sitting in the aisle seat behind a couple of sleeping women, his eyes closed and head leaning back against the chair headrest, his legs stretched out under the seat in front of him, his own chair knocked back a little, but not in full recline. The seat next to him by the window was empty. The seat across the aisle from him occupied by a man who was snoring.

She spotted the tail in one breath, had just enough time to realize who he was, and in the next breath, he opened his eyes, looking right at her.

She grinned, waved her fingers at him, and easily slipped over the top of him to settle into the seat next to him, lightly using the seat backs of the sleeping women in front of him and his own to lever herself up and over. Her move must have surprised him because he didn't immediately do anything. Didn't reach for her or even try to run away. He blinked at her for a few startled moments. Which gave her another few seconds to study him.

Not a large man. About half the size of Christopher in both height and width. A white man with light hair, cut neat and short, dark eyes, and a very narrow face. He was innocuous enough, the sort of person who could blend into a crowd. Go unnoticed. Not handsome. Not ugly. Nothing startling about his appearance at all. No tattoos that were visible around his ordinary clothes—jeans and a long sleeved, dark colored sweater—and no obvious jewelry except a gold band on his right pointer finger. Not a wedding ring, unless he just wore it on the wrong finger, and not an expensive piece of jewelry. Simple gold, not gold plated, but if she were a judge of these things—and she was—she'd say not high-quality gold either.

Outside of the ring, there were no distinguishing features to make him stand out. Nothing a person might glance at and latch onto as something they'd remember having seen before.

His bad luck that she had a great memory for faces and noticed small details as part of her career.

"Did the dragon king send you to follow us or someone else?" she whispered, turning in the seat so her legs were tucked up to her chest and she was half sitting on the armrest by the window, facing him directly while he turned awkwardly in his seat to face her.

The fact that he didn't run away was interesting. And he didn't immediately attack her when she questioned him. Also interesting.

"Not the king you're thinking about," he said.

"You're not a dragon, though." At least, she didn't think he was or Christopher would have spotted him earlier.

"I'm not."

"Why's the Chicago king having us tailed?"

"He's heard rumors."

"I *love* a good rumor. Do tell." She waggled her eyebrows at the man and leaned in.

A human, but not a wizard, she thought. No tingling sense of someone else's magic. And he hadn't thrown up a shield or tried to toss any magic at her. Most wizards she'd encountered—the few she'd had the bad luck to come up against—were quick with the spell casting.

And most wizards had a sort of burnt ozone smell to them, at least in her experience. She was able to wield her particular brand of magic without that scent following her around, but it was mostly because her magic and her spells didn't tend to burn up ozone when cast. Wizards liked to throw around things that sizzled. She just finessed locks and hid her own scent.

The man next to her just smelled like…well, nothing to her. Just ordinary, like the train. Maybe a little sweat? But otherwise, nothing in particular.

So she was going to say ordinary human. Which made sense if the Chicago king wanted to hire someone who could walk around and follow a dragon unnoticed.

"Rumors that one of the New York king's sons might be coming this way," the man said. "Maybe looking to interfere in some… negotiations the king is having with his people."

"Oh, I doubt that last one holds any water," she said. "Why would he want to do that?" She leaned in closer and lowered her voice, as if they were two old friends exchanging gossip.

The man's eyes narrowed, but he said, "Why else would someone like a prince be heading to Chicago now?"

"Vacation? Weekend getaway?"

"Not into another dragon king's territory. Not when you're the son of another king. And not in the company of a notorious thief."

"Notorious? Me?" She'd have assumed this guy didn't know

who she was, though she did have a reputation. But since he did seem to know who she was… "What have you heard?"

"Managed to break into the New York king's hoard."

That was going to follow her around. She was inordinately proud that she'd managed it, but inordinately embarrassed that she'd been caught in the act. So it was hard to preen at having done something most thought impossible.

"Think that's me, huh?"

"We know it was you," the man said. "Impressive."

Would have been more impressive if she'd gotten out unnoticed.

"And you survived," the man added. "Was the bet worth it?"

"I survived," she said with a shrug. But she was annoyed he knew as much as he did. More dangerous, then. And that meant she'd been right to come out and confront him. "What are you intending? Why follow us?"

"I'm not supposed to kill you, if that's what you're worried about."

"Good to know."

"My job is just to see what you do."

"And if we don't want someone seeing what we do?"

He shrugged. "You might be better off just letting the Chicago king know your plans. He'll be less inclined to interfere. Especially if he knows it has nothing to do with his current… politics."

"Politics." Good euphemism for near rebellion in the Chicago king's cohort. "We've got no political interests."

"The Chicago king will want you to make a formal appearance," the man said.

"Of course he would. But we're just here on a weekender. Won't be around long enough for a visit with the king."

"Lovers' getaway?" the man asked.

She kept her expression controlled, but for some reason, that guess hit a little too close to home and made her jittery. "Sure." She tried for a casual shrug.

Must have succeeded in keeping her reaction to herself because the man's eyes narrowed slightly, like he couldn't quite make out whether she was admitting to an affair with Christopher or not.

"You gonna keep trying to follow us?"

"Just doing my job."

"You going to step in and interfere in any of our touristing?"

"Not my job."

"Then we have an understanding." She hopped back over the top of him into the aisle, moving fast enough to make him blink up at her. "Should have gotten the dragon king to at least spring for a roomette for you."

"I prefer coach," the man said, trying to recover from her sudden change of position without looking like he was trying to recover from her sudden change of position. "Easier to keep on eye on things."

"Kind of is, isn't it?" She touched a finger to her forehead in a little solute. "Sleep well."

She slipped silently back down the aisle past the sleeping passengers.

She didn't yelp when a hand grabbed her arm in the gangway between cars, but only because she'd been expecting him.

"What did he say?" Christopher asked near her ear, having hauled her close so they weren't in view through the car window.

"Chicago king sent him. He's just a tail, though. No orders to interfere."

She glanced up at Christopher. It was quite dark in the gangway, so all she could see about his expression were his glittering blue eyes. Even with her excellent night vision. Just two glowing blue eyes with a hint of purple, irises that looked to have more facets and angles than typical human eyes, the pupil narrowed now like a cat's.

In the darkness, his glowing eyes were both compelling and terrifying. Especially since she couldn't really see the rest of his expression.

"Should we shake him?"

They could. Get off the train early. Now even. But she had a slightly different plan. "Not yet. Soon, though."

But things on this already interesting job had just gotten more interesting.

Chapter Seven

They made an appearance at breakfast, where Myra made sure their tail saw them even though he was still trying to be discrete. The dragon king of Chicago hired good people.

The dining car was quiet as she and Christopher had chosen to eat early. Their tail was already there, which made her wonder how long exactly he'd been sitting in the dining car, nursing a coffee. The meal was a decent collection of eggs and cooked meats and toast. Christopher, somewhat to her surprise, didn't like eggs. To no one's surprise, the dragon did eat a lot of the meat put in front of him.

There were less whispers this morning. Too many people too tired and up too early to bother with gossip, but Christopher still drew the gazes of those around them.

She forced herself to sit still through a second cup of coffee and to watch some of the passing scenery, attempting to appear calm and unconcerned that they were being watched and followed. Both she and the tail knew what was happening. He'd know Christopher was aware of his presence now, too. But all three of them were doing a bang-up job of appearing to ignore each other. It was pretty impressive, really, if Myra did say so herself.

By the time she and Christopher left the dining car, though, she was ready to move. She was capable of sitting still. She did often. Or maybe sometimes. But when she was excited, she didn't sit still very well. She gave their tail a little wave on the way out, which startled him into waving back. She grinned at his scowl.

Once back in their suite, without even speaking, she and Christopher gathered up their small backpacks—the extent of their luggage—and bid goodbye to the small cabin. Christopher removed his shirt as they walked down the narrow corridor, stuffed it into his backpack, then slung the pack over his shoulders, centering it. Unlike her wider pack, his was long, and narrow, and not like a normal human backpack. His sat along his spine, leaving lots of room around his shoulder blades.

She studiously ignored the fact that he was shirtless, more amused by the fact that he'd shucked off his shoes the instant they'd returned from their meal and those were already inside his pack. He really didn't like wearing shoes.

At the gangway at the rear of the train, where there were currently no train staff, Myra hunted up the emergency hatch. The thing most people didn't know even existed, but which allowed access to the roof of the train. If she'd been on her own, she'd have had to use some sticky grips on the walls and ceiling to climb up to the hatch and get it open. But with Christopher here…

"Boost me up," she said, turning her back to him. He lifted her by the waist, holding her up as if she weighed less than his shoes. There went those stomach tingles again.

She finessed the alarm set on the hatch with a small spell and then pulled the handle out and down, pushing up on the heavy chunk of metal. That was harder than it sounded because the train was still in motion and that hatch was working against the air friction of highspeed rail travel. She scrambled through the hatch the instant it was open, staying low to the roof of the train and using a couple of her sticky grips to give her secure handholds so she wasn't swept off the fast-moving vehicle.

Once Christopher had pulled himself up and closed the hatch—with impressive ease—she released the spell that held the grips firmly to the slick metal roof and tucked them back into one of the many pockets in her fitted black vest.

The countryside around them flew past, mostly farmlands now. And from here, they had a good view of the lake. The train would arrive in Chicago in only a couple of more hours. Soon they'd be traveling through outer suburbs and the small towns that circled Chicago. In maybe another twenty minutes, they'd pass through one of those towns.

She wanted to be off the train before they got there. And their exit point was approaching fast.

When she faced Christopher again, he was scowling at her, also low to the roof in deference to the wind speed pulling at them.

"You sure about this?" he asked, shouting to be heard above the noise of the train and icy cold wind.

She grinned. "It'll be fun."

She tugged down the straps of her backpack, ensuring it was secured. Then she stood, the wind buffeting her and rocking her on her feet. She looked over the side of the train. Smiled at Christopher. And leapt up and to the right.

A move that took her out over a steep drop into a valley as the train passed over a bridge.

The sharp change in position and motion rocked her and sent

her tumbling, making the freefall hard to enjoy. But she didn't have long to enjoy it anyway. An instant, just long enough to take a deep breath, and then strong arms caught around her back and under her legs, scooping her up.

She grinned up at Christopher's face as he focused on the landscape ahead. His huge wings spread out above them, a shimmering purple that reflected the sun. The light filtered through the thin membranes between thick, trailing bones and the small, more delicate looking bones that stretched like fingers down through the width of his wings. There were little hooks, like fingers at the first joint of the main trailing bone, which were black among the thick iridescent purple and yellow scales.

More purple and yellow scales spread across his chest now, along his collarbone and over his shoulders in a delicate pattern. The partial shift didn't affect much more of him, except for the soles of his feet becoming thicker. Given the beauty of his wings, she was really curious what he'd looked like as full dragon.

He banked out over the valley, catching an air current and pumping his wings in several strong beats to get them higher, above the bridge and train, skimming across the tree tops before rising higher. When they'd reached an altitude he deemed comfortable enough for her to breathe but still put them above the trees and farms, she glanced down at the ground far below, awed by the view. Even from airplanes, she wouldn't get this view, this ability to look straight down to the ground without anything but a dragon shifter's wings keeping her up here.

She straightened and tightened her arms around his neck, ensuring she was secure enough for him to adjust his arm around her back, so it was beneath the backpack instead of across it. The new position put his hand down by her waist. She liked his hand on her waist.

She was also now level with the side of his head, close enough to see he'd shaved very well that morning.

She grinned. "See," she said. "Fun."

He let out a long breath as he banked toward the distant city. She couldn't tell if he was trying to contain a smile or a scowl.

<h1 style="text-align:center">CHAPTER EIGHT</h1>

itching their tail on the train and flying the last few hours to the city proved one of the more unique experiences of Myra's life. One that, in all honestly, she wasn't sure she'd repeat.

Because, as it turned out, she loved flying with Christopher. She felt surprisingly secure and safe, trusted him a lot more than she probably should to not drop her. And that was a problem. Too easy to get used to the cold air whipping through her hair, across her cheeks, the sound of his strong wings occasionally pumping above them, the flutter of air rippling across the thin membranes like a breeze across canvas sails, his body heat keeping her comfortable despite the cold wind of their passage. Even the smell of fresh air and Christopher…

The experience was all so delightful and fun. And fast.

And getting used to it, perhaps even starting to rely on it, would be very very bad.

He landed in a park on the outskirts of the city, but within walking distance to an "L" station, remaining cloaked until they were on the ground and he'd tucked his wings away. Now that they were here, she did worry that flying in might have alerted the dragon shifters that Christopher was in town. The cloaking kept humans from noticing them. She had no idea if dragon cloaks worked on other dragons.

But since the Chicago king had already been tracking him, the dragons here already knew he was on his way. The tail had probably called the Chicago king already to let him know Christopher was off the train and likely flying in.

The dragons were just something they'd have to deal with. But hopefully not until after they'd finished swiping the chalice from the wizard.

Things went smoothly getting her DNA-matched ID card for the building. This wasn't her first time pretending to be cleaning staff. She knew how to play that role believably.

After a great deal of debate—and her search coming up empty on a dragon shifter that bore a close enough physical resemblance to Christopher to pass—she talked Christopher into remaining outside of the building while she went in. It was not an easy conversation. Everything in him rebelled at letting her go in alone and she knew it. But without an ID card, he'd die.

And now that they knew the Chicago king was aware of their presence in town, she worried the dragons inside the building would recognize Christopher instantly, even if they'd managed to score him an ID.

He couldn't wait for her on the roof of the building itself, because it was bespelled with dangerous security magic, too. But she compromised and agreed he could wait for her on a neighboring roof, keeping watch in case her escape plan went sideways.

They wasted some scouting time having this argument, but by eight that night, she was heading into the huge skyscraper in downtown Chicago, a few blocks from the lake, the "L" loop rumbling past just outside the windows on the third floor.

As an employee and cleaner, she entered through a side door, not the main lobby, but like the rest of the building it was protected by spells. If she entered without her ID card, she'd be dissolved. She hesitated before stepping onto the black linoleum floors in the employee lobby, a momentary thrill of fear coursing through her blood.

The security guard at the door, a human woman, said, "You got your card, it's okay, honey. Don't worry. It takes some getting used to for all new hires, but once you do, it's just like working anywhere else. Cleaning's cleaning, right?"

Myra nodded, let out a breath, and stepped into the smaller employee lobby. Smiled at the security guard when nothing happened

"Told you," the guard said with a wink. "Good luck."

Myra thanked her and hurried to the employee elevator and the maintenance office where the cleaners were assigned floors and the cleaning equipment was kept.

So far so good.

Now she just had to get the chalice.

The good thing about working as a cleaner was that most people didn't look up long enough to register a face. Even the friendly people rarely took the time to talk long with someone popping in to clean their office. At this time of night, the day shifts were gone and there were only a few people working late. It was, to her outsider's view, just like any other downtown office building, mostly busy during ordinary work hours and only the ambitious or reluctant to go home staying late into the evening.

Given that a wizard owned this place, she suspected more people were willing to go home than stay, though, based on the relative emptiness of the offices. If she had to worry about her employee card fritzing and accidentally getting fried by magical spells, she'd go home on time every night, too.

Pushing her cart full of cleaning supplies, brooms, mops, and a garbage bag stretched open over one side through the building ensured no one gave her a second glance, though she did get the occasional wave or half smile before people turned their attention back to their phones or inner thoughts.

She walked past a patrol of dragon guards, as well, but none of them paid any attention to her. They made themselves obvious by wearing uniform dress shirts with an embroidered golden dragon on the back. Not very subtle. She ensured she memorized their faces. Knowing the ones working here were dragons that didn't like the Chicago king gave her a bit of information to file away for later use. Always good for a thief to have important information in her mental files.

The elevator down to the subterranean floor where the vault was located was empty, but she continued to play the role of a half disinterested cleaner because cameras were a thing. Someone was watching her. And the more disinterested she was, the more disinterested the watcher would be in what she was doing.

She was a passible computer hacker—part of a thief's job in the modern era—but she hadn't been able to get at the vault cameras from outside the building. So she was going to have to finesse them on the ground. She couldn't bring in a disposable laptop to help with that either, because of the metal detectors getting into the building—what would a cleaner need with a laptop?—and navigating the kill spells everywhere was challenging enough. She'd have to rely on her magic. Her spell for finessing the cameras wasn't as reliable as a physical hack, but it worked in a pinch.

She rolled her cart off the elevator and made her way directly to one of the offices near the vault. There were no connections to the vault from that office that weren't covered in spells, but she had to get rid of the cart and fix the security cameras, and there was a camera in the office she could use to spell into those monitoring the vault.

The space was a windowless square with slick black conference desk in the center that didn't even have any chairs around it. There were some boxes stacked against one wall, that she investigated as she was pretending to dust, but they were mostly blank printer paper. There were high vents in the room, for the connecting air ducts, but those would be spelled, and the carpets were well worn and smelled vaguely like spilled coffee.

It was a depressingly dark sort of room with one overhead florescent light and walls painted an unfortunate steel gray. She had no idea what the room might normally be used for, but she was guessing hatching evil plans to take over the world because why else would anyone have a room this ugly and depressing tucked away in a basement level of the building.

Or maybe it was just supposed to be a storage room that had never fully materialized. Hard to say. And she didn't really care. Once she'd dusted around to the cameras, she slipped the powder from her pants pocket and sprinkled it onto the fluffy fake feather duster. She missed having on her vest with all the pockets, but the cleaner's uniform of tan pants and a short-sleeved navy shirt were a required disguise.

As she dusted the camera with her spell, she wondered how Christopher was doing. What he was doing. Was he sticking to his promise to remain on the building across the road? Had he spotted anything from that lookout perch that might be important? Not having a handy way to communicate was a pain. But she wasn't used to working with anyone else, so she'd forgotten to pick up some of those handy earpieces that would allow them to talk. Probably for the best anyway. She wasn't sure if those would have made it through the security metal detectors unnoticed. And having

Christopher constantly asking if she was okay in her ear would be distracting.

Not that she could be certain that's what he'd do. But he was totally the type to clutter up the communications line with checking to make sure everything was going to plan. And there was only so often she'd be able to say yes without getting annoyed. Especially since she certainly wasn't going to answer that question with a no and risk the disaster of him swooping in to try and rescue her. That had worked that one time but was more likely to get them both killed in this situation.

Once she was certain the camera spell had had sufficient time to set, she pushed her cart to a spot under the camera, where it wasn't visible, and waited for the spell to get a loop of the supposedly empty room that it would play on repeat after she left. She had to wait out the spell doing the same for the hall cameras and the cameras outside the vault.

The spell wasn't full proof, because someone could walk through the shot at just exactly the wrong time, creating a loop of that person moving through the frame in the exact same way over and over again. But this level was supposedly empty, so she was betting the odds.

As she waited, she stripped off the cleaner's uniform, reached under the stack of folded garbage bags on her cart, and redressed in her happy clothes. The black leggings and her multi-pocket vest that were *her* uniform.

After ten minutes, she slipped from the office and went directly to the vault. If her spell hadn't worked, she'd know soon enough when either she liquified from a triggered magic spell or a collection of dragon guards came to collect her. Neither prospect sounded fun. But risks had to be taken in these kinds of jobs. Especially when under a time crunch.

The vault was behind a pretty typical looking door. Round like a bank vault's door, shiny silver steel gleaming under another single florescent light. A multi-layered lock panel that required both biometric scans and a passcode next to a large, multi-pronged wheel for spinning and opening the huge round door. The model was one she'd worked on before, though, so that was one extra layer of research she'd been able to shortcut.

She stood outside the vault, anticipation crawling through her gut, waiting for some signal that she'd been caught. Her ears strained to hear any sound of approaching feet. She'd disguised her scent the moment she was no longer having to pass as a cleaner—if the dragons hadn't picked up a scent from her that would have immediately given her away—but it wasn't her scent that would bring down trouble now.

When she managed to survive those few minutes, and no one came running in to snatch her up, she grinned and went to work on the vault lock. There were spells here, too, but surprisingly, the wizard had relied on the surrounding spells to protect the vault and only inserted a few electrical charge spells onto the door lock. Probably that was a good use of energy. Given the nature of the surrounding spells, and the inability to even get this far in the building without dying if you weren't welcome, wasting power on complicated locking spells probably seemed like overkill.

The spells were easier to finesse than the lock itself. Which took her fifteen seconds longer to crack than she'd accounted for. Fifteen seconds she was going to have to make up somewhere. The heavy locks clicked, the giant tubes of steel pulled out of the interlocking panels in the surrounding walls with a chunking sound, and the door popped open an inch, release a hiss of air.

She never celebrated until she'd gotten the thing she came to steal and escaped, but she did allow a satisfied smile as she wedged the huge door open enough for her to slip inside.

The interior of the vault was a steel-lined square with tiny air vents up at the roof that were so small, nothing larger than a mouse could slip through them and were on their own system, cut off from the rest of the building, the air in here constantly circulating through its independent filtering cycle. A good filter system because the air inside the vault was fresh and crisp. Even a little cold. Actually, very cold, she realized. They had the temperature inside so low she could see her breath.

She hadn't planned on that. Temperature affected a lot of things, including spotting heat signatures on surveillance systems. But there wasn't a heat sensor on this room that she could find in the specs. Maybe the temperature was important to something they had stored here?

She looked around. There wasn't a lot visible inside the vault. There were a series of small cubbies along one wall, like in a security deposit box section of a bank. A miniature version of the main vault door directly across from the entrance, with a series of blinking electronic locks and another biosensor panel. And a plain steel wall opposite the bank of security box cubbies. Nothing in the center of the black marble floor. Not even a logo or other distinguishing feature. There were motion detectors in the floor, but those were only activated when the vault was locked, even though slipping into this model of vault without going through the door was impossible—she'd tried multiple ways. Never worked. This vault, you needed to get in through the big, round, steel door.

She started toward the mini-vault door at the opposite side of the chamber, but her curiosity about what was stored in those cubbies along the wall to her left almost had her exploring. There wasn't enough time to spend on that. The whole operation was timed to the second to ensure she didn't cross over any of the dragon guard patrols, and she'd already lost a few of those seconds on the vault lock. Which was unfortunate. She would have liked to have seen what those boxes held since she hadn't been able to find that in her research. Probably just jewels and money and bonds. Although, it could be spells, since this was a wizard's tower. Or bespelled objects. Maybe that's why it was so damned cold in here.

She forced herself away from the wall of cubbies and to the mini vault door.

This one took her another extra thirty seconds to finesse, which irritated the hell out of her. It wasn't the lock this time, though. Getting the biosensors to register her spelled signature took that tiny bit longer than it should have.

There was that moment, that gut-churning, heart-pounding, adrenaline-spiking moment when she worried the spells would fail and the alarms would sound. Honestly, she sort of loved those moments. The rush was incredible.

The rush was even stronger and more satisfying when the locks finally clicked open, and the miniature vault door hissed open.

She grinned, swinging it wide…

To be confronted with betrayal.

CHAPTER NINE

She met Christopher on the roof of a building downtown, opposite side of the "L" loop from the wizard's tower. The high-rise gave a great view of the lake in one direction, the brightly lit night landscape of downtown Chicago in the opposite direction. The "L" rumbled past far below, screeching against the tracks as it made the turn. There were shorter buildings bumping up against this one, but this one stood tall enough, and had a flat enough roof, to make it easy for a dragon to land.

He was already waiting for her when she arrived, so she wasn't sure if he came in on wings or just used the elevator the way she had. But honestly, she was too pissed off to care.

"He lied," she said, stomping up to Christopher where he sat on the low, stone wall circling the roof, his back to the lake. "Your father lied."

"He does that a lot. I thought you knew he had."

"I knew he lied about aspects of this job," she said, slowly, through her teeth. "What I didn't realize he'd lied about is that there is no chalice here. He sent me on a wild goose chase."

"What?" Christopher straightened. "What are you talking about? The wizard moved the chalice?"

"No. There never was a chalice. It isn't now, nor has it ever been, in the wizard's possession."

"How could you know that? Your own research showed the chalice was there, that the wizard had it."

"And that's a mistake I intend to check into," she said, her cheeks hot that he'd pointed out her own mistake. "How I know he never had it… After I searched every cubby in the vault and nearly got caught slipping out—"

"Are you okay?" He stepped closer to her, but she waved him away.

"That's not the point. I got out. The other lock boxes were mostly empty. There were a few with spells. And one with a relic that I may go back for one day. But no bone and dragon skin chalice. Nothing even resembling a cup."

"What was in the lock box where the chalice was supposed to be?"

"A book. A thick, leatherbound book. A book of spells. The *exact* sort of thing a wizard would store in his most guarded safe. Not a dragon relic. A *wizard* relic. What I'd expect to find in a wizard's safe." She shook her head and cursed, stalking away from Christopher, then stalking back. "No chalice anywhere," she repeated. "So on my way out, I snuck into one of the offices with a computer that had security access. There was never a chalice here. Ever. It's never been on the inventory, isn't part of the security precautions. It. Was. Never. There. I'm not sure the wizard even knows what it is or that it exists. If he does, he's not looking for it."

Christopher's brows lowered, giving him an expression most people would call deadly and probably terrifying. She was too angry to be scared. And a part of her knew she never had to be scared of Christopher, that he'd never physically hurt her. It was a weird bit of knowledge, given she'd known him for less than a week, and she was so fucking angry she could barely think straight.

"I don't understand."

"Me neither. Why the hell did your father send us into the territory of one of his rivals, where you're in danger—and he had to know, given your soft spot for women in a fix, that you'd go with me. He set us up to infiltrate a wizard's tower in the middle of a rival king's territory, when there's infighting going on between the dragons and…"

She trailed off and scowled at the stone roof as her mind worked, churning through what she'd learned and seen. What she knew now that she hadn't before. A cold breeze off the river blew through her hair, brushing strands that had escaped her tight braid across her forehead. She swiped them away.

When she looked up again, Christopher was scowling at her. "Your father is a devious, sneaky bastard."

"He has to be to lead a dragon cohort. He wouldn't have stayed king long if he wasn't devious and sneaky. But I swear, I didn't know he'd lied about the chalice. I thought this was an honest job. The chalice has been missing for decades. I thought he'd finally found it."

"He might have found the chalice somewhere, but it wasn't here. That's not why he sent us."

"Why do you think he send us, then?"

Before she could answer, a dark shadow swooped across them from overhead, cutting off the nightlight for a few moments, an icy gust of wind battering the rooftop as the sound of snapping wings drew both Myra and Christopher's gazes up.

The dragon circled overhead, a full-grown adult dragon with a wing span that blocked out the sky, a thick body, long tail, and suspiciously sharp looking spikes around its long, slim neck. Against the city lights, the dragon was a dark color, maybe blue but possibly red. And its scales caught the building lights, giving it a shimmering glow.

Something that large should not be able to fly in between the tightly packed skyscrapers of downtown Chicago, but dragons, Myra was learning, were amazing creatures with an awful lot more maneuverability than she'd assumed given their size.

The dragon tucked its wings and slid between the high buildings to the north of them, before circling back and landing on the opposite side of the roof, facing them. Up close, the creature was even more intimidatingly impressive, with a long face circled by a sharp-looking ruff of what could be spikes or hair, raised nostrils that steamed, and wide set, black eyes that were impossible to read.

Somewhat to Myra's amusement, Christopher moved to stand in front of her, placing himself between the strange dragon and her. He really was very gallant. It was weird to be on the receiving end of all that gallantry, though.

Because he was guarding their front from the dragon, she took a moment to glance over the side of the building. Long way down to the sidewalk.

She faced the dragon again as it shifted and shrank, its body shimmering in a cloud of sparkling dark fog as it made the change. That was...wild. To be fair, she'd never seen a dragon shift from full dragon to human before. The closest she'd gotten was watching Christopher snap out wings when he needed them.

Again, it occurred to her she hadn't seen Christopher's full dragon form yet. And she was curious enough to wonder what he'd look like.

When the stranger dragon finished its shift, Myra wasn't really surprised to see their tail from the train. She *was* a little surprised he really was a dragon. She'd been prepared to believe he was human as he'd claimed because Christopher hadn't sniffed him out as a dragon. She'd have to ask Christopher about that later. She was also a little surprised the newcomer had approached them in full dragon regalia after trying to pass as human on the train. He could have just used the elevator like she had.

His human form was the same as it had been on the train, so he really did look that way as a human. Innocuous, light hair, dark eyes. Smaller than Christopher in stature, but taller standing than she'd thought on the train. He had clothes on after the shift, which she found interesting. Christopher took his shirt off to let his wings out. Was that only because it was a partial shift or…?

So many questions about dragon shifters. Really, she needed to do more research.

"Long time no see," she called to the man. "You said you weren't a dragon."

"And you said you were here for a vacation," he said, walking slowly toward them, his hands open and at his sides.

She assumed he was trying to look harmless, or at least like he wasn't intending on attacking them. But honestly, he'd landed on the roof in dragon form. Did he really think he'd get away with looking harmless now?

"But you already knew that was a lie," she said. "Are you working with the New York king after all?"

His gaze flicked to Christopher, who'd remained silent and firmly between her and the new dragon. "Not…technically. I was being honest about that at least."

"Oh, I'd love to hear this. Go on. You're here for a reason. Spill the tea and tell us all the gossip."

"We needed a distraction," the dragon said with a shrug. "And information."

"Meaning?" Christopher asked. Given that was the first word he'd spoken, and his voice was very deep and guttural sounding, with just a hint of hiss in it even though there were no "s"s in the word, Myra thought maybe the new dragon should be nervous.

The dragon did flick a quick look at Christopher, then focused his gaze on Myra, his head tilted down at an angle that made it necessary for him to look upward to meet her eyes. It was a strange and awkward sort of angle. She had to assume he was doing that on purpose. And suddenly it occurred to her that might be some sort of dragon deference gesture?

"The wizard is siding with the rebelling dragons in this situation. He's been here in Chicago a long time, and he's always worked here at the dragon king's pleasure. We suspect he'd like to change that balance."

"That's a you guys thing," Myra said. "Why would the *New Yor]* king send us here? Send *me* here?" Especially for so much money, to retrieve something that wasn't here, to help another king. None of it made sense.

"It's to the New York king's benefit to monitor what's happening in Chicago and, if possible, to ensure dragons don't get the idea that rebelling against their king is a viable option."

She could see that. "What's your name?" she asked suddenly. Tired of looking at this guy and thinking of him as a tail. That took on a new meaning when he was a dragon shifter and actually had a tail.

"Archer."

"If I call you Archie, will you growl?"

"Yes."

"Fair enough. He has to be Christopher." She nodded at Christopher, who growled if you tried to call him Chris. Which was fine. She liked Christopher better. "Is that a dragon thing? Not liking your names shortened?"

"You don't know?"

"Why would I?"

Archer paused, then shrugged. "Right." Again his gaze flicked to Christopher but very briefly before dancing away.

"So, why bring in a human thief and risk sending Christopher here? Still not seeing the connection." Actually, she was starting to. But she wanted the explanation from the dragon's mouth, so to speak, to make sure she'd figured this out right.

"Christopher made for a good distraction. The dragons here are whispering. The rebelling ones worried the New York king might involve himself and his cohort."

"Would he?" she asked Christopher. "Seems the kings usually stay out of this sort of thing." Not that she really knew. Archer had made it abundantly clear she wasn't overflowing with the dragon knowledge.

"I hadn't thought he would," Christopher said. "But given this… I'll have to speak with him when we return."

Oh, she'd love to be a fly on the wall during that conversation. Though, if things got spicy and they started throwing fire at each other, she wouldn't want to be caught in that crossfire.

"Christopher is only here because the New York king sent me to retrieve a chalice that wasn't there. Why *that* part of all this?" Although, she'd already guessed.

"To test the wizard's defenses."

"Of course. And the fact that I got in and out?"

"Means he's not invulnerable."

"But also that I'm very very good at what I do and not just anyone and their dragon could have done what I did."

Archer shrugged. "Fair point. But if it's possible for anyone, then it's possible. Which means the wizard and all his dragons are not impervious to consequences while they're inside the wizard's tower."

"You used us."

"It's what kings do."

And she was not at all happy about it. Only good thing was she got paid up front. That money had already been moved to several separate and secret accounts so the king couldn't just snatch it back. Seems her natural paranoia worked in her favor on this job. Except for the part where she actually did a job that wasn't one.

"Now what?"

"You two can go home. Or stay for the weekend. The Chicago king has offered you the use of his suite at one of the luxury hotels if you'd like to use it." His gaze flicked to Christopher again. "Special guests."

"No," Christopher said before she could.

She might love the idea of staying in a luxury hotel for the night, and she definitely wouldn't mind exploring Chicago more at some point. This was not that moment.

She also flicked a glance at Christopher. She was still deciding if he was that company.

Archer just shrugged at Christopher's rejection of the Chicago king's offer. "Suit yourselves."

"Why can't he smell you?" she asked, curious. "Why didn't Christopher know you were a dragon?"

"Ah. That. Well…"

"A genetic anomaly," Christopher answered for him. "Happens in about one in every thousand dragons. His dragon side doesn't create a scent. Just his human side. So dragons…all shifters really, will only register him as human."

"Is that…a good anomaly or a bad one?" she asked both dragons.

"Handy," Archer said. "Easier to fly under the radar. So to speak."

"They often work as intermediaries between cohorts because they don't trigger aggressive territorial instincts in different kings," Christopher added.

Ah. So that's how this all got set up. "You've been passing the messages between kings," she said. "And that's why you in particular where the one following us."

"Christopher wouldn't be able to identify me as a dragon, and I'm the only one outside of the kings who knew what your real mission was, so it made sense I keep an eye on you."

She pulled in a deep breath and let it out in a rush, letting it ruffle the fine hairs on her forehead. "I'd call this a wasted trip, but I got paid, and paid well, so I guess that's something."

"And you managed to break into a wizard's tower and escape unscathed," Archer pointed out.

She wanted to wave that away, but given the wizard's guard spells, she was pretty proud of that accomplishment.

"Since you're not staying the weekend, the Chicago king has something for the New York king. Save me a trip if you could bring it back to him."

Christopher growled low in his throat, which Myra decided meant she needed to do the talking here. "We'll deliver this whatever it is, but that's gonna cost extra. Courier fee."

Archer's mouth twitched. The closest he'd come to a smile. "You can bill the king. He's good for it."

"Which one?"

"Up to you. They've both got the funds."

"You trying to tempt me?"

"Didn't learn from the last bet you took to break into a dragon king's hoard?" Archer asked.

"Fair point. What are we delivering?"

Archer, his gaze fully on Christopher now, shrugged something off his shoulders, slowly.

Myra had noticed the straps over his shoulders, a backpack like the type Christopher wore, that was long and narrow down the spine, leaving room for wings. But she was pretty sure that backpack hadn't been on Archer's back in dragon form. At least, she hadn't noticed it while he was dragon. Though the big teeth and potential for fire breath might have distracted her.

Archer's movements remained slow, and careful, as he pulled the pack around and set it gently on the ground. He proceeded to open it very slowly, his gaze still directed toward Christopher. But now he was kneeling and his head was definitely tilted down. A very supplicant pose.

Myra watched it all, fascinated. She had so many questions. But mostly, just watching dragons interact with other dragons gave her a lot of information. She wondered if they realized they were revealing themselves to her. She also wondered if Christopher would answer some of her many questions.

The backpack fell open. Archer jumped away from the contents, suddenly enough to land about ten yards away.

Okay. She frowned and looked at what the open bag revealed.

Except...

She had to be seeing that wrong.

She leaned around Christopher to get a better look. Nope. She was absolutely seeing that right. Even if she hadn't trusted her own eyes, which she did—one of her magic skills made it easier for her to see through magical illusions—Christopher's quiet hiss would have confirmed her suspicions.

The chalice.

The very fucking chalice they'd been sent to steal.

Chapter Ten

"The Chicago king had it all along?" Myra asked without looking at Archer.

Her full attention was on the huge cup sticking out of the crumbled black backpack sitting innocently on the roof of the high-rise, the lights of downtown Chicago surrounding them. A cold breeze off the lake ruffled her hair and she hardly noticed. She couldn't believe what she was seeing. And yet, she really should have guessed.

Fucking dragon kings.

"How do you think he paid for the New York king's help?" Archer said with a shrug she caught from the corner of her eye.

In real life, the chalice was a pretty impressive relic, even rising up out of the pile of nylon. It was larger than she'd realized, based on the pictures, probably a good two-foot-tall, with a flat, round base, long, thick stem—she'd have trouble getting one hand around it—and a wide, shallow bowl at the top. The rim around the bowl and the rounded base of polished white were the only visible bone parts of the chalice. The rest was wrapped in an iridescent, shimmering material that resembled green, yellow, and purple scales but also looked like stained glass. The skin of a dragon from centuries past, according to the legend around the chalice.

The scales were almost as see through as glass, giving hints of the bone structure underneath. In the pictures, that transparency had been difficult to see. The luminosity of it hard to appreciate. In person, the cup fairly glowed, even in the dim lights thrown by the surrounding skyscrapers. It almost looked like the cup was lit from within, like the skin had a natural luminescence.

It was one of the most beautiful cups she'd ever seen. And now that she was seeing it in person, she realized she'd have had trouble carrying that thing out of the wizard's tower. And also, it was entirely too big for the cubby safe it was supposed to have been in.

Honestly, she should have known she was being played sooner. It was just embarrassing that she hadn't figured it out before breaking into the vault.

"Pretty," she murmured, straightening.

"Dangerous," Christopher said.

"You get to carry it, then." She didn't trust the New York king at his word that touching the chalice wouldn't be bad for her. The scales were glowing. On a cup. Without any internal battery or light. The only things she knew that did that were magic and radiation, and neither seemed like a good idea to touch.

Christopher didn't immediately approach the bag. He stared hard at Archer, the intensity of the stare intimidating to Myra and she wasn't even the focus of it. She looked up at the side of his face. Yeah, he could probably be pretty scary when he wanted to be.

She didn't consider interfering, though. This was a dragon thing. And she couldn't breathe fire.

After several very tense moments, Christopher lowered his gaze to the backpack. "The king thanks you for your assistance in this matter," he said, very formally. "I take possession of the payment for *his* assistance in your matter. We are in accord."

"We are in accord," Archer repeated, his head bowed.

Christopher stalked forward suddenly and Myra rushed to keep up. She wasn't going to touch the chalice, but she definitely wanted a closer look.

"That would have been tricky to carry out of the wizard's tower," she murmured, staring down at the huge goblet, that looked even larger up close. Definitely two-foot-tall, plus, and probably weighed fifty pounds or more. Unless there was some dragon magic that made it lighter than it looked.

Based on the flexing of Christopher's arm muscles as he lifted the entire backpack containing the chalice, she was guessing the cup might weigh even more than she thought.

"Could you have managed?" Christopher asked quietly as he stared at the relic. In his hands, the whole thing looked less massive, still huge, but more like it fit. Definitely a cup designed for dragons the size of Christopher.

"I could have managed. But it would have been trickier. The pictures didn't do it justice."

Christopher pulled the sides of the backpack up and zipped it closed, the chalice safely cut off from the outside world again. He slipped the whole thing over his back. He still had his shirt on, not taking it off when he positioned the pack, so he wasn't going to fly them off the roof.

That was a shame. She liked jumping off roofs.

"When you see them," Christopher said to Archer, "tell the rebels that I stand by what I said. I won't be helping them."

Myra bit her lip to keep from showing any reaction to what Christopher had just said.

Archer didn't show that same restraint. His brows went up high, even though his head remained mostly tilted down. "You assume I'll see them? I'm loyal to my king."

"I'm sure you are. Just pass on my message. I don't want to have to make my point again. Next time, I won't be so restrained."

Myra could actually see Archer swallowing. There were things going on in this conversation that she needed to understand better. But maybe after Archer left.

The other dragon gave a sharp nod, then backed up a few paces and started to shift. Christopher edged Myra backward, so there was distance between them and the changing shifter. Once Archer finished, the huge dragon stood across the roof from them, his wings tucked against his thick sides. Now that she could see him better this way, Myra noted the color of his scales was definitely red, but a dark maroon red.

The dragon, despite the size difference, dipped his huge head at Christopher, then rose onto his hind legs, flapped his wings once, and launched straight upward. The wind from his wings forced Myra backward a step. Christopher caught her arm to keep her from falling over. She grinned up at him, shaking her head.

"You don't even think about that kind of thing, do you?"

"About what?" he asked, his gaze turned upward as he tracked the retreating dragon.

"Nothing." She waited until Archer had disappeared and Christopher looked down at her before asking, "So you met some of the rebel dragons while I was busy breaking into the wizard tower, huh?"

"They came and found me on the roof across from the wizard's tower while I was waiting for you, yes. Which is, I suspect, what both the kings were hoping for."

"What did they say?"

He shrugged and set a gentle hand at the small of her back, guiding her toward the door that would take them inside the building and to the elevator. "They are unhappy with the way their king is running things. They'd like a new king."

"Do they have someone in mind?"

"Me."

She stumbled over the doorway ledge leading into the small foyer where the elevator and stairway were. Christopher caught her again with ease.

She was too surprised to be embarrassed by the slip. "You? You who is already the son of another territory's king?"

"A king who's strong and has good control of his cohort. By having me king here, they'd also get the power and backing of my father. So they assumed. For some reason, they thought that would be a good idea."

"I take it it's not."

They had to wait a few minutes for the elevator to come all the way up to them. The five-foot square foyer around them was utilitarian, gray walls, black linoleum flooring, all easy to clean but not designed to be aesthetically pleasing. She presumed because no one in the building used the roof for much. There was just enough room for her and Christopher to stand side-by-side, but it reminded her a little of the sleeper car on the train. Forcing them into close proximity, close enough to touch.

She didn't actually mind the touching part, though.

"Attempting to combine both cohorts under a dynastic kingship would be bad for everyone. My father has more than enough power as is. Anymore would be…dangerous."

Well. That was an interesting insight. The elevator bell dinged and the silver doors slid open. Christopher followed her inside, but he had to duck to get in.

"So," she said. "Back to New York. Your father gets the chalice after all. We leave the trouble in Chicago here in Chicago. And we go back to our regular lives?"

"What is your regular life?" he asked as the elevator whisked them down to the ground level.

She grinned. "More of this. But in New York mostly."

"And when you aren't stealing things?"

"I like to read." She folded her hands in front of her, smiling at their reflections in the elevator doors. "How about you?"

"Reading is nice. Movies are good, too."

"Go to many movies, do you?" She wondered if he could do movies without drawing so much attention they were impossible to enjoy. She also wondered if the seating would be uncomfortable for someone his size.

"The occasional matinee," he said.

"Sounds fun."

"Want to join me for a movie? After we get back."

Her grin widened. "So long as it's not a heist movie, I'm in."

"No crime movies? I'm surprised."

She shrugged. "I get enough crime in my day job."

Christopher's chuckle tickled along her spine and started that tingling in her stomach again. That tingling sensation was going to get her into trouble. Definitely dangerous.

Good thing she liked danger.

The Dragon Thief Series
The Poisons Book Job
Bestselling author of the Cary Redmond Series
KAT SIMONS

THE POISONS BOOK JOB
BOOK THREE

Priceless artifact, impossible heist... How can a thief resist?

As Myra tries to find her footing in this new world of dragon shifters, one problem clearly stands out above the rest. The dragon king and his dangerous jobs. Avoiding Christopher because of his father proves impossible, though. And when the king offers her yet another job, a heist almost as interesting as it is impossible, she gives in. To both the job, and working with Christopher again.

Pulling off an impossible theft requires focus, precision, and planning. Precision and planning, Myra has down. Focus... With Christopher around, that focus wavers. Ignoring a seven-foot tall, intimidatingly sexy dragon shifter would challenge even the most determined. Myra's determined. Just not determined enough to stay away from Christopher.

But first they have to pull of his father's impossible mission and recover a priceless relic. Without getting caught.

And without letting her feelings get in the way.

Chapter One

Myra slipped across the roofs of the Brownstones until coming to the roof she was aiming for. One that had a low wall and pressure sensors on the roof that were impossible to see if you didn't know they were there.

The Manhattan night kissed her cheeks with chilly air, the sounds of traffic over on Third a quiet hum. This neighborhood was exceptionally quiet at three in the morning, for Manhattan, but quiet in New York wasn't technically quiet. A couple of dogs barked a few streets over, which meant at least two people had to take their dogs out for walks at this time of night. She loved animals, but this is why, if she were to get a pet, it would be a cat. They could pee on their own while she was out working.

A cat burglar getting a cat might be clichéd, though.

The roof she needed to cross was wide and mostly empty, unlike the one she was standing in which was covered in raised stones boxes filled with plants and had a nice set of patio furniture and an outdoor grill. There were even trellises with ivy growing over them, though the ivy was mostly dead at the moment, given they were rolling into winter. The roof she stood on topped a Brownstone owned by a family that sent their two twin girls to private school and had parties up here that they claimed were for family but an awful lot of the mother's associates from the big accounting firm where she was a partner got invited.

Currently, the entire family was out of the country for a ski vacation, and the staff didn't spend the night. Which made this building a safe place to work from.

The roof Myra was aiming for was a wide-open square but for the small raised hut that led inside to the stairwell. The gray stone tiles on the roof looked ordinary and harmless. But her research confirmed they were sensitive enough to detect a pigeon landing on them. Which was probably annoying to the people who had to monitor the activity because there were a lot of pigeons in the city.

She pulled a hook and wire from a pocket of her jacket, and using a little spell to ensure the hook landed against the raised hut on the first throw, she swung and tossed the metal barbs, catching a sharp lip of the hut. She tied off the other end of the long wire to a metal loop fixed into the accountant's roof, a metal loop used to chain the grill down most of the time—for some reason, the residents hadn't bothered chaining the grill last time they'd used it. Maybe they'd assumed no one would try to steal it from off the roof?

There was an irony there since she was an actual thief but *wasn't* going to be stealing the grill. She had something a little different in mind.

She grabbed the wire, her gloved hands protecting her skin, and swung up so her legs hooked over, stretched out so she could use her feet to help her shimmy along the wire. Dangling over the motion sensor tiles, moving fast along the thin wire, she mentally asked all pigeons in the area to stay away for the next fifteen minutes.

The painting she was here for wasn't hanging on any of the walls inside the five story Brownstone. It wasn't kept inside a vault either, which was amusing to her. It was tilted against a wall in a closet on the third floor, one of many gently stacked into the closet, waiting for its rotation when it actually would get a position on a wall somewhere.

The Brownstone was owned, outwardly, by a small agency that claimed to represent artists in the city. Supposedly, all the art inside the mansion consisted of clients' work either given to the agency as a gift, or donated to the agency for resale. In point of fact, most of it was stolen from clients who were having trouble paying rent and buying groceries because their "agents" couldn't get them gallery showings or sell any of their work for more than a pittance.

Myra liked artists. It was a strange, but probably predictable thing, for a thief to have a soft spot for the people who created the things she stole. She never actually stole things from the artists, though. She stole things from the rich people who bought the artists' work.

Or in this case, stole the work first.

And this particular piece was worth a fortune according to an appraiser Myra sometimes worked with, but the agency had told the artist it was only worth a hundred dollars and they were being generous giving her that much. The artist was a single mother about to be evicted. Myra really didn't like that. So here she was, breaking and entering, not for her own amusement this time, but to help an artist out.

She might be a thief, but there were lines. And standards. And she had no compunctions about stealing from other thieves.

The hut was sturdy enough so that when she crawled on to it, it didn't even groan under her weight. Leaving the hook in place for her escape, she used the same lip that held the hook secure and folder herself over and down, hanging in front of the locked door without touching the tiles. Once she was certain her handhold wouldn't collapse, she released one hand and used a little spell to open the door. She could pick the lock in a pinch, but the spell finessed the lock in twenty seconds, saving her time.

Despite the pressure tiles all over the roof, the lock itself wasn't complicated. And the interior of the hut wasn't monitored or alarmed.

Sometimes thieves had blind spots. She liked to take advantage of those.

She slipped downstairs to the closet containing the piece she wanted, the house dark and quiet. No one actually lived here. This was a glorified warehouse and, when necessary, a fancy sort of office for the agency. The head of the agency, a man whose nasal voice irritated every last one of Myra's nerves, entertained wealthy clients here when he had something to sell, and intimidated eager artists here when he was trying to rope in a gullible aspirant.

When not in use, the place had a decent security system in place, but it was focused on entrance and exit points. Windows, doors, the roof. There was an elevator that was locked down when no one was using the house. And the first two floors had cameras in place that could be turned on remotely—and were during events so the agency's security team could monitor and spy on potential clients and customers.

But on the top three floors, the security was limited to doors and windows. A weird system, but it worked for her.

The lock on the storage closet was a cute little biosensor thing that didn't stand up to her spells and lock picks for more than thirty seconds. It tried, though. She was in and out of the closet in moments, waving her fingers over the locks to spell it sealed again.

Locked room mystery, she thought as she hurried back up to the roof.

The hardwood stairs didn't creak under her feet, but they might have if she hadn't had on her specialized shoes, a bit like ballet slippers that were almost like walking in socks, and had a little spell in the sole that helped dampen sound. She'd watched the building all day and knew it was empty, but better to be safe than sorry.

She tucked the painting into the small black nylon backpack she wore, which was just large enough to fit around the frameless one foot by one foot canvas, then opened the door onto the roof and reached up for the wire still taunt overhead.

She didn't scream when someone touched her gloved hand. But it was close. Years of training and practice keeping the surge of adrenaline spiked by irritated surprise from erupting out of her mouth. She looked up, prepared to run back into the house and escape through her alternate exit point.

Then cursed under her breath and shook her head, scowling up at the dragon shifter prince casually sitting on the hut above her.

CHAPTER TWO

Christopher sat on the roof of the hut, his legs crossed, his huge wings tucked up against his back so that all Myra saw of them were the joints rising above his bent head. His blue eyes gleamed in the darkness, catching light from the surrounding buildings where a few windows were lit even this late at night. His dark hair ruffled in the cold breeze, calling attention to the fact that he was shirtless—what she was starting to think of as his flying uniform—the purple and yellow scales over his chest and the wings giving away his nature.

He was a huge man when standing, but like this, and from her current angle standing beneath him trying hard not to step out onto the motion sensor tiles lining the Brownstone's otherwise empty roof, it was hard to see. He needed a shave, she noticed, evening scruff darkening his jaw and almost, but not quite, obscuring the scar there. He had another scar on his forehead, neither of which she'd ever asked him about, though her curiosity was peaked.

He wasn't what most people might call handsome. Compelling was the word she used for him. Something about the arrangement of his features fit together to capture attention when all those individual elements should probably have looked awkward, maybe even ugly on a different man.

On this particular man, everything just worked.

She sighed. "What the hell are you doing here? I'm working."

"You've been avoiding me," he said, his voice quiet even though there was no one around.

"No, I haven't." Except she really had been.

"Why?"

"I'm working. Can we talk about this another time?"

"I'm here to help."

"Help?"

He nodded toward her back, where the canvas she'd just stolen was carefully concealed inside her black nylon backpack.

She narrowed her eyes up at him. "Is this because I'm helping a woman in trouble?"

He shrugged and glanced away but the darkening color along his cheekbones delighted her. He was ridiculously sweet about this kind of thing.

"Damsel in distress," she murmured.

He had a real soft spot for them. Got him into trouble all the time apparently. She thought it was adorable.

"Did you get the painting?" he asked.

She tucked her chin. "Did you really just insult me that way?"

"Sorry." He reached down for her hand.

She grabbed his thick forearm and let him lift her—with such ease it made her stomach flutter—up onto the top of the hut. She settled next to him, her legs dangling over the roof. "What was your plan?" she asked.

"To guard your back and then fly you off the roof to wherever you needed to go."

"Decent plan." And would save her time. "But you probably should have discussed this with me. Ahead of time."

"You've been avoiding me," he repeated.

"No. I haven't," she repeated, the lie slipping out on easily faked offense.

"What are you going to do with the painting?"

"Hand it off to my appraiser, who will sell it and then ensure the artist in question gets the full amount. Less a small fee for me and the appraiser, of course. But in this case, we're both only taking a nominal fee. The artist deserves a good payday after her agents stole so much from her."

"Does your appraiser have a buyer in mind?"

"Would you buy the painting if she didn't?"

He didn't answer but he did hold her gaze.

She grinned. "There is a buyer waiting. But it's sweet of you to offer."

"How much will the painting get?"

"Four million, give or take."

He nodded. "Good. Let me know if the buyer balks at that price."

"I will." She tilted her head and smiled softly at him. "You're entirely too sweet to be the dragon king's son."

He rolled his eyes, but that charming color darkened his pale cheeks again. "Can I see the painting?"

She shrugged and pulled her backpack around, unzipping it enough to show him the canvas.

The square, one foot by one foot, painting was a portrait of a child playing in a garden. The technique was exquisite, photo realistic but with an odd color palette that gave it an almost fairy-like quality. And it was that ethereal element, combined with the photorealism, that had made the work so valuable to collectors. Which the artist didn't realize. Because her agents were crooks.

"Beautiful," Christopher murmured.

"Definitely. And the buyer will treat it, and the artist, with the respect this piece deserves."

"I didn't know you had a soft spot for damsels in distress, too."

She snorted. "Nothing like yours."

She replaced the painting into her backpack and slipped the pack over her shoulders. Then she unlatched her hook and murmured a little spell that released the tied end of the wire from the neighboring roof. The wire snapped back fast, but not quite fast enough to avoid the pressure plates. The first few tips of the wire against the stone didn't produce any reaction. But at the last minute, the wire smacked against a stone, just before retracting fully.

"Oops," she said as she heard the alarm inside the house going off. A similar alarm would be going off at the agency's security office, where a sleepy but diligent guard would be turning on cameras to see if a pigeon was having a party on the roof.

At least, she hoped the guard thought this was a pigeon-related alarm. She folded and tucked the hook into one of her many vest pockets and stood, balancing on the small metal roof. "Time to go," she said.

Christopher rose to his full height which was very impressive and always made her tingly. She had a real soft spot for tall men. He snapped out his wings and she jumped up into his arms. He caught her easily and without comment. When she had her arms around his neck, he crouched low and then launched himself upward, leaping high above the Brownstones. He brought his wings down hard in two strong beats, catching the air currents, circling them up higher and higher until the island receding below, looking more like an elaborate model of a city than a real city beneath them.

He took them so high, the air was cold and thin, but his body heat kept her warm. When he'd flown a few miles from Murray Hill, and the site of her theft, he dropped back closer to the rippling skyline of high rises, moving them smoothly through the canyons created by buildings as he headed toward Central Park.

"Did you really come tonight just to help me steal a painting?" she asked, studying the side of his face as he stared out over the city lights.

"Not just. But I did want to help with this."

"Don't tell me, your father has another job for me?"

His gaze flicked to her, then out over the city again. "My father has another job for you. If you want it."

Did she? The dragon king paid very well. But the last job she'd done for him had been…irritating. Did she want to risk that sort of irritation again?

"Is it a real job this time? I'm actually going to be stealing something and not…whatever that last job was supposed to be?"

"That's what he says," Christopher hedged, not meeting her gaze.

She pursed her lips and considered her options. Saying no to the dragon king was probably a bad idea. But she no longer owed him anything, so she'd only be doing this because she wanted to. The pay would be good. And it was entirely possible the job would be fun.

The fun part was the real trick for her these days.

She gave a brief nod. "I'll hear him out, then. Not saying I'll take the job. But I'll listen." She gave a little wave. "Have to take care of tonight's acquisition first, though."

"I can take you to him tomorrow night. Will that give you enough time?"

"Tomorrow night will do."

"And maybe then you'll explain why you've been avoiding me."

She pressed her lips together so she wouldn't point out again that she hadn't been avoiding him. Because she had.

And it was because of his father.

CHAPTER THREE

S he met Christopher in the open courtyard at the center of Columbia University. It was as good a place as any, because she was still hesitant to let him know exactly where she lived. Not really for his sake. But because she didn't want his father to know.

The dragons had been attempting to track her, but she was used to going unnoticed and slipping away from people. That was part of her job. Her thief magic helped as well because she could hide her scent. This came in handy whenever there were shifters of any kind around.

Dragon shifters had very keen eyesight, though. The kind of eyesight that could pick a human out of a crowd on a sidewalk while they were soaring high above the skyscrapers. That was something she had a harder time hiding from. But if they were in that crowd with her, they couldn't pick out her scent from the other humans surrounding them. And since the dragon king was trying to do this in a low-profile way, he kept sending his dragons in human form to follow her.

She was delighted by the fact that they kept losing track of her. Less excited by the fact that Christopher *could* track her. That he'd found her last night, even though she'd been working. She had no idea how he'd managed it, and that was the worrying part. Also the reason she picked Columbia as their meetup point. She had a feeling he might already know where she lived, but she wanted to keep the illusion going that she still had some secrets from him.

The night was cool but not too cold. That sort of mild, late autumn temperature that made for nice night walks, the soft glow of the city not far away. The courtyard in front of the Low Library was quiet at this time of night when college was out of session for some sort of break. The courtyard itself was lit by very dim streetlamps, softer and pinker than the orange lights on the sidewalks, giving the white stone columns and steps up into the library a glow.

Christopher was waiting for her, sitting on the marble steps, his blue eyes gleaming with a faint purple as she approached. He didn't stand, but waited for her to sit on the step beside him. He was such a tall man, she got the impression he often made himself seem smaller to keep from intimidating the people around him. Unless he wanted to intimidate those people, of course.

Myra didn't mind his height. In fact, she quite liked it. Which definitely complicated things. And made a lot of fluttering and tingling happen whenever he hovered over her.

He was wearing his "flight" suit, which tonight meant he had on dark cargo pants with side pockets that looked empty—what a waste of pockets—but no shirt and no shoes. He really didn't seem to like shoes very much. And the shirtless thing meant he intended to do the partial shift to give himself wings without changing any other part of his body.

One day, she hoped he'd show her his full dragon. She hadn't asked yet. Any more than she'd asked about his scars. And she wasn't going to ask tonight.

Instead, she went right to the point. "Your father waiting?"

"Impatiently. He didn't understand why this meeting couldn't take place last night."

"Because I'm not a dragon who comes at the king's call."

"I did point that out to him."

She grinned. "Figured you did. He hated that, didn't he?"

"To the depths of his soul."

"I'm not going on another wild goose chase," she repeated. "Not doing what we did last time. I hate being used. He crossed a line. I have one more line for him, and if he crosses that, I'm done doing anything for him."

"Fair enough." Christopher stood in a smooth, graceful flow of muscle and sinew that was just rudely sexy and stretched his hand out to her.

She took his hand and used his muscles to leverage herself up and directly into his arms. The fact that he didn't even blink at her suddenly jumping up onto him, that he just caught her automatically, did funny things to her. Made her soft and happy and fluttery in ways that were so so dangerous.

He held her gaze for a long moment as he cradled her close to his chest, and she didn't flinch away from that look. But the longer he held her, the longer he studied her face, the harder her heart pounded. When his gaze dropped briefly to her mouth, it took willpower not to lick her lips. They'd kissed once. Well, technically twice that same night. And it had been a very very good kiss. She wanted to revisit that kiss. She knew he did, too.

But…

It was that internal "but" that kept stopping her. Not because it existed, but because she wasn't entirely sure what it meant. "But" what? She didn't truly understand her own hesitance. She knew it had something to do with him being the dragon king's son. And the dragon king being an ass who seemed to think he could lay claim to her, command her the way he commanded his cohort. This summons was just another reminder that the king *wanted* to be able to claim her as part of his cohort even if she wasn't a dragon.

She didn't like that, didn't like the position it put her in. And kissing Christopher would complicate that situation. She knew instinctively it would.

Unfortunately, self-preservation instincts did not stop her from wanting to kiss him again.

He blinked suddenly, his gaze jumping away from her face. Then he crouched and launched up into the air. His wings snapped out suddenly, the shift so quick, the appearance of his wings so sudden, she gasped.

He spiraled up high over the buildings, leaving her dizzy, her stomach dancing. All of it thrilling, like riding a roller coaster. She could do this with him all the time.

That was another reason for the ill-defined yet definitely serious "but" in all this.

They banked over the northern edge of Central Park, before Christopher headed to the top of Manhattan, to the dragon king's hold.

The mansion was a large complex tucked into thickly wooded lands. The king had no immediate neighbors, though land in Manhattan—anywhere in Manhattan—was at a premium. The mansion itself was a vague cross between a castle with its turreted towers and low retaining walls along the roof, and modern, with its funky architectural arrangement of box buildings and open glass walkways leading between section of the mansion.

The roof of the main building was huge, and flat, with a large grassy area on one side for the youngling dragons to land, and a large stone area on the other side designed to allow fully shifted adult dragons to land, one at a time, with ease. One at a time for defensive purposes. Easily because this was the seat of the king's power, the place the cohort aggregated when they needed to.

The place had been designed to be dragon friendly in every way. Even the proportions of the interior of the mansion were designed with dragons in mind, with the ceilings being that bit taller and some of the corridors wide and high so one of the cohort could walk through in his dragon form, wings tucked against his sides.

Myra's eyes were watering a little as they landed on the roof. Christopher had flown here faster and higher than he usually moved with her, and the air at that altitude had been cold and sharp. She didn't mind. She wanted to get this meeting with the king over with.

"Any idea what he's going to ask me to do?" She brushed her tears away as Christopher set her on her feet on the stone roof. He folded his wings against his back, but didn't shift them away.

"He didn't see fit to explain the job to me. Just...asked me to check in with you about doing it."

"Asked?" She snorted.

Christopher led her past the open, exterior metal gate that would come down if the mansion needed to be sealed off for any reason, and through the elaborate double wooden doors beyond that opened into the mansion. They were huge, those doors, and decorated with carvings and symbols she wasn't familiar with, all inlaid with precious stones, all of which she was familiar with.

She wouldn't attempt to steal any of them, though. Even when she'd broken into the dragon king's hoard on a bet, she hadn't intended on stealing anything valuable. Just a small token to prove she'd done it and win her bet. And she'd intended on putting the token back. A thief only stole from the dragon king at her peril. Only her dumb luck that they caught her before she'd escaped. She had no intention of giving the king any more influence in her life by stealing something else from him. But she did admire all the lovely, winking stones imbedded in the dark wood as Christopher pushed opened the heavy doors with shocking ease and led her inside.

A large ramp led from the doors down to the top floor of the mansion. From there, Christopher walked her directly to the king's throne room. The corridor was lined with slick white marble threaded with gold that sparkled in the lights cast by overhead Venetian glass chandeliers. The audacity of having glass chandeliers in a corridor where a full-grown dragon might walk was, she had to admit, pretty impressive.

The whole mansion had a vague scent of dragon to it, a mix of reptile, faint sulfur, leather and musk. It was hard to describe. Her sense of smell wasn't great, nothing like a shifter's, so she only noticed the undertone of musk and dryness that she associated with reptiles because the scent was so pervasive here. It wasn't a bad smell, by any means, just a lot of it in one spot.

And it hit her lizard brain hard. That lizard brain recognized a predator's scent and kept telling her to run away and hide under a rock so the giant flying death machines didn't find her.

As they neared the entry into the king's throne room, Myra thought her lizard brain might just be on to something.

Chapter Four

The interior of the dragon king's throne room was pretty austere for a place presided over by a dragon who had a hoard of wealth underneath the mansion. His throne was elaborate enough, a seat made of bones and gold and winking stones. Three bones rose above his head in arches that reminded her a little of rib bones, and they too were decorated in leaf gold with rubies and diamonds imbedded in them.

The rest of the room, however, was just a large bare, marble-lined space. The marble here a darker red color with lines of obsidian. And instead of glass chandeliers, the room was lit by a series of sconces lining the walls. They were electric, but designed to look like flickering fire. Here, the underlying reptilian scent receded under a stronger smell of cleaning wax and bleach.

The place hadn't smelled so much like cleaner the last time she'd been here. What had happened that the audience chamber needed a good scrub down with bleach?

Probably something it was better she didn't know about. For her own survival.

She and Christopher stood shoulder to shoulder, or well, because he was so tall it was more like shoulder to thick bicep, but it was the thought that counted. They faced his father who sprawled on his throne in a more indolent slouch than he'd used last time she'd been here. Changing things up. Probably to keep her guessing. The bastard.

They'd been standing in silence since she and Christopher walked into the room. No one had greeted anyone. No words at all had been spoken.

Though she was still woefully ignorant of a lot of things about dragon shifters, she had finally started to do some research, as it looked like avoiding them going forward might be difficult, if not impossible. And she'd confirmed in that research that dragon shifters, at least the more common males, didn't have telepathy. There were rumors that one or two of the female dragon shifters did, but most of what was written about female dragon shifters was conjecture and hypothesis. There were only about twelve of them in the world. They mostly stayed away from other dragons, including each other. And they were so deadly, no one, not even dragon kings, went out of their way to change their minds.

Outside of those twelve females, most dragon shifters were male. There wasn't anything in the online searches she'd done about third genders or nonbinary or transgendered dragons, so she wanted to ask Christopher about that. But in the meantime, she had a few more details about basic dragon shifter biology, more than she'd known when meeting Christopher. And that included the fact that no male dragon shifter communicated telepathically. Not even kings. So the silence wasn't a conversation she wasn't able to hear.

The king was just being an ass.

The first one of them to break the silence was going to wonder if they'd lost. The longer this went on, the more certain she was of that. That they'd ended up in some kind of game the king was playing. A game that triggered her competitive instincts. She had no intention of speaking first. Let the dragons battle it out. And lose.

She did smile, though, when the dragon king's gaze fell on her. The family resemblance to his son was more obvious when they were standing in the same room. But the king was more conventionally handsome. Black, short curly hair with threads of silver through it, eyes that changed from blue to green depending on the lighting, a strong face. Though where Christopher's was long and narrow, the king's jaw and brow were more prominent. Thinner lips. The nose was different, too, she realized. She'd had more time to study Christopher's face since the last time she'd seen the king, and yeah, the nose was definitely different.

The king wore a small version of his larger crown, just a basic bejeweled diadem, nothing fancy—she nearly snorted at her own sarcasm—and instead of wearing elaborate regalia, he wore a black suit, complete with jacket and embroidered vest. During her last appearance in front of him, he'd worn dark trousers and an orange sweater, a color went remarkably well with his pale skin.

The casual wear, with the bejeweled crown as he sat on a throne of bone and gold and jewels had felt like a deliberate choice to throw her off. The change to a dark business suit felt equally deliberate. Though exactly what he was going for this time, she couldn't be sure. Nothing was ever entirely certain with the king. But when a man could shift to a building-sized creature that breathed fire, he could do whatever the hell he wanted.

"Thank you for coming, Myra," the king said, his head tilted in a graciously condescending way.

She held her smile, and her tongue. But the thrill of triumph that she'd *won* whatever game they'd been playing with the silence was very satisfying.

"I have another job offer for you."

Using the word *offer* was a choice. But she let it go. She wasn't going to reject his *offer* before she'd heard it.

"Curious?" he asked, his brow raised.

She was actually—irritatingly—curious what he wanted her to do. "Enough to still be standing here. Not enough to take the job without knowing what it is."

"I like you, Myra," the king said.

"Glad to hear it, your majesty." After their initial introduction, she wasn't so sure his statement was true, but she assumed his liking her meant he wasn't going to try killing her and that was always good.

"A book disappeared from my father's hoard a century before I was born," the king started.

She still had no idea how old the king was, just assumed he was old because he'd been around for a long time—though she assumed the threads of silver in his dark hair were affectations. But the mention of his father having a valuable hoard a century before he was even born was a pretty good indication that the dragons lived a very long time. According to the research she'd finally started, the males could live several centuries if they weren't killed. The trick was the not-being-killed part. Apparently, living to old age for a male dragon shifter was a real accomplishment.

"This is a magic book," the king said.

"Of course,"

"It's resurfaced."

"Don't tell me. A wizard has it." There'd been a lot of wizards going around lately. The last thing the king had sent her after was supposedly held by a wizard. And Christopher had been stolen by shifters working with a wizard. She wielded magic herself, but she preferred to avoid wizards. She had been unable to do that lately. She did not like that turn of events.

"Not a wizard this time, surprisingly," the king said, his thin-lipped mouth tipping up at one side. Not quite a smirk, but almost one. "This time, it's a human."

"A human? That sounds…"

"Impossible?"

"Improbable." An ordinary human breaking into a dragon king's hoard, even a few centuries ago, and stealing something that the dragon king had never found? Though, obviously this wasn't the same human. That human would have been dead for centuries. But the original thief was unlikely to have been a shifter or a wizard if a human had possession of the book now.

Maybe. Or maybe she was making assumptions. Lot of time in multiple centuries for things to happen.

"How'd the book end up with a human?" she asked.

"Sold. Apparently. From the original owner. In a private, underground auction. Which I wasn't invited to." His expression didn't change a lot, but his eyes narrowed, his nostrils flared, and a ripple of movement, a tightening, went through his jaw.

"Or you would have bought the book?"

"I would have…retrieved the book. Yes. Given it is my father's property."

"What's inside this magic book? Love potions?"

"Could be. Depending on your definition of a love potion. According to my father, and the legends, the book is full of formulas for various poisons. Magical ones that can do astounding things."

"Astounding things, like, kill stuff?" That was generally what she thought of when she thought of poisons.

"Kill, yes. But what's poisonous to one being can be curative to another. Especially when magic is involved."

"Curative?"

"A poison that cures illnesses, for example. Or seals up a wound. Or one that extends the life of a human indefinitely."

"You actually believe any of that?"

"I haven't noticed any long-lived humans outlasting their natural lifetimes or swaths of people being mysteriously and miraculously cured from an outbreak of deadly disease, so either the legends around the book's contents are false, the poisons are generally just deadly instead of helpful, or the persons in possession of the book all these years never risked trying one of the spells. Probably for the best if they weren't a wizard."

Yeah, spells of any kind could backfire if you didn't know what you were doing. Even her small thief's magic could do more damage than good if she hadn't learned how to use it properly.

"But the book itself is said to bring great wealth to its owner. That sort of thing is harder to...discern. There have been many fortunes won and lost over my lifetime. Whether those fortunes were due to a magical book or not..." He spread his hands. "Impossible to say."

"How's the book bring wealth if not via a spell?"

He shrugged. "I'm only telling you what I've been told. Obviously, I've never even seen the book."

"But you want it back."

"I want it back."

"Because it was your father's?"

"Because it rightfully belongs to my family, in my hoard, and a human having it in their possession is offensive to me."

The way the king said human was like someone talking about dog shit on their shoe. Nice to know where she, as a human, stood in his opinion. "How much did the book go for?" she asked out of curiosity.

"A hundred million."

She let out a soft whistle. "Someone thought it was worth that amount. Someone thought the legends held water."

"Or just wanted to possess something that no one else had. There are those kinds of collectors."

That was very true. Those were the collectors she stole from the most because it was fun taking a thing they only had because they deemed themselves worthy of possessing it.

And the king knew that a fun, challenging job, especially one that stuck it to a rich collector, would be just the sort of job that tempted her. It was annoying that he had her number that way.

"So is the book currently in someone's mansion tucked safely away in the family vault with grandma's jewels, or did this human get creative?"

"Creative. It's on display. Private museum, security of the highest caliber, invitation only viewing."

"Which you were also not invited to?"

"Actually, I have received an invitation to view the book. Whether the new owner realizes it's a relic from my father's hoard is anyone's guess. But unlike the auction, I was not left off of this VIP list."

Wow, he was really annoyed by being left off the underground auction invite list. "Where's this private museum?"

The king made a small hand gesture, and a man Myra hadn't seen until that very moment stepped out of the shadows in the corner of the room and handed her a manilla envelope.

Myra raised her brows at the man. He was six foot and dressed in a suit, like the king, but was careful about the way he glanced at Christopher, keeping his head tilted down, and kept his gaze averted from the king's all together. He had no such compunctions about staring at her, though, but his expression was unreadable. Professional and neutral. She couldn't immediately tell if the man was a dragon shifter or not, but she suspected he was. Maybe the king's assistant?

"Thanks," she said, raising the large envelope in a little salute.

The man nodded and returned to the corner of the room without once making a comment.

"Everything you need to know is inside that envelope. Including a copy of my invitation so you'll know what they look like. Just in case."

"You still have the original?" She glanced down at the envelope without opening it.

"I intend on attending the viewing, yes."

"Groovy. Alright. I'm going to look through all this and let you know if I'm in. No guarantees. If I get this book back for you, it'll cost you." She named her fee, which was substantial. The book had sold for one hundred million. Her fee was a fraction of that amount. But retrieving something that valuable came with higher risks. Higher risks costs more.

The king didn't blink at her fee. "Done. Paid ahead of time?"

"Not until I confirm I'm taking the job. Then I take the full payment upfront." She didn't trust the dragon king as far as she could throw him. He'd paid her for the last job, but she wasn't prepared to assume he'd pay her this time if something went wrong. Full payment. Upfront. *Then* she'd do the job.

"The exhibition and private viewing are soon. I'll need to know if you're going to do this for me by tomorrow at the latest."

"More than enough time."

"My son will be assisting you again."

Not a question. Not an order either, she realized. Just a statement of fact.

She glanced up at Christopher. He didn't look away from his father but he gave a small head nod, confirming he would be helping her if she took the job.

He hadn't said anything during the audience. Hadn't tried to interfere in any way. Had neither tried to talk her out of the job nor tried to talk his father out of giving her the job.

Either he wanted the book returned to his father, too. Or he was going to save his attempt to talk her out of taking the job for when they weren't in front of his father.

"Tomorrow morning, then." She gave the king a quick, sharp head nod, and turned to leave without waiting for him to give her permission. It was a risky move. Dragon kings were notoriously prickly about that sort of thing. But she needed to make clear, again, she wasn't one of his dragons to command. And she no longer owed him anything. Not even deference.

Christopher moved up behind her before she'd gone more than a few feet. She had no idea if he'd paid his father a curtesy goodbye without words or just followed her. Would have been interesting to see which and see the king's reaction to it all. But better not to look back. Not now.

Now, she had to get somewhere safe, go through the contents of the manilla envelope, and decide if this was a job she'd take.

She nearly laughed at that. Of course she was going to take the job.

She just wanted to make the dragon king sweat.

<h1 style="text-align:center">CHAPTER FIVE</h1>

Myra watched the video feed streaming through to her phone from the pin-sized camera on Christopher's lapel, studying the crowd of mostly humans as he walked through them. Everyone parted the way for him, which was fun to watch from this vantage. A few people even looked up at him, startled, and scrambled to move out of his path in a way that looked very undignified in their fancy clothes.

"Are you scaring people on purpose or just being yourself and that's how people react?" she asked into the earpiece that connected her and Christopher so they could talk during this operation. Thanks to her pointing out his father had a plus one on the invitation, Christopher was there as himself, with his father, all on the up-and-up. Which had made one aspect of this job easier.

"I'm not purposefully trying to intimidate anyone," Christopher said, sounding monumentally annoyed. "But I'm not hiding being unhappy."

"Then you are intimidating everyone on purpose. Shame on you," she said softly and with a laugh in her voice.

Actually, he was playing his part perfectly. Lots and lots of attention on the king of the dragons and one of his sons stalking through the interior of this gallery. Well, the king wasn't stalking around. When Christopher swung around to give her different view of the room, she spotted the king holding court at one side of the huge open space, a dozen humans gathered around him, hanging raptly on his every word.

The old goat had to be loving that.

The gallery itself with inside an old Catholic church, one of the beautifully made stone buildings with flying buttresses and elegant stained-glass windows. The church was designated a historical building and so was preserved almost exactly on the outside. The inside had undergone some renovation over the years. The pews, altar, and lectern had all been removed. The interior was now mostly a wide-open ground floor with inlaid tile floors and decorative stone pillars running the long narrow length of the main room, separating the outer aisles from the interior of the nave.

A narrow gallery circled the main floor from two stories up, a vantage that would give a beautiful view of the tiling on the ground floor and allowed access to the three large wood and metal chandeliers that ran the length of the nave. At one stage there'd been a giant pipe organ up in that gallery, but apparently, according to the information the dragon king's assistant had given her, the pipe organ was out being refurbished and rebuilt from a state of extreme decay.

The fact that the currently owners of the gallery intended on bringing the pipe organ back made her happy for reasons she hadn't tried to explain to Christopher when he'd asked. She just liked when old things were still valued and taken care of—or at least returned to their former glory and *then* taken care of.

The artwork for this particular show was scattered around the ground floor. Some huge paintings were hanging in the large bays that dotted the exterior wall, where there had once been statues of saints behind stands full of burning candles. No candles now. At least not the kind that required fire. Around the open main floor, there were also wooden stands with various objects de art under glass cases. Most of the art, including the pieces under glass, were relics from the seventeenth and eighteenth centuries, the age of Enlightenment. So not as many saints and martyrs and a lot of realism and what people might see as modern art. There were also relics that looked like they belonged in an alchemist's lab.

There were also books under glass throughout the room. Large tomes covered in leather. Some opened to reveal the yellowing pages within, the ink faded but legible—she'd made Christopher stop at a few of them so she could get a closer look—and some were closed, revealing only the well-tended leather and any decorative inlays.

And in the center of the room, a very large display pillar with an empty glass case on top. The future location of the dragon's king's father's stolen magic book.

Future because it was currently being guarded in the crypt by some very large, burly human and shifter guards. About twelve of them. The fact that all that security was dedicated to a book when there were some extremely valuable paintings on the wall of that former church and at least one of the relics in the glass-topped pillars was worth almost as much as the book, just amazed Myra.

Oh, there was other security around. Plenty of alarms on the art and a number of guards casually strolling through the party as if they were guests. Christopher kept drawing their attention. And one of them was in the crowd around the dragon king, laughing at something the king said last time Christopher had swung the camera in that direction.

But the bulk of the security focus was on the magic poisons book that had once belonged to the dragons.

She was pretty sure, although not entirely certain, that the former owner of the book, the auctioneer, and the current owner of the book, all knew that the dragon king's father was the original owner. That was the reason he *hadn't* been invited to the auction but *had* been invited to the viewing.

She'd researched the human who'd bought the book. You spend one hundred million dollars on an old book, you are either a big-time collector of magical relics, or you know exactly what you're buying, and you know it's gonna piss off the king of the dragons, and you're doing *that* on purpose. But she hadn't learned much about the new owner. No one, not even the king, much to his irritation, had been able to find the actual buyer. Not even a picture.

That mystery was as tantalizing as the heist itself.

She'd been trying to see the collector all night, but they hadn't made an appearance yet. "Walk past the empty case again," she said into Christopher's earpiece. "Any sign of the book's new owner?"

"No grand entrance," he murmured. "If they're here, they've come in quietly and not made themselves known."

"Possible." But she doubted it. Waiting to reveal the book. Waiting to make an entrance. All this spoke to the purchaser being the sort who liked to make a splash. Who was dramatic and liked attention. Maybe the wrong kind of attention in this case.

Christopher's camera panned past the dragon king again as he returned to the center of the nave where the awaiting glass case stood under a spotlight. The king was still holding court, so to speak, but his gaze swept Christopher and his mouth turned down in a slight frown, before he let his charming smile out for his audience again.

Myra shook her head. Speaking of someone who liked to put on a performance.

The glass case under the spotlight remained empty. The crowds around it milled as if trying not to look like they were hanging out in the general area of the glass case, but they were definitely remaining in that general area so they didn't lose their position close to the case for the big reveal.

One man actually scowled at Christopher when he approached, as if he'd refuse to move out of the way and whoever was daring to try and dislodge him from his position was just going to have to pick a different route. Myra saw the exact moment the man realized Christopher was nearly seven-foot tall and maybe attempting to hold his ground against a man that size was unwise, followed closely by the realization that the seven-foot-tall man was, in fact, the dragon king's son. The man scrambled away, bowing his head in deference. And Myra had to put a hand over her mouth to keep from laughing loud enough for someone to hear over Christopher's earpiece.

"I can still hear you snickering," Christopher whispered as he approached the empty case.

"Sorry. But people's reactions to you are funny."

"Tiresome."

"Oh, the poor bored prince."

His snort was half amused, half irritated. She grinned even as she studied the case.

The platform that would rise up with the book on it was still locked into position. They hadn't begun the whole dramatic process of lowering that small platform into the pillar, down into the crypt where the book would be placed by one of those dozen security guards onto the platform, before the whole thing rose once again through the base pillar and into the glass case.

The case itself was sealed to the pillar. No way to actually get in or out of it without literally breaking the glass or ripping it off the stand. Which would be pretty obvious. And, according to the security specs she'd hacked yesterday, the unit was strong enough to prevent even shifters from tearing it to pieces. The pillar was embedded in the floor, also impossible to just lift out and fly away with. The tube through which the platform dropped into the crypt was made of titanium all the way down, and that titanium tube was also bolted into the stone floor of the crypt.

There was a single access panel that opened by a security code onto the titanium tube so that the guard could place the book onto the platform. Meaning that trying to snatch the book while it was in transit back up to the case would be impossible.

The only time the book wouldn't be encased in that secured apparatus, it was under the watchful eye of the security team inside a lock box chained to one of the guard's wrists. At least three of the guards were shifters—two lion shifters and an eagle shifter, which was interesting in and of itself—and the guard with the box chained to his wrist was wearing both bullet-proof clothing and a bespelled necklace that protected him from magical attacks. She'd watched the team walk into the church earlier that evening, before the party started. They were not messing around. A team of serious and professional guards, from an agency known for its efficiency and effectiveness.

Myra had seen less security surrounding the crown jewels of monarchs and priceless portraits in hyper-secure museums. She'd seen less security put into place in government buildings and embassies. The book was probably worth more than the hundred million the buyer had paid for it, and a hundred million was a hell of an investment even if that was all the book was worth, but the extreme levels of security meant the buyer knew the real value of the book wasn't in the price.

The real value of the book was in its relationship to the dragon king.

The fact the book was guarded against shifter attack as well as magical attack and mundane, ordinary human thieves just reinforced that impression.

Myra glanced at her digital watch. The watch, like the rest of her clothing, was all black, with a display face of pale blue that didn't throw up too much light and was difficult to see even with her night adjusted vision. A shifter might catch the glow, but she also had a little spell on the watch to prevent that. Her plan required precise timing. And not just her own timing, which she could keep track of without a watch, but coordinating that timing with Christopher. That meant using an actual watch.

"Almost time," she told him.

His grunt was his only response.

"I'm heading in now. Do not pay attention to me."

Another grunt.

She chuckled, tucked her cellphone into her pants pocket, and put on the special glasses she had had made just for this type of job. They had thick black ear bands and thin black rims around medium thickness lenses. Tiny rhinestones decorated the ear bands, a dash of sparkle when hit just right by the light.

Once on, she pushed a point on the ear band, and a tiny view of Christopher's camera display appeared across the inner left glass. From the outside, no one could see that display. There was a special coating for that, but she'd saved herself the expense and just used a tiny illusions spell so the lenses would look like ordinary, clear glass to anyone not staring through them.

She kept the display on, monitoring Christopher's view of the guests, as she finally got out of the plain, gray van she'd parked a block away and headed toward the venue.

Time for the show.

Chapter Six

Myra worked her way to the back door of the converted church where the catering staff were just starting to bring in the hors d'oeuvres after already circulating with flutes of champaign and wine.

She adjusted the collar of her black button-up shirt, straightening the long sleeves over her watch, and dusted her black dress slacks. Though it was cold outside, she hadn't worn a coat, so she could appear as if she'd been part of the staff from the start.

The small room at the back of the church, behind where the altar had been—she forgot what the area was called—was set up with long folding tables topped with temporary food warmers filed with silver trays of various tiny foods. The smell hit her the minute she slipped inside and might have made her stomach growl if she hadn't eaten a big dinner in anticipation of a fun night's work. There were spices and fried dough involved, though, so she might sneak a bite of something when no one was looking.

A man in a black cook's jacket stood behind the tables, directing two people as they loaded up large silver trays and handed them to the line of servers. The servers then pushing through a door at the end of the tables. The minute that door swung open, the noise of too many people talking at once from inside the church washed loudly through the back room, only to be cut back to a din when the door swung shut. Behind the food tables, a standing rack hung with a blue curtain half hid a plain black door with a surprisingly complex-looking series of locks running above the otherwise ordinary round doorknob.

A man with an empty tray pushed into the back room just as another of the servers started to head out. The noise drew everyone's attention as the two servers angled past each other.

Myra took advantage of the noise and inattention to blend into the line of servers waiting on food trays to take inside, adjusting her collar again and trying to pretend she'd been there all along.

The woman in front of Myra, a small, curvy Asian woman with her black hair knotted up in a bun on top of her head, glanced back, gave Myra a knowing look, then leaned in and whispered, "I won't tell them you were late, but you have to cover for me later when I need a smoke."

"Deal," Myra whispered. "Thanks. I've got you. How is it in there?"

"Crowded. Lot of rich twats. Few grabby hands you'll have to watch out for."

"Of course." Myra rolled her eyes and pushed her glasses up her nose.

Christopher, who could overhear the conversation through Myra's earpiece, made a strange sort of hissing sound that was a tad worrying. But since she couldn't see anything that might have caused that reaction through his camera feed, she ignored him. Which she would have had to do anyway with all the other people around.

"Hey, have you heard there are dragons in there?" the woman whispered.

"No shit? No one told me there'd be dragons tonight. What are they like?"

"Wild. Tall. The *king* is in there. And one of his sons."

"Oh fuck." Myra pressed her lips together. "What happens if I spill a drink on one of them?"

"Count on losing this gig and all future ones."

"Shit. Okay." Myra made a show of attempting to pull herself together, straightening her shirt and swallowing hard. "First time I've been in the same room with any dragons."

Christopher snorted. She ignored him.

"I've done it before," the woman said. "They're okay. Just, you know, don't piss them off."

That was very good advice. Advice she wished she'd given herself when she'd made the mistake of taking a bet and breaking into the dragon king's hoard.

She was handed a tray of tiny bites of food—she was pretty sure they were miniature empanadas, but they were so small it was hard to tell. Could have also been miniature egg rolls. As she headed toward the door into the church proper, she glanced briefly at the locked door half-hidden behind the standing curtain.

Then she pushed through the doors and into the din.

Each server moved into the throng and spread out to ensure maximum coverage of guests. She went in the opposite direction from where she knew—even without hearing his voice—that the dragon king held court. She didn't approach Christopher either, letting another server—the woman who'd warned her about the dragons—take his section of the gathering. A section where, Myra was pretty certain, her new friend would be safe from any "grabby hands" guests because Christopher would snap the wrist off of anyone disrespecting the staff.

Myra liked that about him.

She wound through the crowds, studying the people she'd seen earlier through Christopher's video feed. The dual view of seeing the venue in person and through his feed inside her glasses' lens gave her a pretty thorough impression of the place. When not filtered through Christopher's earpiece and camera, the noise was louder, the dim lighting from the overhead chandeliers carried more ambiance, the scent of so many different perfumes and colognes strong even to her ordinary human sense of smell, and the spotlight on the still empty glass case where the book would be seemed even brighter. Very obvious that something important was going to be in that display case. Eventually.

She subtly glanced at her watch. They only had a few more minutes.

Myra made her way past the display case, giving it a glance, but pretending to pay more attention to the guests as they plucked the tiny bite-sized pieces of food off her tray using the toothpicks sticking out of the food, leaving behind the miniscule bits of lettuce on which the food sat.

One guest turned suddenly and grabbed three of the bites at once, making a yummy sound that surprised Myra. She backed up a step from the man's gleeful expression and bumped into the currently-empty display case, setting one hand against it to hold her balance as she attempted to keep the food tray from clattering to the ground.

The case was solid as stone and didn't even wobble when she hit it, but a few people nearby gasped, and a man Myra was sure was one of the circulating security people stomped up to her and pulled her away from the pillar.

"Watch it," he hissed under his breath. "There are alarms on all these cases. The owners will be ticked off if you set one off on accident and cut the party short."

Myra quickly adjusted her glasses and nodded frantically.

The guard gave her a brief nod, took one of the hors d'oeuvres off her tray, and released her arm, giving her a gentle pat. "Just be careful," he murmured before weaving back into the crowd.

Myra did the same, angling away from the empty display case and the bright white spotlight on it. "Ah. He seemed nice."

"Focus on your job," Christopher murmured.

She chuckled. "My part is handled. How are you doing?"

"Almost in place."

Through the feed on her glasses, Myra watched Christopher approaching his father's location at the rear of the church, not far from the door where the servers were still moving in and out in a steady flow of full and empty trays.

A little wave of hushing and quiet murmuring moved through the crowd. Myra positioned herself with her back to the wall so she could watch the dais where the altar had once stood at the head of the church.

Gasps erupted around her as all the lights but the spotlight on the empty case dropped suddenly.

And when they came on again, a woman and a man stood on the dais, smiling like triumphant warriors at the startled yelps followed by loud cheers and applause.

Myra shook her head, stopped just short of rolling her eyes. So dramatic.

Chapter Seven

The woman standing on the dais at the top of the church was a medium sized older white woman with bright silver hair done up in an elegant twist. Her jewelry sparkled and winked in the chandelier lights. Diamond earrings, an emerald and diamond necklace, and a series of diamonds woven into her hair. All of which made Myra's thieving heart yearn. Dressed in a long emerald silk gown, the woman wasn't slim but she wasn't heavy either. And her silver heels gave her both stature and excellent posture.

The man next to her was dressed more austerely in a black suit, white shirt, and silver tie, though every bit of clothing looked tailored to perfection on his rail thin body. He was also white, with an expensive artificial tan, his hair a dark brown that didn't look like its natural color, and his features were cut sharply in a long face. Very few lines showed around his eyes and none appeared on his forehead or around his mouth. He was, Myra supposed, technically handsome, though the kind of handsome that required some maintenance and work to keep it up. And looked too artificial to her to be really handsome.

Unlike his companion, he wore no jewelry except for a substantial gold and ruby ring on his right pinky. A ring that drew Myra's interest almost more than the woman's jewelry.

As the crowd continued to applaud the dramatic entrance, the woman waved an appreciative hand, then gestured for everyone to quiet. Though the church was quite large, when the woman spoke, her voice carried throughout the venue, and Myra realized she was mic'd up and there were speakers in the rafters. The speakers gave the illusion that the woman was talking right next to her. She didn't even have to raise her voice.

"Welcome, welcome. I'm delighted to see so many distinguished guests grace our small gallery."

"That's the gallery owner," Christopher said into Myra's earpiece. "The man is her husband. They aren't the ones who purchased the book at auction."

"You're sure?"

"Sure."

Huh. She'd been certain they were the purchasers. Or at least one of them was. The one thing none of them had been able to ferret out was the identity of the person who'd spent one hundred million on the book. The underground auction took anonymity seriously. The records Myra had been able to hack, which were surface because her hacking skills only went so far—she should probably find someone better at that to help more often but she didn't like working with other people—revealed a shell corporation as the buyer. They all knew that wasn't the purchaser. Myra didn't know this gallery owner on sight either. She'd never robbed this place before, which was a bit strange in hindsight, and there weren't any pictures in the records.

She realized as she let the woman's droning welcome speech

wash over her that there were no cameras inside the church either. No phones snapping pictures of the big reveal. No press documenting the event. That might have been a dictate from the dragon king. There were no pictures allowed of the royal family. But not even a small contingent of press to document the event and carefully *not* take pictures of the dragons…? Seemed odd now that she thought of it. Explained why there probably weren't any pictures of the owners, though.

But if there were no pictures, how did Christopher know them?

"Been to one of their showings before?" she asked.

"A few."

Well. He could have told her that ahead of time.

The droning speech ended with a dramatic flourish of popping lights around the dais and some smoke slowly creeping out across the tiled floor. That was fun.

"The dragon has come," the woman said, her tone low and ominous.

Myra did roll her eyes this time. She just couldn't help it. "Well, you did invite two of them," she murmured. Christopher snort-laughed in her ear.

She searched the room for the location of the other servers, trusting Christopher and the king to be in their places by now. Most of the servers had stopped and were standing as unobtrusively as possible against walls, or pillars, behind the crowds so they wouldn't obstruct anyone's view. Just as she was doing.

The faux smoke reached Myra and spread past her, cold against her lower body. Definitely not dragon's breath, she thought. That was supposed to be hot.

A lot of show and drama, but Myra didn't mind. She liked a little show and drama. Especially when it helped her plan.

The two gallery owners moved down through the crowd, the crowd parting for them as they made their way to the still empty case. Its spotlight looked even brighter now, with the smoke catching in the light beam. The whole thing made a sort of haze around the case that looked very mysterious.

Myra smiled as she saw the little panel inside the case slip to one side. Here comes the prize. She set her mostly empty tray behind a pillar, checked her watch in the darkened corner, and started making her way around the edge of the nave.

The book rose slowly into the case, first the top corner, then inch by inch the rest was revealed. There hadn't been any images of this online either. Not even from the original underground auction house. Just a line item on a list. So this was the first time she'd gotten to look at the magic poisons book that had once belonged to a dragon.

It didn't disappoint. The tome was huge, easily a foot wide and two feet long. Covered in a shimmery black leather that was so smooth it could probably be a mirror. On the front, in gold leaf, a symbol of some kind, nothing she could see clearly from her position near the edge of the crowd, but it was circular and looked like it required a lot of that gold leaf. In the middle of the gold symbol, a bright red ruby winked at the crowd like a drop of blood had dripped onto the center of the cover. All of it shimmered and glowed and sparkled.

There were no other outer markings on the book that she could see at this distance. But the black metal lock on the side of it was interesting. And the page ends had been coated in a dark red color she assumed was supposed to look like blood, same as the ruby.

That looked so much like a magic book it was almost ridiculous. If she were going to make a magic book of poisons, she'd make it look ordinary, plain, something no one would guess was an actual magic book. That puppy screamed *I'm a valuable and dangerous book!*

Although, maybe that was the point? And to be fair, it had once been in a dragon hoard. It might not have found its way there if it had been too ordinary looking.

Still, just to be sure… "That it?" she asked Christopher.

She looked across the crowd at him. He was easy to spot at nearly seven feet tall, a head over most of the people here, and he had taken his position by a pillar close to the display case but not right next to it. He glanced at his father, who'd come to stand closer to the case, his full retinue of sycophants in tow.

The king gave a little nod, without even looking at his son. Christopher said into her earpiece, "That's it."

Excellent. "I'm setting the lures," she murmured, continuing to work her way around the edge of the church. No one glanced her way. No one paid any attention to anything but the raised display case and the mysterious, magical book.

The woman who was the gallery owner turned to the king, which drew everyone's attention to him. He was good at being the center of attention, Myra noticed. He preened and puffed himself up even more and, because he was tall, looked down his nose at everyone. She wasn't sure if that was an exaggerated show for the crowd and for the sake of their plan, or if that was really him—but she suspected it was a combination of both.

"Majesty," the woman said. "What do you think?"

"Stunning," he said, and his deep voice carried throughout the crowd easily. Without needing a mic like the woman.

The gallery owner smiled. "It truly is. Worth every cent it earned at auction."

"And more," the king confirmed. "But as it's stolen property, it must be returned to the original owner."

Myra smiled. You tell her, majesty. Myra slipped past a series of valuable paintings and pressed more of her little button sensors against the wall, ensuring they were stuck in place before moving to the next display.

If Christopher had done his part, the display cases around the room also had those little sensors stuck to them. She'd placed the one on the poisons book's display case personally.

She did actually sort of trusted Christopher. He could have done it. But he was too obvious in this crowd.

The "sort of *trusted*" Christopher part of that thought was going to give her some feelings later that night when she looked back on all this.

By the time she reached the far side of the nave and was near the servers entrance again, the debate over ownership between the king and the gallery owner had reached a substantial volume, and every eye in the place was on the debate. The fact that the gallery owner was still smiling, even if her smile was a bit brittle, and her husband still looked mildly bored, meant they'd been expecting, maybe even hoping for, this show. It just added to the event. Otherwise, they wouldn't have invited the king.

Smoke still covered the tiled floor and had filled in the entire nave now. An added bonus Myra hadn't counted on. She glanced at her watch.

"Ready?" she asked quietly.

"Ready," Christopher said. He moved to stand just behind his father's shoulder, a very prominent location where he couldn't be missed.

And *everyone* in the room, even the servers, were staring at the scene.

Myra loved a good scene.

She counted quietly to ten. Then pressed a button on her watch.

And every piece of art in the gallery flickered and disappeared.

Chapter Eight

The gasps started near the king and Christopher. The first shout indicating something was wrong came from someone in the king's collection of sycophants at his back. "The book! It's gone!"

More gasps throughout the church. Then the yelling and shouting really got started.

"It's gone, too!"

"Where's the art?"

"What's happened?"

"Is it magic?"

"It's the smoke! They've rigged the smoke."

That last one was one Myra hadn't had on her bingo card.

The chaos and smoke and dim lights made it all so much better. People moving and shuffling around. The security guards in the room shouting for everyone to stay where they were. "*No one move!*" Except everyone was moving. Everyone but Christopher and the king, who stayed perfectly still, glaring at the crowds, demanding explanations even as the security guards swarmed around them.

The door back to the caterer's station swung open. Another stream of guards came bursting into the room. The dozen from the crypt. Myra smiled. The shifters flew past her, going right to the king and Christopher.

And Myra slipped through the door and back into the caterer's area. The cook and any staff who'd been back here had already hurried into the main part of the church when all the noise erupted. No one even back here having a smoke.

She slipped through the multi-locked door that had been left open when all the guards came charging upstairs. And why would they bother to lock it? There was nothing down there anymore. All the art had been upstairs, including the book. Which was now vanished.

She circled the stone stairs that led into the crypt, running her now gloved fingers lightly over the stone wall. It was even colder down here than it was outside, which was nice after the heat in the gallery. The air was a bit stale and musty, but not as moldy as she'd have thought for someplace called a crypt. And it was well lit and bright, the white stones reflecting the overhead fluorescents so the place felt a bit like an office building.

She shuddered at that.

The crypt itself was relatively small. A low-ceilinged room with stone floors and walls. Where once there'd been plaques for the dead buried there, the walls were now blocked by stacks of wooden crates and painting boxes. The specially designed, high tech titanium tube which protected the book as it rose up into its display case, the protective barrier that was supposed to prevent theft, was bolted into the stone floor at the very center of the room.

There was a lock on the hatch that allowed access to the interior of the tube, a simple number coded panel with raised push keys, metal and without any biosensors. And there was a small up and down button beside that.

Myra pressed the down button, rocking on her heels as she let her gaze travel over the small room. Christopher would bash his head on this ceiling.

She heard a little chu-chink sound from inside the tube. Then she hit a button on her glasses and the view of the chaos upstairs through Christopher's video feed switched to a blue display that analyzed the lock panel.

Residual heat from the guard who'd entered the code to open the panel rose, allowing her to see four numbers had clearly been pressed. The code required five numbers so one of those four was a repeat. If she entered the code wrong once, she'd have twenty seconds to enter it right or an alarm would go off. Given the noise from upstairs, filtering all the way down here, she wasn't sure if anyone would even hear the alarm, but it would give away the game if they did.

She studied the heat signatures, the numbers pressed. And made a guess based on one number having a slightly higher signature.

A grating beeping sound when she got it wrong.

Damn. Okay. One more try.

She held her fingers over the lock pad and whispered a spell. The spell couldn't open the pad, but it could move her fingers true. It wasn't always as reliable as just figuring the code out herself, but she didn't have time to try and fail again.

Her fingers danced over the pad, pressing buttons. She smiled when she heard the lock give.

The panel clicked and lifted out of alignment with the tube, then with a quiet buzz moved to one side. Inside the tube, the platform from the case upstairs. With the magic poisons book sitting on it, the shiny black leather binding winking at her. The gold leaf and ruby in the center of the book's cover glittered in the bright crypt light.

She took off her cloth belt, gave it a shake. It opened into a sturdy, black cotton backpack. Only just barely big enough to hold the book, but it would do.

Clicking her glasses back to the view above, she confirmed things were still chaos and noise up there. Christopher stood just behind his father's shoulder, facing a guard Myra hadn't seen earlier —one from the crypt she was sure—and behind the guard, the gallery owner and her husband. Everyone but Christopher was pointing and talking in harsh, demanding tones. The guard had to hold his arms out to keep the woman from stepping too close to the king. And since he was her guard and not the king's, that was a telling gesture.

Myra grinned as she slipped the book from the tube and eased it into her backpack, then slipped the narrow straps over her shoulders. Heavy. But not as heavy as all that black leather and the winking ruby made it seem like it might be.

She closed the panel and sent the platform back up into the display case above. Then hurried up the crypt steps, listening intently, prepared to run all the way back down if she heard noise from the door. But all the noise and all the attention was still focused on all the missing art in the gallery.

The caterer's area was still empty when she slipped back out of the half open door. The servers and cook must be having a great time watching all that mayhem. She couldn't see any of them through Christopher's feed, but if she were an actual server, she'd have been in the middle of that room watching the drama.

Slipping out the same door she'd slipped through earlier to join the catering crew, she started to tell Christopher she was out when a puff a smoke to her right and the distinct scent of tobacco stopped her with her mouth half-open. Her server friend stood against the stone wall of the church, in the dark beyond the circle of light from the security lamp above the door, puffing away.

She motioned Myra over. "How's it going in there? Anyone kill anyone yet?"

In her camera feed, Myra could see some of the guards heading back in the direction of the catering area behind the altar, back toward the door leading into the crypt. Christopher turned slightly, keeping them in view long enough for her to confirm their direction.

"Everyone was still screaming when I slipped out," she said to her smoking friend as she leaned against the wall beside her, her backpack pressed into the stones.

The woman offered Myra a cigarette from a pack she had tucked into her jacket pocket. Unlike Myra, the woman was wearing a coat, an oversized black wool coat that looked a couple of sizes too big for her. Myra took the proffered cigarette and let her friend light it while keeping half her attention on Christopher's feed and some of her attention on the door to her left.

"Figured I could slip out for a smoke and no one would notice," the woman said. "Who d'you think figured out a way to steal all that art? That had to be magic, right? The way everything vanished?"

Myra shrugged. "Don't really know. Wizards, maybe? If it was magic, though, that was a big security hole, right? I mean, wasn't that book supposed to be magic or something?"

The woman shrugged and took a deep drag. "All I know is I still better get paid. My feet are killing me."

"Same." Myra took one long drag at her cigarette and let the smoke out slowly in a long stream as the back door swung open and slammed against the stone wall.

Both she and her new friend looked at the three men pushing out of the door, one of whom, Myra confirmed, was one of the lion shifters. They searched frantically around the narrow courtyard behind the church, then looked toward Myra and her friend.

"You ladies seen anyone come out this way?" the lion shifter asked.

He was a little shorter than the other two guards, broad and dressed in a black suit, black shirt and even a black tie. His sandy hair was cut short and his beard trimmed neatly. Not much about him screamed shifter until he sniffed the air, his head turning in a very not-human way as he scanned the area with his nose. That and the long narrow slit of his pupils inside golden eyes. His pupils whirled open as she watched him come farther out into the darkness behind the church.

Myra took another puff of the cigarette and blew the smoke into the air, leaning more heavily against the stones at her back. "No one but us," she said.

"Bad habit," the woman said, lifting her own cigarette. "Any idea what happened in there?"

"It's being handled." The shifter stayed a few feet away, his nose twitching, his nostrils compressing. "You don't need to worry, though. There's no danger."

"Thanks for that," Myra said. "Seems pretty crazy."

"Garet," one of the other men said, drawing the lion shifter's attention.

"Thanks for your help, ladies," the shifter, Garet, said, looking back at his companion. "I would recommend remaining out here or in the catering area until everything is settled." He faced them briefly. "You should have worn your coat." He nodded at Myra.

"It was so hot in there," she said, "feels good out here without it. But I'll be fine, sir. Thanks." Myra flashed her most innocent smile and let the smoke from her cigarette fill the space between her and the shifter, keeping her back firmly to the wall so her backpack wasn't immediately visible, its black straps blending into her black shirt in the darkness.

Garet nodded, his companion called him again, and he turned away, rushing around the church to the front of the building.

"What a mess," her new friend said. "Someone's gonna get fired."

"So long as it's not us," Myra said. She snubbed out the remaining half of the cigarette against the stones behind her. "I'm gonna take off. They're not gonna start serving again, and I don't want to waste a night getting questioned by those guards over and over again."

"You sure? They might get suspicious if you disappear before someone asks you what you were doing when it happened." She lowered her voice and said the last in a gruff, exaggerated tone that Myra took to be a joke.

She grinned. "I was questioned already, though, right? We both were by that guard."

The woman nodded. "True enough. Might take off in a minute myself."

"Good luck. Thanks for earlier, covering for me. And for the cigarette." She waved over her shoulder as she headed around the church, same direction the guards had gone.

"Hey," the woman called, "you forgot your coat."

Myra turned, though she kept walking backward. "Forgot it at home. Never had one." She waved. "Have a good night." And slipped around the church.

The front of the gallery was crowded with people in fancy clothes all talking over the top of each other while some of the security team tried to keep them from leaving. There was a lot of shouting and pointing and demanding and raised hands trying to hold back the tide. The guards who'd pounded out the back door, including Garet the lion shifter, were among the people trying to keep the guests from leaving. None of them looked her way.

She slipped down the road to the closest side street, then turned a corner. Once she was out of view, she took off at a jog that brought her several blocks to the south. She didn't bother returning to the van she'd left parked two blocks from the building. She could get that tomorrow. She hadn't left anything behind to point to her even if someone decided it was suspicious and searched it.

Instead, she headed to the bright green and white globe of light over the nearest open subway station. "Heading underground," she said to Christopher, glancing at her watch. "Illusions will cut out in twenty-six more seconds."

"I'm ready," Christopher murmured.

From his feed, she could see he and the king were still facing off with the gallery owners. She wanted to hang out long enough to watch their faces when the illusions broke. The buttons she and Christopher had pressed against the walls around the gallery, into the bases of the various display cases, all those temporary spells flickering out and all the "missing" art reappearing. She wondered exactly how long it would take everyone to notice the one and only thing *really* missing was the book. That everything else had just been covered by an illusion that made it seem like they were missing.

But she couldn't hang around and watch the show. She did get one last view from Christopher's feed as the various spells started to flicker out around the nave and the gallery owners standing in front of Christopher and the king turned in a circle, looking at the returning art, their mouths hanging open.

She chuckled as she slipped underground and hurried through the turnstile to make her train.

Chapter Nine

Myra met Christopher on a rooftop in Midtown, the same rooftop they'd landed on after she'd rescued him from his kidnappers those many weeks ago. And he'd rescued her from tumbling to her death. Though she didn't remember that part because she'd been hit by a wizard bolt and was unconscious for most of her fall.

She was looking out over the tightly packed skyscrapers, the lights inside windows bejeweling the skyline, noise from traffic below distant but distinct. Up here, the air was fresher, and colder as the wind cut through the canyons created by the buildings. The night had grown overcast, turning the sky a funny orange color as the clouds reflected the city's night light back down to it.

She heard the sound of his wings, felt the brush of air at her back from his landing. She didn't immediately turn to face him, instead leaning against the waist-high brick retaining wall circling the flat roof.

"Is the book safe?" Christopher asked, his voice quiet to match the late night.

"Got it stored. We can bring it to your father in a couple of days, after the chaos dies down."

"He'll want it tomorrow."

"He'll have to wait. He might be the dragon king, but that won't keep people from investigating. Especially when the stolen artifact just sold for a hundred million at auction. Better for him to have no idea where the book is, and even be mad about that, when the police do show up to question him. They'll buy his outrage better that way."

"Good plan. He'll hate it."

She grinned. "What happened once the art reappeared?" she asked, her attention still on the lights in the building across the street. She felt him come up beside her, saw him lean against the retaining wall next to her from the corner of her eye. He had to lean down a lot farther to reach it.

"Confusion and chaos. Exactly what you wanted."

"How long before they realized the one thing really missing was the book?"

"About ten minutes. My father got impatient and pointed it out."

She raised her brows. "Huh. That probably worked in your favor."

"It did. He roared about it missing and started shouting at the owners about their shoddy security. Made a huge scene, even bigger than the one he'd already caused."

"Perfect. He carries that energy into a meeting with the police, and we'll get away with this without a hitch." She tilted her head into a gust of cold wind blowing across her face. "The king was really good at his role in all this."

"I think he enjoyed it a little too much."

She chuckled. Finally turned to look at him. He was also staring out over the city. The wind blew through his messy dark hair. In profile, his angular face took on a sort of nobility, the kind of thing she'd seen in marble statues in the Met. He was still wearing the dark dress slacks he'd worn to the event, but he'd stripped off his shirt and he had taken off the loafers he'd worn earlier in deference to humans' preferring for footwear at fancy parties.

His wings weren't out, though. He's done the partial shift and looked fully human now. Even the purple and yellow scales that covered his chest and shoulders when he shifted to just having wings were gone. He looked like an ordinary, handsome, very tall man. Who should probably be cold standing around with so few bits of clothing on.

She didn't bother asking him if he was cold. His dragon metabolism kept his body temperature up, so most places actually felt too warm to him. The nippy night air probably felt good.

"Did the person who bought the book ever show up?" she asked the side of his face.

He kept his gaze out over the city. "No. Not that we ever saw. If they were there, they stayed inconspicuous. They didn't come out accusing the gallery owners of losing valuable property. There will probably be all kinds of insurance arguments after this, though."

"Weird the owner never made an appearance. You'd think after going to all the trouble of buying the book out from under the king, then taunting the king by inviting him to the gallery showing, that whoever is responsible for this would want to be present to see the king's face."

"I'd have assumed so. Maybe they thought it was safer to taunt him at a distance."

She snorted. "That shows a great deal of intelligence, if true."

He smiled softly, briefly, but he still didn't look at her.

She let the silence stretch, but only for a few moments.

"I haven't been avoiding you because I didn't want to spend time with you," she said, speaking as softly as his smile had been. Even with the echo of noise from traffic below and the wind whistling past, she knew he'd hear her. "But your father... The king..."

"He's complicated things because he keeps asking you to work for him."

"He has. For exactly that reason."

"I'll tell him to stop." He finally faced her.

The determined expression that hardened his jaw and set his mouth in an uncompromising line made her stomach dance. In a good way. Like freefalling off the side of a building, those moments before the harness caught and slowed her descent. Everything inside her tumbled around, chaotic and messy. A bubble of excitement and fear mixing together in her gut.

Breathless.

Sometimes Christopher looked at her like that and left her breathless.

"Will he listen?"

Christopher's jaw worked, like he was grinding his teeth. "I'll convince him. But..."

"But?"

"Are you certain? You've made a fair amount on these last couple of jobs for him. Do you really want to cut off that source of income?"

She raised her brows and for a moment wasn't sure what to say. Then she chuckled. Then she laughed. "I don't need his jobs. I'm perfectly capable of finding my own jobs. And I don't need the money. Anymore."

"There's a story in that anymore."

"There is." But not one she was going to talk about yet.

When she didn't elaborate, he nodded. "Still. He could be a very...useful benefactor."

"I don't need a benefactor. In fact, I'd rather stay off the king's radar all together. Breaking into his hoard was one of the stupider things I've done in my life. Before that, he didn't even know who I was." And that had been better. In a lot of ways, that had been better.

"If you hadn't, we wouldn't have met."

Which was the one thing she would have regretted. "It's not you that's the problem," she said instead because she was afraid of the implications of admitting she would have regretted not meeting him. "But you is…complicated."

"*We*," he emphasized, "don't have to be. *We* can just…"

"Just?"

He held her gaze and she couldn't have looked away if the building fell out from under them. Knowing that, even if it did, Christopher would catch her. How was she supposed to resist that?

"We can just go see a movie," he said after a moment. "Like we'd planned." His half frustrated, half hopeful shrug made her stomach flutter.

Well. And wasn't she used to taking chances? Didn't she *like* the thrill of not knowing for sure what could happen?

Usually, she didn't take that thrill-seeking, adventure-chasing attitude into personal relationships. But she also didn't allow many personal relationships that went past a superficial level. And she had a feeling, with Christopher, things were heading—maybe already well past—somewhere beyond superficial.

"Bit late for a movie," she said. It was after three in the morning.

A slow smile brought his mouth to life and that was impossible to resist, too. "Do you trust me?"

She almost gave the glib response. The one that should have been true. Instead, she gave him the real truth. "I do."

She didn't trust anyone. But she trusted Christopher. At least a little. She trusted him to catch her if she fell. And for her, that was a lot of trust.

He straightened away from her and snapped his wings out, the shift happening so fast it was if his wings had already been there and he'd just opened them. She was still learning about dragon shifters—had been doing covert research ever since meeting him—and she knew that not every dragon could do that. Not all of them could even shift partially so they had wings on a human body. A little less than half of them were capable of it. And even fewer of those could do the shift fast.

His wings stretched out behind him, glorious and huge, the thin purple membrane between the thick, hollow bones not quite see-through, but delicate enough she could see a series of veins, yet thick enough to tackle long distance flight without issue. The dusting of purple and yellow scales that crossed his chest and shoulders spread with his wings, almost like a cloak covering him.

Like this, it was impossible to pretend he was anything but what he was. And she liked that about him. She didn't have to pretend to be anyone else with him either.

"If you're up for it," he said, "I have a surprise."

She raised her brows. "I like surprises."

Without warning him, she jumped up into his arms. He caught her easily, as if he'd been expecting her, one of his arms secure under her knees, his other around her back. She liked this about him, too.

"Where to?" she asked.

"Short flight."

He dipped, then launched himself upward, the suddenness and stomach-dropping thrill of it making her chuckle. She tightened her arms around his neck. But not because she worried he'd drop her.

They banked out over the city, Christopher keeping lower than usual, flying in a slow tilt between the skyscrapers, moving along the street-carved canyons. They reached a building that rose several stories higher than its neighbors but was far from the tallest building in the neighborhood. From here, she could see out to the Hudson, and beyond that, New Jersey spread out in a series of low lights outlining the landscape.

Christopher could probably see the individual houses that made up all those lights. What would it be like to have that kind of vision?

As they lost altitude, she finally glanced down. A huge, flat patio beneath them stretched away from the top story of the building. The roof was a series of water tanks and some decorative stonework and wrought iron designed to hide those water tanks. The patio was a long, wide stretch of white stone circled by a red brick retaining wall that had actual gargoyles stationed at intervals along it. Plants spilled out of giant terracotta pots and long, narrow planters lining the base of the retaining walls.

As Christopher gently touched down, she saw the giant white screen stretched over the redbrick wall that led into the building. And in front of that, two huge and cushiony recliner seats pushed closed together, covered with thick blankets, and bracketed by small, marble and wrought iron tables already topped with popcorn. A thick pole behind the chairs had what looked like a projector fixed to the top. And beneath the tables, red coolers with white lids. The kind people used to take cold drinks to the beach.

She glanced up at him. She was still in his arms, and not in a hurry to get down, so she didn't loosen her hold on his neck yet.

"Where are we?"

"My home."

She raised her brows. "The one with the hoard?"

"No," he said with a deadpan. "Do not try to break into my hoard."

She laughed. "Aw, so I don't get a tour?"

For reasons that both delighted and confused her, an adorable blush crept across his strong cheekbones.

"You really need to learn more about dragon shifters," he said, his voice gruff.

"I'm trying." She narrowed her eyes. "What have I missed?"

"When a dragon shows someone their hoard voluntarily…? It means something. Most dragons only do that with their mate. Their long term partner."

She rolled her lips into her mouth and stared out wide-eyed at his patio so she wouldn't have to look him in the face. "Didn't realize that."

"I understand."

"Wasn't implying…"

"You don't need to panic about that now."

Panic? Yeah, that's what this was. Some panic creeping in.

But she was still in his arms, and this was his home, and she didn't want to panic now. She wanted to focus on this moment and not worry about what it meant or what might happen in the future.

Which meant a change of topic. "Is that a movie screen?" She nodded to the white rectangle sheet stretched over the redbrick wall.

"It is."

"Is it always there?"

"It is not."

"Set up for us?"

"I was hopeful."

She grinned. Her panic dying away, replaced by a race of tingles throughout her body. "You were confident."

"Hopeful," he said, a little twinkle in his blue eyes. The awkwardness of moments before gone.

"What's showing?"

"Old school rom-com. No heist movies."

She smiled softly. She'd told him no crime movies the last time he'd asked her to a movie—a date she'd proceeded to avoid because things felt…complicated.

This still felt complicated. It felt like things could get out of her control fast. She might like thrills, but she also liked control. She was used to controlling her life, used to answering to no one. With Christopher that was going to be a problem. And not just because his father liked to control everyone around him.

But for tonight, she wanted to forget that complication, too.

"I love a good rom-com. But it better be a real one. Not one that pretends to be a romance and then one of the romantic leads dies at that end."

He looked at her in genuine horror. "On what planet would something like that be called a rom-com? Where is the com in any of that? Or the rom?"

"You'd be surprised."

"No. Not in this house. Rom-com here means romance and comedy. Not...whatever else that is you just described."

She chuckled. "Okay, then. Old school rom-com with popcorn and... What's in the coolers?"

"Soda, water, and champaign. Wasn't sure what you'd prefer after a night's work."

Oh.

Yeah, this was definitely going to be complicated. That melty feeling in her chest didn't bode well. And yet, as her gaze dropped to his mouth, she decided this was the kind of thrilling fear she could definitely learn to live with. So long as she didn't think too hard about what was happening.

Still carrying her, he strode across the patio to the chairs. When he finally loosened his hold on her legs so she could slide back down to her feet, she went reluctantly, and didn't let go of her hold around his neck. This meant he had to lean over when she was on her feet. And this meant their mouths were remarkably close.

He wrapped his arms around her lower back, tugging her closer, lifting her this time up onto her toes so they were pressed together.

That started a whole lot of tingles in her stomach and lower, and did nothing to fix the breathless problem. Not that she minded.

"Anyone else here?" she asked, her voice breathy and quiet. "Staff? Roommate?"

"No roommates. No staff."

"Now or ever?"

"Ever. Prefer my privacy."

She did, too. "So no one will interrupt. The movie."

His gaze moved over her face, down to her lips. "No one will interrupt. The movie."

"Good plan."

"Glad you approve."

"Should we…start the movie?"

He nodded. "In just one minute."

His mouth angled over hers, settling gently at first, a testing touch that gave her room to move, room to decide how much of a kiss this was.

She wasn't sure she made the decision consciously, or rather, this seemed like a decision she'd already made. Weeks ago. Right after they'd met. She tightened her hold on his neck, pressed harder into him, and let the kiss get serious, deep. Exploring what he offered of himself and returning a little of herself. His lips were soft, his hold on her hard. He tasted like the wine from the gallery reception and a flavor like heat that she couldn't quiet describe.

One of his big hands crept along her spine and then cradled the back of her head, holding her close. Having his big body wrapped around her, feeling that heat and a strange combination of fear and security, sent a rush of warmth through her. Without his wings and scales, he felt like an ordinary man under her sensitive fingertips, his skin smooth, his chest hair soft. She traced a line along his shoulders, where the scales appeared when he had the wings. Studying the difference in texture. The similarity in heat.

His hand on her head remained a gentle cradle but the one on her lower back tightened, clenched at her shirt, and she found herself pressing even tighter against him. Wanting…more.

Dangerous. This whole thing was very very dangerous.

There were feelings here. And not just the physical, lusty, wouldn't-mind-getting-his-pants-off feelings. Emotional, personal feelings. The sort of feelings that made him blush and her get awkward just at the mention of mates. The sort of feelings that could be even more complicated than the situation they were already in.

And there was a part of her, a very serious part of her, that was thrilled with that danger. With that possibility. With the rush of fear and adrenaline and terror.

She'd have to be careful of that part of her nature. Or she'd get in too deep too quick and get hurt. But…

But as he eased back, his breathing ragged, and set his forehead to hers, she closed her eyes and just absorbed the moment. Let his scent fill her. He had that faint smell of sugar cookies again. A yummy smell that made her hum.

Maybe this didn't have to end in heartache. Maybe this could be…something.

Or maybe she was a crazy adrenaline junky who was doomed to fall off a very high building attempting this.

Scarily, she felt absolutely positive, if she did fall, Christopher would catch her.

"So how do we start the movie?" she asked, letting humor and some of her lust into her voice to hide the deeper emotions.

His muscles loosened slowly, and his hold on her eased gradually, and after a moment, they both stepped back enough to allow some air to move between their bodies. She could still feel his heat, though, even when he wasn't pressed up against her.

"Remote," he said. He snatched a small, white, rectangular

remote she hadn't seen earlier off the table by one of the chairs and hit a button. The projector started, and the movie flickered to life on the screen.

She grinned and bounced into the recliner, shoved a handful of popcorn into her mouth as he sat. His smile was a little smug, but she could forgive him that.

"Do you always watch movies this way? I thought you said you went to matinees to avoid attention."

He pulled a can of soda from the red cooler under his table and cracked the top. "I do go to actual theaters sometimes. But I thought this would be better. After tonight's reception. And since it's three in the morning."

"Right. Good idea." She pulled up one of the thick blankets, getting cozy in her seat as the cold evening air brushed her cheeks. "This is better."

Privacy, a fun movie, popcorn and sodas. A little of the champaign as the sun rose.

And the company of someone she wanted to spend more time with. A lot more time.

Even if it meant tumbling off the top of that very tall building.

The Dragon Thief Series
The Vault Job
Bestselling author of the Cary Redmond Series
Kat Simons

THE VAULT JOB
BOOK FOUR

What does a wizard want from the dragon king…

And what do they both want from Myra? Questions she asks herself, repeatedly, while trapped in a vault. A circumstance that leaves her questioning all her life choices. Unfortunately, curiosity bit her again. Because both the dragon king and the wizard lied to her about this job.

A job to steal a relic with nefarious powers.

A job that Christopher doesn't know about.

Myra trusts the wizard and the king about as far as she can throw them, but she also desperately wants to know what they're up to. And why Christopher's father cut him out of this scheme. She also needs to know what the dragon king really wants from her, once and for all. Because her feelings for Christopher grow with every passing moment. Only one thing keeps getting in the way of exploring those feelings. The king.

But before she can get her answers, she has to survive her current job.

And she has to escape the impenetrable vault before time, and her air, runs out.

CHAPTER ONE

Myra contemplated all the mistakes that had led her to this moment, staring down the barrel of a gun held by a very angry wizard inside a sealed steel vault. Everything that had led her here. Not every*thing*. Every*one*. One someone. One mistake.

One big, huge, fucking mistake.

A mistake she'd have to deal with later because now she had to prevent a panicking wizard from shooting her. Which was going to be complicated by the fact that they were both sealed inside this vault, and at any moment, they'd be discovered by shapeshifters. Who would be equally as upset to find Myra and the wizard inside the vault as Myra and the wizard were to *be* in the vault. And since those shifters had a problem with the wizard, and the wizard had a gun—currently pointed at Myra—none of this was good.

She didn't even have a convenient roof to leap off of to save herself. So irritating.

"You did this," the wizard hissed. "You did this on purpose."

"Get sealed inside a vault? You think I arranged *this*? To what end?" She wanted to search the area around the door, see if there was anything she could tweak to get the door opened again. But she couldn't move because gun in her face and angry wizard trapped with her.

"So they'd catch me. This was all a ruse. You're working with the shifters, aren't you?"

Not the ones he was referring to, but that was a technicality that could get her shot. "No. I am not working with these shifters." Absolutely true fact. "I would very much like to not get caught inside this vault by them. Or anyone for that matter. But I can't figure a way out of this while you're pointing a gun at my face."

"How can you get us out? We are *locked inside an impenetrable vault*."

"Yes. I am aware. But impenetrable is… Maybe not the right word here. Let's just call impenetrable a suggestion." At least to her. She had managed to break into some of the most impenetrable places in the city and its surroundings. That's what she did.

Also one of the things that had led to this mess. She'd never regretted that bet to break into the dragon king's hoard more than she did in this moment.

"What does that mean?" the wizard snapped. "A suggestion? No one can get out. We're trapped. If they find us, we're dead. If they don't find us, we'll suffocate. We're dead, one way or the other. If I shoot you, I can blame you. Someone might hear the sound and come get me out. And at the very least, I'll have more oxygen while I hope someone gets me out."

"But you'll be stuck in a tight space with a dead body. Not fun. Trust me. And anyway, if you shoot me, you have no hope of getting out of here without getting caught. I'm good at getting out without getting caught."

"You're caught now. I'd say you suck at it."

"*I'm* not the one who tripped the backup alarm that sealed the door shut." Though, she should have been watching this asshole closer to make sure he didn't trip that alarm.

She still wasn't entirely sure what had happened, how it had happened. She'd had her back to him for all of forty seconds. Next thing she knew they were both staring at the vault door as it slammed shut. And honestly, she'd had no idea a door that big and thick could swing shut that fast. It had taken a hefty heave to get it open once she'd unlocked it. Taken her and the wizard to move the huge round door to one side.

The instant the wizard—his name was Glen. A wizard named Glen. Instead of Astrid or Angelino or something. That felt strange to her—the instant Glen had triggered the backup sensors, Myra had taken one step toward the door, thinking she had time to keep it from sealing. Or at the very least, slip out before the three foot thick ode to engineering closed. She'd have been able to get it to open again from the outside. Maybe a little trickier. It was designed to seal in thieves until the authorities arrived. But she could do it. Wouldn't have been the first time either.

But then the door swung shut too fast for her to get out. So fast, if she'd tried, she'd have been flattened. Squashed dead between the door and the steel frame. Not an end she was excited about.

She didn't particularly want to be shot either.

"Listen," she said with as much patience as she could muster. "I need to examine the door. I might be able to tweak something. But I can't even attempt that while you're pointing a gun at me. So we need a little truce." She shrugged. "Think of it this way. You can always shoot me later."

That thought obviously mollified him because, though he narrowed his already narrow dark eyes at her, he did lower the gun. Without the gun raised, Glen was a much less intimidating man. Wizards could be that way. Almost innocuous. Very ordinary and human looking. You couldn't just look at someone and assume they were a wizard—wizard was a gender-neutral term despite *some* people's insistence a wizard had to be a man. She'd met wizards who were women, who were nonbinary, who were transgendered, who were gender fluid. Gender had nothing to do with wizard magic. The term wizard applied to the *type* of magic someone wielded.

For example, she would never be referred to as a wizard because she didn't wield wizard magic. She had a different kind of magic. The kind that made breaking-and-entering a very successful career choice.

Glen, on the other hand, had a pretty decent amount of specifically wizard magic inside that wiry body. But it wasn't obvious.

He was taller than her, which wasn't hard, but not a giant. He was razor thin, even a little emaciated in his face, with sharp cheekbones and a narrow nose on which perched small, round, purely decorative glasses. In the right circumstances, he could have graced catwalks because he had that sort of haunted, interesting quality to his face. Not handsome. His eyes were too close together and his jaw too pronounced for handsome. But interesting enough she could see some designers wanting to drape him in their clothing.

He'd tied his long blond hair back into a low tail. And he'd dressed in black trousers and turtleneck for their heist, which was both a bit clichéd but also practical. She was wearing all black, too.

Not that the dark colors were going to save them inside a vault lit up so brightly she'd had to blink a few times when walking through the door.

While the interior of the vault was shockingly scentless, so without scent as to be noticeable even to her when she'd stepped inside, the stench of Glen's stress sweat was starting to permeate the air. That level of panic wasn't good for either of them. But at least he wasn't pointing a gun at her anymore.

"Don't try anything funny," he said, taking a step away from her. "I can shoot you before you can get the gun from me."

"I don't like guns anyway."

She really didn't. And never used them unless absolutely necessary. In her line of work, it was almost never necessary. Guns were messy and made noise and drew attention. All the opposite of what she did or wanted to do when working.

Once she was sure Glen wasn't going to shoot her the moment she moved, she eased up to the vault door.

The interior of the vault wasn't huge. It was maybe eight by ten feet, lined with security deposit boxes, most of which were just filled with people's wills and family treasures—things like thumb drives with pictures and backup files. Very few would contain anything worth stealing for a thief and a wizard.

One of the boxes, however…

The reason the vault door was impenetrable was because all the family treasures and wills and miscellany belonged to shifters. This wasn't an ordinary security vault. It wasn't on the property of a bank, like human security deposit boxes.

This vault occupied space at the back of a law firms' offices in a mid-rise building in Midtown. A building that blended seamlessly with its neighbors, a couple of high and mid-rise, glass fronted buildings that held office space mostly. The building next to this one had offices on the lower levels and a hotel on the upper floors. Two different elevators. Not that she'd cased that building before.

Okay, she'd cased that building before. But that was just a coincidence. And had nothing to do with her current job. She'd cased a lot of the buildings in this city at one time or another. She was a busy thief.

The building with the law firm's offices was shorter than its neighbors by a few stories, but not enough to look awkward. The front was covered in dark brown, almost black glass, that reflected whatever sunlight got down the tunnel of the Midtown street. There was a coffee shop on the ground floor, and mostly lawyers and accountants in the upper floors, though one level was taken over by a budding new fashion designer's business.

She'd been tempted to sneak in there, just to see what the designer had for next season. Myra wasn't very into fashion for herself personally, but she liked the accessories that went with fashion and tended to keep up on the scene as a sort of side hobby, so she'd know what rich people were into at any given point.

The law firm with the vault was outwardly like any other firm in the building. Except that it was run by Shifters for Shifters—the non-dragon shifters. Dragon shifters had…other avenues of dealing with legal matters. But the average shifter in the city couldn't take advantage of dragon resources and had to do their own thing. The city tolerated shifters and wizards because they had little choice. Especially when the dragon king lived here. But that didn't mean they had to look out for the shifters.

This law firm, one Janu Peters and Schlotz, had an entire floor in the building to itself, and offered this vault for their clients' most prized possessions, because traditional banks could be bigoted toward shifters if they realized a shifter was a shifter. There were laws of course—that's why Janu Peters and Scholtz were in official business—but laws weren't always *helpful* in the ways one might think.

So she was currently trapped in a space full of things a shifter would love, inside a vault designed to withstand shifter strength— even dragon shifter strength—and to block most wizard magic. Wizards and shifters had a very mixed-bag sort of relationship. They either worked together well—with "well" being a subjective term because when they did work together that usually spelled disaster for other people—or they were enemies. There was very little in the way of neutral ground between them. Allies or enemies. No indifferent acquaintances. Ever.

In this case, she was dealing with a wizard whose relationship to shifters was…unknown. That made their position, trapped inside a shifter vault, particularly dicey.

She shouldn't have taken this job. She should have refused. She'd walked into the sort of job she *knew* better than to take.

But when the dragon king asks, it's so hard to say no.

Especially when you have a crush on, possible a budding relationship with, the dragon king's son.

Though, if Christopher knew where she was right now, and that she was here because of his father, he'd be so pissed.

She was pretty ticked off herself, to be honest. But that anger had to wait for later.

First, she had to find a way to crack open a vault from *inside*.

She'd never had to break out of a vault before. Usually, she was breaking into them.

Chapter Two

Myra had never driven into the dragon king's compound before. The first time, she'd taken a subway to a nearby station, then hiked up the steep hills to the base of the compound, where she had found a way to sneak into the hoard undetected. At least, undetected long enough to get inside and wander around before someone caught her.

Mistake number one. Taking the bet that she could break into the king's hoard.

Mistake number two. Getting caught.

The other times she'd come to the compound, she'd been flown in. But only by one dragon shifter. Christopher. The thought of letting another dragon shifter carry her the way Christopher did gave her the icks. It felt… Weirdly, it would feel like cheating. Not the sort of cheating she might do at cards. Not the sort of cheating that she occasional felt when using her magic to break into things. She did like old school breaking-and-entering to ensure her skills were up to scratch.

This sort of cheating was the type that had more to do with private relationships and romance. Which…

Well, that part of things between her and Christopher was still delicate. Not quite settled. There was potential there. A tension that was almost as fun as it was spooky. Thinking about Christopher gave her a fluttery feeling in her stomach and being around him gave her tingles and she was pretty eager to explore those tingles with him. But also…

Still hesitating. Still uncertain.

He was the dragon king's son.

And the dragon king was a huge complication to… To everything.

Because of this thing with Christopher that she couldn't label yet, the idea of another dragon shifter holding her in his arms and flying her around the place felt disloyal to Christopher. Like cheating.

She had no idea if the dragons would have viewed it that way. As she'd understood things, the only way in to the mansion was to be flown in. Someone went to the front entrance, they never got past the gates. But instead of sending a dragon to fly her in, or sending Christopher to get her, the way he usually did, this time the dragon king had sent a car for her. A big, long, shiny black limo. She'd never ridden in a limo legitimately before. Snuck into them. Driven them when pretending to be a chauffeur. Hidden in the trunk to sneak in somewhere. Yes.

Invited into the backseat and driven around like she belonged in the car? No.

Driving into the compound gave her a completely different perspective on the place. It was huge when looking at it from above, spread out over the hills on the upper tip of Manhattan. Surrounded by forest. Looking like an ancient castle. The white and golden sandstone walls reinforced by modern steel. Some flat rooftop spaces, which Myra realized while flying in with Christopher were designed to allow airborne dragons a place to land since the surrounding trees did not making a dragon-landing easy. Also, those few flat spaces made for good defense against any potential attacking dragons.

Except for those flat roofs, the main mansion did look very much like a human palace or castle from the air.

Inside, though, the proportions were odd, better suited to beings that weren't entirely human. Strangely large corridors with ceilings twice as tall as ordinary. Long spaces, double-sized doors, no tight corners or small rooms.

Entering from the ground level, driving in through thick metal gates that rolled back only after the car was scanned by a device set into the wall over the gate, the weird proportions of everything were more obvious. The gate was wide and tall, set into a stone arch in a curtain wall that was topped by spikes. And, she knew from researching to break into the hoard, those spikes weren't just decorative or to prevent pigeons from landing on the wall. They were sharpened, set very close together, and tipped in poison. The kind of poison that a tiny scratch resulted in death.

Climbing the wall and trying to get around the spikes was not a good option for breaking in.

Once through the gates, the drive up to the main building wound through the thick forest, trees crowding the road and making the long limo feel awkward. She kept expecting it to scrape against a branch, kept wondering why the king used a car this long on these tight bends when something smaller would make the switchback turns easier.

Still, the limo made it up the hill and didn't once scrape against a random tree branch or tip out over the top of a gapping drop. Which was pretty impressive.

"Nice driving," she said to her chauffeur, who hadn't spoken the entire time.

He did not disappoint by speaking now. Just held the back door open for her as she climbed out.

She respected that level of commitment to the job.

Looking up at the main, ground-level entrance to the mansion was yet another reminder of the odd proportions. The front door was a double wooden door that looked both wide and tall enough to allow in a big rig truck. Reinforced by steel beams, looking like something from a medieval castle, but with a remarkably ordinary set of modern doorknobs on each door. Brass, ordinary size for human hands, round. The knobs were at the level of her head instead of anywhere a human might have put them, but otherwise, pretty ordinary doorknobs.

The chauffeur pushed one of the two doors open, swinging it inward with what looked like a pretty significant heave of muscle, and let her proceed him inside. She expected him to follow and continue leading her to the king.

Instead, the door closed behind her and she was left standing in a large foyer decorated in dark woods and a brass chandelier hanging from the too high ceiling. This foyer had a different aesthetic to the parts of the mansion she'd seen on prior visits. It was more in keeping with the impression of a medieval castle, right down to the tapestries covering white stone walls.

Myra didn't have a great sense of smell, but the compound smelled strongly of that elusive scent of dragon that was hard to define. Bit dry and reptilian. But also musky, like a mammal. A touch of leather. And with just a hint, very faint and hard to detect on its own, of sulfur.

She couldn't explain it and didn't have a sensitive enough sense of smell to describe it. But it was very distinctly dragon shifter. If there were real dragons in the world still flying around—they were supposedly mostly asleep—Myra imagined they'd smell like this, too.

She stood in the huge foyer wondering why she'd been left alone to wander around, since the first time she'd been here, she'd broken into the king's hoard. Then movement in the shadows of a set of wooden pillars against one wall. The pillars were decorative, as far as she could tell. But maybe not. Because suddenly she was standing in the foyer with someone who hadn't been there a moment ago.

It took her brain a full beat before she realized she was looking at the dragon king himself.

She'd seen him multiple times at this stage, both here and out in the city. The familial resemblance to Christopher was obvious. While the king wasn't quite as tall as his son, he was no slouch in the height department. The angles and planes of his face spoke a similar story to Christopher's. But where Christopher wasn't what one would call conventionally handsome—she thought of him as compelling—the king defined the term.

His dark hair was peppered with silver. His eyes were a changeable blue or green depending on the lighting, with creases around the edges. The first time they'd met, he'd called Christopher a youngling and Myra had assumed she was going to steal a kid back from his kidnappers. Christopher was no a kid. But the fact that his father still spoke of him that way had either been a manipulative lie or the king was just that old and considered Christopher a child still.

Hard to say with the king. Because manipulation and lying were part of his DNA.

"Clever trick, finding me," she said by way of greeting.

"My son isn't the only one who is…intrigued by your movements. And yet neither of us know where you sleep."

She shrugged. "Woman's got to have some secrets. I hope you didn't bring me here to hit on me."

The king tucked his chin, flashing her a sardonic look that was frankly insulting. But also understandable. He was a king. She was a nobody. She liked being a nobody. She did better at her work being a nobody. She'd gone to a lot of trouble cultivating a life of being a nobody to anybody who might be looking. Having a crush on the king's son was bad enough for that nobody status.

She did wonder how both of them kept finding her when she wasn't in her hidey hole, though. Well, Christopher always found her. This was the first time the king had sent someone other than Christopher to get her. Which meant the king was also keeping tabs on her.

Which was *very* inconvenient.

"I require your services again," the king said.

"But you didn't send Christopher to find me."

"That is becoming... A problem."

"A problem, huh? I suppose you're going to tell me how it's a problem. Whether I care or not."

His mouth twitched, and then he smiled fully. "You're clever and sneaky and capable. I do like that about you. I do not like that my son likes you."

More insults. She supposed this wasn't completely unexpected, but somehow, she was still taken by surprise by the turn in this conversation. She honestly hadn't thought the king cared about his son's romantic life enough to bring it up.

"He's the son of a king," the king said, as if reading her mind. "I have...plans."

"Does he know about these plans? Might want to clue him in."

"The time isn't right."

"Gonna have to get it right soon, then. But I'm not sure what any of that has to do with me."

"My son likes you."

She chuckled. "I've read Page Six. Christopher has *liked* a lot of humans over the years." Though, she hadn't known any of that before meeting him. She'd done a crash course in learning all about this particular son of the dragon king after meeting him. And discovered a lot of rumors and innuendo and assumptions and speculation.

And not an awful lot of real information.

That had done more to pique her interest than put her off. She loved a good puzzle.

And a dragon shifter with a soft spot for damsels in distress who also happened to be the son of the dragon king was a definite puzzle.

She narrowed her eyes at the king. "Do you chase away everyone he sees?"

She was going to say dates, but in truth, they'd only been on one date so far, and that had been to one of his apartments to watch a movie. Nothing else had happened that night. She'd fallen asleep. Found herself waking up alone in a scrumptious bed with a note that told her to eat anything she liked and that he'd enjoyed the movie even if she'd fallen asleep.

He hadn't been anywhere in the apartment when she'd gone exploring, and she had to commend him his bravery leaving her alone with all his stuff. She hadn't stolen anything. But she had snooped. That had been a fun few hours, actually.

Still. What was happening between her and Christopher couldn't be called much yet. There was chemistry. There was intent. But there were also nerves and hesitation—mostly on her part. So the king making an issue of it already was strange. Unless he did this all the time.

She idly wondered how the prince Christopher had once dated dealt with this level of interference.

"My youngest does a very good job of chasing off most of his paramours himself," the king said.

"Rude. Does he know you talk about him this way?"

"It's not an insult. He has never gotten serious about any of his past lovers and does all the work of leaving when things get serious. I do not have to interfere."

She couldn't tell what the king was getting at. Was he warning her that Christopher was a short term thing and not to pin her hopes on more? Because she'd have to have hope for more for that to be necessary, and honestly, she didn't know what she wanted or hoped for yet. She liked Christopher. A lot. She wouldn't mind taking him to bed. But beyond that...

"Is this the entire reason I'm here?" she asked. "So you can warn me away from your son for...reasons. Because I do have better things to do." Like plan her next heist. There were many many rich people in the world with too much stuff, and she liked to redistribute that stuff. Or just prove she could swipe it before giving it back. Depended on the rich person.

"As I said, I have a job for you."

"Why don't we get to that, then." She didn't want to do another job for the king, but letting him tell her about it was better than discussing Christopher with him.

Anything was better than listening to the king trying to dissuade her from a relationship with his son.

Chapter Three

The vault door was a solid block of steel, three feet thick and secured into the surrounding brick wall by twelve thick steel pipes. There was a spell on the outside designed to keep wizards from just bespelling the lock open—which honestly most wizards couldn't do. That was a her-skill, not a wizard-skill. But the spell also seemed to block wizard's magic inside the vault too.

Which was why Myra's jumpy wizard accomplice had a gun.

She really disliked working with people who carried guns. So messy. So much room for disaster.

Already a disaster since they were locked inside a vault.

Maybe she should have encouraged the king to keep discussing all the reasons she shouldn't see his son.

From outside, she'd been able to finagle the code lock and had a spell that worked on the paw-print screen, disguising her ordinary human hand as a wolf-shifter paw. Fortunately, the paw print requirement wasn't specific to any one wolf-shifter. That would have made things much more difficult. She suspected that was an oversight by the lock designers. Or else no one knew how to program biometrics to more than a general shape for a shifter's print. Since she hadn't encountered a biometrics paw scan that was specific to individual shifters yet, maybe the techs hadn't figured that out yet.

Even the dragon king hadn't had a specific hand print biometric lock on his hoard. The eye scan had been interesting, since it *was* specific to a dragon's eye...

She shook off the thoughts for later research. She'd only started working more around shifters and wizards—usually she avoided both as much as possible and stuck to breaking-and-entering human facilities and houses and such—so some of the finer details hadn't crossed her work situations before.

In fact, she hadn't even known all that much about dragon shifters until that unfortunate breaking-into-the-king's-hoard incident. Since then, because of Christopher mostly, she'd really been trying to learn more about dragon shifters. And hadn't *that* been eye-opening research.

These weren't dragon shifters, though. Most of the lawyers and two of the three firm partners were wolf-shifters. So the paw print being wolf-shifter made sense. And, again fortunately, the shifters hadn't considered blocking *her* kind of magic. Just wizard magic. She had a feeling shifters and wizards knew as little about her magic, the specifics of it at least, as she'd known about dragon shifters.

That had made breaking into the vault a lot easier. But the breaking out part...

The blocks on magic inside the vault were a lot stronger than the ones on the outside. Maybe those increased once the interior alarm had been triggered. She hadn't tried to use any of her thief magic inside the vault before the alarm and the door sealing shut again. She hadn't actually had much time to do anything but look for the specific security box they needed. She hadn't even attempted to open that box yet when the door closed.

Now, she realized that the blocks inside the vault were doing a number on her magic, not just Glen's. When she tried to sense her way into the lock from this side, she came up against a blank wall. That was not normal. A touch and she could usually "read" a lock. Even if she used more traditional methods to crack it—which she often did, especially if the lock was challenging—she could get a read on the type of lock it was and how best to get through it.

She could usually sense a magic trap on a lock as well, which had saved her tripping an alarm more than once. Spells on locks weren't uncommon. Even humans bought those. So she tended to check automatically.

With the inner vault door, though, she couldn't sense the lock, couldn't pick up any spells. Actually felt a lot of blankness when she tried to use a small spell to even reveal the locking mechanism. Nothing.

Her magic was officially useless inside the vault.

Shit.

She could do this the old-fashioned way. Maybe. But as she'd never had to break *out* of a vault before, she wasn't sure what the old-fashioned way was because she couldn't even see the locking mechanism.

She cursed in her head again, but rolled her lips into her mouth so she didn't curse out loud. Her companion was jumpy enough as is.

Okay, so. She couldn't get at the door locks from this side. Yet. Maybe there was something else in here that would help. Or maybe she could find the spell that was blocking her magic. If it wasn't baked into the vault walls—in which case she'd be well and truly fucked—then it would have to be set into something, a device of some kind. That's how this kind of thing had to work. Couldn't just have a spell floating in the air. It had to have an anchor. Otherwise, it dissipated. If that anchor was something she could find—and not the vault walls—maybe she could dismantle the spell.

Did they have time for that?

No one had opened the vault yet, so hopefully. Not that she'd mind the vault door being opened. She'd rather face the shifters than slowly die of asphyxiation in a room with a wizard holding a gun, who might shoot her to conserve the oxygen. But having time to break out of the vault without anyone being the wiser would be better.

She started a methodical search, checking the walls, hovering a hand over the various deposit box doors. When she reached the door of the box they'd been sent for, she hovered a beat longer. But not too long. She expected the wizard to say something, to say they should get what they were there for and then worry about getting out. But he didn't comment.

Maybe he didn't want to get caught holding incriminating evidence if the shifters found them before they could escape.

What was that called? Plausible deniability. He could make up any kind of story to get out of this if caught, but not if he was holding something he wasn't supposed to be holding.

Still, she was surprised he didn't mention anything about the box when she paused at it. Not even a suggestion they look inside and make sure what they'd come for was even there. She was tempted by that logic herself. But she wanted a way out first. *Then* she could get on with the theft part of her night.

She didn't sense anything from the specific box that was any stronger or more pronounced than any other box. They all felt like blank slates to her. Black holes of nothingness. The fact that the box they were aiming for was just as blank and protected in the exact same way as the other boxes, some of which held nothing more than pictures and wills and maybe a few family heirlooms, was interesting.

Because either the law firm applied the same security to all their boxes, no matter the content, or the contents of the box she was here for were not what she'd been told.

And wouldn't that just be a kick in the pants.

She hated working for the dragon king.

She missed Christopher.

That last thought was incredibly scary, though, so she pushed it aside. Better to be angry with the father than to dwell on her softer feelings for the son. She got soft, she was going to get killed. Or worse…

Have her entire life taken over by the dragon king.

That was starting to happen already. And she hated it. But again, a problem to deal with when—*if*—she got out of this vault.

The search of the boxes turned up nothing specific. She glanced at the vault door again. No hint that someone was outside waiting to get in. She scanned the vault for a camera, something recording them, but couldn't see any obvious signs of one. Didn't mean there wasn't one, just that if there was, it was well disguised.

She hunted around the base of the walls, near the floor. The room was a steel case reinforced by brick, reinforced by titanium in the outer layer. Again, designed to prevent shifters from breaking in, and some of those shifters had the kind of strength that made pulling a traditional vault out of a brick wall possible. The extra layer of titanium *outside* the brick and steel exterior of the vault was the real kicker.

When nothing suspicious or useful turned up around the baseboards, she searched high, near the ceiling. At first from the floor. Then she brought out some of her climbing suction cups from her multi-pocket vest that she went nowhere without, and climbed up the two it took her to reach high enough she could study the line where wall met ceiling.

The wizard watched all this with a scowl, his gun lowered but his finger hovering too close to the trigger along the barrel. At least he wasn't stupid enough to stand around with his finger on the trigger. One loud noise and he'd shoot his foot off, and then she'd have to deal with that. Blood was messy and obvious. Hard to explain away blood.

She hit a corner of the vault, studying the spot where all the angles came together, and finally spotted a camera or recording device of some kind. A tiny device, very advanced, with an illusion spell to keep it disguised. It was little more than the size of one of those button batteries, easy to overlook even without the illusion spell. The spell itself was pretty simple. Anchored to the camera, but not designed to stand up to close scrutiny. Just to hide from casual observers.

And now her face was in it. Which meant somewhere, someone had a recording of her face, close up. That wasn't great news, but she could mitigate that issue. She touched a finger to the little camera. Studied the spells around it.

The realization hit her a moment later—longer than it should have taken her to realize—that the illusion spell was working up here, when other magic inside the vault was dampened. And she could sense the illusion spell. And study the camera with a touch.

Her magic worked up here.

She glanced down the few feet below her to where Glen was silently glaring up at her.

The minute she made eye contact, he said, "What did you find?"

"Camera."

She dislodged the button, taking the illusion spell with it, and hopped off the suction cups she'd been using as toe and finger holds while she studied the ceiling. Because of the magic dampening in the vault, she'd had to manually move those suction cups around to study different locations. That was less efficient. Also a bit irritating.

Once she was back to floor level, the illusion spell on the button camera broke. She felt it break. Not just dissipate or stop working. It actually *broke*, like thin glass shattering, the shards falling to the floor. That left the camera exposed, an obvious circle of silver on her fingertip. But also revealed something about the way the magic dampening effects worked inside the vault. Any spell she'd come into the vault with, anything *active* she'd brought inside the vault with her, would have broken the instant she was inside.

Interesting.

Now she was even more determined to find the source of the spell. And maybe take it with her so she could study the spell at her leisure.

So long as she could get out of the vault of course.

Chapter Four

The dragon king led Myra through a series of corridors she hadn't seen before, keeping her in suspense about his reasons for bringing her here, and the job he wanted to hire her to do, because he was a drama king as well as a dragon king. She should have expected the suspense.

The conversation about her relationship with Christopher still had her reeling though. Off balance. Because her relationship with Christopher, whatever it was and was developing into, also had her off balance and reeling a bit. She wasn't prepared to discuss this with his *father*. That his father didn't like the relationship, whatever it was, didn't bode well. But also, it was none of the dragon king's business. And she was just obstinate enough to want to see Christopher just to annoy the king.

Except…

She didn't want her…whatever was happening with Christopher to be something she got involved in just to irritate the king. She *liked* Christopher. She wanted what was developing between them to be between them. With no irritating, domineering third party having any influence or say over the matter.

The corridors through the palace were remarkably empty. They usually were when she was here with Christopher, too. The occasional shifter in human form passing, but most of the time, just empty hallways with weird proportions—very high ceilings and oddly wide walls, but in a way that almost felt narrow. The wooden floors gave way to marble floors in a few hallways, then returned to wood.

The walls in one corridor were decorated with huge hanging pictures of dragons, and landscapes, and the occasional battle scene —she'd have liked to study those closer because she suspected they had hints of actual dragon history in them, but the king didn't let her linger. In other corridors, the walls were hung with tapestries, or displayed ancient weaponry in display cases. And in one notable corridor, the white walls were as empty and blank as the black marble floors. That was one of the most disorienting corridors because it felt so blank, like it was half finished and awaiting the final details.

The underlying dragon smell permeated all of it. No matter where they went, that collective smell of dragon lingered in the air. She was a little surprised by how pleasant the scent of dragon shifters was, even with the very faint hint of brimstone at the base. That was probably down to how she felt about Christopher, though, and that she associated that smell with him. Well that and the smell of sugar cookies. That Christopher sometimes smelled like her favorite cookie amused her.

Finally, after what felt like a purposefully long walk to show off his mansion—to a thief!—the king led her into small conference room. Small being a relative word. The room still had inordinately high ceilings. But it was more roughly human-sized otherwise, like a boardroom in a Manhattan office building. Dark blue carpets covered the floor, the walls were wood paneled on three sides and a bank of floor to ceiling windows made up the fourth wall. The windows looked out over the forest, down into the valley below the hill the mansion sat on. Beyond the hill, she could just see the rising cityscape of Manhattan. She thought of that as "below" them since it was heading downtown. But also, given the king's compound was up on a hill, there was the illusion of the city being "below" the king's perch.

The center of the room was taken up by a large wooden conference table surrounded by cushiony black desk chairs. A rectangular device in the center of the conference table probably controlled audio-visual equipment, but she didn't see any screens or TVs or anything to display charts and graphs. Her experience with conference rooms was usually confined to creeping through them in the dark on her way to steal something, though, so maybe the screen or TVs were hidden.

She didn't see any closets or hidden panels at first glance, but after wandering to the windows to pretend to take in the views, she spotted the hidden panel in the wall to the left and the subtle cameras placed in the four corners of the room.

"Nice." She turned to face the king.

He was also looking out the window and he nodded briefly at her comment so he'd made the assumption she'd wanted him to— that she'd been talking about the view.

"We attending a board meeting or something?" She gestured to the table.

"I need you to retrieve a necklace from a vault," the king said abruptly.

Okay. So. Right to the point. She was good with that. This tour of the mansion felt like stalling and she didn't like stalling when she wasn't the one doing it.

"What sort of necklace, and why, and why haven't you just

bought it?" She'd seen his hoard, probably one of the few humans to have, and she knew it wasn't just random piles of gold and free gemstones. There were plenty of necklaces and piles of jewelry. "What makes this necklace special enough you need it stolen?"

"It's not for sale," he answered the most obvious question. "It's magical." Which sort of explained why it was special, but the king also had other magical necklaces. "And it is dangerous."

"How so?"

"It's held in a vault guarded by shifters."

"It's not like that amulet you already have, right?" The amulet the shifters who'd kidnapped Christopher had wanted in exchange for Christopher's return. An amulet that would essentially turn shifters into monsters. Bad bad bad. If this was something like that, then yes, it was dangerous.

"No. Not precisely." The king let his gaze travel over the room as he said that.

He thought he was subtle, and a good actor. And he actually did do a good job of being himself in public in a loud and obviously bombastic way. He was also good at court machinations, according to Christopher, which were all about deceit and hiding motivations. So she wasn't entirely sure if that refusal to make eye contact meant he was really hiding something or he was attempting to make her think he was hiding something. Either way, he was attempting to intrigue her. Which was the way to get her to take a job she didn't necessarily want to take.

If she'd been a shifter, she'd probably have been a cat shifter of some sort, and then along with the usual cat burglar jokes, she'd also have to deal with her mental "curiosity killed the cat" jokes because her curiosity was definitely an issue. Also, that subtle sense of challenge got to her.

The king was entirely too skilled at manipulation and she was afraid he had her number.

"Where's the vault?"

"Midtown building. Lawyers' office suite."

"Not a bank?"

"These lawyers specialize in handling shifter cases. It can be hard for a shifter to get good and fair representation among human lawyers." He sneered the word human.

She tried not to take offense, even if he meant to give offense. "Not sure why that means they need a whole vault in their offices and not one inside a bank." But that didn't matter much to the job. "Why is it better for you to have this necklace rather than it staying nice and safe and unused inside a vault?"

"The necklace is dangerous and there are others after it," the king said. "It will be safer inside my hoard."

She'd heard that story before. But in this case, she suspected "safer" meant "I'll have it and no one else will" because in the grand scheme of things, the king was still a dragon who hoarded valuable things for the sake of hoarding valuable things.

"Why not just negotiate that with the lawyers, then?" A test of sorts in that question. "Why steal the necklace? Why not buy it."

"As I already said, it's not for sale."

"But if it's dangerous, and your hoard is really the safest place for it, wouldn't the owners *want* it to be safer?"

"The owners do not realize the necklace's potential."

Of course not. "And you do?"

"I have been fully briefed on the situation."

"By?"

The door to the conference room opened again and a new man walked into the room. Tallish, though not as tall as the king, very thin, high cheekbones, dark eyes, long blond hair hanging loosely around his shoulders. He wore a business suit in a dark charcoal gray with a white shirt and purple tie. A pair of tiny round glasses perched on his nose, glasses she could tell at a glance were for effect rather than necessity, and he kept his hands clasped in front of him.

He looked innocuous, very human, and probably the sort of person no one would look at too closely.

She pegged him immediately as a wizard.

Chapter Five

Glen leaned in close to Myra's finger and pointed at the silver button she held on the tip. "That doesn't look like a camera."

This close, Glen's nervous sweat stink was a bit stronger. The man was seriously stressed. If she could smell him, with her not great sense of smell, things were bad. If the shifters caught them now, they'd probably be hit in the face with that sign of his fear.

"It's called a button camera and mostly it's a short distance device for recording. It will be motion activated, which means it turned on the minute we got inside the vault, and the recording it's making is probably nearby in a security room or security closet."

"How do you know that?" Glen barked, glaring at her.

She ignored the glare, frowning as she glanced around the vault interior again. "Part of the job to know these things. Standard operating procedure. The button doesn't have a strong signal. The recorder would have to be close."

Outside of the camera, even searching baseboards and ceiling, she hadn't found the magic dampening device. There weren't a lot of hiding places inside the vault. It wasn't that large. And any spells in spots lower than the ceiling would have broken so there wasn't anything being hidden by an illusion.

She hadn't been able to sense anything from the safety deposit boxes lining the walls. But those were the only option for hiding the magic dampening device. She glanced at the locked vault door, still decidedly sealed against exit. No one busting in to stop them or catch them or kill them. But would they allow her time to search all the deposit boxes?

Maybe they didn't think she could open them.

Magically breaking locks was far from her only skill. And she liked doing things the old-fashioned way. Testing her abilities. Seeing if she was good enough.

Most of the time, she was.

But safety deposit boxes were tricky. They took two different keys. And all the keys were different. This required a bit of technology if she wasn't using magic. Fortunately, she'd brought the technology—a sort of key imprinting and replicating machine— because she'd thought she'd need it for the deposit box that was their goal. She hadn't intended on opening more than the one box, though.

Opening every single box would take all night, maybe a couple of days. She was certain they didn't have that kind of time. The air in the vault would run out. She estimated they had about five more hours of breathable air. Then they were dead.

She planned on being out of this place before that. But she didn't have enough time to search every single security box in the meantime.

Where to start?

She considered the little button camera on her fingertip. Did she smash it or keep it? Smashing it might set off an alarm—though so many had probably sounded by now that hardly seemed something she needed to worry about—and it might bring the shifters sooner rather than later. That had the benefit of getting them out of the vault sooner, but the drawback of getting them into a different sort of trouble sooner too. And without the prize they'd come for.

If she didn't smash the camera, the shifters would be getting a recording of everything she did. And that could be used against her in a court of law. Which she had no intention of being in. Dealing with the recordings they might already have was an issue she had to see to after they got out. So far, the only thing she could be accused of was breaking into the vault and getting stuck. She hadn't technically stolen anything yet and could plausibly deny being here to steal things if she never tried to open a deposit box.

But she had to open at least a few of the deposit boxes.

So. Smash camera or put it in her pocket. She couldn't tell by looking at it if it was also recording voices. Voice recordings would be as bad as video evidence, or nearly so. She suspected Glen would have a hard time not asking questions, and since he had a gun, he wasn't exactly ignorable.

Okay. She really had little choice. Crush the camera. If someone showed up, they'd be free of the vault. If no one showed up, she'd have time to check for the magic dampening device and hopefully also retrieve the item they were here to get.

She dropped the little camera to the hard linoleum-over-steel-and-concrete floor and smashed the button with the heel of her soft-soled shoes. She felt the stomp reverberate up her calf. Heard a satisfying crunch. She ground her heel down harder into the button, just to make sure. If she'd been wearing harder soled shoes, she'd have known the button was completely shattered with that first stomp, but her shoes had been selected for their ability to limit any sound she made, not crush small electronic devices.

She lifted her foot to see a nice collection of tiny bits of metal and wires flattened into the gray floor. If that thing was still recording, it would be a miracle. Or magic. And the magic couldn't work down here.

Myra glanced at the vault door and held perfectly still for a full three minutes, waiting on signs someone was going to open that door and rush in to arrest them. Or kill them. During that three minutes, she had to shush Glen once. But only once. Which she counted as progress.

He rubbed a hand across his mouth, the gleam of sweat on his upper lip obvious in the vault's mercilessly bright lighting.

At the three minute mark, when it became obvious no one was rushing in to stop them, she turned her attention to the security boxes. She still wasn't sure where to start looking for the magic dampening device. She had to find that if she had any hope of breaking them out of the vault from the inside. But she hadn't a clue which box to try first.

She did know which box she was here to rob, though.

She decided to start there. She could move on to checking other boxes after. She really didn't want to get caught red handed with the very thing they were here to steal, but she also didn't know where else to start.

From inside one of the many pockets in the black vest she wore over her black yoga pants and black t-shirt, she pulled out the small rectangular device she used for making keys. It was a sort of 3D printer, printing whatever she pressed into the memory foam type substance inside the box.

She needed something for it to copy and print, though, which was where the little tube of super soft, malleable clay-like substance came in. It was stiffer than the foam inside the box, but could be inserted into a lock to form the ridges and contours that would make up the key necessary to open the lock. The substance was nowhere near strong enough to actually open anything. It took the impression of the key, but if she twisted it in an attempt to open the lock, all she'd do is twist the impression and mess the whole thing up.

Carefully, she inserted the tube into one of the two locks keeping the security box sealed. She counted to five, then gently slid the tube back out again, working hard not to flinch or turn it in any way. The impression had to be perfect, or the resulting key would never work, and for that to happen, she couldn't afford to introduce any flaws.

Once out, she examined the impression. Looked clean. She gave the substance a few seconds to harden enough it could be copied. A little warm rub of her fingers and it would soften into the malleable clay-like substance again. But it was just stiff enough after a few seconds to press into the memory foam grid and get an impression that the tiny printer could replicate exactly in a hard plastic.

The hard plastic key would work in the lock.

She went through the procedure twice. Making one of each of the keys necessary to opening the deposit box. Then she returned her little printer to her pocket, and neatly slid the two keys into their respective locks.

When the box clicked open, Glen finally made a noise. A sort of hissing, quiet cheer, like he was trying to keep in a gleeful shout. Myra appreciated his attempt to keep his enthusiasm in check.

"I didn't think you'd be able to pull that off," he murmured.

Why he was whispering, she wasn't sure. The vault was too thick for their voices to carry outside it, and she'd smashed the one camera she'd been able to find. If there were any other listening devices inside the vault, she hadn't found them.

"Trust, Glen. You need to have some faith."

"In a thief?" He snorted.

"Rude. But yes. I'm a very good thief. You should have faith in my ability to steal things."

He didn't comment. Probably for the best.

She slid out the small metal box that occupied the cubby, and swung around to open it while Glen was watching. Last thing she needed was him deciding she'd palmed something to screw him over if what they expected to be inside this box wasn't inside this box.

"Ready?" she asked him.

He nodded, his full attention on the rectangular metal lid. "Open it."

She did.

CHAPTER SIX

"The king said the job was to steal a necklace." Myra stared at the wizard, then looked at the dragon king, then glanced back at the wizard. This didn't feel like a good turn of events. And she was definitely not happy about the wizard's presence.

"It's actually a locket, not a full necklace," the wizard, Glen, said. "The locket is the important part." He glanced at the dragon king, but the king kept his attention on Myra. The king hadn't spoken since Glen started explaining the specifics of what they were after.

Myra ignored the king's stare outwardly to keep her attention on the wizard, but she was very aware of his gaze and that focus made her skin itch.

Behind Glen, through the wall of windows at his back, the distant skyline of Manhattan sparkled, sunlight reflecting off the tall, mirror-windowed buildings. At this distance, over the top of a forest, the city looked almost like a fairytale land. And she was in the palace, looking down at it. Except she sat in a very modern boardroom, at a large wooden conference table, across from an actual wizard, with a dragon sitting at the head of the table.

Her life was a little weirder and more fairytale like than she'd prefer. Not like those sanitized-for-kids fairytales either. But like the real fairytales where people cut off their own toes and the fairies sucked poor, unsuspecting humans dry.

Myra repressed a shiver, glad that, as far as she knew, real fairies didn't exist. Dragon shifters and wizards were bad enough.

"It's ancient," Glen continued. "Used to belong to wizards in eons past. But it disappeared. Became more of a myth."

She'd encountered those sorts of relics before. Stolen a few of them over the years. A lot of them ended up in private family collections, passed down with other wealth, and the wealthy people in possession of them usually didn't even know what they had. Which would explain why the king had said the owners of this locket didn't know the locket's potential.

Myra had built a career on stealing those kinds of things. Forgotten things. Things no one realized were missing until too late.

"It's turned up again in the possession of a wolf-shifter family," Glen said of this missing locket. "The locket does not belong to shifters. It's dangerous for shifters to possess it."

She'd heard that story before, too. "Except I understood they didn't know what they had. Or was I misled, and they do know what this locket can do?"

Glen flicked another glance at the king. This time, Myra felt the king's gaze move away from her. She knew without looking when the king's attention landed on Glen because the wizard flinched and looked away quickly.

"They don't know what it is, what it can do," Glen said. "At least, from what I can tell, they don't. They're keeping the locket in a vault inside a law firm. The firm represents shifters who can't find human lawyers who will work with them."

Glen's lip curled just a little, but Myra couldn't tell if he was sneering at the shifters or the humans who didn't want to work with them.

"Since they don't know what they have," Myra said, watching Glen closely even as she felt the king's attention move back to the side of her face, "why is it dangerous for them to have this locket? It seems the safest place for something dangerous is locked away in a vault with no one worried about finding it or using it."

Despite the king's assertion the artifact would be safer in his hoard, she wasn't seeing the logic. Leaving something dangerous safely locked away from the world, in the possession of people who weren't going to use it—in this case because they didn't know what they had—was always better than having said dangerous thing out in the world in the possession of people who might use it.

She had no illusions that whatever this locket did, Glen would just lock it away safely and never use it. He wasn't going to all this trouble for nothing.

"The lawyers are suspicious," Glen said. "The ones who have the vault in their office. They know…something. I'm not sure how much. But if they discover the truth, it'll mean bad things for all wizards."

"Do I get to know what these bad things for wizards might be?" she asked, and finally turned her attention on the king. "And what all this has to do with the dragons?"

"I'm merely here as a facilitator," the king said, his gaze steady on hers. "Glen came to me for help."

Except that the king wanted this necklace-locket in his own hoard and not in Glen's possession. She wondered if Glen knew that part.

"Why? Why would a wizard come to you?"

They both looked at Glen.

"Why come to the dragon king," Myra asked him directly,

"another shifter, for help retrieving something you don't want shifters to have?"

Glen did this thing with his shoulders that might have been a shrug. "The king has resources that I don't have access to. Like the name of a good thief."

She didn't wince at that. But she wanted to. This didn't bode well if word had gotten out the king had a thief on the books, ready to do jobs he assigned her. That wouldn't do at all. No. She didn't work for the king. She wasn't one of the king's dragons. And she was not on retainer with him. She worked alone, for herself, and intended on keeping things that way.

She glanced at the king. He blinked slowly at her, but that was his only reaction.

"And I can't go to other wizards," Glen added.

This wasn't entirely unexpected. Wizards working together was a bit like wizards working with shifters. They either did and were tight allies, or they didn't and were basically mortal enemies.

She was starting to believe the problem here was the wizards.

"Why not?" she asked anyway, wondering if she'd get a specific answer or some hand wavey excuse.

She got the hand wavey excuse. "None of them understand the danger. They don't care enough to help me."

Glen was lying. That was interesting.

"But it's important to get the locket back into wizard hands," he finished, his gaze dancing to the king before settling on her again.

She turned to fully face the king. "You think this is important enough to ask me to do the job?"

"I think it's best if this locket is not in possession of the shifter law firm," the king said. Very carefully.

"Whose paying me?" She looked between the two men, swiveling a little in her chair.

Glen did another of those quick glances at the king, then said, "I have some money to pay you. It's not a fortune, but it's something."

She didn't like anything about this. Her hackles were raised. Her suspicions up. Glen had some secret purpose he wasn't discussing. The king had his own agenda in this. And she'd get caught in the middle if she took this job.

A wise thief would say no. She was a wise thief.

But she was also a dangerously curious thief.

"Wire the money to my account by the end of the day. The king has the details. We go in in three days. I'll need the time to research and set up the heist."

Glen blinked hard a few times, opened his mouth, closed it again. Glanced at the king. Faced her again.

She nearly smiled. She liked keeping people on their toes.

"You'll do it? You'll help me?"

"If I can't get into the vault, I'll let you know and refund your money less my research fee." But she was sure she could get into the vault.

"I'm coming with you," Glen said.

She frowned. "No. I don't work with other people."

She ignored the slight eyebrow raise from the king she could sense more than see in her peripheral vision. She knew he was thinking about Christopher. Because she had been working with Christopher lately. But that was unusual. She didn't usual work with other people except as occasional contract labor when she needed help with new tech or a computer hack she couldn't manage on her own.

"I'm going with you. That's part of the deal. I need to be there. I need to…to retrieve the locket myself. I just can't get into the vault on my own."

"Don't trust me to get the locket for you, Glen?" she asked with a small smile. She wouldn't necessarily trust her either if she didn't know her so well.

"It's not that." Glen's gaze once again flicked to the king and back to her. "I need to be there. The locket would be dangerous for you to touch. You'll need a wizard to handle it. You'll need me there."

A jumpy wizard who was telling her any number of lies, might have lied to the king, and whose real motivation in all this was pretty sketchy along for the ride during a break-in.

Yeah, that would turn out well.

But if he was right and the locket needed a wizard to handle it safely, she was going to have to take him along.

She hated working with amateurs.

Chapter Seven

Inside the security deposit lock box, resting on a small purple silk patch of material, sat the very thing Myra had broken into this vault to steal.

There hadn't been any pictures of the locket when she'd researched it. In fact, there'd been no information on it at all. Glen hadn't really given her enough to find the locket in the histories, and since the shifters didn't know what they had, there weren't any more modern stories about it. She'd come across one single, possible story of a wizard locket that possessed mystical powers to control time. But that was the closest she'd managed to find. And there'd been no descriptions or images of that locket.

So finally getting to see the locket was a moment for pause.

It was round, about half the size of her palm, which made it larger than she'd been expecting, and was made of a greenish polished stone, with swirls of purple and gold color in it like marble. The stone was surrounded by a silver frame, with a pattern of twists and folds in the silver that gave the whole thing movement. It wasn't hanging on a chain of any kind, despite the king having called this a necklace. But there was a little hook of silver at the top where a chain could be strung. There weren't any runes or etchings in the stone's surface or woven into the silver frame. The locket just looked like a pretty, if large, pendant.

"It opens?" she asked Glen with her attention still on the locket. She assumed it did since Glen called it a locket and not a charm or medallion, but she couldn't see a clasp in the silver frame.

"It does. But only for a wizard." Glen reached into the box to retrieve the artifact.

When she looked at his expression, she didn't particularly like what she saw. The gleam in his eyes. The avarice. She'd known this job was hinky from the start. She still wasn't sure if the problem with it all was the king or Glen. Though, given his expression, she was certain Glen was *a* problem now.

She hadn't touched the charm on purpose, because Glen had claimed that would be dangerous. But as she watched him stare wide-eyed at the locket, she did reach in and touch the silk pouch the charm had been resting on, to see if there was anything there she could read. Her magic mostly worked to pick up things like spells and traps set to keep locks secure. She wouldn't be able to just feel wizard magic and know what it was for. Her magic had its limits. But she'd sense a spell or trap if that's what the locket was.

She picked up a few sparks from the silk, but nothing she could clearly identify.

Except... Except she could pick up the magic.

Her magic wasn't being blocked anymore.

Frowning, she hurried back to the vault door and touched the area near the lock. There. She could sense her way into it now. Sense the lines and follow the paths that took her to where she needed to go to get the door open from this side.

Whatever had been dampening magic inside the vault wasn't anymore.

She looked back at Glen. He still held his gun in one hand, but it was pointed at the floor and he seemed unaware that he still held it. His full attention was on the locket. He was smiling, rubbing his thumb over the green polished stone in the center. He murmured a spell under his breath, too quiet for her to catch the words, and the green stone shimmered and seemed to fold backward in a way that wasn't possible for regular stone, revealing an inner chamber, a small depression inside the larger stone.

In the depression, a diamond the size of a corn kernel winked in the overhead florescent lights. Rainbows danced along its surface, reflecting on Glen's tiny round glasses.

Glen's smile grew.

"You can open the door now?" he asked without looking up at her.

"Yeah. You ready to go?"

He nodded. "Oh yeah. I'm ready."

She had no idea what the diamond was—beyond probably worth a tidy sum all on its own—and what the locket really did, but she did want out of this vault sooner rather than later so questions and concerns about the locket could wait.

And since no security had come charging in the minute they opened that box and retrieved the locket, she was starting to suspect no one had been monitoring the vault's camera, or that any alarms had gone off when she'd crushed it under her shoe. There could still be people—security guards or police—on their way. But if they were out there somewhere just beyond the vault door, they'd have probably opened the door by now.

She still had time to get out of this cleanly. Or at least cleanly enough to deal with what dirt was left behind. But she sensed in her little thief soul that her window for escape was closing.

She went to work on the vault lock, using her magic to burrow down into the layers of security. It took her longer from this side, almost a full minute to crack the code. She didn't need the biosensor's paw print this time, though. Probably because, without magic, no one would be able to pick the vault lock from this side of the door.

When the steel bars clicked and clanked out of the wall, sliding into the door, Myra smiled. She gave the big, heavy circle a shove and the door hissed open with a release of air. The fresh air from outside the vault rushed in, brushing the fine hairs that had escaped her bun. She pulled in a deep breath, only then realizing how stale the air inside the vault had been getting.

Wow, they'd had less time than she realized. That would be a terrifying thought later if she chose to dwell on it.

She eased around the door, searching the office beyond.

Empty.

Weird but also she was going to accept the gift horse, as they say, and just get out while the getting was good. They'd even gotten what they'd come for. In the moments after the vault door had closed and locked them in, she'd worried about that part.

"This way," she whispered and motioned Glen to follow her without looking back at him.

She crept forward on noiseless feet, waiting for the telltale sound of running security guards. She reached the office door that moved them into the corridor beyond, and paused again to listen. At one end of the long hallway, an emergency staircase led out of the building. At the other, a private elevator. Offices of various sizes and a couple of conference rooms lined the hall. There was one side corridor that branched off the main one and led to the partners' offices. To the left of the private elevator was a reception desk and small foyer. To the right of the private elevator, a glass door that led out to a bank of public elevators.

The private elevator inside the offices was a pretty unique

feature of the building. A security issue, she'd have thought. But where there's money…

Given the law firm often represented shifters pro bono, she was curious where the money came from. Had to be some high profile and wealthy clients in there somewhere.

Which meant she'd probably left at least one security deposit box full of actual valuables back in that vault. Shame.

She eased open the door when she didn't hear anything and studied the corridor. It was dark, with only a set of emergency lights on over the private elevator. Light from the public elevator bank came in through the glass doors, but the rest of the office was dark. Still no signs of security.

They'd set off an alarm, locked themselves in the vault, found and crushed the only camera in the place, and they were still being left alone with no cops arriving to arrest them?

Something about that was…wrong.

Her every instinct hummed. Not that this job had felt right from the beginning. She knew Glen had been lying to her from the start. But the fact that he'd been so willing to shoot her inside the vault, his panic sweat, his visible fear, that would have been hard to fake. She knew he'd panicked. That the vault locking them in wasn't actually part of the plan.

At least, she was pretty sure it hadn't been.

But what she was certain of was that the lack of response to all the alarms they'd triggered was super suspicious. And something was not right.

"Private elevator," Glen said.

That had been her original plan. It was locked down with codes and paw print bio scanners, like the vault, but she could get past those exactly as she had with the vault.

Then she'd be stuck inside another metal box with a jumpy wizard who still had a gun.

"Stairs," she said.

"They'll expect that."

"*They* should already be here to arrest us," she said. "*They* are not working according to plan." Which meant she couldn't make assumptions about what would happen next. The only thing she knew was that she didn't want to be stuck in another metal box with Glen and his gun.

"I'm taking the elevator. That was our plan."

"Help yourself." Their plan had also not involved getting locked inside the vault and Glen having a gun. "You got a way around the bio scanner and lock panel, be my guest. I'm taking the stairs."

She eased out of the door and into the corridor, searching right and left, before jogging on quiet feet to the stairwell door. It was alarmed, of course. It was for emergency use only. And given all the other alarms she'd set off that night, she really shouldn't worry too much about this one, but this one connected to the full building security, not just the law firm's security, so she was a lot more likely to draw attention if she set this one off.

Last thing she needed, getting humans involved. She was still worried none of the law firm's security were bearing down on her. She'd feel better if she'd had to make a daring escape. This being left to break and enter and escape was making the hairs on her arms rise.

She expected Glen to make a show of heading to the elevator, before following her into the stairwell. He didn't even do that much, just trotted after her.

She made short work of the door alarm—it was standard motion sensor triggered, something she'd dismantled many times before—and slowly pressed the bar to open the door. When no alarm sounded, she smiled and pushed the door open fully.

The stairwell was dark, but lights flickered on when she moved onto the landing, revealing cream walls and black concrete stairs.

The stairs circled up two flights to the roof and down the eighteen flights to ground level.

She glanced down the column of space in the center of the stairwell, around which the stairs circled. The lower levels were shroud in darkness. She could barely see the landing below them, and only a little of the landing above them. The roof was as hidden in darkness as the ground.

No one else moving in the stairwell. No other lights triggered.

In an emergency, she assumed all the lights came on. But without triggering the alarm the building probably saved money by keeping the lights on motion detectors only. It was a very handy way for her to know if there were others moving around in the stairwell.

Glen bumped up against her back, looking downward, too. She held on to the rail, and glanced at him. "You looking to jump?" she asked.

He glared at her. "What are you waiting for? Let's get out of here before we run out of luck."

Luck. That's what he wanted her to believe was happening here?

He started toward the stairs heading down. She let him get halfway to the first turn before she went the other way, heading up.

"Hey, where are you going?" he hissed, a sort of shouted whisper that nevertheless echoed in the stairwell.

She didn't bother to answer. She took the steps two at a time, hurrying up to the door that would lead out onto the roof.

Glen's much louder footsteps came after her, a rush of noise that echoed off the concrete walls.

There was another alarm on the roof door. She took the time to disarm it as well, time that gave Glen a chance to catch up. He was puffing and panting as he stumbled up behind her.

"What the hell? How are you planning on getting off the roof?"

"This was always the escape plan. I have an exit. Don't worry."

"I can't fly like your boyfriend," he hissed.

There was a lot of anger in that comment. More than was really called for.

She thought back to the way he'd kept glancing at the king during their meeting. The way he'd gone to the king for help. The way the king had been looking at Glen.

The whole situation stunk, right from the start. Especially the king bringing her in without letting Christopher know about it all.

The locket Glen had retrieved blocked magic. It had to be the reason her magic started working again once they'd retrieved it. Glen's magic should be working now as well.

But he hadn't put the gun away.

"You got a problem with dragon shifters, Glen?" she asked as she pushed open the roof door and studied the flat expanse beyond.

Nothing much up here but extractor fans and a flat, black-tarred surface. The retaining wall around the roof was low, but only two sides were open. The other two butted up directly against the neighboring buildings, both of which were several stories taller than this one.

At the back of the building, there was a gap over an open parking lot with cars in a stacker, six levels high. The front of the building opened up onto the street below. They were half a block over from Lexington, and even at this time of night, the sounds of traffic were clear. The street below, however, was quiet, with crosstown traffic down to a minimum.

Most of the surrounding buildings were dark except for the occasional light in random scattered windows. The building across the street was a sheet of gray-tinted glass with no lights at all showing through.

She made it to the low retaining wall on the side of the building facing the street before she heard the click of Glen's gun.

Myra expected the shot to be fired before she could turn, before he had to look her in the eyes. She'd assumed he'd just shoot her in the back and be done with this.

When he didn't shoot immediately, she turned to face him.

Glen was smiling faintly, his lip lifted in an expression that could more accurately be called a snarling smirk. His tiny, pointless glasses reflected the faint glow of ambient city light.

"So fucking clever," he said. "In and out. If I hadn't triggered that alarm on accident, this would have been done already, wouldn't it?"

"If by *this* you mean the theft, yes. If by *this* you mean shooting me… I can wait longer for that."

He chuckled. "Shame I have to kill you. You really are very good at what you do. But this doesn't work if you survive." He shrugged. "The plan's already screwed up enough as it is. Can't afford to let anything else go wrong."

"Gonna explain the plan or just shoot me?"

He lifted the gun. "Just shoot you."

"I'm going to be dead. Sure you don't want to explain your nefarious plot? I'd like to know why I'm being killed."

"Sorry. Not inclined on discussing it further. Just know, the war will take care of them. You'll be happier dead than watching your boyfriend and his kind die."

Well. None of that sounded good at all. She leaned against the low retaining wall. It came just to the level of her butt, which meant it was really short. Behind her, she could feel the fast breeze of open air, the cold kiss of wide open space, and a long drop.

Glen's eyes narrowed. He lifted the gun so it pointed at her head. "I'm a good shot," he said. "Especially for a wizard. You can't get away."

"Fair enough."

She smiled. Glen frowned. His finger twitched against the trigger.

She leaned back until she felt gravity take her over the edge of the building, was aware of a bullet whizzing past just above her face, heard the sound of the gunshot as she hung for a split second in the open air.

And then she fell.

CHAPTER EIGHT

A̲ir whooshed past Myra as she dropped toward the street. But she didn't freefall for long. Not a high enough building for that.

She heard his wings, the sound of his approach like canvas sails in a breeze, before she felt his arms come up around her, before she could even fire off her grappling hook gun to stop her own fall.

Christopher swooped down to almost road level to catch her, rising up under her. The breathless feeling of his arms snatching her out of the air, the jolt as her drop stopped abruptly. She wrapped her arms around his neck, and the swift beat of his wings pulled them both high up above the rooftops.

She grinned up at the side of his face. "Well hello there. Fancy meeting you here."

He glanced at her, his blue eyes sparking with hints of purple in the night lights. "You okay?"

"Perfect." She held tighter, luxuriating in his warmth. He was shirtless, so his wings could spread out, the partial shift allowing him to keep most of his body in human form as he flew. Before meeting him, she'd had no idea dragon shifters could do this. But it did have its benefits.

The layer of purple and yellow scales over his shoulders and chest were warm and silky. His dark hair was a mess from the flight. If she could see his feet, she knew he'd be barefoot. His jaw was tight, and he looked as angry as she'd ever seen him.

For her part, she'd never been so delighted to see someone in her life. And it wasn't just because he'd swooped her out of the air, stopping her freefall to the hard sidewalk below.

She touched his jaw. "You're okay, too?"

"I've been better. Why didn't you tell me about this job?"

"Honestly? Because your father chose not to tell you. I wanted to see what would happen."

"What happened was you almost got shot."

"Yeah. The gun was a bit of a surprise from a wizard."

He angled high over the building where she and Glen had just robbed the law firm. They both watched as the wizard, looking quite small from this height, hurried back inside. She wondered if he even realized he hadn't killed her. Had he rushed to the edge, to make sure he'd shot her, to make sure she hit the ground? Or did he just shoot and then decide to run?

"Do you know what all this was about?" she asked Christopher as they circled the buildings, waiting for Glen to come out onto the street.

"I found out about the meeting you and my father had with the wizard from a friend in the mansion. It took some digging to find out what the wizard was up to."

"Which was?"

Below them, a few cars moved along the dimly lit cross streets. And if she turned to look over Christopher's shoulder, she'd probably see the louder traffic over on Lexington and Park. But this late, it was remarkably quiet. No horns or loud buses. They were too high up to hear the rumble of the subway, though Christopher might be able to.

The air at this height was cold, sharp. The taste of the city and a chilled breeze off the East River mingled with Christopher's scent —a mix of dragon musk and a really nice soap tonight. She tightened her arms around his neck, soaking up his warmth. He was really warm tonight. Or maybe she was just cold because she'd nearly been shot and she hated guns.

Or maybe she just really loved Christopher's heat.

"Glen wants to start a war among the shifters. To eliminate them all."

"Ah." She nodded, though she was still a little surprised by the sheer scale of Glen's plan. "One of those wizards." No neutral ground. Either allies or enemies. And Glen was the kind of wizard who was an enemy. "Why the hell did your father arrange for me to help Glen then? Why did Glen go to your father?"

Christopher let out a low, hissing growl that actually made the hairs on her neck tingle. Wow. She wasn't sure that sound boded well for either Glen or the king.

Before he could answer, though, a small shape hurried out of the building onto the street. Glen paused, turned in a circle, ran one direction, looked up at the roof, then searched the street again.

So. He'd thought he'd shot her or at the very least she'd hit the ground and gone splat. He probably should have researched *her* better before getting her involved in all this crap.

Christopher tucked his wings and arrowed toward the street. The feel of the sudden drop, the speed of the air passing as they plunged downward, made Myra gasp. She tightened her grip as her stomach bottomed out and her heart hammered. She had to make an effort not to giggle. The thrill like riding a roller coaster, charging adrenaline and endorphins through her system.

He snapped open his wings and stopped their dive only a few

feet above the street. When his feet touched the sidewalk, the landing was gentle and she barely felt the transition between flight and standing. He kept his wings wide behind him, a move that would make him look even larger than he already was.

Glen's back was to them for a split second. Then he turned. Spotted them standing only a few feet away, appearing as if out of nowhere. And stumbled back several steps, nearly landing on his ass in the process. He didn't have the gun in his hand anymore, having tucked it away somewhere. But Myra watched his fingers twitch like he wanted to reach for it.

Given the anger pumping off Christopher in waves of heat, Myra thought it better for Glen's sake that he didn't reach for that gun if he wanted to keep his limbs attached.

Glen looked between Christopher's face and hers, his eyes wide, the panic making his already pale skin sheet white. "How?" he said, though so quietly, she wasn't sure he was actually asking them. Just trying to figure it all out.

"Assuming you could arrange a meeting with my father and endanger the life of someone close to me without me knowing was a mistake," Christopher said.

She resisted the urge to look up at him when he said "someone close to me." He was still holding her in his arms, and she hadn't released his neck so he could put her down. This meant his hands were occupied, which wasn't optimal if Glen decided to pull that gun out. But she also didn't particularly want to let Christopher go now that he was here. And her heart did a funny sort of flutter at the "someone close to me" comment.

The quiet hiss in his voice didn't bode well for Glen, though.

"This won't change anything," Glen said, his eyes wide as he hunted the surroundings for an escape.

"You think my father didn't know what you were trying to do?"

Christopher said. "You think he hasn't already started to hunt down your accomplices?"

"He can't stop us. Not all of us."

Myra would sure *love* to know what was going on. But she thought interrupting to ask questions might derail the conversation. If she didn't get answers, soon, though, she was definitely going to grill Christopher about all this later. After kissing him. Maybe after kissing him for a while.

When his hands tightened on her legs and around her lower back, she decided the kissing part would definitely happen before the questions.

"And you can no longer use the locket against us," Glen continued. Which was convenient of him. "It's mine to control now."

"Blocked magic," Myra murmured to Christopher. "At least that's what I think it did. Neither of our magic worked inside the vault until he held it."

"The shifters didn't know what it was," Christopher murmured back. "They knew something in the vault screwed with the illusions they used to disguise their camera, unless they kept the camera at the ceiling. They didn't know which of the things in the vault was responsible for the problem."

"But Glen did." Glen knew which safety deposit box to check, too. That he hadn't told her sooner to open that box so she could use her magic to escape was a question she wasn't sure she'd get an answer to. Maybe he was hoping she wouldn't figure out what the locket did. Not that it would have mattered if he'd always intended on killing her.

"The time of the dragons is done," Glen said with a snarl that he probably thought hid his fear.

"If you come near my people or those I protect again, I'll kill you and hang your body from the top of a Midtown building as a warning to all."

Myra's eyes widened at the threat. She'd never heard Christopher be quite so blunt about killing. She knew he had crisped at least one wizard and some shifters once. The ones who'd kidnapped him and then nearly killed her. She knew killing was within his skill set, so to speak. But the level of violence in his tone made her shiver.

His arms tightened around her, like he was trying to warm her up. Or maybe keep her from running? Not that she'd run from him. She really didn't want to be anywhere else just then but in his arms.

"This isn't over," Glen said. "You can kill me, but more will rise."

"This attempt at starting a war between shifters will not happen. It was a bad plan to begin with. Why do you think there's no shifter security bearing down on you?"

Ah. She'd wondered about that. Obviously, the king had let them know the theft was happening and to let it go. Which meant the shifters were talking, and if the people you were trying to convince to start a war with each other were actually communicating, it was harder to trick them into going to war over a misunderstanding. Bad news for Glen.

Glen hunted the surroundings again, his eyes wide with panic. She didn't have Christopher's sense of smell, but she'd bet he could smell the panic sweat rolling off Glen just then.

"The wizards working with shifters will destroy us all," Glen said. "They need to understand. They need to know."

"Know what?" she asked, curiosity getting the better of her. Again.

"That the shifters will betray us all!" Glen snarled.

And to Myra's utter surprise, he pulled his gun and fired it, so fast, all she could do was blink.

The blink, the hesitation should have cost her. She wasn't usually surprised by people, but Glen had looked so panicked, and he was facing a fucking dragon shifter, that she just assumed he'd run. Especially from Christopher. Especially after attempting to betray the dragon king—even if the king suspected betrayal all along.

She'd made a mistake, assumed Glen would try to get away. And if he attacked, she'd assumed he'd attack with magic. He was a fucking wizard after all.

She had not been expecting the gun. Again.

That mistake, that oversight, should have gotten her shot. Maybe even killed.

Thankfully Christopher didn't suffer from the same oversight.

Or if he did, his hesitation lasted a fraction of the second hers lasted.

He moved so suddenly, and so fast, Myra's stomach bottomed out. A faint nausea gripped her before it was replaced by the thrilling jolt of adrenaline. The same adrenaline she'd gotten freefalling off the side of a building.

Her surroundings blurred. And then they were standing in front of Glen.

Christopher had stepped so close to the wizard, he was inside the man's outstretched arm, the one with the gun. And he didn't give Glen time to adjust to the fact that someone was suddenly standing so close.

Christopher released Myra's legs, and she swung them around to wrap around his waist as he used his now free hand to grip Glen around the neck and lift him off the ground. Christopher's hand was very large compared to Glen's throat. And Christopher was very tall compared to Glen. With his arm stretched straight out in front of him, he held Glen a foot off the ground.

Myra heard the gun clatter to the sidewalk behind them. She

patted Christopher's shoulder and dropped her legs. He let her slip down, keeping his arm around her back until she was balanced, then released her.

He never loosened his grip on Glen, who was kicking and wheezing and clawing at Christopher's fingers.

She ducked behind Christopher's wings to retrieve the gun. Once she had the safety on, she stuck it into one of the many pockets in her vest. Then she faced the wizard.

"I'll take that locket now," she said. "I'm not sure what you intended, but you having it is probably bad. And I was paid to steal it, so I think I'll just finish that job."

Glen was too busy trying to breathe to stop her when she took the locket from his pants' pocket. She was a decent pick-pocket, but it wasn't her best skill, so she appreciated that she didn't have to bother.

When she stepped back next to Christopher, pressing her back to his free arm, he finally set Glen onto his feet, though he didn't take his grip from Glen's throat.

He leaned down and put his face in the wizard's face. "I do not appreciate that you tried to shoot me or my companion. And the only reason you aren't dead is because I do not want to deal with the paperwork tonight. But know this. If you come anywhere near my people, or those I'm close with again, if you attempt to start this nonsensical war, I will find you. I will not be this lenient."

Glen's eyes were starting to roll back into his head. Even on his feet, Christopher's grip left no room for breathing.

"Nod to tell me you understand," Christopher said, very quietly. There was that hiss in his voice again. And the heat pumping off his body was like a furnace at Myra's back.

Glen nodded, proving he wasn't as stupid as Myra thought he might be.

Christopher released him so abruptly he stumbled backward. By the time Glen straightened, she was in Christopher's arms again and they'd leapt into the sky, strong dragon wings beating the air to bring them above the buildings.

She looked down at the shrinking form of the wizard, watched him dropped to his knees on the sidewalk as he presumably sucked in desperately needed oxygen.

"Is he going to…live?" she asked.

"This time," Christopher said, his voice still very deep and that growling hiss quality still lurking beneath the human words. "He tried to shoot you. Twice. I should have killed him."

She patted his cheek. "If he acts up again, you can always kill him then." She considered the side of his face as he banked over the skyscrapers and turned toward the Hudson. "Why didn't you? Out of curiosity."

He flicked her a look, then focused ahead. "I didn't want you to watch me kill someone."

Ah. That was interesting. "You killed before while I was around." But she was unconscious when he had.

"You didn't have to watch."

She nodded, letting this insight into him settle as they flew over the Manhattan skyline.

CHAPTER NINE

Christopher swooped through the tunnel of skyscrapers, moving across the island of Manhattan in the time it would take a bus to move a block in traffic. Faster, really. Myra was only a little surprised that he took her to his apartment—the one she knew about. The one she'd fallen asleep at when they were watching a movie on his patio, snuggled up in comfortable lounge chairs, her belly full of popcorn after a very successful heist.

For some reason, she thought he'd take her to a random rooftop, which is where they'd normally go after a completed heist, or if they needed to talk. But now that she'd been here at his apartment, maybe this was safer.

She didn't mind. She was just happy to see him again.

He set down on the balcony, jogging a little as he came in for a landing, stopping slowly. Greenery filled planters lined the brick wall circling the patio, but most of the space was open. Plenty of room for a partially shifted dragon, maybe even room for his full dragon, though she hadn't seen him in that form yet. There was a light on inside his apartment, so she could just see the marble floored living room beyond the double glass doors leading inside. But the balcony was otherwise dark under the night sky. Giving a sense of seclusion and privacy even though they were surrounded by other buildings.

As the cold night air brushed against her cheeks and neck, she became very aware of Christopher's warmth again. Not just warm. He was hot. Not sweating. His skin was just very…hot. A kind of delicious heat that made her want to groan.

He held her gaze without releasing her and putting her on her feet. She stared back, wondering what he was thinking.

"You're hotter than normal tonight." She touched his shoulders when he raised his eyebrows, a look that made her chuckle. "Your skin, I mean. Is that the anger?"

"Right now? No. That's not why I'm hot."

He released her legs so she slid to her feet, but he held her close, which meant she slid along his body, the glide downward full of friction and intent and possibilities.

"Innuendo?" she asked, feeling a little breathless herself by the time her toes touched the ground. "Or fear."

"Now? Innuendo."

She grinned. "Good." Then she stretched up and met him as he bent his head down to her.

The brush of his lips was gentle at first, gentler than she'd expected, but the minute she sighed, the minute she sank fully against him, tightening her arms around his neck, the kiss went from gentle to hard and urgent. Delicious.

He cupped the back of her head with his big hand, she angled her mouth over his to taste him better. Swiped her tongue against his, tasted that unique flavor she couldn't quite place, but that *tasted* the way Christopher smelled to her. Not just the musk and dragon now either. But that scent of sugar cookies that she sometimes got from him. A rich, vanilla flavor, so delicious she wanted to gobble him up.

Her pulse pounded as her own skin warmed and heat pooled in her belly and her nerves demanded she rub against him. His groan filled her with a sense of satisfaction, but also left her wanting more.

Yet…

She buried her fingers in his hair, trying desperately to stave off that "yet" and just savor his kiss, his hands on her, his taste, his scent wrapping around her as surely as his heat. She didn't want to think anymore. She'd been thinking about this for weeks now. Ever since meeting him.

And if he was anyone else, she'd throw all caution to the wind and drag him inside to the nearest soft surface where she could strip off the only clothing he currently wore—a pair of dress slacks—and celebrate the fact that she hadn't died tonight with mutual orgasms.

But he wasn't just anyone.

His father had set her up tonight. In a way that could have gotten her killed.

That wasn't something she could ignore. If they kept kissing, if she did take him inside, it took things that one last step toward… something serious. Something his father disapproved of. She couldn't fool herself into thinking sex with Christopher would be a casual fling. Not for her anyway. She was in deep already. Big time crush. Maybe more.

She was already destined to get hurt here. She needed to deal with the fact that his father had set her up to be killed before she let things go any farther.

She still took longer than she should have to ease away from him, to break the kiss, to put some of that cold night air between their very warm bodies.

He held her gaze, looking intent, his jaw tight. He was breathing hard, color highlighted his sharp cheekbones, and his erection had pressed against her belly before she'd stepped back. He still had one hand cradling her head, his fingers tangled in her hair, loosening her bun, but he didn't pull her close again. Just stared down at her, watching her with those sharp blue eyes.

She let him see as much of her, of what she was feeling, as she was able, though years of practice hiding herself from others made that level of vulnerability difficult. Almost impossible.

Finally, he dropped his hold completely and straightened to his full height. Which was significant. She had to crane her neck to look up at him.

"We need to talk," she said.

He nodded. Gestured to the cushion covered lounge chairs. They weren't facing the outer wall of his apartment now, like they'd been for the movie date night, but instead were turned so when they sat, she could see the sky overhead and the building across the street. There weren't many lights, but a few started to pop on as they watched. It must be five in the morning. Getting close to the time people with ordinary jobs that kept ordinary hours would start to wake up.

"Your father tried to get me killed tonight," she said, jumping directly to the big problem.

"I'm not sure he intended for you to die," Christopher said quietly. "More likely this was a test."

"A test?" She scowled at him. "What kind of test?"

"A test to see if you could survive. If you were…worthy."

"Worthing? Of what?"

"His notice." Christopher held her gaze. "Me."

"Isn't that your business? Deciding if I'm worth your time. And my business deciding if *you* are worth *my* time?"

"It is. My father is…bad with boundaries."

She snorted. "He told me, at the meeting when he introduced me to Glen, that he had plans for you and I wasn't part of that. What was he talking about?"

"I have no idea." Christopher's frown and blank confusion looked sincere enough. "But I'll ask him when I take tonight's situation up with him."

"What will you say? About tonight."

"That if he tries to pull something like this again, with you, I will not let it go passively. Even if he's my father and my king."

"Will that get you killed?"

"No."

He sounded certain. She was…less certain. "You don't have to start a full family war over this. Just let him know I'm not working for him again. Ever. This was the last job. I don't like being made a pawn and he's done that a couple of times now. There's not enough money in his hoard for me to tolerate that."

"I'll tell him."

"Glen wants a war between the various shifters. Why did your father humor him? Why did he even go to your father? Why didn't Glen tell me what the locket did sooner so I could get us out of the vault?"

The way Christopher had talked to Glen, she knew he'd figured out most of the machinations in the background. Now that she was safely away from guns and possibly being arrested for breaking-and-entering, she really did want to know what tonight had been all about. She'd gotten a little of it. But the whys still eluded her.

"Why he didn't tell you what the locket did, I don't know," Christopher said. "Maybe because he didn't understand your skill set and that it would be to his advantage in getting out of the vault."

She smiled a little at that. She didn't mind being underestimated. Gave her the element of surprise.

"As for the war, my sources tell me Glen wants it because he hates shifters, because he thinks wizards are being usurped by them, and because he wants to clear the way for wizards to…rule. To rise to prominence."

"What does a locket that blocks magic have to do with that?"

"He could influence the other wizards, manipulate them if he possessed something that prevented them from using their magic."

"How was all this supposed to start a war between shifters?"

"Your relationship to me, to my father, is… More people know about it now. That you've worked for him a few times. That I'm… That I like you more than a casual acquaintance."

She grinned suddenly. "Really stumbling over how to define this thing between us, aren't you?"

"You able to do any better?"

"Nope." That earned her one of his quick grins, the humor softening some of the hard lines of his angular face. "Keep going." She waved a hand. "Word's getting around that I can be hired by the dragon king. That's probably bad for me. What does that have to do with Glen?"

"Why bad for you?"

"Too many people aware of me. Of who I am. What I do. Hard to be a successful thief when people…see you." He scowled again, but she nudged him. "What does all this have to do with the wizard?"

"From what I could learn, his plan was to have you caught breaking into the vault, trying to escape. The shifters would assume my father arranged the theft—I'm not sure how Glen intended for them to make that assumption—and that would start tension and arguing between the shifters involved. There have been…rumors spreading. Rumors attempting to pit the various shifter groups against each other. The fact that shifters were involved in my kidnapping, and were looking to gain that relic from my father's hoard to turn themselves into monsters only added to those tensions."

He ran a hand through his hair, already messy and windblown, making the strands stand out in a wild disarray she found extremely sexy.

"I assume Glen is part of those rumors," he continued. "He went to my father because he needed a link between my father and the theft. He wanted the locket. The plan was to kill two birds, so to speak. Get the locket he could use to manipulate his fellow wizards, leave you and the dragon king on the hook for the theft. I'm not sure if Glen intended on killing you from the start."

"He did. He said I needed to die for his plan to work. So, yeah, that was part of it."

Christopher's eyes flared, a dangerous anger tightening his jaw. Almost without thought, she reached out and ran her fingers over his arm, down to his hand, tangling her fingers with his. His expression eased, a little, but a muscle in his cheek still jumped.

"At any rate, he tried to convince my father he wanted the locket because it was dangerous to him in shifter hands. My source in the mansion said Glen was not a great liar, though. He stank of his deceptions. So there was never a chance my father didn't know what was happening."

"For a man who hates shifters and wants to get them fighting, he probably should have done better research on how to keep his nefarious plans secret."

"Probably." Christopher's fingers tightened on hers. "My father went along with it out of perverse curiosity, and to get the locket. But also to see what Glen would do."

"And didn't particularly care if that put me in harms way," she said, nodding. "And he kept it from you because if you knew, you'd have either gone with me or tried to stop the charade before it got started."

"Tried?"

"Well, ultimately, the decisions about which jobs I take or don't take are up to me. Even when I know they're dodgy and the people hiring me are lying to me."

"You knew?"

"I knew the whole thing was a con of some kind. Like your father, I went along with it to find out what was going on."

"You could have been killed." His fingers tightened so hard on hers, she winced. He relaxed his grip instantly, tried to pull his hand from hers.

Her turn to flex her fingers, tightening her hold on him briefly, so he'd know he didn't have to let go if he didn't want to. She waited him out, waited to see if he'd slip his hand from hers or continue to hold her hand.

When he relaxed and left his fingers gently wrapped around hers, she let out a breath. Her shoulders relaxed.

The rush of uncertainty and fear that brief exchange had caused left her shaken, though. She was really in a lot of trouble with this man. They didn't even have to fuck for her to be fucked here.

She tried to refocus on the other issues, because she wasn't sure how to confront that moment of panic she'd felt waiting to see if he'd let her go.

"I wasn't," she said, clearing her throat because her voice sounded gruff and shaky. "Killed that is. I knew the risks. I knew one or the other of them was trying to play me. I've been doing this for a long time, Christopher."

"You fell off a building. He tried to shoot you. Twice."

"That second time was a bit shocking, I won't lie. I expected him to run. Or try to anyway. But I was ready for the first attempt. I went over the side of that building on purpose."

He let out a low breath. "I saw the grappling hook you tucked away after I caught you."

"It was more fun getting caught."

"You're an adrenaline junkie."

"You're surprised?"

He shook his head.

"Besides." She rolled her lips into her mouth, studied the building across the street. "I like when you catch me. I like flying with you."

"I like flying with you too."

They sat in silence for a few minutes, both of them staring at the building across the street as the lights came on and the sky overhead turned that deep purple that was almost darker than night before the sun finally peeked over the horizon.

She lifted his hand and brought it to her mouth, giving him a brief kiss without looking at him. Then said, "We have to deal with your father. Before…before this thing between us goes any farther. If it goes any farther. You need to talk to him about…whatever the hell plans these are he has for you. And make sure… Just. Make sure you're free. For this."

"This hard to define thing between us that leaves us both stumbling over our words?"

She laughed and met his gaze. "Exactly." Her smile faded when she said, "I don't want whatever this is to end. But I can't allow it to go on longer if, in the end, it's something you can't…stick with."

She'd almost said commit to, but the whole concept of commitment was foreign to her and she wasn't even sure if that's what she was looking for from him. Especially so soon, so quickly. She just knew she wanted Christopher in her life without worrying that his fate or destiny meant she'd have to give him up whether she liked it or not. Whether they made the decisions to stop seeing each other or not.

"As far as I'm concerned, whatever my father's plans are, they're his idea, not mine. I have no intention of going along with them."

"Okay. That's fair. But you need to make sure he knows that. Because if he doesn't, he might try to set me up to be killed again."

"I won't allow that."

She believed he'd try. He meant what he was saying. But he wasn't omnipotent. If his father really wanted her dead, it was only a matter of time before the king succeeded. Better to just ensure he wasn't trying to kill her.

"I'll talk to him," Christopher said. "I'll make sure the situation is clear."

"As clear as it is to us?" she asked, with a teasing lilt to her voice, trying to take some of the edge off the conversation.

He snorted. His gaze traveled over her face, searching for something in her expression. Then he said, "I'll take you wherever you want to go. But… If you're not too tired, would you like to watch the sunrise with me?"

"Another date?"

"We could call it that."

She nodded and settled back into the lounger, wrapping her arms around his one big arm, cradling it against her because she didn't want to let him go. "A date, it is. I like watching the sunrise."

She especially liked watching the sunrise with him.

The Dragon Thief Series

The
Femme
Fatale
Job

Bestselling author of the Cary Redmond Series

Kat Simons

THE FEMME FATALE JOB
BOOK FIVE

No one saw her coming...

After the last job for the dragon king, Myra vows never again. No more. But for Christopher, and for whatever these feelings developing between them might be... She can't say no. Especially if the job involves a damsel in distress. Myra's dragon shifter prince just can't resist rescuing people in trouble. And when he needs a thief to do that, Myra happily jumps in. The job might be skirting the line between working for the dragon king and not working for the dragon king, but Myra willingly walks that line for Christopher.

What starts out as a simple case of helping one woman rescue her career, though, quickly turns into something Myra never expected, something no one expected. A foe so deadly, so terrifying, that if they get this wrong, the entire Island of Manhattan could burn.

Pitting a magical thief and her dragon shifter prince against one of the most terrifying creatures on the planet... How can they possibly survive?

By stealing something of course.

Before everything goes up in flames.

CHAPTER ONE

Myra strolled under the canopy of trees, the bright winter sun filtering down through evergreen branches along the paved path through the middle of Central Park. The Bethesda Fountain was ahead of her, Strawberry Fields behind her, and most of the tourists clumped up in those places so that her stroll was pleasantly people free. The lake to her left peeked out around raised black rocks and greenery, but she didn't take the diverted path to watch the paddle boats. Though it was the middle of winter, the air crisp and frosty at the moment, the lake hadn't frozen, and there were just enough tourists willing to take out a paddle boat even in the cold to keep the service open a little longer.

The Boathouse restaurant wasn't far away, but she wasn't heading there either. She was ambling. Enjoying the day. No where specific to be.

Waiting for him to find her.

It didn't take him long. He never took very long finding her. In fact, he had an uncanny ability to find her even when she hadn't given him a place to look.

He fell into step beside her, a very tall presence, standing easily a head or more over everyone else around them. He had a good foot and a half on her, which might have been awkward, but she had a real soft spot for tall men.

She had an even softer spot for Christopher.

She glanced at him from the corner of her eye. He was wearing a shirt. A button up business shirt in a soft pink color under a long tan coat. And instead of the dress slacks he normally wore, he was wearing jeans. It was a strange sort of combination, nothing she'd seen him in before. She'd mostly seen him in his flight outfit—pants, no shoes, no shirt so he could shift enough to release his wings. The fact that he was wearing a coat, which she didn't think he needed, and shoes, which he didn't like to wear, made it obvious he was attempting to appear human. Or at the very least, blend in with the humans so he didn't draw too much attention.

Given that he was nearly seven foot tall, it was impossible for him not to draw attention. But it was always possible the tourists assumed he was a basketball player. This was New York after all. Lots of people could be found walking the paths through the Park.

She bumped his arm with her shoulder, using the excuse of getting that close to him to breathe in his uniquely Christopher scent, that mix of dragon shifter—heat and musk and a very faint hint of brimstone—and some sort of soap that she associated purely with him. No sugar cookie scent at that moment, but she liked when he smelled like this soap of his, too.

"You look good in business casual wear."

"Thank you," he said, his voice deep and rumbling. He tilted his head slightly toward her. "I'm not sure the camouflage is working as well as I'd like."

"It would help if you weren't as tall as some of the trees."

"I can't be sorry for that," he said. "Because you like tall men."

She huffed, tried to swallow her pleased laugh. "I do."

She let her gaze move over the path, skim the scattering of people walking around them. Christopher was drawing stares, but most people looked away quickly. She couldn't tell if they recognized him or not. There weren't any pictures of the royal family allowed in magazines and newspapers. But he did occasionally show up at events with his father, and sometimes in gossip columns. Or at least, he had shown up in the gossip columns at one stage, by name, but he hadn't been in them recently.

Even if people didn't recognize him as the dragon king's son, though, they might still recognize him as a dragon shifter. A lot of the dragon shifters were hard to miss, even in human form.

Not that she'd known that much about them before meeting Christopher. She'd gone out of her way to avoid all things dragon. She mostly stuck to robbing humans, and rich humans at that. Like her soft spot for tall men, she also had a soft spot for stealing from people who already had more than they could keep track of and often didn't even notice when some of their stuff went missing. There was something very satisfying about taking a valuable object from someone like that. And then making herself a small fortune in the process.

Keeping under the radar so she could do her job, though, meant staying under the radar of the movers and shakers in the city. The powerful people.

The dragon king.

She'd blown that up by taking an ill-considered bet and breaking into the king's hoard. A challenge she hadn't been able to resist. The hoard was supposed to be impossible to break into. And if she hadn't been caught standing in the middle of all that wealth, perusing all the fine objects and valuables, looking for something tiny and relatively worthless to take to prove she'd been in the hoard, she wouldn't have ever gotten tangled up with dragon shifters. She would have happily continued to avoid them and everything about them.

But then the king had sent her to rescue his "youngling." That youngling turned out to be a fully grown man. Who was distractingly tall. And strangely attractive in a way that couldn't be described as handsome.

And her life hadn't been the same since.

She regretted getting caught breaking into the king's hoard. She didn't like at all having the dragon king think she worked for him now, or that she was somehow beholden to him. She hated that the dragon king thought of her as one of *his* people.

She did *not* hate that she'd met Christopher.

Unfortunately, his father was a problem. One they needed to deal with before the undefined and very new thing between them went any farther than the few kisses they'd shared and the two technical dates they'd been on. One watching a movie on a screen he'd set up on the balcony of one of his apartments. The second, just a few nights ago, when they'd sat on that same balcony watching the sun rise.

She wrapped her black wool coat around her a little tighter, not because she was cold but because she needed something to do with her hands so she wouldn't automatically reach for his.

"Let's go disappear into the Ramble," she said. "Easier to talk without you drawing all this attention."

He nodded, his own hands stuffed into his pockets as they strolled at a measured pace to a section of forest that spread across the middle the Park. Winding dirt paths twisted through thick, dense woodlands, though the oak and maple limbs were bare now, giving the area a lovely stark effect. Dark rocky outcroppings rose up around corners in the bending paths, and sun flittered down to the fern and vine underbrush.

They followed the paths, encountering a handful of birders as they moved deeper into the woods. The feeling of being in a city disappeared. Even the smell was all nature, dirt and trees, dried leaves and pine. Myra could almost believe they were walking through the woods in Upstate New York, far away from everything they had to deal with.

When she was certain they were alone, with no random people around the next bend, she broached the reason for this meeting. "What did your father say?"

Christopher's mouth tightened. "Not as much as I wanted. He refused to acknowledge what he told you about having plans for me. He won't admit to any such thing. He's a stubborn old bastard." This last said under his breath, with a twist of annoyance to his mouth.

"Did he tell you I lied about what he'd said?" She was more curious than offended. The king was used to manipulations and lies. She wouldn't put it past him. Especially since he'd made it clear he disapproved of her relationship with Christopher, even as he kept attempting to make her one of his "humans," one of the humans known to work for him.

"He didn't, actually. He claimed you misremembered."

"Huh. I would have expected him to just say I lied."

"I found the hedge interesting, too. He likes you."

"No, he doesn't. He set me up to be killed." The last job the king had hired her for had put her in the way of a wizard who'd tried to shoot her. Twice. That wasn't usually something a person who liked you did.

"*Like* is maybe a strong word. Admire. He admires you. And I was right. That job was a test. A test he claims he thought you'd pass."

"If I survived, I'm worthy, right?" She snorted, a sardonic sound of her own.

She didn't want the king's admiration or to be worthy in his attention. She didn't give two fucks about whether he found her worthy or not. She just wanted him to leave her alone now.

"That fits with his way of thinking," Christopher said on a sigh.

"And when you told him I'm not working for him again?"

Christopher let out a hissing sort of growl. A sound she associated with dragon shifters. A sound no human made. "He smiled," Christopher said. "He claimed you'd change your mind."

"Wow. He's never been so wrong about anything before. I do not intend on changing my mind."

"I know." Christopher's shoulders hunched as he scowled down at the dirt path, his hands still firmly in his coat pockets. "He mentioned something…"

"Another job?" She narrowed her eyes at him.

"Not…technically. But, it's a situation that…" He trailed off and looked out at the trees, turning his face away from her.

But not before she saw the color rise in his cheeks, the red blush coloring his high, sharp cheekbones.

He was blushing. That could only mean one thing.

"There's a damsel in distress, isn't there?"

She pressed her lips together so she wouldn't grin. He was sensitive about this particular soft spot of his. Her attempt not to smile failed miserably, though, so she just gave in. She loved that he was a dragon with a soft spot for damsels in distress. In fact, it was one of the things about him she liked the most.

But the character trait got him razzed by the other dragons. The trait had also been exploited by the people who'd kidnapped him.

"There might be," he mumbled.

"You know he's manipulating you, right? To get you to do what he wants you to."

"Yes." Still a mumble.

"But you'd like my help saving this damsel anyway because this is a damsel in distress situation?"

"Yes." He admitted with a sigh.

She bumped his arm again. "For you, I'll help. But not for the king. For you."

Without looking at her, he took one hand out of his pocket and stretched it out to her. She only hesitated a beat before taking hold of his hand and twinning her fingers with his. His hand was so much bigger than hers, he completely engulfed her. But he was also exceptionally gentle with that size and strength. She never worried about him hurting her.

He squeezed gently and she felt his muscles relaxing as they walked.

"My father *claims* he will no longer attempt to hire you," Christopher said. "He *says* he understands you prefer your independence and do not want to accept the protection of the dragons."

"Protection?" She snorted. The king had a funny idea of the word "protection" if he thought sending her on a job to get killed qualified.

"He hasn't given up on trying to pull you into his permanent employ," Christopher said. "He'll likely keep trying. But for now, he's pretending to let you go your own way."

"I see." She did. It was a game for the king. But…

Where did that leave her and Christopher?

Chapter Two

T hey reached a rocky outcropping just off a path, the black collection of stone forming natural seat shapes as it rose above the dried leaves and dirt of the thickly wooded Ramble. Without a word, they both settled on the rocks, close enough Myra could feel Christopher's body heat along one side of her body, a warm contrast to the cold stone under her. In the distance, she could hear the bubbling sounds of the manmade stream running through the Ramble and quiet bird twittering overhead. Good day for the birders.

She turned to face Christopher, pulling one leg up onto the rock and wrapping her arms around her knee. "Tell me about this damsel and her current distress."

Christopher pulled in a deep breath. She ignored the way that made his shoulders and chest expand to stretch the fabric of his tan coat tight. For a moment she worried he'd tear through the thick wool.

"Her name is Issa and she works for a couple of plastic surgeons on the Upper East Side. Receptionist, not a nurse, but she's currently in school to get a degree in medical billing so she can move jobs."

Myra rested her chin on her raised knee, watching Christopher's expression closely as he spoke. Tension around his jaw, faint lines around his narrowed eyes. Yeah, definitely a distressed Issa had him unhappy.

"Is she human?" She could be a shifter. She could be a wizard. She could be a human with other magical skills that didn't fall into wizardcraft, like Myra's own touch of thief's magic. Or Issa could be one of the millions of ordinary humans just trying to get through the day.

What she wasn't likely to be was a dragon shifter.

Because Myra had known so little about dragon shifters before meeting Christopher, she hadn't realized there were so few female dragons in the world, that they were so fundamentally scary and violent, that they lived a hell of a lot longer than the males, and that they were, most of them, currently sound asleep. Like the few real dragons that existed in the world. Something to do with living for millennia encouraged centuries-long naps, apparently.

Among the ordinary—if that word even applied—dragon shifters walking around not sleeping, there were apparently a number of nonbinary individuals, and a lot of males. But at the moment, few to no females.

In rare quiet moments, Myra did sometimes wonder what a female dragon shifter would be like in real life. But then she remembered the dragon king, and how much of a pain in the ass he was, and thought better of her curiosity. A curiosity which as often as not got her into trouble. In this, though, she considered the common phrase "leave sleeping dragons lie" a good way to stay alive.

"Issa is human," Christopher said. "But she was involved romantically with a dragon shifter a few years ago. The relationship didn't take. They separated. But they'd had a child together. And it seems like her son is a dragon shifter."

More fascinating facts she hadn't known before meeting him. That there were so many males running around the place because dragon shifters could produce offspring with humans. In fact, having a dragon shifter mother was apparently very very rare for most of the living dragon shifters. They almost all had one human parent. The dragon king himself had had a human mother. The king's age was a mystery he encouraged, but Myra knew he was old enough that his human mother had passed a long time ago. As far as she knew, his father had passed away also. But since that involved Christopher's family, she hadn't actually asked him about his grandparents yet. Or his own mother.

There were certain topics they just…seemed to avoid without making a conscious effort. Details about families had been one of those topics.

"Because he's a dragon," Christopher said, "he's entitled to an annuity from the king. Until he's old enough to start collecting his own hoard. He'll receive a dragon mentor to help him with all things shifter when he's old enough, too. Right now, he's only five and won't be ready to start shifting and flying for another five to ten years, depending on the youngling."

Myra listened in rapt fascination. Some of this she hadn't known. Like the fact that the king financially supported young shifters until they were old enough to strike out on their own. The insights into the more private aspects of the dragons were captivating. She didn't want to interrupt Christopher, even to ask a question, though she had many.

Primarily, what was Issa's problem that she was what Christopher considered a damsel in distress?

"The annuity means Issa can raise him comfortably while still affording school for her career change. Turns out the surgeons she works for are not great people. There are two partners, both of them arrogant, but one in particular is…difficult. Edgy, angry, abusive. She sometimes sexually harasses Issa and the other administrative staff, though she apparently doesn't do the same with the nurses. And her demands are beyond what can be expected of human beings to accomplish in any given time period."

"Sounds like a fun boss," Myra said, with a snort.

Christopher's tense mouth twitched. "There's a reason Issa is in college and planning a career move."

"Can't blame her. The other partner bad, too?"

"More indifferent to the bullying and harassment of his business partner. He sees his patients, makes a fortune, and leaves. Not concerning himself with the details of the business or the happiness of his employees."

"Lovely."

This time Christopher let out a full snort-laugh at her sarcastic assessment. "At any rate, Issa is often responsible for contacting insurance companies and working out copays for patients. They have an outside company that issues the actual bills, but she is involved in the practice's billing and insurance procedures." He let his gaze travel over the surrounding trees, most of them maple and oak so the branches were bare fingers of wood stretching toward the blue sky.

A small frown bunched his forehead and he held a finger to his mouth.

She glanced around, keeping quiet, looking for danger. A few minutes later, a small group passed, three adults and two kids. The kids were charging ahead of the adults, holding miniature binoculars, pointing noisily up into the trees. The adults, with cameras and their own binoculars hanging on straps around their necks, followed more slowly, smiling at the children and chatting quietly.

They didn't acknowledge Christopher and Myra, sitting a few feet away on the rocks, but one of the adults did glance their way briefly.

Once they'd passed, and Myra could no longer hear the kids, she said quietly, "You heard them coming?" His shifter hearing was excellent.

"It isn't like anyone will know or understand what we're talking about," he said. "But I prefer to keep these details between us."

"Fair. I'm assuming the issue has to do with the surgery's billing practices."

Christopher's grin was quick and so sudden, Myra's heart started to thump harder. He had a very sexy smile. Something about the way his mouth curved…

She blinked when she realized her mind was wandering toward thoughts best left for when they weren't in public.

"You would be right in that assumption. Turns out the practice is…manipulating the bills so that the insurance companies are paying out for things that aren't being done, and patients are paying copays where they don't need to. All pretty subtle. If Issa hadn't been learning all about medical billing, she wouldn't have noticed the discrepancies."

"Has she gone to anyone? Talked to anyone?"

"She contacted the Department of Financial Services and the Health Department last week. Both have hotlines for suspected medical billing fraud and are supposedly confidential. The next day she came in to work, all the dodgy bills had been removed, patient records had been changed, and there was no sign of the evidence of fraud there'd been just two days before."

"Someone tipped off the partners and they cleaned up their books."

Christopher nodded. "Or at least, they hid the actual paper trail and subbed in false documents to make it look like things were on the up and up if their records were audited. Issa has no idea how they did that in just two days, but she suspects the evidence is still there. They haven't had enough time to fully cover up their fraud."

"This all sounds like something the various government agencies and their forensic auditors are supposed to deal with," she said hesitantly. "And Issa's filed reports were confidential, right? So no one in the office knows she was the whistleblower."

"Seems the same insider person who tipped the practice off to the fraud reports so they could clean up the paper trail also found out and revealed Issa's identity. The more difficult of the partners has fired Issa. And intends on making sure she can't get a job anywhere in the medical field in this city again."

"That sucks. Big time. All around. Issa should get a lawyer and sue." She paused. "But what does this have to do with you and me?" she finally asked. "What do you think we could do to help?"

"Issa knows the practice is still misbilling people and skimming money, and she strongly suspects some evidence of this is still inside the office because there really hasn't been time for the partners to erase everything. They got rid of the person they thought could tell what was and was not fraud, so now they'd have less reason to worry about hiding the evidence."

"Won't someone from the state be investigating them?"

"The fraud reports were closed, without investigation, marked as without sufficient evidence to pursue, even though they never really investigated Issa's claims."

"So whoever is helping inside the state and health departments is also part of the cover up?"

People went to an awful lot of trouble to make a few extra dollars. And her form of thievery was considered the "bad" kind. At least she was an honest thief who only stole from people who could afford to lose what she took.

"Seems likely," Christopher said.

"Still waiting to hear how you think we can help."

"I want to break in to the practice and get the evidence Issa needs. Then hand it over personally and officially to an investigator, as a representative of the king. So they can't afford to cover it up without causing a…diplomatic situation. Issa having a dragon son gives her status in our community, and puts her under the protection of the dragons. But I need the actual evidence or I'm just hollowly threatening public servants."

"A bad look."

He nodded.

"So. A little light breaking and entering. And you need a thief for that."

"It would help," he said with a shrug. "If you'd rather not, if this is too close to feeling like you're working for the king, I'll understand."

It might well be too close to working for the king. The king had obviously told Christopher about this knowing he'd want to help a single mother in distress. And that he'd tell Myra about the situation. Or maybe this was another test. To see if Christopher would tell her things not specifically meant for her. Maybe the king wanted to see what Myra would do for Christopher.

Unfortunately, what she'd do for Christopher went a lot farther than what she intended on doing for the king. No more working for the king. But helping Christopher when what he needed aligned with her particular skill set…

"Yeah, I'm going to help," she said with a little head shake. "Maybe I have a latent damsel in distress issue, too."

His mouth quirked up at one corner, the small smile making her giddy. "Either damsels in distress or dragons in distress. I'm still deciding."

"If the dragon is you… That makes a difference."

Chapter Three

Before breaking into the plastic surgeons' practice, Myra wanted a meeting with Issa. If she had to look for evidence of medical billing fraud, she needed to know what she was looking for. And she wanted to take the measure of the woman. Someone who'd actually had a relationship with a dragon shifter, had a child with a dragon shifter. And now, even though she was no longer with that shifter, still kept ties with the dragons because of her son.

Myra didn't allow herself consciously to consider *why* she was interested in Issa's personal life and situation with the dragons. But she was…curious.

They met at a café on the Upper West Side, putting the entirety of Central Park between Issa and her former place of employment. And still she seemed antsy and jumpy, sitting at a table at the halfway point of the narrow coffee shop. Since this was one of the funky, independent businesses, and not a chain coffee store, the wooden tables and floors were delightfully scuffed, the walls covered in opera posters, displaying shows put on at the Met, and the counter and coffee was handled by two employees, one with extensive piercings and tattoos, the other with glasses and a tight, high bun.

Myra strongly suspected the two women were also in a romantic relationship based on the way they smiled and danced around each other. But her tendency to people-watch when in a coffee shop had to be curtailed. She did keep half an eye on the other three people in the place. A woman working on her laptop, and two men with their heads bent together as they talked quietly. Outside of the initial startled glances at Christopher—it was hard not to notice when a man nearly seven feet tall walked into a room—no one paid them any particular attention. Even the initial startlement was shrugged off quickly and everyone returned to what they were doing with no more attention paid to him.

Myra loved New York and New Yorkers.

"They are definitely still embezzling," Issa said, as she toyed with her coffee cup, circling it between her hands without sipping on it. Plain black coffee in a bowl-shaped ceramic mug with a pithy saying on the side. She'd refused a pastry.

Myra had not refused a pastry—fruit and cream filled tart that was delicately flaky and not too sweet—and her coffee was a cappuccino with a lot of yummy foam on top.

"Before I was let go," Issa said, "I saw at least one more bill for a current client that wasn't right. But I wasn't given time to look at it closely before Dr. Butler fired me. But if that bill hadn't been disposed of like the others I'd actually reported on, I'm sure there are more in the office still. Dr. Butler thinks she's smarter than she is."

This last was said with a snarl as Issa glanced down into her cooling coffee.

Issa Abarca was a tall woman, thick and curvy, with black hair she currently had twisted into a series of braids held up in a bun. Under soft, subtle makeup, there was a scattering of freckles across her pale tan nose. The makeup didn't hide the circles under her dark eyes, or the worry lines bracketing her mouth. Myra guessed her to be somewhere in her mid-thirties.

Not for the first time since they'd sat down, Issa pressed a finger to her left eye, rubbing gently. Myra couldn't tell if it was a nervous tic or if Issa had something in her eye.

When Issa looked up and noticed Myra watching her, she said, "I've got something in my contact lens. Can't seem to get it out." She shrugged. "I'll rinse it later."

"How far back does the embezzlement go?" Christopher asked, quietly. He'd slouched a little in his seat, the wood creaking under his weight, but Issa didn't seem to be bothered by his height. She hadn't given him that double take that people often did.

The reaction made Myra wonder if it was just that Issa was used to dragon shifters or if she and Christopher had met before. Christopher hadn't mentioned it if they had.

"I'm not sure," Issa said. "A few years. Maybe more. But I only noticed the discrepancies in the last eight months of billing, so maybe less?" She shook her head and rubbed lightly at the edge of her left eye again. "I have a kid to look after. And my tuition for the next semester took out my reserves. I only have this one semester left. But…" She closed her eyes briefly. "I've spent all this money to get this degree, so I can do a different job. And now I might not be able to get a job in the field because of a crook." She sighed. "I don't want to move. My son's father lives here. They're close. I don't want to screw that up. But if I can't work…" She spread her hands around her coffee mug before gripping it tight again.

"Is Dr. Butler's partner involved in the embezzlement?" Myra asked. "Or does he just go along for the ride?"

"His billing seems standard. I never saw anything suspicious there. Doesn't necessarily mean anything. He profits from his partner's actions." She tugged at her left eye again and cursed quietly. "Sorry, I'll be right back. I have to get this rinsed."

She stood, taking her purse with her, and headed to the back of the narrow coffee shop, weaving past the table with the two men talking to reach the single bathroom.

Myra watched her go, frowning a little when she turned back to Christopher. "What do you think?"

"I think she needs help, and I think she doesn't know what to do next."

"Agreed. And I think she's telling the truth." Which wasn't always the case with people Myra encountered in her line of work.

The door to the coffee shop opened on a dinging bell as another customer walked in.

Christopher lowered his voice so that it was difficult to hear him over the sounds of the espresso machine. "I'm not sure we'll find what she's looking for at the offices, though. Knowing one of their employees figured out the embezzlement scam means Dr. Butler might be more careful for the next few months."

"Maybe. But it also sounds like she's pretty arrogant. And thinks she's covered by whoever she knows at the Health Department or Department of Financial Services that warned her about the whistleblower report. People like that don't tend to cover their trail as well as they think they do." Myra leaned back in her chair. It did not creak the way it did under Christopher's weight. "I'll start at the practice offices. If I can't find anything there, we can always try Dr. Bulter's home."

"Don't write off her partner either," Christopher said. "If he's okay with Butler's crimes, he might be okay with helping her cover them up."

"Fair point." Myra frowned at the still closed bathroom door.

"Would Issa be able to move, to get a job, given who her son is related to? She said she didn't want to, but…would your father, or her son's father, try to stop the move? Is there…a legal issue with her moving?"

"No more so than if the boy's father were human. It depends on the custody arrangement they have. My father might…discourage a move. Having loyal dragons in his immediate territory is good for his power base. If Issa moves for work and takes her son into another dragon king's territory, it would be possible her son would shift loyalties to that new king. But my father can't legally prevent her from moving."

"She didn't sound like she wanted to."

"She shouldn't have to because an embezzler blackballed her."

"Agreed. So we'll break into the office first, then if nothing there, we'll try other avenues of tracking down evidence." Myra tapped her fingers against the wooden table top, running her short fingernails in a tipping pattern as she thought. "But once we have the evidence, what do we do with it? We can't turn it over to the very people who are already covering for Dr. Butler. I know you said you'd put the weight of the dragons behind a formal report but that doesn't stop Butler from interfering in Issa's job prospects. How do we get the woman to leave Issa and her career alone? Do we actually do anything to stop Butler's scam? Or are we just getting the evidence to use as…blackmail to make the good doctor back off?"

She glanced away from the bathroom to look at Christopher. He was frowning, his forehead bunched into creases she had the irrational urge to smooth with her fingertips.

"I think we let Issa decide what to do with the evidence," Christopher said. "It's her life, her future. She should decide how she wants to proceed."

Myra smiled as Christopher's gaze swept down to her. "Good plan."

The bathroom door finally opened and Issa came out, blinking a few times. She gave Myra a little smile on the way back to their table.

But before she reached them, the two men who'd been sitting with their heads together, talking quietly, stood suddenly, blocking Issa.

For a split second, Myra just assumed they were rude, getting up to leave and not paying any attention to the people around them.

Then she saw the gun in one's hand. The widened, panicked look in Issa's dark eyes.

And before Myra could even push her chair back, the man with the gun had his arm wrapped around Issa's neck, the gun at her temple, using her as a shield in front of him.

His companion stood behind him, also with a gun. His pointed at Christopher.

"Don't try anything," the man with the gun at Issa's temple said. "Or we'll kill her."

Myra raised her hands, palms facing the men. "What do you want?"

"We're taking the woman for a little chat with our boss. You want her released alive, you'll look out for a message."

"Ransom," Myra said, rising slowly.

The second man, whose gun had been aimed at Christopher, shifted the barrel to point the gun at her.

She kept her hands raised and her gaze on Issa and the gunman behind her, trusting Christopher to watch the second man. "Who do you think she has to pay a random? She's just a single mom. Working hard. Just been fired. There isn't money for a ransom."

The man snorted. "Boss knows who her son's father is." He flicked a glance at Christopher. "What that connects her to. You want her alive? You want her to see her son again? You back off looking into the boss's business, and you make sure that ransom gets paid when you get it. No tricks." He glanced at the side of Issa's face. "Shame for her son if his mother was killed."

Issa's eyes widened, her skin paled, her hands were visibly shaking, and her breath came in such hard, fast gulps, Myra worried she'd pass out. Her bottom lip quivered and she looked like she wanted to scream, to cry, to say something. But she remained silent and trembling and staring at Myra with such desperation in her gaze, Myra's own hands twitched to reach out to her.

The two gunmen eased around the narrow path between tables, keeping Issa between Myra and Christopher and themselves. The second man kept his gun trained toward Myra and Christopher. The first never moved his from Issa's temple.

Tears tracked down Issa's cheeks as they reached the front door.

The two women behind the counter had ducked down, out of view. The woman on her lap top had folded herself into the corner, using her table and laptop as cover. The silence in the café was broken only by Issa's quiet whimpers and the sudden sound of the coffee machine grinder going on.

"Call the cops on us," the man said, "and she's dead. Just do as instructed, she'll live to see her son again."

They backed out of the café's glass door, onto the busy sidewalk. Half a dozen people screamed at the sight of the guns. A few walked past without even noticing. A black SUV pulled up onto the sidewalk, which drew almost as many gasped and outraged yells and screams as the two men with guns. The back door opened and the two gunmen pushed Issa inside before jumping in behind her.

By the time Myra and Christopher reached the sidewalk, the SUV had sped away, racing up the avenue, honking and whipping around the rest of traffic, running a red light. It screeched around a corner. Disappearing from sight.

Myra glanced at Christopher. He stripped his shirt off without a word. She jumped into his arms as his shirt dropped to the sidewalk and his wings snapped open behind him.

They were airborne an instant later, leaving the sounds of more shouting and gasps on the sidewalk below.

So much for being inconspicuous.

Chapter Four

Christopher banked, following the road below, keeping the black SUV in sight as it sped through the streets of the Upper West Side, and launch up the West Side Highway. The cold afternoon air whipped across Myra's cheeks. Christopher was flying fast enough the rush of air made her eyes water. She clung to his neck, but kept her gaze on the SUV. Afraid if she looked away too long, she'd lose it in the traffic.

And with it, Issa.

"They'll know you can follow this way, won't they?" she asked, speaking loudly to be heard above the rushing air and the noise of protesting traffic below. "They knew about Issa's connection to the dragons even without saying it aloud."

"They might know," he acknowledged. "But will rightly assume we won't try anything while they have guns on Issa."

"What are we going to do?" she asked. She was a thief not an expert in rescuing kidnap victims.

Though, technically, that's what she'd done with Christopher. She'd reframed it in her mind, though, to fit her skill set. She'd gone in and stolen him back from his kidnappers. She could steal things. That's what she *did*.

Rescuing people on the other hand…

"First, we make sure we know where they're going. Then we get Issa back."

Christopher's voice was hard, and very deep, and that underlying, inhuman hissing growl was there under his words.

"We could just pay the ransom and then I can steal the money back after Issa is safe," Myra suggested. "Your father would front the money, right?"

"That's what they're counting on."

Yeah, Myra sort of thought so, too. Especially after they specifically referenced who Issa's son was related to and glanced at Christopher. They knew the boy's father was a dragon shifter and that by extension that meant the dragon king would be involved in the situation. The dragon king had more than enough money to pay a ransom, even a big one.

The question was, would the king *really* pay the ransom for one random human woman?

The boy's father was still around. The boy's father was a dragon shifter. The king might *want* the boy to be raised by his father, away from human influence.

Though, if that were the case, he probably wouldn't have "mentioned" Issa's problem to Christopher, knowing Christopher would want to save her.

The SUV headed down the West Side Highway, barreling through the snarl of cars, shoving them aside physically to get them to move if it had to. The time of day was leading into rush hour, so things were starting to get heavy, but not as bad as they'd been in about an hour.

"They're heading to the tunnel," Myra said.

It was a ways to go downtown to reach the Lincoln Tunnel.

Going up to the George Washington would have been a lot closer from where they'd started. But on this route, short of heading into some specific place in Lower Manhattan, she couldn't imagine where else the SUV would be going.

They'd hardly stay in Manhattan where the king and his dragons could more easily hunt them down.

There were a lot of places in New Jersey for a black SUV to disappear. The king's sway in the state wasn't as powerful as in New York. And she and Christopher would lose that specific car in the tunnel since Christopher couldn't safely fly *through* the tunnel.

"Do we stop them before they reach it?" she asked.

"If we try to, they might just shoot Issa."

"Can we land on the car and…ride through the tunnel that way?"

"They realize we're there, they'll shoot up through the car. Or shoot Issa."

"We're fucked if they make the tunnel."

Christopher banked low, so close to the roofs of the cars, Myra actually gasped and clung tighter to his neck. Usually, he stayed well above traffic when he flew her around the city, often above the buildings. From that height, the only thing they were likely to hit was an errant flock of birds.

This close to the cars, the possibility of electrical and phone wires, or even big delivery trucks, felt a lot more imminent.

She didn't close her eyes when he flew directly up to, then whipped around a large delivery van, but she did have to press her teeth together so she didn't squeal.

A giddy rush of adrenaline hit her bloodstream hard. And it took a great deal of effort for Myra to hold in her laughter. This wasn't a laughing situation. Issa's life was on the line.

But hot damn the rush in this kind of danger…

Christopher swung up behind the SUV, close enough Myra

could see into the back windows, see Issa's head bracketed by the two men from the café through the dark tinting. There had to be at least two more people in the SUV. The driver, and whoever had opened the back door for the gunmen and Issa to get into the car. But Myra couldn't see either of those two people from this vantage.

What she could clearly see was the SUV's plates.

"Got the number." Christopher gave his wings a heavy downward sweep and heaved them higher above the cars again.

The change in direction and sudden rise making her stomach drop and an edge of nausea clench around her middle before everything but the adrenaline rush settled.

"Now what?" she said as they went back to trailing the SUV from a higher altitude, skimming over the tops of wires, and reaching a height that felt less like they might run into a bridge or big truck.

"Now, we follow at a more discrete height and let them believe they've lost me in the tunnel."

"Your eyesight that good?"

"Yes."

That was scary. "Is that how you always manage to find me?"

He paused long enough she wondered if he'd even answer. Then, "Sometimes. But not always."

He had found her when she wasn't out in the open more than once. So she knew his scary good eyesight couldn't explain it all. She'd even searched herself for a tracking device at one stage. Nothing. Christopher just had an uncanny knack for finding her, no matter where she was. It would probably be more disconcerting if she didn't enjoy the moments when he did find her.

"You ever going to explain the times that have nothing to do with your eyesight?" she asked.

"One day. But not while we're chasing a woman in danger."

Well. That was fair enough.

CHAPTER FIVE

Christopher banked out over the Hudson as the SUV disappeared into the line of cars inching into the Lincoln Tunnel. Below them, ferries and tourist boats chugged down the slow, dirty water of the river, neatly avoiding the smaller sailboats and occasional fishing boat or kayak.

How people went kayaking in this weather was beyond Myra. Even when she wasn't mid-flight, the winter weather was frosty. Out over the water, the temperature dropped another few degrees. The thought of being that close to cold water made her shiver.

"You're cold," Christopher said.

She shook her head. "You're pumping out enough body heat to keep me warm." His skin felt like he'd just come in from sitting in the sun, the scattering of purple and yellow scales over his shoulders and chest radiating heat.

While she'd read that ordinary dragons, what few were left, could be cold blooded and therefore needed quite a lot of heat to warm their huge bodies, dragon shifters, even in dragon form, were warm blooded. She got the feeling from Christopher that they could control that body heat better than the average mammal, warming themselves up when they needed to. Or when their emotions got the better of them.

Helped keep her warm midflight, too.

"I was thinking it's too cold to go kayaking," she explained.

"I have to agree." He adjusted his arms around her, lifting her a little closer to his body, and she tightened her hold on his neck.

"Am I getting too heavy?"

He glanced briefly down at her, his brows lifted in such a smugly sardonic expression, she rolled her eyes.

Since he'd once flown her from the back of a train all the way to Chicago, a flight that had taken hours, she realized her question was silly. Still, she felt rude not asking.

He took a flight path that circled them around to the far side of the tunnel, where cars were rushing out onto the more open Jersey freeways.

"There are hundreds of black SUVs down there," she said with a sigh. "Not a bad plan, disappearing through the tunnel. Hopefully they don't know how good your eyesight is."

"We'll know soon. There they are."

He stayed high, gliding over the SUV as it moved toward Hoboken. The car had slowed to a reasonable speed, keeping pace with traffic now instead of ramming through and rushing past other cars. From above, it looked like every other car driving along the freeway, nothing to make it stand out. Even the dents on the front, where it had rammed other vehicles to move them out of its way during the earlier chase didn't stand out as particularly obvious because, even at this height, Myra spotted at least two other vehicles with damage.

This was why she mostly stuck to the subways. Cars were a menace.

The SUV eased off the freeway and headed into a residential

area. Myra half expected them to drive to one of the many houses that looked like doll houses below her, but the SUV kept driving, moving from the residential area into a more industrial part of the city, where warehouses took up large swaths of marshy land, the shades of grays broken up by the occasional winter-brown tree planted along a sidewalk.

They watched the SUV pull into one of the industrial complexes, with a series of gray-white buildings scattered around empty parking lots. The car drove to one of the far buildings, a smaller one with large loading bay doors. The lot and building looked empty. There weren't even any trailers parked at the loading bays.

Christopher circled down to a flat rooftop with a low retaining wall that looked across to the building but was far enough away, the kidnappers would have to have excellent eyesight to see them. He got them onto the roof and they both ducked low to the retaining wall before anyone even stepped out of the SUV.

The driver was first, getting out and scanning their surroundings as he closed the car door. They were much too far away for her to see him clearly or to hear anything that was said, so she asked Christopher, "He have a gun, too?"

Christopher nodded without speaking, his eyes narrowed.

After a moment of scanning, the driver opened the back door, keeping his gaze on the surroundings as he let the people in the back out. First came one of the men from the café. The taller of the two, the one who'd kept his gun trained on Myra and Christopher.

He was taller than the driver as well as the other gunman, but only by a few inches, and leaner than the driver, who was wide shouldered and thick through the middle. Both men were white and had dark hair, but that was the best she could do at a distance. Her memory of the two men in the café was that they'd been ordinary looking. Dressed casually in jeans, with their black coats still on as they'd hunched over their table talking. Since she hadn't bothered to take her jacket off inside the coffee shop either, she had noted the coats but not found it particularly suspicious. It really was cold outside.

No obvious external features to the two men either to make them stand out. Neither even wore glasses. And she hadn't noticed any obvious jewelry, which was something she did make note of on all the people around her, though usually subconsciously.

Old habits.

Issa was next out of the car. She stumbled a little when she hit the ground, and the man who'd gotten out first braced her with a hand on her arm. He dropped his touch the minute she got her balance and jerked free, then stepped to one side so she could move out of the way for the last man in the back seat.

Who climbed out still holding his gun in his hand.

As far as Myra could tell, neither of the other men had weapons in their hands. But Christopher had confirmed even the driver had a gun.

Lot of guns between them and Issa. And Myra was pretty sure Christopher wasn't bulletproof. She definitely wasn't bulletproof.

She hated guns.

Reaching inside the multi-pocketed vest under her coat, she pulled out a tiny pair of binoculars.

"Is there anything you don't carry inside that vest?" Christopher asked as she set the binoculars to her eyes.

"Nothing that might be useful."

"Binoculars are regularly useful?"

"In my job? Yes. All the time."

She felt more than saw his head tilt in a shrug.

Scanning the men and Issa briefly, she confirmed Issa didn't appear injured. In fact, now that they were all out of the car and walking toward the building, none of the men even touched her. The first man from the coffee shop who'd taken her hostage walked behind her with a gun pointed at her back, but that was the only method of restraint. No cuffs or ties. Nothing to keep her from screaming. Though out here, with no signs of life anywhere nearby, screaming probably would seem pointless.

Myra swung her binoculars back to the SUV. She was certain there was at least one more person in that car. Someone had to have opened the back door. The driver couldn't have. But only the three men and Issa had gotten out.

"There's someone still in the car," she said. With the magnified vision, she could barely see movement inside the tinted windows. A changing of light coming through the windshields to indicate the car wasn't empty. The SUV was parked in the shadows of the building, so there wasn't enough light hitting the windows to light up whoever was inside.

"Can you see them?" she asked Christopher with his superior eyesight.

"One person, no one else, but I can't tell much more about them. Tint has something in it that's distorting my vision."

That was interesting. He could see into the car, but not as clearly as he might be able to without the tint. That there was a way to tint car windows that affected dragon shifter eyesight was a new fact for her. Something else to research.

She swung her binoculars back to the quartet as they headed inside the building, climbing a short set of metal stairs to a door that had an obvious lock panel beside the doorknob. The driver entered a code, waited a beat, then turned the knob and opened the door wide enough to let the other two men and Issa proceed him inside. He continually scanned his surroundings as he waited for them to pass, only taking his gaze off the lot and other buildings when he finally ducked inside and the door closed.

"Code lock but no cards or keys or biometrics," she murmured.

"You can handle that?"

"I can handle that."

"Good. Smashing in the door would be too noisy. Give away our element of surprise."

She lowered the binoculars to look at the side of his face. The door in question was thick and metal and looked pretty substantial. "You could smash in that door?"

"I could smash in that door," he said without glancing at her.

"Not sure if I'm impressed or appalled." He was very strong. No wonder he'd looked at her like she was ridiculous when she'd asked if she was getting too heavy.

"The person in the SUV getting out?" she asked as she swung her binoculars back to the car.

"No. But there's another vehicle coming."

"There is?" She lowered her binoculars again to scan the area. She could hear traffic and cars in the distance as a low drone of background noise amidst the quieter hum of wind around the industrial park. But now that she paid attention, she could hear a more distinct motor separating from the distant background drone.

Sure enough, a heavy engine sports car motored around the corner of a building, growling up to the SUV. Pretty and red but that was the best Myra could do. She did not specialize in stealing sportscars, so they weren't in her expertise.

The sportscar parked on the far side of the SUV, doors opened and closed. Even with her binoculars, she couldn't see who had gotten out until they came around the back of the SUV. At which point, the driver of the little red sportscar revealed himself to be a medium height, middle aged man, his head shaven, his beard scruff artful, his skin artificially tan, and his short-sleeved polo shirt entirely inappropriate for the weather. He looked irritated as all hell, pointing at someone still hidden behind the SUV, and speaking loudly enough Myra could almost hear him.

"What's he saying?" she asked Christopher without taking her eyes off the man. Through the binoculars, he was easy enough to see but not someone she recognized.

"He's yelling at the person behind the car about getting him involved in all this. It's their fault. He's an innocent bystander. Blah blah blah."

Myra pressed her lips together to keep from laughing. Her huge dragon shifter companion saying, "blah blah blah," struck her as remarkably funny for some reason. Also, his obvious annoyance with the newcomer couldn't have been clearer.

"Do you recognize him?" she asked.

"No. But I will bet that's the second doctor from the practice Issa worked at."

"Not taking that bet. I think you're right." She watched for a moment more before saying, "What do you bet the person we can't see, the remaining person in the SUV, is Dr. Butler?"

"I'd bet my father's hoard."

She grinned. "Not your hoard, of course."

"Of course not."

The absolute afront in his response did have her quietly chuckling.

They watched another minute, with the sportscar man continuing to yell, before the person he was yelling at finally came into view.

And the absolutely stunning woman that stepped up to him, with strappy black heels so high they made Myra dizzy and an elegant sweep of jet black hair, struck the man silent.

The woman wore very dark sunglasses, so Myra couldn't see her eyes. But even at a distance, it was obvious she was a beautiful woman. Slim, dressed in a long white coat that wrapped snuggly around her small waist, her long legs encased in stockings that sparkled in the winter light. Even her hair looked glossy and perfect.

For a moment, Myra had this odd feeling that the woman was not real. That she had stepped out of a magazine, airbrushing and all, to exist in the real world and yet not be of the real world.

The woman stepped up very close to the man who had, just moments ago, been blustering and yelling at her, and he lowered his head as she got near. She stuck her finger under his chin, lifting his head, but he still didn't meet her gaze.

Through the binoculars, Myra could see the woman's lips move, close to the man's face. "Can you hear her?" she asked Christopher. There was no hope of her hearing the woman. All she heard was the whistle of a sudden gust of wind through the complex.

She felt more than saw Christopher shake his head. "She's speaking too quietly. Whispering. I get the sound, but not the words."

"That you even get the sound is impressive."

After a moment of this whispering, the woman stepped away from the man, the man lowered his head again, looking properly chastised, and the woman smoothed a hand down her coat before gesturing at the door where the gunmen and Issa had gone. The man nodded his head rapidly, then extended and arm for the woman to proceed him which she did.

The whole thing couldn't have lasted more than two minutes. But it felt like Myra had just watched a fully half hour drama in those minutes.

Once the woman and man—presumably Dr. Butler and her practice partner—had disappeared inside, Myra lowered her binoculars and scanned their surroundings. The area was silent now, no more cars growling into the lot. Just the distant sound of traffic and the whistling breeze.

"See anyone else?" she checked with Christopher and his superior eyesight and hearing.

He shook his head, then stood and let his wings unfurl from where he'd kept them tight to his back while crouched out of sight. "Can you open that door quickly?"

"I can open that door quickly. But let's see if we can find a window first. I want to know what the interior of the warehouse looks like."

"Issa might not have that kind of time."

Myra was worried about that too. "If we see or hear anything, we can always go crashing in through a window. Create some chaos."

She tucked her little binoculars away into their pocket, and without a word, jumped up into Christopher's arms. He swept them up into the air an instant later, as if they'd practice this move so often it was habit, well trained muscle memory.

For reasons, that made Myra all soft and giddy inside.

Chapter Six

They swept around the perimeter of the building, gliding on a cushion of air just above the ground. There were a few windows high up on the two story structure, but when Christopher flew close enough for them to see inside, all Myra could see were stacks of wooden and metal crates.

Anxiety and worry for Issa clawed at her gut, and she suspected Christopher was impatient to get inside and rescue Issa, too. But he'd been kidnapped once when he rushed into a situation to rescue a damsel in distress. Myra refused to be responsible for him getting kidnapped again, or worse, because they didn't know what the situation was inside that warehouse.

The situation inside, however, was something they'd only figure out once she got them through the code lock on the door.

He set them down gently at the top of the staircase, his feet settling onto the metal so lightly, he didn't make noise. Given he'd made the wooden chair in the coffee shop groan, Myra was impressed.

The code lock took her about twenty seconds and she used a

spell to do it because they didn't have the extra ten seconds she would have needed using an old school heat scanner to pick up the buttons that had been recently pushed. The spell basically did the same thing, lighting up the buttons pressed, and there were enough of them for the type of lock she was looking at to indicate no repeat numbers.

The lock snicked open, but Myra stopped Christopher before he rushed in. She eased the door just wide enough to listen to what was happening beyond. When she couldn't hear anything immediately, she crept inside, taking in her immediate surroundings with a sweep of her gaze.

Red painted metal stairs leading back down to ground level. Blue concrete floors. Boxes and wooden crates piled on the floor. A few stacks of larger, metal shipping crates. It wasn't a giant building, but was tall enough for the shipping crates to stack two high.

She eased down the metal staircase, and headed immediately to the cover of a nearby stack of wooden boxes.

Christopher leapt from the stairs landing right beside her behind the crates, hitting the ground with the lightness of a cat.

She rolled her eyes. Show off.

She touched her ear with a finger and narrowed her eyes up at him. He gave a brief nod and headed in one direction. She followed, quietly, trusting his hearing to pinpoint the location of everyone.

That she trusted him, anyone really, to guide her through the building was a revelation. She trusted Christopher to catch her when she fell. She trusted him to lead her in the right direction in intense circumstances. She...trusted him. At least with her physical safety.

Unprecedented.

They stayed behind cover, easing through the warehouse. Reaching a point where even Myra could hear voices. A quiet whispering female voice. Issa's denials. A man lifting his voice in an almost shout before he also quieted.

As they neared, the words got clearer.

"You shouldn't have brought the dragon king into all this," the woman said.

"I didn't." Issa, sounding like she wanted to cry. "I just told Havier I would have to move after Dr. Butler fired me. He informed the king. I didn't do anything."

Myra frowned. She'd been assuming the woman was Dr. Butler and the man was Dr. Butler's partner. But… Something about the way Issa mentioned Butler made it sound like she was referring to someone else completely. Not the woman with the quiet voice who'd shut the sportscar man up with a look.

Okay. So. Something more going on here. And not just two people trying to shut up a whistleblower.

Somewhere around here, there were also the three gunmen.

"I told you," a man said. "I told you this was a bad idea."

Myra guessed that was the sportscar man, but couldn't see him yet to be sure.

"The king sent his son," the woman said. "His son would have found out everything. This wasn't a situation I could let go."

"What could they do? She destroyed everything. All the evidence is gone."

"And the king's pet thief? You don't think she'd have found anything?"

Pet thief? Myra mouthed at Christopher, her scowl fierce.

That was *exactly* what she'd been afraid of. People starting to think she somehow *belonged* to the king and his cohort just because she'd done a few jobs for him. Bad enough the *king* had started to think that. Other people thinking that was both bad *and* wrong.

Probably the fact that she was…on her way to being… romantically involved with the king's son didn't help that perception, but that was another issue. As was her stuttering over what to call her relationship with Christopher.

"There's nothing for her to find," the man insisted. "But now you've made things worse! Kidnapped a woman in broad daylight. While she was with those two. They'll find us. The king will know. The police will know."

"My men lost the king's son. He's not some sort of omnipresent god. None of them are. Despite what the king would have people believe."

Wow. Sounded like there was some history there. But also, hadn't the woman heard of license plate numbers?

"I won't stand by for this. We can't just kill her. The police will come looking at our practice first. They'll *know*. They'll figure it out."

Shit. Okay. Wanting to kill Issa was bad. Issa's quiet whimper and plea for her life after that didn't help.

"I have a son," she said brokenly. "Please. He needs me."

Heat pumped off Christopher from Myra's side, his anger obvious even without having to look at him. She set her hand against his arm to keep him from rushing in and it was a bit like touching a fire. Not quite hot enough to burn. But since they weren't flying and they weren't outside in the cold air, the heat felt like it would burn if he got much hotter.

She understood the reaction. She wanted to run in and rescue Issa, too. Had wanted to since she'd first been kidnapped. But there were still those three gunmen.

Given the conversation, Myra was now certain the man talking was the sportscar man, and he'd confirmed he was Dr. Butler's partner. Where the hell Dr. Butler was was a hanging question. But they could sort that out after they got Issa out of this. Hopefully without Christopher lighting the whole place on fire.

Against Christopher's ear, in a whisper so quiet, she wasn't even sure she was speaking aloud, she said, "We have to see what's happening. The gunmen."

He jerked his chin in a nod. When she leaned back to look at him, his jaw was set, his eyes fairly glowing in the dark, a yellow glow over the blue, and he looked like he could chew rocks.

But instead of running headlong into the situation, he tapped his nose.

She assumed that meant he could smell something important.

Then he pointed to their left and right.

Okay. She was going to interpret that as where the gunmen were. She mouthed, *gunmen*? Just to be sure.

Another jerky nod.

So. One to their left and one to their right at least. But the third had to be with Issa. Either that, or the woman had a gun they hadn't seen earlier.

Christopher leaned in close to whisper in her ear. It was like stepping up to the very edge of a bonfire. "I'll take care of the two gunmen not with the group. Be right back."

Before she could stop him, he was gone, moving so fast she blinked. Shit.

She knew, because he was a shapeshifter, because he was a dragon, he could move very fast when he wanted to. She'd flown with him at speed. But this was the first time she'd really seen him move so fast she'd been unable to visually follow him.

The realization he could do that was disorienting.

More disorienting was how fast he returned.

She blinked up at him. *Are they dead*? she mouthed.

Brief head shake. "Unconscious," he whispered against her ear. "Guns destroyed."

He'd done all that and done it in complete silence? In less than a minute. Woah.

Okay. Maybe they could get Issa out alive after all.

She motioned him to the left, so they could move around the crates and get a view of the situation around Issa. The remaining group were still talking, with the man arguing with the woman in quiet but intense tones and Issa quietly crying. The sound of her soft sobs went right through Myra. She could only imagine how bad this was for Christopher.

They reached a spot where, with a quick glance around one of the metal shipping crates, Myra could see the group. The woman, the sportscar man, the remaining gunman, and Issa on her knees at the center of them all. The gunman had his gun pointed at the back of Issa's head.

They needed a distraction for the gunman. Christopher, with his apparent super speed, could race in there and remove Issa from the middle of the group, but not if the gunman startled and got a shot off first. Even if he missed Issa's head, he'd hit...someone.

Myra pointed to the metal crate. Mouthed, *I'm going up.*

Christopher scowled at her.

Distraction.

More scowling. She wasn't sure if the scowl was because he didn't understand or because he didn't want her to be the distraction. He didn't have much choice if it was the latter, but if the former...

You, go in and get Issa. She made gestures to emphasize her mouthed words, hoping he got it. *I'll make sure the gun is pointing somewhere else.*

This would be easier if she could just say the words to him, but they were so close to the others now, she didn't want to risk it. Reading lips, even with careful enunciation, still left room for error.

She tried a final time since Christopher was still scowling at her. *You...* She pointed at his chest. *Get Issa. I...* She pointed at her chest. *Will distract the others.*

No.

She wasn't entirely sure what he was noing. Him going in to rescue Issa or her distracting the others so he could. She had a feeling it was the latter, though, because this was Christopher after all.

She grinned at him and pointed upward. *Be back soon. Don't miss your opening.*

And just because she felt like it, because he was pumping off heat like a boiler and looked so fierce and angry, she rose up on her toes and kissed him. Light and quick. On the mouth. Then spun around the back of the crate before he could stop her.

Technically, she thought as she found the ladder up to the top of the metal shipping crate, he probably could still stop her. Given he could move in a blink. She hoped he'd trust her to do her part as she was trusting him to do his. This was a team effort here.

That she was working with anyone else, even one other person, was astonishing.

That she didn't mind…

Unprecedented.

CHAPTER SEVEN

Myra shimmied up the flat ladder stuck to the side of the metal shipping crate, careful of her footing and ensuring she made no sounds. The roof of the crate was tricker, inclined to bend and creak if she wasn't careful. That would work for her, but she needed to time things right.

Below her, the woman was still lecturing the sportscar man about how he'd fucked everything up. The sportscar man was arguing that they couldn't afford any more bodies on their hands. And since Issa had whistleblown on embezzlement and not murder, the fact that there were *more* bodies involved was news.

Issa remained on her knees in the middle of the group, quietly sobbing into her hands, her face covered. At the mention of *more* bodies, she shivered hard and shrank farther in on herself. The gunman stood behind her, his gun pointed at her head, his attention on the man and woman yelling at each other, his expression bored.

Unfortunately, for all the boredom, he didn't look like he was going to point the gun elsewhere or drop his arm any time soon.

Somewhere below and hidden, Christopher waited, pumping off

so much heat in his anger, Myra worried he'd melt the side of the shipping container.

The lights inside the warehouse were dim in most sections but bright enough in this part of the space Myra had to be careful she didn't cast shadows from her perch up on top of the shipping crate, so she kept low, inching over the metal to get into position.

"The king will come after us for sure if you do this," the sportscar man hissed. His artificially tan skin looked pale and pasty in the bright overhead lights. His bald head was dotted with sweat even though it wasn't that warm inside and he was still only wearing a polo shirt.

That the partner was here but not Dr. Butler had Myra pretty curious, since Butler was the one whose supposed embezzlement had led to all this.

"Her son is a dragon," sportscar man said, flinging a hand at Issa. Issa flinched.

"And he has a dragon father who will take care of him," the woman said dryly. "The king will probably prefer that anyway."

This close, it was easier to see the woman's flawless complexion, smooth and pale under expert makeup. Her black hair, twisted into an elegant bun. The spikey heels she stood on looking even higher and spikier up close. Myra would definitely break an ankle on those.

The woman hadn't loosened her white coat yet, so it was still wrapped around her like a dress. Her sparkling nylons gave her long legs a sheen that weirdly reminded Myra of the way Christopher's scales caught the light when he did his partial shift. A sort of soft sparkle. But Christopher's scales were purple and yellow. The woman's nylons were an ordinary tan color.

Her age was just as difficult to pinpoint this close up. That vaguely mid-thirties sort of age that could mean she was anything from a mature-looking twenty year old or a well-preserved fifty year old. The woman's body posture and clothing screamed money to Myra—who was used to assessing these things—a kind of casual wealth that still, nevertheless, wanted people to know she was wealthy.

Lot of old money people dressed in ordinary clothes, ripped jeans and worn t-shirts and, depending, expensive converse or inexpensive wellies. Old money, the ones secure in their wealth and station in life, tended to show up in the world like ordinary people, with a few hints that the money was there in the background.

People who wanted people to know they were wealthy, people who *needed* others to know they were rich, always looked the part.

And made great marks for people like Myra.

This woman, though… Myra was having trouble reading her. It was like this obvious wealthy appearance was a sort of act. A costume she'd donned for a point. Myra couldn't even say what details about her were making Myra assume that. Outwardly, she seemed to be exactly what she was. But Myra was used to studying people, their dress, their body language.

Something about the woman wasn't adding up.

"Please," Issa sobbed into her hands. "My son needs me."

The woman glared down at Issa's bent head. "Sons do not need their mothers that desperately, woman. You should consider that falsehood. Dragon sons need their own people. But not their mothers."

Myra narrowed her eyes. Yeah. Something was definitely up with that woman. She knew an awful lot about dragon shifters, and had some very specific opinions.

Who the hell was she?

Whoever she was, it was time to get Issa away from her. And the man with the gun pointing at Issa's head.

Myra lifted her head a little more, a darting motion before she lowered back to the container roof. She shifted to the left. The metal roof creaked.

"Someone's here," the gunman said. The first time he'd spoken.

The woman's eyes narrowed and she lifted her head.

Myra lifted enough to be seen again, dropping as fast. A quick sort of motion. Like someone trying to avoid being seen.

Then moved slightly right. Another creak on the metal roof.

The sound of a gun firing was so loud in the confined space, Myra covered her ears when she ducked. Though the sound came at the same time as the bullet whizzed over her head.

"Up there," the woman shouted. "It's the thief. Get her!"

Nice to be recognized?

No. Myra did not like that the woman had recognized her at all.

She crab-walked backward along the metal roof as more shots rang out over her head and more shouting came from the group below.

She realized they expected the other two men to hurry to them, or at least expected the other two men to be there. Using that, she slithered down the side of the shipping container and made an obvious dart between it and another pile of boxes moving in the direction where one of the now disabled men had been.

Hoping when Christopher had left him unconscious, he done a thorough enough job the man wasn't already getting to his feet. And that Christopher had checked for more than the one weapon.

More bullets. Ricocheting off the metal containers. Thunking heavily into the wooden crates. A few whizzed too close over her head as she made herself a target.

She hated guns.

Then a sudden flurry of noise and shouts. A change in tone. A scream.

Of outrage.

Myra risked a look around the edge of a crate. The woman, the sportscar man, and the gunman all stood together, backs to each other, searching the area. The sportscar man rubbed a hand over his head and looked ready to bolt. The gunman looked a little panicky, too.

The woman just looked pissed.

Like…really pissed. Like her face getting so red and her fingers so tightly clenched in a fist she might just explode from the anger.

"How did he find you?" she snarled at the gunman. But there was something in her voice… A sort of…

Hissing.

Myra blinked hard. Her stomach bottomed out.

She'd heard that sound before. That hissing beneath a growl that human voices didn't make. A combination of sounds that would be impossible for a strictly human throat to produce.

Christopher sometimes made that sound when he was angry.

She'd only ever heard that sound from dragon shifters.

But…that was impossible. There were, what, twelve dragon shifter females in the world. Only twelve. They kept to themselves, too. They were elusive. They were secretive. Most of them were supposed to be asleep.

One of them should not be standing in the middle of a warehouse in New Jersey threatening to kill a human woman over the insurance fraud committed by a Manhattan plastic surgeon.

What the hell was going on?

Chapter Eight

With the revelation that she might well be looking at one of the very few female dragon shifters on the planet, Myra froze for a full ten seconds. When there were shifters involved. When there was still one man holding a gun. When there was a woman's life on the line.

Ten seconds was a long time.

Ten seconds before she realized that Issa was no longer in the middle of the group trying to kill her. Ten seconds before she realized because the woman knew Christopher was here, Christopher had gotten Issa away from the people trying to kill her.

Ten seconds to realize Myra had to get the fuck out of that warehouse now.

Time for them all to escape.

She hoped Christopher had gotten Issa to safety. His need to rescue people meant he might come back for Myra, or even not leave without her, and while she admired his desire to help, she didn't want him anywhere near that female dragon shifter who looked like she wanted to explode with rage.

Myra wanted them all very far from this warehouse as soon as possible.

Ducking behind more boxes, she kept her movements as silent as possible as she hurried toward the door they'd entered through. There weren't a lot of ways out of the warehouse that weren't sealed and locked shut. And any of those options involved cracking locks and making noise—like lifting one of the docking bay doors—so she had to hope the original escape route was still clear.

The fact that it was. That nothing stepped into her way. That nothing went horribly wrong by the time she reached the exit door, forcing her to change her plans, forcing her to fall back on one of the various contingencies she'd planned out of habit, left her a little…

Uncomfortable.

Happy of course. She took the stairs two at a time and pushed out through the door, taking a hit of cold air to the face. She was delighted not to have to fall back to a backup plan.

Right?

Except…

No. No. This was fine.

She raced to the nearest building that would provide cover and hunted the skies, the surrounding roofs.

He had to be around here somewhere.

A swooping noise, the sound of rushing air. The feel of heat cutting through the cold.

She turned in time to see Christopher drop out of the sky, flying low to the tarmac in the parking lot. He wasn't carrying Issa, though.

Myra had only a moment to worry about that, to wonder about that, before he reached her and she jumped into his arms at the same instant he scooped her up.

"Issa?" she asked, watching the ground recede below her rapidly.

"Safe. For the moment. We have to get her and hurry. To my father's compound."

"That woman… She really is a…" Myra looked from the ground to Christopher's face. "She's a…"

He looked grim, his mouth a flat line, his jaw tight. Under her hands, his shoulders were tight and hard as rocks. The scales that covered his skin when his wings were out seemed more solid than usual.

Almost like armor.

"She is," he said simply.

He pumped his wings harder and they flew fast, the wind cutting sharp against Myra's face, making her eyes water. They'd flown fast to get here. She'd been with Christopher when he'd been moving very fast. But she wasn't sure she'd ever experienced flight this fast. Everything blurred around them.

She blinked. "You're cloaking?"

He hadn't cloaked much when flying with her before this. He'd cloaked after rescuing her when a wizard had nearly killed her, and he'd cloaked briefly when they'd flown into Chicago because it was another king's territory. But because it blurred their surroundings, he didn't do it much with her. She liked to see the landscape.

The fact that he was cloaking now confirmed just how serious this situation was. And how potentially deadly.

"We'll reach Issa soon," he said, ignoring her question. "I'll need to carry you both to my father's, but that will require…"

When he didn't finish, she looked at his face again, ignoring the blurring whip of Hoboken below. "Require what?"

"To carry you both safely, and reach my father's mansion fast, I need to fully shift."

Myra blinked. She'd never seen his full dragon form before.

She'd seen a few others in full dragon, of course, but most dragon shifters didn't reveal themselves like that to humans. Not casually. Not just randomly. They cloaked if they had to fly in full dragon form over the city. And if they did go full dragon around humans, they often ensured it was done at a distance so it was difficult to tell just how huge they were.

They were careful not to make their true natures really obvious to humans on a regular basis because if they remained in mostly human form, humans often forgot how utterly terrifying it was to live shoulder to shoulder with beings that turned into giant fire-breathing creatures of myth.

A dragon shifter appearing full dragon to humans happened. Of course it did. It just didn't happen all the time. It was kept to rare occurrence. On purpose.

And Myra had never seen Christopher in that form.

She'd assumed, when she did, it would be… She wasn't sure. She had this idea that he'd revealed his dragon to her in some sort of formal way, in a field somewhere. Weird assumption. She'd learned a lot about dragon shifters since meeting him, but there was still a lot she didn't know, and she supposed she still harbored some strange ideas about the whole thing.

Since he'd kept his dragon form to himself this whole time, she'd just assumed revealing it was…cause for ceremony or something special or… She wasn't sure. Something anyway.

"How does that help us?" she asked trying to keep her voice even and business-like, as if this was just part of the plan and not a complete revelation. A mildly terrifying one.

An intimate one.

"I can carry you both easier in that form. My…hands are bigger. I can fly faster in that form, too."

He didn't glance behind him, but Myra did. She looked over his shoulders, past the sweep of his wings. She couldn't see the warehouse. She couldn't see anything but a blur of the landscape below.

But there was this sense of knowing. Knowing that a dragon shifter female was back there.

And she was mad.

They reached the rooftop of a multi-story apartment building near the river. At least three miles from the warehouse. He'd flown there, and back to get her, and here again, in a matter of minutes.

Issa hurried out from behind an air duct where she'd been hiding. "I can't believe you two came for me."

"We're not safe yet," Christopher said. His voice was very deep, deeper and more guttural than normal, and full of that hissing sound underneath that human vocal cords couldn't make. "We're going to the king. We'll be safe there."

"My son. She'll go after my son."

Christopher pulled his cellphone out of the back pocket of his jeans. He tapped in a few things on a text screen, then replaced the phone. "Your son's father and another emissary from the king will collect your son from his school. They'll meet us at the compound."

Issa closed her eyes, let out a long breath. "Thank you."

"I need to shift," he said, holding Issa's gaze. "You understand?"

She nodded. "Nothing I haven't seen before." Her smile looked forced.

Myra couldn't even force a reassuring smile. The fact that Issa had seen a dragon shifter in full dragon form wasn't technically surprising. She'd had a son with a dragon shifter. *Myra* had seen a few dragon shifters in full dragon form. At the king's mansion. In Chicago. Once or twice over the city.

She just hadn't seen *Christopher's* dragon form before.

And she kept latching on to the word "intimate" to describe the experience. Which didn't feel like it should be shared. At least this first time.

But needs must, right? This had to be done. Now. And fast.

Christopher caught her gaze. "You okay with this?"

She nodded, though the gesture felt jerky and awkward. "Hurry. We have to get out of here."

She wasn't sure how long it would take the female dragon to track them down, if she was even now currently airborne and hunting for them. No time to waste on her weird feelings. They could talk about all this when everyone was safe.

Maybe. She might not want to talk about the way she felt about this part. Maybe not ever.

Christopher narrowed his eyes at her, but then turned to look over his shoulder, in the direction of the warehouse. Even three miles away, it felt too close.

He stepped away from them, to the far end of the flat roof. There was one of the old water tanks up here still, and a lot of air vents and ducts. But enough open space on the roof, she hoped, for him to shift.

When he let his wings out, they just sort of snapped out. Appearing as if they'd been there the whole time, and he just had to unfurl them.

This was different.

A sort of swirling purple and yellow fog built up around Christopher, continued to swirl and sparkle around him, catching light, moving outward. Inside the swirl of colored fog, she saw Christopher's body convulse, heard noises that sounded like grunting. A flicker of light. More shimmering. Something that sounded like a crack. The wings along his back extended outside the fog, growing larger, longer, until they were so wide they spread the length of the roof.

The body they were attached to seemed to have grown

significantly, too, though Myra couldn't see clearly through the swirling, sparkling, colored clouds. She picked up the shape of a snout. Some spikes. Definitely a lot of scale covered muscle emerging.

And then the swirling fog went higher, encompassing something much, much bigger. So big, nearly half the roof was filled by the fog obscuring the body beneath. A talon poked out of the mist, long and sharp, attached to a giant, five fingered hand covered in purple scales.

A roar came from the center of the swirling fog, a sound that reverberated across the roof and through the surroundings. She heard the screech of tires below. Knew that this transformation wasn't going unnoticed.

And then the fog swirled down, fast, collapsing back in on itself, to reveal…

The most magnificent dragon Myra had ever seen.

CHAPTER NINE

T he dragon was easily three stories tall, even though he stood crouched on his hind legs, with a long, spike-lined tailed curling around those folded back legs. His body was thick, muscular, covered in mostly purple scales with a wash of yellow along his sides and over his stomach. The scales caught the weak winter sunlight, turning the dragon into a sparkling spot of unreality.

Myra blinked as a creature that could swallow her whole and barely notice lowered his huge head to her, bending his long neck nearly in half to get his raised snout down on her level. Though the dragon kept his mouth closed, she was acutely aware that there were a lot of teeth inside that mouth.

Turning to one side, the dragon stared at her with one eye, transparent inner lids whisked over the huge, purplish-blue iris, making it look like his eye shimmered. That faint purple glow over blue… That reminded her so sharply of Christopher she gasped.

"So," she whispered, wondering if his hearing like this was as good as when he was in his human form. "This is you as a dragon, huh?"

A small head nod and a little puff of smoke from his raised nostrils. She expected that smoke to smell vaguely of sulfur, a hint of brimstone to remind gawkers of the fire that could escape that mouth.

Except, he didn't smell like sulfur. Or even a reptile. There was a bit of Christopher there, surprisingly. But also…

"Does he smell like sugar cookies to you?" Myra asked Issa.

Issa gave her a look. A frown. Then a slow smile. "No. He doesn't. First time seeing his dragon form?"

Myra nodded, curious but too awed to ask why Issa was smiling at her. Most of her attention was still on the dragon.

A sound, in the distance, like the roar Christopher had released but louder, deeper, and distinctly more angry sounding, echoed across the buildings. Myra glanced toward that sound. Coming from the general direction of the warehouse.

That was bad.

"How do we travel this way?" she asked Christopher, panic making her less worried about the dragon in front of her who did not want to eat her because the dragon on its way just might.

He stretched out both his huge front hands. Each finger was thicker than her entire body and tipped with long, sharp talons like a ginormous hawk. Without hesitating, Issa climbed up onto one of those giant hands, and Christopher gently closed his dragon fingers around the woman, cradling her in his grip as she wrapped her arms around the digit that looked most like a thumb.

Myra looked at the hand stretched out to her. Then the eye focused on her. The little wink of the inner lids. Okay. So. He intended on carrying them this way. Took that whole saying of having someone in the palm of your hand a little literally, but she could do this.

Her heartbeat pounding, the rush of fear sent a spike of adrenaline into her blood. And the charge sent another bolt of excitement hot on its heels. The fear and excitement left her a little giddy. The knowledge that Christopher wouldn't drop her tipped the balance toward excitement and she scrambled into his palm. Her eyes widened as the huge fingers closed in around her, gently, giving her a comfortable cage to ride in. She did as Issa had done and hugged her arms as best she could around his thumb.

Beating wings that could knock over a building if he wasn't careful, the dragon launched into the sky. More cars screeching below. A few shouts. Then that blurring around them. And with a pump of his wings, they streaked across the sky. Out over the river before she could blink. High enough to see the island of Manhattan below. So high, the air was sharp and a little hard to breathe. Her ears popped as he dropped again a moment later, spiraling downward at such dizzying speed, even Myra had a moment of vertigo.

She gripped his thumb tighter and leaned out enough to see the ground rising up to them fast. To see the king's compound already beneath them. Wow. That had taken less than two minutes. Like he'd stretched his length and they were already here.

The sound of Issa's squeal reminded Myra that she should probably be afraid of the rapid decent. They were coming in fast and hard and the landing roof on the top of the king's mansion was approaching so rapidly it took up most of her vision.

But this was Christopher, even in this terrifying form. And in her soul, she knew he'd keep her from hitting the ground.

He swung upward at the last minute, giving his huge wings a strong beat, and settled onto his hind legs on the open landing area on the roof as lightly as if he'd just floated down.

The multiple and sudden changes in both speed and altitude left

Myra both dizzy and a little nauseated. She liked a good roller coaster as much as the next girl, but that one had been a bit much.

Still, they were at the compound now, and there were other dragons here. And the king. That female dragon would have to go through a lot of other dragons to get to them. The nausea and disorientation were worth the distance they'd put between themselves and the female.

Christopher set his taloned hands down on the red sandstone roof, opening his fingers so Myra and Issa could scramble off his palms. Behind him, there were already about a dozen men hurrying up onto the roof. Dragons didn't drop in on the king unannounced. Certainly not at the speed Christopher had.

But they all must have recognized his dragon because no one had tried to shoot him out of the sky with whatever weapon they had in the two guard towers flanking the mansion. Something to do with fire. She knew enough to know she didn't want personal experience with those weapons.

Instead of firing on him, the twelve men formed up in a wide circle around Christopher, like a guard, and waited.

She recognized some of them as people she'd seen around the mansion on her few visits here. But she hadn't been introduced to any of them so didn't have names.

The swirl of purple-yellow smoke that had accompanied Christopher's shift to his dragon swirled around him again. Both Myra and Issa stepped away, all the way to the line of the circling guards. The swirl hid most of the shift, a reverse process of what had happened on the apartment roof in Hoboken. Large taloned hands shrank into the fog, tail and wings compressed so they were no longer visible, the fog itself shrank, and shrank some more.

When everything settled, the sparkling fog vanishing in a whisp, Christopher stood in the middle of a wide open space on the roof, wearing basically what he'd had on before. His jeans. No shoes now. No shirt. His dark hair mussed. His blue eyes still holding a faint glow of purplish gold.

He wasn't even breathing hard.

And for some reason, she still smelled sugar cookies.

She was going to have to ask about the sugar cookies. He didn't always have that added element to his scent. Just occasionally. Mostly he just smelled like the soap he used and that faint leathery-reptilian underscent of his dragon. There were hints of vanilla all the time, but the smell of actual *cookies* was so strong in that moment, she started to crave cookies.

This was not the time for cookies!

Christopher strode over to them, his brows lowered, giving him a fierce, almost mean look. The scowl bracketing his mouth tight. Issa pulled in a sharp breath and took a step backward.

Myra gave her a look. She'd been okay climbing up into his hand when he'd been gigantic and could breathe fire, but his scowl made her nervous? Weird.

Myra noticed the guards were also straightening and their gazes darted away from Christopher. She just couldn't see how everyone was so intimidated by a man who currently smelled like sugar and vanilla.

She looked back at him. To be fair, the scowl was pretty ferocious. He was not a happy dragon.

"We need to get inside," she said, stepping close to him. "Get Issa away." She lowered her voice. "Her son?"

Christopher glanced at one of the guards.

The guard snapped even straighter, if that was possible, and said, "Arrived moments before you, Highness. They're inside."

Myra heard Issa's sob and turned in time to catch the woman before her legs collapsed out from under her. "Yeah, we need to get her inside."

At a brief nod from Christopher, the guards formed up tighter around him, Myra, and Issa and escorted them all inside.

The roof was an open space, half grass for the younglings to land on, half red sandstone, circled by a low wall decorated with dragon statues. Under normal circumstances, it was a pretty space, giving great views of the surrounding woods and, in one direction, the high spears and lights of Manhattan far below.

But with the threat of an angry female dragon looming, Myra was just as happy to get off the roof.

The entrance to the castle from the roof was through a low ceiling ramp that could be closed off with titanium doors infused with fire-resistant magic. You wanted to defend against dragons, you had to use fire and defend against it.

For the most part, though, dragon shifters fighting dragon shifters hadn't been an issue in Myra's lifetime. She was glad the king had built this place with that possibility in mind, though.

The door rolled down behind them as soon as they were all inside, sealing off the roof entrance. The lights inside came on in a flicker of brightness and then...

"Mommy!"

A tiny whirlwind zipped past Myra and right into Issa's arms. Issa caught the whirlwind with only a single grunt and then a lot of tears and petting dark hair and kissing little cheeks.

The boy looked about seven or eight in human years, but Christopher had said he was only five so maybe he was just big for his age. Myra wasn't much of a judge for kid ages, though. It was good to know what a proper youngling looked like. She realized as she watched the mother and son reunion, this was the first time she'd seen a dragon shifter kid who she knew for sure was a dragon shifter.

Another man strode through the guards and up to Issa and the boy. He was tall, a reasonable sort of tall. Just over six foot. Not as huge as Christopher. Thickly muscled, light blond hair, brown eyes, skin a few shades browner than Issa's. Myra spotted a tattoo along the back of his neck, but she couldn't see the details.

As far as she was aware, shifters lost their tattoos every time they changed shape, so to keep one meant regularly reapplying the tattoo. Lot of time in a chair with needles for body art. She admired the commitment.

"You okay?" the man asked Issa quietly, setting a gentle hand to her back, sort of hugging both Issa and the boy.

"Fine. Fine now. The prince and Myra saved me."

Myra appreciated being given a name in that exchange and not just referred to as "the thief."

The man looked at her and Christopher, bowing his head a little and dropping his gaze to the ground. "Thank you," he said.

Christopher nodded sharply. "Please take Issa to the rooms prepared. You can all rest there."

The man nodded, and Issa, her son, and the man who was obviously the boy's father walked through the circling guard and disappeared around a corner in the mansion.

That Christopher knew there'd be a room ready for the small family spoke well of the mansion staff's efficiency.

"Any signs of the female?" Christopher asked one of the trailing guards as the rest of them turned down a different corridor, heading toward the throne room and the no-doubt waiting king.

"Nothing on radar yet. We've warned air traffic control towers in the area."

"Good thinking," Christopher muttered.

Yeah, Myra thought, last thing they needed was a giant female dragon knocking commercial airliners out of the sky.

She'd read that female dragon shifters were huge, but after seeing Christopher up close and personal, she wondered just how big a female really was. Since they were a lot larger than the males, and Christopher was the size he was in dragon form, that meant the female could be as large as the entire island of Manhattan. And that was utterly terrifying.

"You ever encountered a female dragon before," she murmured to Christopher as they stalked through the corridors. The guard around them peeled off as they went, she presumed to take up defensive positions.

"Not in person," he said.

"Why didn't she…smell you in the warehouse?" Dragons had a good sense of smell. They weren't like werewolves or some of the cat shifters, but their sense of smell was still significantly better than a human's. Christopher and the female should have been able to at least smell each other, right?

"That's complicated." He gave her a sideways look. "There are some things about dragon shifters that aren't…public knowledge."

"Not public knowledge?"

"You'd have to be part of a dragon shifter community to know."

"I see. Is this something you can't tell me?"

"No. It's not that. It's…complicated."

A wash of red swept up his pale cheeks, a blush that for the life of her Myra couldn't understand.

"Later," he promised. "After we deal with the current crisis."

Her curiosity was bursting for answers. But she pressed her lips together to keep them in. He was right.

They had a crisis to deal with first.

CHAPTER TEN

The few times Myra had been inside the throne room, the place had either been empty or a handful of dragon shifters had filled it. It was a huge, high ceiling room with the king's actual throne—a big piece of gold and bone furniture encrusted with precious jewels she hadn't figured out how to steal yet—on a dais across from the giant wooden doors that led into the room.

This day, there were at least a dozen men moving through the room, a sort of controlled chaos of passing around information, working on tablets and phones, everyone seeming to talk at once. There was a table against one wall that hadn't been there before, set up with computers and what looked like a radar system. There was beeping, and shouting, and talking, and so much noise it echoed off the high ceilings.

But it all seemed controlled. The shouting was just to be heard above the din. The rapid-fire conversations intense and focused. The movements around the table and back and forth to the king or out the door calculated and well-choreographed so no one bumped into anyone else.

The king stood to one side of the room, looking at documents put into his hands, or studying something on a tablet held up for him occasionally. His throne was empty, and while she knew it wasn't the time, Myra did indulge in one longing glance at all those imbedded precious stones currently going unnoticed by anyone else in the room.

Christopher hooked a hand through her elbow, which made her wonder if he'd realized where her mind had momentarily strayed, and hurried up to his father. The king currently had his head tilted toward another man who was nearly as tall as Christopher and bore a remarkable resemblance to the king. Dark hair, light eyes, pale skin, a certain cut to his jaw and nose.

Myra's gaze jumped between the man with the king and Christopher. Yeah. There in the mouth. The nose. This must be one of Christopher's brothers.

He had a bunch, apparently, but no one knew quite how many sons the king had, or what they all looked like. Some were known by name in the gossip columns, like Christopher had once been. But even those didn't apparently encompass all the king's offspring. As the king had said on that first day he'd commanded her to go rescue Christopher, there were no pictures of the royal family allowed. Many people knew the king on sight. He was hard to miss and he usually ensured those who saw him knew he was the king. People talked about his looks even if there were no pictures. But the appearances of most of the sons were still illusive and vague.

Coming face-to-face with one of Christopher's brothers sent another bolt of curiosity through her. Shame they had the female dragon to worry about. She had a lot of questions she couldn't ask yet.

Christopher paused at the radar screen, watching the small

glowing green dot on the darker green background. There were other, smaller dots on the screen, all moving away from the larger dot.

"All planes in the area are landing or diverting to other airports, Highness," the man sitting in front of the radar screen told Christopher.

"Good. Is she on her way?"

"She's remained in this spot—" the man gestured to the singular dot, "—the entire time I've been monitoring her. We're not sure what she's doing."

Christopher gave a brief nod, then moved to join his father and —probably?—his brother.

"Tell me," the king said without preamble.

Christopher went over everything that had happened that day, their meeting with Issa at the café—the king cast Myra an unreadable look at that—Issa's kidnapping by the two gunmen from the coffee shop, the chase, the New Jersey warehouse, the sportscar man, and finally the woman.

The king nodded as he listened, his mouth pursed. He snarled at Christopher's description of the woman. His eyes narrowed and, somewhat surprisingly, he cursed under his breath.

She'd witnessed the king angry. Witnessed him pretending to be angry. Seen him barely controlling that anger.

She'd never seen him…nervous.

"That would be Jasmin," he said after a moment. "One of the younger females."

Which, given females lived millennia, could still mean she was thousands of years old. "Young" for a female dragon was relative, so Myra had learned.

"What's all this have to do with a plastic surgeon and insurance fraud?" Myra asked into the silence following the revelation of the female dragon's name.

The king's gaze flicked to her. "Jasmin gathers wealth the way we all do, but she prefers to do it in ways that…give her a charge."

"Illegal stuff," Myra said, shrugging. She got that. She was a thief after all. Though, she didn't really do it for the money anymore. She did it for the fun and the challenge. And the adrenaline rush.

"Illegal," the king murmured. "But more than that. She takes human partners. Manipulates them. Kills them when she's tired of them or they get in her way. Bodies build up around Jasmin when she's working a con." Another unreadable expression crossed the king's features. "All this might be forgiven in another era, but in modern times, given our treaties with the humans, this can be… awkward. She keeps a low profile most of the time. And usually doesn't tangle with other dragons as part of her schemes."

"Maybe she didn't realize anyone at the plastic surgeon's practice had ties to the dragons here." Issa *was* human after all. "At least not when she started her con."

Because Jasmin had absolutely known Issa's son was a dragon by the time they got to that warehouse.

"Incoming," the man at the radar shouted, and everyone in the room stilled.

The silence that fell rang in Myra's ears. People never really thought about it if silence wasn't part of their profession, but *silence* had both weight and sound to it. Sometimes the sound of a space's silence was hard to describe. At that moment, Myra had no trouble describing the silence that had just fallen over the throne room.

It was the silence of collective dread.

The king exchanged a look with the son he hadn't introduced yet. Then with Christopher. All three men looked grim.

Myra glanced between them and the radar screen which had started beeping. The beeping increased. The sound was loud in the quiet room.

Myra wanted to do something, but most of her instincts were the run-and-hide sort. She was a field mouse to this circling hawk, and she very much wanted to go to ground and get very still and wait for the hawk to fly over, hoping it didn't see her.

Except the dragon already knew who she was, and where she was, and there was no hiding from this.

Probably a good thing she was a mouse with a lot of smaller hawk friends. Still. What could even an entire dragon cohort do against one angry female dragon.

Nowhere in anything she'd ever researched had she learned how a female dragon could be killed. The males could be killed. They lived centuries and were incredibly *hard* to kill. But it could be done. Nothing she'd read, that was publicly available, had hinted at a way to kill a female dragon.

Was it even possible?

And, given there were only twelve in the world, was it…right? Jasmin didn't sound like a nice person. Actually, she sounded like a serial killer to Myra, though it was hard to judge dragons by human standards. But she was one of twelve. One of so very few living female dragons. Even if they could kill her, *should* they try?

Would Jasmin even give the cohort a choice?

The beeping had gotten so loud, so persistent, Myra could practically feel the presence of the dragon overhead. Circling the compound, a shadow over the city. Her heartbeat seemed to have sped up with the beeping too, until it was pounding so hard in her chest it almost hurt. She liked a good adrenaline rush and that touch of fear as much as the next person, but this was too much, even for her.

"What do we do?" she finally blurted out into the tense silence.

The man who the king hadn't introduced yet, who might well be another one of his son's, said, "We negotiate with her and hope she leaves."

Myra looked toward the radar screen and the incessant beeping. "That doesn't sound…"

"Likely," Christopher finished for her.

"And what would you have us do?" the possible brother asked Christopher. "We can't remain locked down inside the mansion forever. There are innocent humans in the city we have to worry about if she gets very angry."

"She doesn't want to bring the human world down on her," Christopher said, sounding very reasonable. Myra latched onto that reasonable tone of voice to calm her fears. "Having human militaries from around the world hunting her will never suit. She won't be able to rest. And if she destroys this world, or rallies the other females to try, it will leave her with no games to play." Christopher shrugged. "There's also the very real likelihood one of the other females will not take kindly to the way Jasmin courts disaster."

Oh. Wow. The thought of another female dragon fighting with Jasmin seemed like it might not go well for all the unfortunate human settlements below them.

"Then we negotiate," the possible brother said with a firm nod.

"Negotiate what?" Christopher said.

"We turn over the human she wants," the brother said.

"No," Christopher and Myra said at the same time.

Where Christopher had that hissing growl in his voice, Myra's sounded almost like a snarl. Given the circumstances, she was surprised she could snarl at a dragon shifter who stood easily a foot taller than her and was twice as wide and could snap her like a twig. But given what was circling overhead, the possible brother seemed like less of a threat.

That was saying something.

"We negotiate," the king said, his voice firm. "We turn over no one as sacrifice." He glanced at Christopher. "The time of feeding virgins to dragons is done."

Myra was glad to hear that. Not that she was a virgin. Nor was Issa for that matter. But still, she appreciated the confirmation.

"What do you intend on offering her, then, father?" the now confirmed, but still unnamed son asked.

The king's gaze dropped to Myra, and Christopher immediately stepped in front of her.

"I said we turn over no sacrifices," the king growled, his eyes narrowing at his son.

"Myra has done enough," Christopher said. "She's not part of this."

"Jasmin knows of her. She is now."

And didn't that just suck.

"Jasmin gathers a not insignificant amount of her wealth in a hoard in New Jersey," the king said. "If she knew that hoard was vulnerable, she would be willing to negotiate a…compromise."

Myra noticed he didn't say a peace. She had a feeling Jasmin didn't do "peace."

"Where's this hoard and how hard is it to break into?" Myra asked. She knew a job offer when she heard one. "Also, I do this for you? This is absolutely the last job. Got it?"

The unnamed son frowned and looked between her and the king. Christopher remained standing in front of her, but he didn't speak up or try to prevent her from considering the king's suggestion.

"Her hoard is…not as difficult as mine was to access. She's a female. No one would dare try for her hoard. Not even master thieves."

Myra's mouth twitched with a smile she refused to release. And no, she wasn't preening or delighted by the king calling her a master thief. This was not a preening situation. It wouldn't do for the king to know he could compliment her into taking one of his jobs either. Bad enough he knew her soft spot for a challenge.

"Also, the location of her hoard is not generally known, whereas mine…is."

"But you know where she keeps her hoard," Myra said.

"This part of it anyway. It is not her only collection. But any of them being vulnerable will…give her pause."

"Pause long enough for the rest of us to grow old and die before she decides to start making trouble again?"

"Long enough for her to not lay siege to Manhattan for another century."

That sounded good. Myra was likely to be dead by the time that century passed. Jasmin would be someone else's problem then.

She cut off any thought of where Christopher would be in a century. That was a long time off and they had more than enough to think about right now.

"Okay." Myra straightened her shoulders. She could do this. If this would get Jasmin to go away and leave everyone, including Issa, alone, then she could do this. This was even better motivation than a bet. And she'd only sworn off breaking into a dragon *king's* hoard. She'd never promised herself she'd stay out of *all* dragon hoards. "Where am I going? Specifically."

"I'm going with you," Christopher said, quietly. But his voice carried through the mostly silent throne room.

Except for the beeping that indicated a terrifying female dragon was circling overhead and the conversation the king, his two sons, and Myra were having, the rest of the throne room remained silent. Watching. Listening.

Waiting.

CHAPTER ELEVEN

Getting to the wooded area not far from Trenton without being seen sneaking out of the king's compound by the female dragon circling overhead had proved less complicated than Myra had feared. The king went out onto the roof to negotiate with Jasmin. Jasmin had landed and shifted.

And the minute she was in human form instead of dragon form, Myra and Christopher had taken flight from a position much farther down the hill. An exit that, ironically, was only accessible through the king's hoard.

Christopher watched her closely as they went through, which, if she were being honest, was a little insulting. Yes, yes, all the piles of sparkly shinys were a bit distracting. But not when the potential for all of Manhattan to be laid waste by an angry female dragon was on the line.

Christopher had cloaked and then flown at that speed she hadn't realized was possible until the escape from Jasmin. A speed that blurred the surroundings and made her cling tight to his neck as much for the warmth of his body as the worry about just how fast they were going. She couldn't even really enjoy the adrenaline rush, the speed of it all, because she was too aware of what she'd left back at the king's mansion.

The hoard was in an underground compound, accessed by a single door hidden in the woods, at a specific set of coordinates the king had given Christopher and which he seemed able to pinpoint without GPS, which was pretty impressive. But the location was surrounded by tightly packed trees and difficult to get to by flight. Christopher couldn't just land next to the door without risking the delicate membranes stretched between bone on his wings. He had to find a clearing, and they had to hike in to the door.

Door was maybe a little grand for the entrance. More like a secured metal cover over a hole, similar to a manhole cover, only bigger. Roughly four feet in diameter. If there wasn't some sort of hydraulic mechanism that lifted that big slab of copper, she'd have had a hard time lifting it out of the way without Christopher.

The copper plated disk wasn't just locked either. The minute Myra hovered her hand over the thing, she felt the crinkling static of magic. Lots of magic. More than the typical dragon usually had around their things.

"Do female dragons do magic?" she murmured as she explored the spells with her eyes closed, teasing out the base of them so she could find a way to crack them.

"Not like wizards. Or even you. Not spells."

"She hired someone to do this, then," Myra said. "Because this is thief magic." Not wizard magic. This magic had the…flavor, she supposed. The flavor of her own special brand of power. And it was old. These spells had been here for a while.

"Can you break them?" Christopher sounded worried.

"So little faith," she muttered as she dug through the spells, looking for the key to the lock and… Ah. There it was. Tricky tricky, former thief whoever they were.

It took a bit of finessing and a lot more of her own magic than she usually had to use. Picking at the spells and teasing them far enough apart to insert the metaphorical magic key took her a good ten minutes. Much longer than she would have liked. But to rush this would have set off an alarm. An alarm she was certain Jasmin would know about instantly.

The king was giving her time by negotiating with Jasmin. If Myra tipped her hand too soon, the entire plan was ruined and the king might end up dead before Myra even knew she'd fucked up.

Thinking about the consequences usually screwed up her concentration, so she kept her focus on the magical tangle and when she finally broke through the spells, the mental *click* was supremely satisfying.

She eased back onto her haunches and pressed the center of the disk. It hissed open, lifting about an inch before stopping.

"You're up," she said to Christopher. "You can safely lift it off and set it aside now. Please and thank you."

That last earned her a small smile.

Christopher lifted the heavy disk like it weighed a few pounds instead of probably closer to several hundred pounds, and Myra tried not to admire his muscles as he did because, again, not the moment.

The opening beneath the disk revealed a long, round tunnel and ladder which went so deep into the ground, the darkness closed in like a fist, the sunny winter afternoon light barely reaching four feet into the concrete pipe. She pulled a glow stick from one of her vest pockets and cracked it, letting it drop into the tunnel.

It went a long way down.

The sound of it hitting the ground was also very faint.

Along the way, it lit up the narrow pipe and ladder. She'd be able to slip down the tunnel easily enough, but it was going to be tight for Christopher. She supposed that was on purpose, as only another dragon was likely to want to break into a dragon's hoard. Humans were not typically that suicidal.

She wasn't either. Just…more motivated by challenge than the next human.

Glancing back at Christopher, she confirmed he'd shifted his wings away. Then pulled out another glow stick and broke it, looping it through a cloth tab in her vest so she had her hands free to climb down the ladder.

"I'll go first," Christopher said. "In case there are traps below."

"What if they're magical traps? Probably specifically designed for dragons since this whole set up seems designed to keep dragons out?"

His jaw worked as he looked over her shoulder into the concrete pipe. They couldn't see the glow stick below anymore. She'd barely been able to see it before hearing the *chink chink* sound of it hitting the ground. She considered that Christopher might be able to still see it. Or he could see in the dark well enough, he had a good view down the tunnel. Her night vision was excellent, a part of the magic that made her such an excellent thief, but her vision didn't compare to a shapeshifter's.

"You can guard me from above, if someone tries to follow us down the tunnel," she said, by way of mollifying his need to protect. "Will that help? Make you feel better?"

"No. But you can go first." He tilted his head to one side, then the other, as if loosening muscles in his neck. "There's no way for me to open wings in that pipe."

"I know. On purpose. We'll be okay."

She rose up and gave him a very solid, very firm kiss right on the mouth. A move that startled him enough he didn't react immediately. Then he pulled her into a tight grip, his hands on her waist, bringing her up on her toes. The height difference between them was sometimes ridiculous, but she loved it. The power, the strength so casually displayed, the desperation just under his kiss all made her blood sing.

She pulled back as quickly as she'd jumped in. But now her skin tingled. Her body buzzed with energy. And the fear coiling in her gut tipped toward excitement.

"We've got this." She grinned and patted his bare chest. "It'll be fun."

He didn't smile back. His hands flexed in her vest, tightening around her convulsively, before he let her go.

She slid down onto the ladder, tempted to just slide down the rails to the ground because it was so far below, but she worried about traps along the way, so a slow descent it was.

Relatively slow. They only had so much time.

As much time as the king could manage to stall an angry female dragon.

Before she decided to just light the world on fire.

Chapter Twelve

T he darkness closed around Myra, leaving a tiny halo of fading sunlight above which was mostly blocked by Christopher as he moved down into the tunnel. The green light from the glow stick fastened to her vest provided a bubble of illumination, enough for her to ensure her grip and footing on the ladder, enough she could search for traps in her immediate area. But she couldn't see very far below her feet.

Myra was comfortable in the dark. She loved the dark. It hid all sorts of comings and goings and made her job infinitely easier. She *lived* in the dark.

But this was a different kind of dark. She'd heard this kind of dark, the blackness that had weight to it, called stygian darkness. That word had never felt more appropriate than it did just then.

She was *aware* of the earth beyond the concrete pipe that cut through the soil. She was aware of the weight of that earth closing in around them. A little too aware that this tube with its narrow circumference and thin ladder had been built by a dragon shifter determined to protect the wealth buried beneath. The entire thing could be a trap, seal off, burying her and Christopher alive.

Myra hadn't ever really thought about being buried alive. Her jobs had never taken her into places that gave that impression. Even the king's hoard, buried as it was beneath his mansion into the rocky foundation of the hills on which the compound sat, hadn't given her this feeling.

There had been something…open about getting to the king's hoard. A sense that she could get back out again.

This space felt like it was swallowing her. The darkness devouring and dissolving her until she would cease to exist.

The feeling was so strong she started hunting for illusion spells and panic spells on the ladder.

"You feeling this?" she murmured up to Christopher. "A kind of panic as we go deeper?"

He grunted, a sound which could mean anything but she interpreted it as a yes.

If he was feeling this dread, though, it probably meant magic. But she couldn't feel anything in the ladder. She would have picked that up immediately.

Spells like this needed an anchor. She called up a warning to Christopher and then paused to set her fingers against the pipe's wall.

Well shit. "Spell in the concrete. All of it. The entire pipe is bespelled."

"We should get out."

"It's a panic spell. Designed to drive us back up. Only way out now is through. So to speak." She let her own magic drift through the puzzle of the spell on the walls. "Yeah, I can't break this. It's too extensive. But it's not dangerous. Technically. It's just designed to fuck with your thinking. So just… Ignore your own thoughts until after we reach the bottom."

"My own thoughts are telling me what we'll find at the bottom will be worse than this spell."

"Exactly what they would be telling you under the influence of this spell." She started back down the ladder.

Ignoring panic and fear and the sense of being destroyed the farther down the tunnel she went was not as easy as she'd made it sound. The feeling grabbed onto her lizard brain, triggering her flight instincts so strongly she had to clamp her lips tightly together to keep from shouting up at Christopher to climb out of the tunnel again.

She physically had to force herself not to scramble back up the ladder. Force herself, rung by rung, to keep moving downward.

Given the level of wealth and treasure beneath her, the desire to run away was so contrary to her natural instincts, it was amazing. That contrast, that disconnect from how she'd usually face these sorts of situations, allowed her to keep moving when the panic pushed her so hard it made breathing difficult.

They reached the ground suddenly, the light from her previous glow stick having winked out already. Not even a faint glow, which was weird. Like the darkness ate light.

She realized the glow stick in her vest was fading fast too and quickly cracked another one. She only had a few more after this, so she had to hope whatever was eating the light down here—probably the dread spells worked into the pipe walls—still gave her enough time to get them back out again.

The pipe ended in a dirt floor and…nothing else. No obvious doors or exits or passages into the other parts of the hoard. She knew this wasn't the end of it. If she hadn't had the kind of magic she had, she might have been fooled. Might have thought she'd forced her way through all that horrible fear and panic for nothing.

But her fingertips were tingling and anticipation hummed in her gut. There was treasure here somewhere. Nearby. Close enough she could practically smell it. And she didn't have a shifter's sense of smell.

"Dead end?" Christopher asked, sounding appalled.

He was still on the ladder because there wasn't enough room at the bottom of the pipe for them to both stand on the ground without being wrapped around each other. While that sounded delightful in a different setting, she needed room to study the walls and ground.

"There's something here," she murmured. "I can feel it. Just have to find it."

She studied the walls, squatted to run her fingers over the dirt floor. As she neared one particular part of the floor, at the joint where the ground met the pipe, she felt an increase in the dread and panic. A punch to her lizard brain that robbed her of breath. It was like getting hit with a shock of electricity, but electricity made of panic that wrapped around her most primitive instincts.

She grinned. There it was.

Running her fingers over the spot, ignoring the churning in her gut and the way her body hair raised, she dug around until she found the metal ring. Like a thick chainlink, imbedded into the dirt. She tugged it up and into view, dirt drifting around it and throwing up the scent of dry mustiness and sand. A quick study confirmed a small locking spell on the link. Nothing complicated. Just a lock that made pulling up the full chain impossible.

She only needed thirty seconds to crack the spell, though she had to wave Christopher to silence once before he broke her concentration. Once she had the spell cracked, she grinned up at him and tugged hard on the link. A chain rose up out of the ground.

And a crack appeared at the base of one section of the pipe.

"Here, you pull this. You're the one with the muscles."

He raised a sardonic eyebrow at her, which she could only just see in the fading green light. She was tempted to crack another glow stick, but they were so close to getting out of the pipe, she resisted. They might need those sticks later.

As Christopher pulled on the chain, dragging it up through the dirt like a magic trick, the tiny bit of space that had appeared grew, raising an entire section of the concrete pipe until a person-sized doorway appeared.

Beyond that doorway was more darkness. But Myra's fingertips were tingling hard now. Treasure. Close.

She tried not to giggle because, really, this wasn't her normal sort of heist. But still. She was breaking into another hoard. And there was something so *satisfying* in that accomplishment.

Christopher stopped her walking through the black hole in the tunnel with an arm across her chest. She looked up at him with a raised brow.

"Breaking in is the point," he said. "We aren't here to empty her hoard. Just get one thing to prove we've been here."

"Same as when I broke into your father's hoard," she said with a shrug. "I realize making an enemy of a female dragon is a bad idea."

Even though it was already too late. She'd already made an enemy. One she really didn't want. But the job was done. This was just the icing on the hate cake.

"This is to make a point," Christopher reiterated. "One that will force Jasmin to back off. We hope. So we don't take anything too valuable that she'll miss."

"I get it," she told him. "I do. Don't worry. I know what I'm doing."

The difference here was that Jasmin didn't have a cohort of fellow dragons to capture Myra in the act. Female dragons were loners, independent, kept to themselves. There was no cohort. And Christopher could take care of any unlucky humans Jasmin might have hired to live down here and guard her hoard.

Even that seemed unlikely, though. Dragons did *not* like anyone inside their hoards. Even guards.

Christopher held her gaze for a beat, then nodded and finally dropped off the ladder, landing lightly on the dirt floor next to her. They were still inside the pipe so they were pressed tight together. The feel of his heat enveloping her was exactly as delicious as she'd expected. Also a little distracting.

Still, she leaned into him, and he set his hands to her shoulders, holding her close for a moment as they both contemplated the black hole opening before them.

"More traps?" he murmured against her hair.

"Probably. But not on the doorway." On the other side… She'd have to go through the doorway to see.

"Can I at least go first this time?"

"Nope." She had to go first to look out for spells still. "You guard our backs, big guy. I've got our fronts. We've got this."

She felt his chest expand and contract behind her with his deep breath. The release of that breath ruffled the top of her hair. The bun she'd wrapped her hair into had loosened enough over the course of the day for fine strands to stick to her temples. The air at this depth should have been cold, freezing even. And it was chilled. But not as cold as it should have been. And between that and Christopher's heat at her back, Myra felt sweat start to trickle down her cheeks.

She gave in to the need to see, cracked a third glow stick, and held it in front of her as they moved through the black doorway. Christopher kept his hands on her shoulders, ready to pull her away from danger. She tried not to think about the danger, to concentrate on the treasure ahead that she could *feel*.

But she was very grateful she had Christopher at her back.

Chapter Thirteen

A short, dark, metal tunnel that Christopher had to duck to walk through closed in around them as they passed through the black doorway. Myra wasn't claustrophobic, but the tightness of the space made her very aware of all the earth above. She wasn't sure if that awareness was part of the magical panic she'd felt coming down the ladder or if this was just common sense and survival instincts, but she was glad the tunnel was short this time.

It opened out onto a larger room, with enough space for Christopher to finally stand his full height. The room was just a giant steel box. Without much to recommend it. A dry, dusty smell, so no mold which was good. And a low level of heat seemed to emanate from the walls. Not enough to make her sweat, though she was doing that thanks to Christopher's heat at her back, but enough to keep the room from being as chilled as an underground bunker should have been.

"That heat a spell?" she asked, moving closer to one of the walls to hold her hand in front of it. Definitely warmer than buried metal should be. "Not, like, deadly radiation or anything, right?"

The tingle of a spell along her palm helped assure her this was magic. Still, she glanced back at Christopher with her brows raised in question.

"Not radiation," he said. "That would kill Jasmine eventually, too."

Interesting to learn something would kill a female dragon. Even if it did take a while. "Only if she spent enough time down here."

"This is part of her hoard. She spends time here."

That peaked Myra's curiosity. "Do you hang out in your hoard a lot?"

"There doesn't seem to be a hoard of anything here," he said, avoiding her question. She suspected if the light hadn't been green from her glow stick, she might have seen him blush.

"There's another door around here," she said. "This would be an antechamber. Like in mummy tombs and stuff."

"How do you know that?"

"I know treasure rooms," she said. She'd been in a few in her time. "Your father has a nice antechamber for his hoard. Designed to look like you've found the hoard with lots of valuables in it. Pretty clever actually. If a thief didn't know better. Lot of traps in that room."

She glanced at Christopher long enough to see his mouth twitch, but he schooled his features before she could tell if he was about to grin or scowl. Shame. She could have used his grin at that moment. Scowl could have been nice, too. He looked sexy either way.

She continued walking the perimeter of the room, her hand out to her side, hovering just in front of the wall without touching it. The tingles of magic were pleasant, like the feel of the warmth from the wall. Nothing stinging or irritating or sending out little electrical shocks. Or even the dread she'd felt in the vertical pipe.

"Glad it's not lighting up my lizard brain anymore," she muttered.

"That was…uncomfortable."

She snort-laughed. "Understatement. Ah. Here we go." She ran her hand above an area of wall that definitely felt different. Less heat. Less magic tingling over her palm. No, not less. Different. There was a different magic here. Not dread or warning, though.

"The lock." She wagged her eyebrows at Christopher.

She was probably having too much fun, given what was at stake. But being on the scent of treasure, now that she had a lock to crack, with untold riches just the other side of the door, the thrill of the hunt thrummed in her blood. She'd felt similarly cracking the lock on the copper disk covering the tunnel up in the woods. But now she *knew* she was close. *Knew* the hoard was just beyond this wall.

Only one more trap. One more lock. The king was right. This wasn't as hard as breaking into his hoard had been. Not easy. But not hard. For someone like her.

Christopher walked up behind her as she had her eyes half closed, working her way through this last trap.

Quietly, most of her attention on the bespelled lock, she said, "Jasmin depended on the dread spell worked into the concrete of the vertical pipe. I can see why. Most people wouldn't have been motivated to work their way through that even with the treasure at the other end."

"Would you? If you didn't have your current motivation of preventing Manhattan from burning?"

She shrugged. "Maybe. Oh. There we go."

She felt the little snick as she hit the spot in the trap that released the pressure and let the spell dissipate. She wasn't entirely sure what would have happened if she'd triggered the spell rather than broken it. Probably killed her. But she thought better of mentioning that out loud.

One more check. Nothing in the way. She set her hand to the pressure plate in the wall and pushed. A lot of clicking and whirring and noise echoed around the room. The entire room.

She stepped away from the wall, to the center of the square space. She'd been expecting a door to open, like an ordinary door. Instead, the room all around them creaked and hitched and slid. Metal over metal. Churning clink of metal chains and things spinning.

The room folded back on itself, starting from the ceiling, folding open, then down the walls, the room disappearing panel by panel until it had folded completely into the floor.

Myra blinked. "Huh."

She held up her glow stick. The light broke through the darkness now surrounding them, but not very far. Only enough to reveal the room they now stood in was immense, rising up high above them and spreading out around them.

They'd been led into the center of a chamber, into a box that had been *inside* the huge, cavernous room. And with that box gone…

The hoard spread out around them.

Her glow stick only revealed the edges of it. The piles and piles of…sparkling stuff. Myra sighed and her heart beat harder. So many sparkly things. Even the edges of the treasure awed her. Made her yearn.

She loved treasure.

"Beautiful," she whispered. And even her whisper echoed.

"Are you going to cry?" Christopher asked.

"Maybe."

She eased forward, to the closest pile of stuff. Gold goblets, and boxes, and bars of gold all draped with gold chains and coins. And in the middle of all that gold, multi-colored precious and semiprecious stones winked in a rainbow. And where there were clear diamonds, they caught the green light of her glow stick and made strange prisms.

"We need something that will assure Jasmin we've been to her hoard and not just picked up something from another hoard," Christopher said.

"I suppose that would have been an option for someone who has a hoard." She glanced back at him, eyebrows raised.

He didn't rise to the bait this time either. "That necklace. The one with the diamond medallion on it. That's old. Older than the things surrounding it. That would do."

She nodded, shrugged. But she'd spotted something she thought might work better. "How about this?"

Lifting the little cut diamond dragon from the middle of all that gold, she held it up to her glow stick. Green light skittered over the cuts in the miniature statue. The dragon was exquisite. Each angle and curve intricately detailed. All the detail turned the diamond dragon into repeating prisms of light inside light. The dragon was sitting on its hind legs, its tail wrapped around its feet, like a cat. Wings open and angled backward, but not spread out to the side. Thick body, long neck, head arched down so the dragon looked like it was looking at something near its feet.

"There's another statue that goes with this one," Myra said.

"How do you know that?"

"Guessing, but the way the dragon is looking down? Just gives that impression." Years of studying valuable objects gave her an instinct for that kind of thing, too. She searched the pile they stood before with a sweeping gaze and didn't see anything immediately that might fit the bill. "We don't have time for a thorough search, do we?"

The longing in her voice was a little embarrassing.

"No. That'll have to do. Let's get out of here." He turned in a slow circle. "How, exactly, do we get out of here?"

The short tunnel they'd moved through to get to the box that had now disappeared was nowhere to be found. Neither was the vertical tunnel they'd climbed down to get this deep underground.

"That's a cloaking spell," she said. "The tunnels are still there. Just invisible."

"Why can't I see through the cloak?" he asked.

"Could you normally?"

"Normally. It's part of dragon physiology, the cloaking, but there are hints that other dragon's pick up."

Interesting. "This isn't a dragon cloak. It's a sort of illusion spell. So maybe that's why you can't see it."

She returned to the area where the box had been and Christopher followed, still frowning at their surroundings. "You do know how to leave, right?"

"I know how to leave," she said.

Escape plans were always part of the plan. Though sometimes she had to make those plans in the moment and under duress. But she was always looking for the ways to get out.

She stepped close to the area where she'd found the pressure plate to lower the steel box and pressed her foot to the floor in a few places till she found the pressure plate there. This one wasn't bespelled or trapped. It was just there. But if you didn't know what you were looking for, this would be the last level of trap. A thief got in, but then couldn't find a way out.

Only a non-thief would assume that. Which was good for her and Christopher. Jasmin wasn't omnipotent in her security.

The instant she pressed the floor plate, Myra stepped back close to Christopher, tucking her diamond dragon statue into one of her inner vest pockets where it would be safe. Another series of chunking sounds and heavy chains running fast, and then the walls started to come up again, plates unfolding around them, reforming the box room. It was a fun old process to watch, though she did worry about Christopher's head. Fortunately, the box was tall enough for him.

Once it reformed, the opening for the short passage back to the pipe leading up to the ground level opened. It had been there, invisible because of the cloaking spell, but sealed. The box room was necessary to opening that passage to the pipe.

This time, there was no hesitation. From short tunnel to already open antechamber, from antechamber into the narrow pipe, and up the ladder as fast as they could manage to reach the light. If she could have slid up that ladder, she would have.

There was no more dread going in this direction either. In fact, there was almost a push of exhilaration. *Yes! You're going the right way now. Get out. Get out now!*

When she hit the top of the pipe, she scrambled out into the late evening sun, so low now, the forested area was deep in shadows and the sky was starting to turn that shade of purplish orange that came with sunset. The cold air felt like a needed slap in the face after the heat underground.

Or maybe that was just the heat of her anxiety.

Now that they were out, now that she'd done the thing, instead of triumph, all she could think about was Issa and her son in the king's mansion. And Jasmin on the roof facing the king.

Enough time had passed, the entire island of Manhattan might be alight, despite their efforts. A low level of panic started to crawl across her nerves, making her jumpy and jittery.

Christopher emerged from the pipe right behind her, leaping up to the ground from the top ladder rung rather than just crawling out the way Myra had.

Show off.

His wings snapped open instantly, but they still couldn't just fly upward from this position because there were too many trees and tree cover in the way.

"Let me carry you," he said. "We need to move fast."

"You can run fast, too? I thought dragons weren't as fast on the ground as in the air." She jumped into his arms without hesitation, though.

"We're like crocodiles," he said, pausing long enough to meet her gaze. "Slow on the ground is a relative description."

She blinked and he was running. Fast enough she tightened her hold around his neck.

They hit the clearing in a rush, his wings snapped open behind him, and he leapt upward in the space of a heartbeat. They were airborne before Myra's stomach had caught up with the rest of her body.

Laughter would have been inappropriate, but it bubbled in her throat nonetheless because that sort of adrenaline rush was a hit of dopamine to her. But as they climbed, as Christopher blurred their surroundings with his flight speed and cloak, the anxiety returned. There were no signs of smoke or flames on the horizon. Manhattan wasn't on fire. Yet.

But as they raced back to the compound, Myra kept her full attention on the hill where the mansion was. She couldn't see anything clearly at this speed.

Didn't stop her watching anxiously for the red and orange flickering of flames.

Chapter Fourteen

The mansion was still standing by the time they reached it, circling overhead once before landing on the roof.

Which was now, ominously empty.

There'd been no signs of Jasmin's dragon in the air. And no one on the roof anymore. Which was why Christopher chose to land there instead of returning the way they'd left, through the secret passage that went through the king's hoard. Part of Myra was sort of disappointed about that. She'd wanted to see the hoard again. But most of her was focused on…

"Where is everyone? What's happening?"

Christopher didn't answer—he couldn't know any more than she did, obviously—but his jaw tightened and a muscle there jumped.

They landed lightly, but Christopher didn't put her down immediately and she didn't try to get down immediately. If they had to take flight again quickly, better to be ready to go. The large door that led into the mansion was closed. Christopher didn't move closer to it, just waited.

A heartbeat that felt like an eternity, and the door *kachinked* and then slid upward. Myra's pulse pounded so hard she could hear it, knew Christopher would hear it too. They watched as that door got high enough legs were visible beneath. Beautiful legs in high heels.

Not the dragon king's legs.

Myra swallowed. She was about to pat Christopher's shoulder, encourage him to take off again. Except…

His father. His brother. Issa and her son and her son's father. They were all in there. Somewhere.

When the door fully opened, Jasmin stood in the center of the wide entrance, in human form, her mouth turned down.

And behind her, the dragon king flanked by his son and a handful of his guard.

Myra felt such a shudder of relief she was glad she wasn't standing. Her knees would have given out and that would have been embarrassing.

Jasmin walked toward them, her gaze intent, but she didn't shift and she didn't hurry. The king followed, at a slower pace, Christopher's brother at his side. The remaining guards waited inside the tunnel.

When she was within fifty yards, Jasmin said, "Did you do it?"

Myra flicked a glance at the king. He lifted his chin in a brief nod. She felt Christopher's arms tighten around her back and legs before he set her slowly onto her feet. He remained at her back and she could practically feel his coiled muscles, ready to move.

Myra didn't approach Jasmin. She reached, slowly, into her pocket and without a word, pulled out the diamond dragon. Held it up for Jasmin to see. It caught the dying sunlight, winking and sparkling like fire.

Appropriate.

The silence that followed felt like it should have caused birds to take flight and animals to scurry into holds. The kind of silence that came with shadows of dread. That sort of silence that meant the hawk was passing overhead.

Myra didn't pull the dragon back but she didn't try to hand it to Jasmin either. She stood with her hand extended, watching Jasmin watch the light dancing in the miniature statue.

When Jasmin looked up and met Myra's gaze, her eyes were black. Solid, impenetrable black.

"You did it."

Myra held perfectly still, unsure what to do now. Christopher moved close enough to her back she could feel his body brushing against hers. There was some comfort in his heat, in the wall of muscle and safety he represented.

Some comfort.

Jasmin glanced back at the king.

The king shrugged, a sort of *I told you so* gesture.

Jasmin's jaw tightened, her full lips pursed. She looked back at Myra. "You win."

Win? Win…what, exactly?

"Keep it," Jasmin said, nodding to the diamond dragon. "It doesn't work without the other part."

Wait, what? Work? What was she talking about?

Myra frowned, but before she could so much as open her mouth to ask, and with a suddenness that had her stumbling back into Christopher, Jasmin shifted to her full dragon form.

The female dragon was…just huge. Myra had thought Christopher was big, but Jasmin's dragon was so tall, her shadow covered the hillside. Her scales were a blackish purple, with lines of orange across her stomach. There were spikes along her back, and tipping her long tail. And her wings. Her wings were so wide, they filled Myra's view. Black as a bat's wings, with a shimmering iridescence that reminded Myra of a geode.

She'd barely had time to take in the massive creature, when the dragon launched into the air, smoothly and so gracefully, there wasn't even a buffeting breeze. By the time Myra looked up, the female was gone. Cloaked or flew away just that fast, she wasn't sure.

Didn't matter.

The female dragon was gone.

Myra blinked up at Christopher. His gaze tracked through the sky for a moment longer before he looked down at her.

"What just happened?" she murmured.

"You won the bet I made with her," the king said, pulling both Myra and Christopher's attention back to him.

"Bet?" she asked.

"I learned that from you. Fortunately, this time, it worked."

And the dragon king smiled.

Chapter Fifteen

They settled in a comfortable room that was half library, half recreation room. Decorated in dark woods and thick patterned carpets over hard wood floors polished to a shine. Half the walls covered in floor to ceiling bookshelves packed with books. The other half of the room contained card tables, a pool table, a couple of dart boards, and even a few old-fashioned arcade games, though Myra wasn't sure how arcade games and comfortable seats to read went together. The lighting was low, the fire was lit, casting a warm glow around the large but cozy room. And the whiskey was plentiful.

Myra didn't drink often. Dulled senses irritated her. Most of the time. But this was one night when a drink and dulled senses seemed preferable.

The king, his other son—who's name she still hadn't gotten—Issa and the father of her son, along with Christopher and Myra sat in soft, cushioned chairs in the library side of the room, near the fire. Issa's son was being entertained by two of his father's friends. This wasn't a conversation for a child.

"I can't believe she accepted a bet," Myra said, taking another sip of her whiskey.

The idea that the king had pulled that off… It felt like a coup. Like he should win an award for thinking of it. The fact that he gave her credit for the idea instead of claiming it was all his own brilliance left her feeling a little edgy, though. She didn't trust him, or his motivation for crediting her. Felt like a trap of its own.

She was just too tired to sort that part out.

"Jasmin didn't believe any human could possibly manage it," the king said with a shrug. "She didn't believe me when I said you'd broken into my hoard. And she was smug when I bet her that you would breach hers." He shrugged and swirled the whiskey in his cut-crystal glass. "Her arrogance has always been her weakness."

"She's really going to leave me alone?" Issa asked. "Our son?"

"She really is," the king assured. "There's nothing to be done about either of your former bosses I'm afraid. If she didn't kill Dr. Camden before giving chase earlier, she will go kill him now. Dr. Butler was already dead when Jasmin's people picked you up."

The story made Myra's head spin. Or maybe that was the whiskey.

Jasmin had partnered with Dr. Butler to test the waters of a larger insurance fraud scheme she had in mind. It was a game for Jasmin, making money at the expense of other humans. And this particular scheme apparently appealed to her. The plastic surgeons practice was her testing ground to ensure things worked.

When Issa blew the whistle on the scam, Jasmin blamed the two partners for not sufficiently covering their tracks. She'd killed Dr. Butler over it already. She'd kidnapped Issa for information, so the same mistakes weren't made the next time she attempted the scheme. Then she'd intended on killing Issa and the other partner in the business, the man Myra had been thinking of as sportscar man but whose name was Dr. Harry Camden.

Probably they should have tried to save Dr. Camden's life. But by the time Myra learned that his life was in danger, it would have been too late. And anyway, he'd endangered Issa and her son over greed. Myra wasn't particularly sorry he was no longer a threat.

Myra understood greed. She embraced her own. She was a thief after all. But she drew the line at her avarice destroying other people's lives. It's why she stole from the already obscenely wealthy. She didn't take some poor working mom's last dollar. She stole valuables from the people who wouldn't miss them and from corporations that hoarded wealth. She picked her marks very carefully.

Which was why she only worked for herself. Or had until the dragons came into her life.

She glanced at Christopher, the one dragon she wanted in her life. He sat next to her in a large, low backed chair, slouched in the seat, his long legs stretched out in front of him and crossed at the ankles. He looked relaxed enough outwardly, but she saw the tension in his fingers as he cupped his own whiskey glass in one hand, tapping it gently on the chair's armrest. His gaze was turned down, focused on the slight bounce of liquid in his glass, not looking at the others. He didn't look happy. But no one in the room looked happy, even though they'd technically won the night.

Jasmin had gone. Everyone—or most everyone—was safe. Manhattan hadn't been burned to the ground by an angry female dragon. And Myra had, yet again, pulled off a heist no one thought she could do.

And she got a pretty, sparkling diamond dragon statue out of the mix.

She would love to know what Jasmin had meant by "it doesn't

work without the other part" but she intended on researching that when she got home.

The somber mood was probably just shock, she realized. Everyone a little shellshocked from having to deal with a female dragon. Even the king didn't look nearly as smug as he should have after besting Jasmin.

Issa blinked hard at her mostly untouched whiskey and then looked up at her son's father. No one had introduced him yet either. The dragons weren't very good at introductions.

"We should go check on Matias," she said.

The father nodded and offered her his hand as he stood. Myra hid a smile in her drink. Nice to see two parents who weren't together anymore get along like that. And who knew…

She was sometimes a hopeless romantic. She glanced at Christopher again. Her heart did a little dance in her chest, making her feel giddy.

Yeah. She was definitely hopeless.

He caught her gaze, his brooding expression softening. "If you're ready, I can take you home now, too." He glanced at his brother. "Just need a few minutes."

"Take your time. Didn't have any appointments tonight."

By which she meant, she was still in the planning process for her next theft. Although, after today's dragon hoard raid, her original heist seemed so much less challenging as to be pointless now.

Christopher stood slowly and his brother followed suit, walking ahead of Christopher out of the room. Chistopher stopped beside her before following his brother, setting a hand on her shoulder and giving her a gentle smile.

"Last job for my father," he said. "I promise."

The king snorted but didn't otherwise comment. Christopher and Myra ignored him.

She was too caught up in the expression in Christopher's gaze, that hint of something warm and promising. And suddenly she was smelling sugar cookies again.

She followed him with her gaze as he left, and mostly to herself, she murmured. "Sugar cookies…"

Issa's quiet chuckle drew her attention.

"What is the sugar cookie thing?" she asked Issa.

Issa glanced at her son's father. They both grinned. The father asked, "Do you like sugar cookies?"

"Love them. They're the best cookie. Why?"

"He'll tell you when he's ready," the father said.

"What the hell is your name?" Myra asked suddenly, tired of not knowing and too confused to be polite.

"Havier," he said. "And thank you for helping Issa. I'm not sure we can ever repay you."

She waved that away. "I already got paid." She patted the pocket with the diamond dragon in it. "You're fine."

Issa's grin widened. "You fit in well with them."

She stood with Havier and left before Myra could determine if what Issa had said was a compliment or an insult.

With Havier and Issa's exit, that left Myra alone in the library with the dragon king.

She'd only been alone with the king that one time when he'd walked her through his mansion to a meeting with a wizard. And then, they'd been in public corridors where they passed staff and other dragons regularly on their way to that ill-fated meeting.

"A bet, huh?" she said. "Pretty clever."

"I have my moments." He swirled his whiskey again. The liquid was lower than it had been when his older son had handed him the drink, but she couldn't recall seeing the king take any sips of the alcohol.

"I'm not working for you anymore," she said, bluntly. Because they were alone, she felt like she could be more blunt than she might be allowed in front of witnesses. "I can't. People are already starting to think of me as *your* thief. That can't happen."

The king's eyes narrowed, his only change in expression.

In the firelight, his changeable eyes were more green than blue. And there seemed to be more silver in his dark hair than there'd been the last time she'd seen him, but she still wasn't sure if he'd been adding silver dye to his hair or not, so she wasn't sure if this was just to deepen the effect of him looking older and distinguished or not.

"Our association could be very profitable for you," the king said. "Already has been." He nodded to the pocket where she'd tucked her new acquisition.

"The jobs you talk me into have gone consistently pear-shaped, been lies, or put me in the way of people who try to kill me. I can do profitable on my own, without that added hassle."

One sardonic brow rose, but then his expression turned brooding, a frown turning down his mouth.

The look had her nerves tightening. She'd had more than enough of dancing around volatile dragon shifters tonight. She didn't *want* to be on the king's bad side. But she needed to put an end to him thinking she'd work for him anymore. Here and now.

When he met her gaze, his expression made her stomach tight. She couldn't explain why. He looked angry maybe. Or resentful. Definitely broody and annoyed.

"You'll continue to see Christopher?" he asked.

The comment felt like a change in subject, but she went with the flow. "I will. If he wants to keep seeing me."

Not that they'd reached the stage of anything...official. But after everything they'd been through, she knew she wanted something more, wanted all those promises that buzzed between them and she'd been putting off exploring. She trusted Christopher.

In a way she trusted very few people. Maybe no one else since her parents. All on its own, that was an experience she wanted to explore more.

And if that involved getting the huge, hunky, sexy Christopher naked finally, she'd be open to that, too.

The king growled at her, the growl containing that quiet hiss that was such a dragon sound. The hairs on the back of her neck prickled.

But she didn't back down. She wasn't going to be scared off from seeing Christopher. And she wasn't going to work for the king anymore. And he was just going to have to get used to both ideas.

She did grip her glass a little tighter, and she grew very aware of the distance between her seat and the closed library door.

The king stood abruptly, so fast, Myra scrambled to her feet, too. Not even sure what she meant to do. Run away? Her instincts thought that might be a good idea. Her logic knew the effort would be futile. The king was a shifter. He moved a lot faster than she did.

The library door opened at just that moment, Christopher standing in the doorway.

The king snarled at her and then at his son. "Fine," he spit out. "But only because *he* smells like sugar cookies."

The king stalked out, his half-full glass of whiskey perched precariously on the armrest of the chair he'd abandoned so abruptly. Christopher stepped aside to let him leave, then turned back toward her, frowning.

Myra was left with her mouth hanging open. She shook her head at Christopher's raised brows. "I don't know how to explain," she answered his unspoken question.

Christopher came fully into the room, walking toward her slowly, giving her time to admire him. She loved watching him move. There was a subtle grace and strength. Sexy as sin.

"So," he said, when he stood close enough she had to crane her neck up to meet his gaze.

"So." She smiled. "Interesting day."

"Wrong kind of interesting."

She chuckled. "Everything okay with your brother?"

"Fine. I think." He shook his head. "It's nothing."

Sure. Nothing. But if he wasn't prepared to talk about it, she'd give him his privacy. Her curiosity did not give her a right to all his secrets. Even if she wouldn't mind knowing a few.

She did ask, "What the hell is his name? You all suck at introductions."

Christopher's mouth quirked. "We...offer our names to each other when we're ready to allow another dragon to know it. There are formal aspects of dragon naming and exchanging dragon names. That social instinct means we sometimes forget to offer our names to the humans we interact with."

"Oh. Shit, have I been breaking dragon protocol or something by asking everyone for their names?" She just realized she'd demanded the names of a bunch of dragons in passing because she got tired of not knowing what to call them. That included Christopher. She hadn't realized she was doing something the dragons considered rude.

But Christopher said, "It's not a custom that applies to humans. You haven't done anything wrong. We just forget to introduce ourselves, that's all."

"Okay. But since it is a custom, you don't have to tell me your brother's name. It's fine."

"Like I said, the custom doesn't apply to humans. His name is Thomas."

"Not Tom."

"Not. Tom."

Her lips twitched. There really was a dragon thing about names.

None of them wanted their names shortened and got very growly about it all. "Thomas. Will he be offended if I call him by name since he never introduced himself?"

"No. He'll assume I told you. Or the king."

"The king gives me no names." He hadn't even called Christopher by name when sending her to rescue him.

"What did the two of you talk about?"

"How I wouldn't work for him anymore."

"And he said?"

"I think that last barked 'fine' before he stomped out was in reference to that. But also it could have been in reference to me telling him I would continue seeing you." Her gaze danced away from his as a strange bout of shyness swept up her cheeks, heat she was afraid was a blush. "If you want to, of course."

Christopher lifted her chin, gently easing her face up so she had to look him in the eye. "Of course I want," he said quietly. "I thought you realized that."

"I suppose I do. Obvious, isn't it? But... A lot's happened. I don't want to assume anything."

"I was worried, after you saw my dragon, you wouldn't want... anymore."

"Your dragon is beautiful. Terrifying of course, but that's dragons for you." She tried to force a smile. Tried to lighten the moment. The seriousness of it all made her antsy even as she wanted Christhoper to be serious about her. Because she was quite serious about him.

"You're nervous, though," he said.

"Not of your dragon."

Of what this meant between them? Yes. Especially knowing his father did not approve. If Christopher was just anyone, she wouldn't care about parental approval. As it was, she didn't care enough to back off from whatever this was with her and

Christopher. But him being the son of the dragon king, and the dragon king not liking their more personal relationship, was a complication.

A complication they'd one day have to confront.

But maybe not tonight. Maybe not all at once.

"You want to go for a night flight?" she asked, leaning into him so their bodies were pressed together. His arms came up around her automatically, as if that was just naturally the thing they did. She loved that.

"Haven't had enough flying for one day?" His soft, sexy smile melted her. In a good way.

"Never," she said. "Not with you."

That was as close as she'd gotten to some kind of declaration. But it was enough for now. And obviously enough for him, because his sexy smile deepened and he pulled her closer and lowered his head to her. She rose on her toes to meet him. His lips were soft. His hold firm. And that melty feeling that had started moments earlier got infinitely more melty.

She sank into the kiss, opening to him, letting the play of her tongue against his and the grip of her fingers on his shoulders show him what was difficult for her to say. Heat washed through her, a good kind of heat that made her comfortable and restless at the same time. Left her breathless. And needy.

And happy.

By the time they pulled out of the kiss, Myra was breathing hard and had forgotten where they were. Not hard to do when Christopher had his mouth on hers.

"Let's fly," he said.

She grinned, nodded, and took his hand when he led her from the library.

"You ever going to tell me about the sugar cookie thing?" she asked, bumping his arm and giving him a sideways look.

He also looked down at her from the corner of his eyes. "You haven't figured it out yet?"

She scowled. "Should I have?"

His rumbling chuckle had her skin tingling, reminding her of the feel of his lips on hers, the way he tasted, the way his warm, hard body felt pressed against hers. He glanced down at her again, his brows raised slightly, his smile sexy enough to make her stumble a step.

"I'll explain it," he said, as he led her outside onto the roof.

The cold night air cooled some of the heat in her cheeks and body but not enough. She still felt weak-kneed and restless and she needed to be in his arms. Needed to be soaring over the city with his wings above them, her arms wrapped around his neck.

She jumped up into his waiting arms, which put her face close to his. "You will?"

"Eventually." He hugged her tighter to his body as his wings snapped out behind him, the rush of scales over his shoulders under her hands a soft tickle.

Okay. More dragon shifter stuff she'd have to wait to learn. "When you're ready," she said more than asked.

He glanced toward the sky, then met her gaze. "When you are."

And he launched into the air, leaving Myra's stomach far below. And her heart firmly lodged in her throat.

THE DRAGON THIEF SERIES
THE SCAVENGER JOB
Bestselling author of the Cary Redmond Series
KAT SIMONS

THE SCAVENGER JOB
BOOK SIX

The past might save her future, or destroy everything…

A ten-year-old secret, a holiday season, and a walk down memory lane. Myra hopes to share these things with Christopher, because life is short. Especially if you're a magical thief falling hard for the dragon king's son. She wants to stay in Christopher's life, which means being in Christopher's dragon shifter world.

But first, she needs him to know something about her past. Secrets never shared. And a treasure left hidden for a very long time.

Somehow, old wrongs always come back to disrupt even the most sentimental journey for Myra, though. Endangering this one very important job. And this time, her past, not the dragon world, threaten their lives as Myra and Christopher race to solve an old mystery.

Keeping Christopher by her side is the only thing Myra wants for the holidays, and the one thing that might be beyond her reach.

Because even a magical thief can't steal a heart.

Chapter One

Myra clung to Christopher's shoulders, her arms wrapped tightly around his neck as they soared over the city, his wings spread out above them, the nighttime New York City skyline below. The last day had been strange and complicated. And she was still deciding how she felt about it all.

Not that the last couple of months hadn't all been complicated and strange. Breaking into the dragon king's hoard had thrown her into a world she had never planned on visiting, nonetheless staying. And yet now, here she was. Happy to be in Christopher's arms. Happy they'd survived the last few days.

But leery of the world she now seemed to be part of because she wanted to stay in Christopher's arms.

The night air bit sharply at her cheeks. Winter in full swing now. But the cold felt good. And Christopher's body temperature was so warm, she was comfortable in his arms during the flight.

A flight that had been her idea. They'd been dancing around their feelings for each other for the last few months. Or rather, she'd been dancing. In and out. Not sure if she really wanted to let more happen between them because it would mean staying at the edge of the dragon shifter world. Also not prepared to stop seeing him. Since they'd first met, she'd been attracted to him. Now, what she felt was...more. Enough she was willing to try something she never did.

They banked over Midtown, angling toward the west side of the island and his apartment at the top of one of the many high-rises in the area. Not the tallest building, but tall enough that his large open patio on the top floor gave him plenty of room to fly in and land. No need for elevators when you could do a partial shift and have wings.

As his feet settled onto the stone balcony, he tightened his grip on her, as if he didn't want to set her down. She didn't mind. She wasn't in a hurry to get out of his arms either.

"You're sure about this?" he asked.

Myra nodded. "Never been more sure of anything."

And after the last day, she meant those words with her whole being.

THE WATERS OF THE UPPER BAY FLOWED PAST AS MYRA LEANED over the edge of the ferry rail, enjoying the cut of the cold air and the whip of wind. When she looked up, the grand lady herself, the Statue of Liberty, stood glimmering in the sunlight across the water. Despite living in New York her entire life, she'd never been out to the statue. Maybe one day.

Now, she had other plans.

Which started in, of all places, Staten Island.

She loved riding on the Staten Island ferry, but she rarely got off and went into Staten Island. She hung out in St. George station, maybe got an ice cream, and then got back onto the next ferry returning to Manhattan. Mostly, she did this for the free boat ride.

She could afford other options, she supposed. But when she was a kid, this free trip was what they could afford, and it had been one of her favorite things to do with her parents.

Still one of her favorite things to do.

"You're going to fall into the water." A deep voice behind her. "And if you do, I'm not rescuing you."

She could hear both his worry and his hesitance. "Of course you will." She chuckled. "You couldn't resist rescuing me if you tried."

She smiled as she turned to face him. At nearly seven foot tall, Christopher's head came perilously close to the top of the roof on this lower deck. He sort of hunched to accommodate the occasional crossbeam, but it didn't help hide his size.

Nothing could really hide him when he was out among humans. Even without pictures of him out in public, she'd heard the others on the ferry whispering that he must be one of the dragon shifters. Which, he was. But fortunately, no one realized he was one of the dragon king's sons. There were no pictures of the royal family allowed in public. She hadn't understood why when the king had first informed her of the dictate. Now, after spending more time with Christopher, she realized it was a blessing for his sons, to have some semblance of privacy in a world that was *intensely* curious about them.

He really wasn't the kind of man who blended into the background, though. Dark messy hair, deep blue eyes, wide shoulders. There was a lot of potential for classical handsomeness to him, and yet he wasn't. The angles of his face were too sharp and the assembly of those features could have been described as awkward. No, not classically handsome. But compelling. Hard not to notice. Impossible not to look at twice.

She liked to think of his face as interesting. She was certainly interested in that face. Interested in the rest of him, too. And that interest had moved past simple lust now. Way past. Which was one of the many reasons for this trip to Staten Island. Even if he didn't realize it yet.

"I will absolutely let you fall into the river if you keep leaning so far over the rail," he said, hands on his hips.

She laughed. "First of all, we both know you wouldn't." He had a thing about damsels in distress. Couldn't let them remain in distress. Had to help. Some of the other dragons considered it a character flaw. She loved it about him. "Secondly, I can swim."

"Why am I not surprised."

"You're not? Damn, I'm becoming predictable."

"Never." His expression softened into a smile that made her stomach dance. She loved that smile. "Are you going to tell me what we're doing now?"

"Nope. It's a surprise."

"I'm not crazy about surprises."

"I know. But you'll love this one. I promise."

"Are we stealing anything?"

"Nothing that will be missed."

"That doesn't instill much confidence."

She winked. "You want some hot chocolate? It's a ferry tradition for me in the winter."

She was bundled up in a long wool coat, gloves, scarf, and thick wooly cap. Beneath she wore her work clothes. Black yoga pants, black shirt, her trusty, multi-pocket vest. But the coat, scarf, and hat were all bright. White coat. Red hat and scarf. Green gloves. She was a beacon of winter colors.

The expression on Christopher's face when they'd met at the ferry station, and she'd shown up wearing something that wasn't black, had been a delight to witness. The shock. And then the slow sweep of his gaze that had set those now familiar tingles dancing in her stomach. She had her hair down—which was rare—and had gone to the effort of wearing makeup. She even had mid-height, chunky-heeled boots on. The heels did nothing to get her anywhere near his height. He still had at least a foot and a half on her. But the heels made her calves look good in her tight leggings.

It was fun surprising him. She managed it occasionally. And she enjoyed it every time.

He was dressed for show, too. She appreciated that he'd even worn shoes so he didn't stand out too much. He hated wearing shoes for too long. His black wool winter coat and a scarf he sort of threw around his neck gave a nod to the winter. He needed neither. He could control his body temperature—most of the time—and didn't feel the cold the way a human might. When you flew and spent a lot of time at altitude with nothing but a few scales between you and the biting air, you needed to be able to stay warm.

He looked her over as another icy breeze blew across the open side of the bottom deck. There were only a few hearty souls out here. Most remained in the relative protection of the inside cabins.

"Hot chocolate would be good if it means getting you off that railing."

"I am not *on* the railing," she said, bumping her shoulder against his arm as she led him back inside. "If I were *on* the railing, I'd be closer to your height."

And she was not trying to draw that kind of attention on this trip.

With only a couple of days left till Christmas, there were a lot more tourists on the ferry than usual for a winter afternoon on a weekend. If there was no compelling reason to take the ferry in the winter—like going to and from work—a lot of locals gave it a pass. But the ferry was, nonetheless, packed with people. Crowds inside making the lines at the snack stands surprisingly long. There were a few decorations up around the stand, some red and green tinsel, a menorah in honor of Hanukah, some fairy lights winking in white around the order window.

Myra loved this time of year. She liked the cold. But she also loved all the lights and twinkling colors. Not unlike actual treasure. Which she also loved.

The hot chocolate was delicious, though so hot she burned her tongue with her first sip.

"Can't take the heat?" Christopher asked, with a sexy smile.

"I can take heat just fine," she said, trying not to fall into his gaze and failing miserably.

"Need any help with the burn?" His gaze dropped to her mouth. "I could kiss it better."

Yeah he could.

A little purple light played over his irises, and his pupils were narrowed from the bright sunlight spilling in through all the windows lining the cabin. They'd taken a seat near a window that looked out toward the bridges. She loved the view of Lady Liberty, but watching the Brooklyn, Manhattan, and in the distance, the Williamsburg bridges was pretty stunning too. Definitely in New York with that view. But in that moment, all of her attention was captured by Christopher. And that faint purple light in his eyes.

Her stomach tumbled with now-familiar giddiness. Very soon they were going to have to do something about all this tension between them. And for her, very soon was sooner now than it had been a few months ago.

"We'd better wait on that kissing," she murmured. She was a little afraid if they started, she'd embarrass herself by forgetting they were in public.

That "forgetting herself" part had become increasingly more likely. And her resistance to forgetting herself increasingly thinner as the weeks rolled past. Everything about Christopher hit her lusty buttons and left her swoony. From his inability to resist a damsel in distress to his impressive height to the way he accepted her just as she was without trying to force her into a more conventional box.

Things with his father might be easier if she were a more ordinary human. Her being a thief, and a magical one at that, meant she was useful to the dragon king, but not his first choice for his son's romantic interests. Christopher didn't seem to care. And his father seemed to have given up any thought of interfering. At least, he'd made a show of giving up. Whether he had or not was anyone's guess. It was impossible to tell with the dragon king.

But the king had stopped attempting to hire her. Finally. Stopped trying to make her one of "his" people. Stopped trying to control her.

And that had made all the difference.

Now she just needed to do this one thing. One thing before "forgetting herself" completely.

Chapter Two

The house was a few blocks off the subway, which made getting there easy from the ferry station. But Christopher's impressive baring made the journey a little more obvious than it might have been if she'd gone on her own. Even sitting down, people couldn't stop staring at him. No one knew he was the king's son, but most ordinary humans deferred to dragon shifters if they recognized them. Something about the ability to breath fire inspired deference.

Christopher had been offered a seat the minute he stepped onto the subway. Which he'd proceeded to give up the moment a pregnant woman pushed a stroller into the carriage. And when the train reached her stop, Christopher and Myra got off the train so he could help the woman get her stroller up the stairs. Which meant they'd had to wait for another train.

None of which Myra minded. The stairs were icy—it had snowed two days earlier, melted just enough to get everything wet, and then the temperature had dropped so everything froze over. The stairs would have been perilous for the pregnant woman. Myra was delighted Christopher even thought to help.

And, being completely honest with herself, his inability to *not* help was a complete turn on for her.

The snow started falling again as they waited on the open platform.

"We shouldn't have gotten off," Christopher said, hovering over her as if he could shield her from the snow.

She grinned up at him, letting some cold flakes hit her cheeks. "I like the snow. You think we'll still have any by Christmas?"

"The way the weather's been going, more likely a frozen East River and gray slush on the sidewalks."

"Hey, but then we could ice skate half way to Staten Island."

"I could have flown us here." He held his coat up so it acted as a makeshift umbrella, protecting her from the snow. The way he used his coat reminded her of the way he sometimes folded his wings over the top of her.

"I like the ferry."

"And the train?"

"Yes."

He dropped his chin and gave her a look.

"I do! But also, if we hadn't been on the train, who would have helped the pregnant woman get her stroller up the stairs?"

He shrugged and looked across the tracks to the platform opposite. But she didn't miss the color reddening his cheeks.

She leaned into him, letting his natural body heat keep her warm and pretending she liked the protection of his coat covering her head when what she really wanted was just to get closer to him.

They managed to stay on the train until their own stop this time. The walk was cold, the wind as sharp as it was when she flew with Christopher, but she barely felt that chill with him standing so close to her. He even held her hand for part of the way, ostensibly to keep her gloved fingers warm.

The feel of his huge hand wrapped her hers did more than keep her fingers warm.

When they reached the house, Myra spent several long moments just looking up at the place. She hadn't been here in years. She should have. She should have at least dropped in once or twice in the last ten years. But sometimes it was easier to leave all the past in the past.

She had kept tabs, over the years, checking in from a distance. Enough to know this was still the house. But standing here on the sidewalk, looking up at the narrow, two-story building, the white siding in need of a paint, the little front porch decorated for Christmas with twinkle lights around the overhand and some red ribbons circling up the posts beside the short staircase up to the porch. There was even an inflated snowman in one corner of the porch, bouncing around in the cold wind.

Myra couldn't decide if the decorations, slim though they were, made her happy or sad, so she chose happy that they were still there, and released Christopher's hand to walk up to the door.

Christopher hung back, following, but remaining on the stone pathway at the base of the stairs rather than following her up. Snow dusted the two narrow patches of grass that bracketed that path, but Myra remembered summers here when those tiny squares of grass were bordered by flowers and seemed like a huge yard to her.

She hesitated with her fist raised to knock, a beat of uncertainty, before she gave the door a solid whack. She kept her hands out of her pockets, at her sides, ensuring they were in full view.

A few moments passed. She heard Christopher move behind her, remaining back but a tellingly restless movement. The door remained solidly closed, though Myra knew someone was at the peephole. She wondered if this was all she'd get after ten years. If this was her answer.

But then the door creaked open. Harry Goldsmidt stepped out.

Myra remembered thinking he was a huge man when she was a little girl. Towering and strong and indominable. A rock. He still had that craggy rock look to him, though older now, his pale skin creased in more places, his hair and trimmed mustache gray instead of brown. His glasses were thicker now, too, though still inside thin-rimmed frames. The thick cigar hanging out of his mouth was unlit. He was dressed in plaid pajama pants and a thick Irish wool sweater. The years had been kind. He wasn't hunched or too thin. He still looked sturdy and healthy—despite the cigar.

He just wasn't as huge as Myra had made him in her mind. Only a few inches taller than her. Shoulders she'd once thought broad enough to carry the world were narrower than in her memory. Looking at him through adult eyes without the nostalgia of kid memories to color what she saw, Harry looked like a perfectly ordinary older man. Glaring at her from his porch like he was about to shake his fist and tell her to get off his lawn.

That image made her smile. "Hey, Harry," she said. No matter what happened now, she was glad to see him, to see he was doing well. Glad she'd made this trip after so long.

A few moments of him scowling and staring at her. A moment when she worried she shouldn't have come back after all these years. Then his smile broke out huge around his cigar, and she found herself pulled into a bear hug. The familiar smell of his Old English deodorant and cigar smoke sank into her like coming home. A home she hadn't been to in a while.

"Myra, girl," Harry said, patting her back. "It's been a long time. Too long." He pulled back to take her shoulders in his hands and stare her in the face. Then he gave a brief nod. "You look like you've been doing okay for yourself. That's good. That's good. Your old dad would have been pleased."

"That's why I've come to talk to you, Harry. Though, I am sorry I stayed away so long." She gave a little shrug and had to look at the snowman on the porch when she said, "Memories are hard sometimes, you know."

"I know. I know." He glanced past her. "You've brought a friend."

"Harry, Christopher. Christpher, Harry."

"Nice to meet you," Christopher said, and there wasn't even a hint of curiosity or suspicion in his tone.

Myra found that very impressive given how curious and/or suspicious he must be at this stage.

"Yeah." Harry raised a shaggy gray brow at her. "A dragon, huh?" he murmured. "That'll take some telling. Though I'll leave it to you if you want to."

Harry had been as close as brothers with her father. The only real family they'd had beyond each other. An uncle, a confidant, the one they all knew they could rely on. And still there'd been secrets. Still there'd been a lot her father never told Harry. Things Myra had never told Harry even though she knew he was the one person she could trust. Harry understood that. Understood the secrets.

It was the reason her father had trusted him with everything.

She didn't respond to his curiosity about Christopher because that wasn't why she was here. "Can we come in for a few minutes or are you busy?" She'd been afraid if she called instead of just showed up, either he or she would have found an excuse to delay this reunion.

He nodded toward the house and stepped back inside, holding the door for them. Christopher ducked a little when he stepped inside. The door was barely tall enough for him to fit, but the ducking had to be habit at this stage.

The house was a little different than she remembered because ten years would do that to a place. The hardwood floors in most of the house were covered in a deep blue carpet now. That carpet had been a paler gray color the last time she'd been here. And where there was exposed hardwood in the entryway, that was covered with colorfully patterned Turkish rugs. Where there'd been a wood table in the narrow entryway with a bowl for keys and mail, there was now a series of hooks for coats, a larger hook for keys, and a smaller round table for the mail.

He'd once had a long mirror hanging near the door. There'd been a safe behind that mirror. The mirror was gone now and the wall smooth and painted. If the safe was still back there, it was even more cleverly disguised now.

A narrow staircase across from the door led up to the second floor. Past it, a narrow hallway that led back to the kitchen, which used to take up the whole back half of the house. There was a living room to the right. And a utility closet to the left. Upstairs, there were two bedrooms and a bathroom. Above that, a finished attic.

Narrow and simple. All he said he ever needed. Yard easy to take care of. Not a lot of maintenance. Easier to heat in the winter. All the excuses he used with her father when her dad had come into enough money to get Harry a bigger house.

A part of Myra was glad Harry never moved. This house had been the only consistent home she'd ever known.

"I've been nursing a pot of coffee all morning," Harry said. "You want to sit in the kitchen or the living room. I could start a fire. Got gas a few years ago." He grinned. "Get a fire whenever the mood strikes now."

His gaze danced to Christopher, a very large, hulking presence in the narrow hallway. Probably thinking Christopher could make a fire anytime he wanted too, but didn't need gas.

"Whatever's most comfortable for you," Myra said. "I need to talk about my dad, so…maybe the kitchen."

Harry narrowed his eyes a little behind his glasses, the low light in the hallway catching glints on the lenses and making it hard for her to read that narrow look.

"This way." He led them down the narrow hall to the kitchen, and Myra swore Christopher had to suck in his shoulders to get past the staircase.

The kitchen had changed since the last time she'd been here, too. Harry had upgraded his appliances to shiny chrome. The counter was still a light blue Formica, but the gas stove was newer. He also had a very fancy coffee machine on the counter that hadn't been there before. An open space, with a square wooden dining table against one wall, the fridge and stove against another, and a back door that led down two steps into the backyard.

Myra remembered thinking Harry must be rich to have such a grand backyard. She'd been four at the time, so everything seemed big. But that was before her dad had bought them one of the houses they'd lived in, when they'd still been living in an apartment and she'd thought only rich people had yards.

Harry gestured to the table, and one of the four high-backed wooden chairs around it. "Make yourselves comfortable. Do you want some coffee? I'll brew a new pot. I love this thing. The coffee is perfect. I make coffee all day in this thing."

"When did you get it?"

"Present from a lady friend for Hanukah last year. I still can't get enough of it."

Myra smiled. "And the lady friend?"

"Still around. Visiting one of her kids and his family upstate this week." He puttered around the kitchen, getting the complicated-looking machine going on a new pot of coffee. "Your timing was bad if you wanted to meet her, good if you wanted a private chat."

He glanced at Christopher, who hadn't spoken beyond the introductions, but didn't comment. "You take anything in your coffee now that you're an adult?"

She grinned. "Still like it milky and sweet, thanks."

"You?" Harry asked Christopher. "Or would you prefer tea?"

"I don't want to put you out," Christopher said. "Coffee is fine. Splash of milk is good."

Harry raised a brow. "If you're sure. With my new machine, boiling water is a snap."

Christopher's mouth twitched at one side, like a smile fighting to get out. "Tea then. Thank you."

Harry hummed as he worked at the coffee machine, seemingly delighted to give it multiple tasks at once.

Myra grinned at Christopher and he smiled softly back, but she saw all the many questions in his eyes.

Harry brought over a small white ceramic pot with white and brown sugar cubes in it.

Myra raised her brows. "Fancy," she teased.

"Earned it after all these years," he said with a wink.

By the time they had their coffees and tea and everyone was settled at the table, some of Myra's nervous energy and worry had settled. But she still had a little flutter in her stomach as she met Harry's gaze and announced her reason for the visit.

"I need my dad's stash, Harry. I'm ready for it now."

Chapter Three

Harry leaned back in his chair, the wood creaking faintly as he considered Myra over his steaming mug of coffee. The mug was a larger one with a picture of Florida on the side, something kitschy and touristy. Myra tried to hold his gaze as he studied her, tried not to blink. But it was hard after ten years. Especially when she was here for something she'd ignored for all that time.

"You sure, buttercup?" he asked.

The use of her old nickname nearly had tears welling. She forced them down. "I'm sure. It's time. I'm ready."

"Okay, then." He set his mug aside, placed his palms on the table, and levered up. "You two wait here. I'll be right back."

They waited quietly in the kitchen, each sipping on their tea. She heard the attic stairs come down, heard Harry walking around two floors up. When he'd been gone for a full five minutes, Christopher finally asked a question. "Why am I here?"

It wasn't the question she'd expected him to ask. She'd assumed he go right for the "what's happening" or "who is this" or any of the other many questions he no doubt had. The fact that his first wasn't to questions what she was doing, by why *he* was included was something she found…interesting.

"There's something I want to show you. It's important."

"Important," he said softly. Then nodded. And went back to drinking his tea.

Harry came down a few minutes later carrying a large wooden box. An ordinary one, not a fancy one. Something her mother had made in the early days, when she was new to woodworking and hadn't integrated it into her art yet. Just an ordinary square, dark wood box, with ordinary silver hinges and a ridiculous slip lock like you might find on a diary. Not even really a lock. Just a latch to hold the lid down and keep the contents inside from falling out.

"Here you go, buttercup," Harry said. He'd managed to pick up another cigar from somewhere, still unlit, hanging out of his mouth again as he set the box on the table in front of her. "Your dad wasn't sure you'd ever want this. Considered tossing it away. I wouldn't let him."

She smiled, ran a hand over the worn wood, smooth but dusty, the edges of the lid a little wonky. "Thanks for keeping it."

"Docs this mean I'll be seeing more of you around finally?" He sat down across from her again, set his unlit cigar next to the one he'd left on the table earlier, and picked up his coffee mug.

"You sure you want to? New life. Nice woman. No thieves coming and going to complicate things."

"You are who you are. Your dad was who he was. I take people for who they are. We're family. And ten years was too long."

She nodded, tightening her jaw to hold in the hot wash of emotions— guilt, love, regret, a little anger. "It was," she said. She flicked a look to Christopher, then back to Harry. "Still have a lot going on in my life that you might…prefer stayed well out of yours."

Harry's gaze jumped to Christopher, too. "Oh, I don't know. Been missing a little excitement in my life. So's Geraldine. Can't wait for the two of you to meet. Suspect you'll really like her."

Myra chuckled and dipped her head, her hand smoothing over the box lid again. "I need to go, to take care of this. But I won't stay gone this time. Maybe after Geraldine gets back, we can…visit."

"She'd like that. I've been telling her about you."

"You have?"

"Of course."

"And she still wants to met me?" Myra tried to joke but she was feeling a little choked up and the joke didn't land well.

Still, Harry took it for what it was. "Like I said, I think you two will get along well."

Something about the look in Harry's eyes, that twinkle that reminded her of back in the day, with Myra's dad… "I suspect you're right," she said.

She stood and took her coffee mug and Christopher's tea mug to the sink, only realizing she'd fallen into the habit half way to the open kitchen. When she returned to the table, she caught Harry smiling into his mug.

"Thanks again for this." She picked up the box. It wasn't heavy. Sturdy though. Not an aged cardboard about to fall apart. Her mom had used good wood. Wood her dad had somehow "found" for her.

Harry walked them to the door and Myra hesitated on the step, reluctant to leave, even though this was something she needed to do. The snow had stopped again, leaving barely a dusting on the ground under the sidewalk trees.

"I'll be in touch after the holidays," she said, attempting to memorize Harry's face as he was now. Not the man in her memory, but the living, breathing Harry Goldsmidt of today, with his unlit cigar tucked between his teeth on one side of his mouth, his thick-lensed glasses. His soft sweater and plaid pajama bottoms. The additional lines on his face. The gray in his hair and mustache. "It's good seeing you again, Harry."

"You too," he said. "Good luck with that." He nodded to the box. "Hope we get a chance to talk about it after."

On the walk back to the train, Christopher held his questions. Once they'd gone down the stairs and were waiting on the platform heading back to St. George station and the ferry, he stopped waiting. There were no other people on the platform. The traffic on the road above was light. The open valley that made up the station and tracks left little cover if it started snowing again. But since it wasn't, Myra walked them to the end of the platform so they could be on the back of the train.

"Where now?" he asked. Moving to stand in a way that blocked her from the wind.

She hid her smile, but she did wonder if he even realized he was doing that. It didn't look like he was aware of making the adjustment. "Now we get somewhere quiet and I open the box."

"This is what you wanted to show me? The important thing."

She nodded.

"Something inside the box. What it is?"

"Ah, that's the trick. It's not so much what's inside, but where it leads."

His brows snapped down over his eyes, which looked particularly blue in the winter's gray-white lighting. "Where does it lead?"

She grinned outright this time, because she was talking to a dragon shifter. "Treasure."

Chapter Four

Myra picked up their tail about two minutes slower than she normally would have, and she kicked herself for that oversight. She had been lost in thought—about Christopher, her parents, Harry—and thinking about the box on her lap. She had only peripherally noticed the man who joined them on the platform. Habit meant she'd taken in his bearing—middle height, thick with muscles, dark hair, pale skin made red in the cold. He was dressed in jeans, jacket, boots. Nothing really stood out about him except for maybe the tattoo on his neck poking up above his collar, but otherwise, just a man on the train platform.

She should have guessed something was up, though, when he moved back through the doors between train cars to join them in their mostly empty rear carriage. Did, as it happened, realize something was up. Just about two minutes slower than she should have.

Leaning into Christopher, like she was snuggling with him, she reached up and gave him a kiss on the cheek, then whispered, "Dark haired guy with the gray puffy coat."

"Spotted him."

Of course he had. And that only made her more irritated with herself for realizing so late.

"Any idea why?" Christopher whispered in her ear, making it look like he was nuzzling her neck.

Myra had to work not to get distracted by the nuzzle, though. The feel of his breath on her skin sent a shocking spear of desire shooting through her. Shocking because he wasn't even trying.

She smiled and hummed and tried to look like she was so into her companion she wasn't aware of anyone else on the train— barely a leap given how the feel of Christopher's light kiss on her ear sent sensation zinging through her.

She turned into him so their mouths were a breath apart and said, "The box." Her hand tightened on it convulsively.

"Someone wants whatever is where that box is leading?" Christopher murmured before setting his lips to hers.

The kiss, soft and gentle and obviously part of a play to fool their tail, nevertheless robbed her of thought for a full forty seconds. She just wanted to sink into his kiss, sink into his heat, and it took her brain too long to remember she couldn't yet.

Then, "All I can think of. Unless someone else is tailing us for an unknown reason." She couldn't think of any immediate person who might want them followed. Except maybe… "Your father?"

"That's not a dragon," Christopher said, dragging his lips along her jaw, to the sensitive spot just under her ear.

Wow, was concentrating tough when they did this. She blinked up at the subway ceiling, pale, lined with air vents currently not on. Metal hand olds bending over the row of seats against the wall…

"Your father would know you'd pick up a dragon following you. Would he send a human?"

Christopher growled. The sound did nothing to ease the heat coursing through her. In fact, it ratcheted up the melting sensation.

"He might," Christopher admitted. "But why follow us out here?"

"He's nosy?" And he didn't approve of their relationship. And maybe he was just worried she'd lead his son into trouble.

Which…might happen. But honestly, she'd been in more trouble lately because of the king himself. And Christopher was well able to get himself into trouble all on his own thanks to his soft spot for damsels in distress. Neither of them needed *her* to stir up danger.

"I could always ask," Christopher said against her ear.

She shivered. She just couldn't help it. "We could," she said. "Or we could see what he does." She was curious enough to let the tail follow them for a bit just to see what he attempted. But she didn't want him following to her father's "treasure." That was one of the reasons this box had remained in Harry's attic all these years.

The train pulled into the next station. The man stayed seated while two teenage girls with very big hair got off, three men in construction gear got on, and another man who seemed to be alone got on, his face in his phone.

The face in the phone was actually a pretty good way to appear harmless. Myra had used it herself more than once. It didn't work this time. But mostly because she was on guard now that she'd spotted the other tail.

"Two now," she murmured, smiling up at Christopher and batting her eyelashes.

She watched his mouth twitch like he wanted to smile, or laugh at her lashes move, but then a crease formed between his brows in a frown.

"We should get off," he said. "See what they do."

"Yup. Also put fewer people in danger if they aren't just keeping tabs on us for your father." And with two of them on the carriage now, she doubted this was just a find-and-report for the dragon king. This was something else.

The three construction workers and the remaining older woman with her dog tucked into a large bag could be in danger if things went sideways. Neither Myra nor Christopher wanted that. And Christopher could get hurt trying to protect innocent bystanders.

They continued to pretend to be completely absorbed with each other—not much of a stretch, really not that much of a stretch for her—and waited until the train slowed and pulled into the next station. They weren't that far from the last stop, but the ferry station would have a *lot* more innocent bystanders around.

Christopher stood and helped her to her feet as the train bounced to a stop. Then they sauntered off as if they were in no hurry and had nowhere in particular to go, Christopher with his arm slung around her, keeping her tight to his side, her with her parents' box tightly clenched in her arms.

The man with his face in his phone got off while still making a show of reading his phone. The gray puffer jacket man rushed off just as the doors were about to close, like he'd forgotten this was his stop. The two men walked ahead of her and Christopher, not looking back at them as they all slowly moved toward the stairs at the other end of the platform.

Letting all the other people who'd gotten off get safely away from whatever happened next.

There were a handful of people across the track on the other platform, but the train going in the opposite direction pulled in just then, giving them more cover.

"I could always just fly us away," Christopher said as they watched the two men in front of them.

"Then we wouldn't know who sent them and why they're following us," she pointed out. Though she was tempted.

If the dragon king had sent them, it would amuse her to slip the tail. If it was something to do with her parents' box, she didn't want them continuing to tail her and Christopher.

But knowing which of the two options applied—or if there was some third, so far unknown, option—was a bit of information she didn't want to let go.

Her job, her life, hinged on information. Leaving without knowing who these guys were and why they were following her and Christopher might put her and Christopher in danger later.

Once the opposite train pulled out of the station, Myra looked around. No one had gotten off, and the few people who'd been there had gotten on the train. The two platforms were currently empty. Except for the two men, and her and Christopher.

Almost as if they'd all decided they were in the clear to talk now, the two men turned, simultaneously, to face them.

Myra smiled. "Good afternoon, boys. What can we do for you?"

The man with the phone tucked his phone into his pants' pocket as he simultaneously pulled out a gun from his coat pocket. "You can give us that box."

Chapter Five

Well, Myra had her answer. The two men following her and Christopher wanted her father's secrets. She only realized she'd kind of been hoping this was just the dragon king being a pain in the ass when she saw the phone-guy's gun. She wasn't crazy about guns. Definitely didn't like having them pointed at her. Or at Christopher.

Especially at Christopher. Because he'd tried to save her from a bullet. He wouldn't even be able to help himself.

The air on the open platform was cold against her skin, but Christopher was like having a furnace at her side, he pumped off so much heat. The sky overhead was gray, but no new snow fell. She wasn't sure if that was good or not. Would snow help or hurt their chances of getting out of this without that gun going off?

The second man in the gray puffer jacket also pulled out a gun. And Myra sighed. Two guns definitely made this more complicated.

"The box is a Christmas present from my dad," she said, scanning their surroundings casually, looking for options. "I'm afraid I'll have to say no to your polite request to take the box. Anything else we can do for you?"

"You could die," the man in the puffer jacket said. His voice was gravely and low. And something about it was vaguely familiar though he, himself didn't look familiar to her.

"No thank you," she said with a grin. "I'm having too much fun to shuffle off this mortal coil just yet."

Christopher, true to his nature, stepped just a little in front of her at the threat from puffer jacket, and the hissing growl he issued was that distinctly dragon shifter sound that no human vocal cords could make. The sound always made the hair on her neck rise, but also did a little melty, tingly thing to her insides because he usually made that sound to warn off people threating her.

He was so sweet.

"Your father stole something from us," the man who'd been on his phone on the train said. His dark hair barely fluttered as a cold wind blew down the tunnel of the train platform, a sign of some very impressive hair product. "We want it back."

"It won't be this." Myra patted the box. "Whatever he stole, he stole it years ago and probably sold it off a month after he took it. I'd suggest looking elsewhere."

"We know exactly what's in that box," Phone-Guy said.

"That's impressive, since I don't." Which was, technically, true. She didn't know precisely what was in the box. That was really the point. But if she didn't, she was certain they didn't. Even Harry might not know exactly what her father had tucked away into that box, and Harry had had the thing in his attic for ten years.

"Your father was a fucking thief," Puffer Jacket said.

Myra shrugged, nodded, and frowned all at once. "Yes. Yes, he was. I thought that was already well established." She nearly made a Captain Obvious joke, but thought better of it, what with all the guns.

Puffer Jacket opened his mouth again but snapped it shut at a raised hand from Phone-Guy. "We don't have time for this. Hand over the box or we'll shoot you."

Christopher issued that growling hiss again. And really, the two men with the guns should have been more aware of the danger they were in. But she had no idea what happened if Christopher got shot. Whether it was deadly for him or some shifter trick would let him survive. She wasn't sure if bullets would even have any impact on him.

In dragon form, traditional bullets were less than useless. They just bounced off dragon scales like cotton balls. That was one of the main reasons world governments had negotiated truces and treaties with dragon shifters when they'd come out of their caves and into the open. Who the hell wants to tangle with something that breaths fire and can't be shot down? Everyone made good faith deals, and humans and dragons had been living relatively peacefully side-by-side ever since.

The other shifters had come out after, and at different times. The magic wielders interspersed throughout that same period. And the world had gotten very interesting in the fifty years since. She'd always known a world with shifters and magic wielders existed. But Harry had told her stories of a time before, when the magical part of her father's skills had to be kept quiet.

Puffer Jacket flashed Christopher a teeth-heavy grin. "Wanna try something there, big boy? You think you can take us when we got two guns. I don't see any scales."

"He breaths fire, you know," Myra said matter-of-factly, but with a little confusion. Antagonizing a dragon shifter when you realized they were a dragon shifter was just…what? Suicidal? Yeah, suicidal seemed the best description. "Are you trying to get killed? Is that the thing here? Suicide by dragon? That's a bad idea."

"Shut up," Phone-Guy said.

She couldn't tell if he was talking to her or his accomplice, so she just grinned and kept talking. "Listen, you guys aren't getting this box. Whatever my dad stole from you—and I'm not denying he did, by the way. He was a very good thief—but whatever it was, it's well gone. My dad didn't keep loot. He sold it. And used the money to buy things and do things. None of it was left when he died. So this box isn't going to help you."

"He wouldn't have been able to sell this," Phone-Guy said. "And our boss wants it back."

"A mysterious boss now? Groovy. But I'm telling you, he didn't keep anything."

Which was true as far as it went. This box did lead to his treasure. But his treasure wasn't all the things he'd stolen for money.

And there was a difference between the things he'd stolen for money and the other things he'd stolen. She just couldn't imagine these guys would be ten years' worth of committed to anything her dad had stolen for non-money reasons.

"He kept this," Phone-Guy said, sounding very sure of himself. "And we've been trying to find it for ten years. We want it back. His daughter is gonna get it for us."

"Or what?"

"Or we'll turn you over to the cops."

She actually laughed. "For what?"

She committed lots of thefts, of course. There were any number of things that could get her sent to jail if there was actually evidence of the break-ins. But she didn't leave behind evidence of break-ins.

"We'll come up with something," Phone-Guy assured. "Notorious daughter of a notorious thief has a lot of skeletons in the closet, right. And everyone knows it was you who broke into the dragon king's hoard. Cops won't have trouble believing anything we feed them."

The dragon king's hoard thing was really going to follow her around. Probably good no one knew about the female dragon's hoard but the dragons.

"Good luck," she said.

"You ain't worried?"

"Why should I be? I'll either go to jail, or I won't." She shrugged. "And you still won't have found whatever it is you're looking for because my dad didn't have it. Though, maybe, if you tell me what it is you've been looking for, I can find it for you. Get it back. For a price."

Christopher didn't glance back at her, or growl, or comment. But she noticed his shoulders stiffen and wondered if he thought she was being serious.

"We'll just take the box. And maybe we won't kill you."

"As I said, even if you took the box, it'll be no good to you. You won't understand the contents." She might not know *exactly* what was inside, but she knew her father, and she knew it wouldn't be obvious to anyone what it was.

Phone-Guy waved his gun at her. "Set the box down and walk backward. I'm done talking."

"So are we," Christopher said.

And the hairs on Myra's neck stood up. His voice was deep, gravely, and the hiss was more obvious.

He took one step forward, putting a foot of distance between her and him. She nearly closed that distance, afraid he was going to try taking a bullet for her.

But in the next instant, his coat shimmered, a swirl of purple fog whipped around him. And she thought he was going full dragon. A move that was…probably bad on the narrow train platform.

She heard the click of guns. Heard Christopher's growling hiss. And then his wings snapped out behind him.

Myra had half a beat to realize he'd done the partial shift

without even removing his shirt and coat. And then she was in his arms and they were heading toward the sky.

Behind her, she heard gunfire, but it sounded very far away.

Chapter Six

"Well," Myra said once her heart dropped from her throat back to her chest after the rapid ascent. "That was unexpected."

Christopher's wings beat the air three times before he even glanced down at her. At this height, the wind was brutally cold, biting at her cheeks and making tears leak from her eyes. She leaned farther into his warmth. Except he wasn't just warm. He was hot. Like leaning into a furnace. Which meant there were a lot of emotions happening just then.

He was shirtless now, too, with just the layer of purple and yellow scales across his shoulders and upper chest. But given the amount of heat he was pumping out, she knew he wasn't cold.

She clutched her parents' box to her stomach with both arms because Christopher hadn't even given her enough time to get one arm around his neck. Not that she needed that. He cradled her with one arm beneath her knees and one around her back and she felt perfectly secure and safe.

The amount of trust she had in this man still stunned her. That she knew in the depths of her soul he wouldn't drop her.

They were far above the train station now, well out of range for the guns the two thugs had had. She was a little sorry they hadn't revealed what they were after, but she couldn't be upset with Christopher for getting them out of there.

"Are you cloaking now?" she asked.

He grunted once, still not looking directly at her. That was a little worrying. But the cloaking at least meant the men couldn't follow. To them, she and Christopher disappeared into the air. And there was no telling where they'd end up.

They were safe. So why was he avoiding her gaze?

"You gonna tell me what's wrong while we're up here or after we land?" she asked, louder than she might have on the ground, but the wind was noisy up here.

"Nothing's wrong. Where are we going now?"

He sounded strange. And something most definitely was wrong. But obviously they'd have to deal with that when they landed.

"Anywhere we land is fine for the moment," she said. "I need to open the box, so somewhere with relative privacy would be good." She scanned the island below, looking for a convenient rooftop. There weren't the number of skyscrapers and high-rises here in Staten Island. But there were enough tall buildings to give them a few choices for landing. "Head west. See that building." She pointed. "Top of that should do."

Christopher banked and headed toward the multi-story brick building without a word.

When they landed, he folded his wings against his back, but didn't reverse the partial shift that had produced his wings. He set her on her feet gently. He was always gentle. But his jaw was tight, and his mouth a hard line.

He did not look like a happy man.

"Okay," she said with a sigh. "Before I open this, spill. What's with the angry face?"

"Two men just tried to shoot you. That tends to spark my anger."

"Not the first time." Though, to be fair, when they'd first met and a wizard had hit her with magic and almost killed her, Christopher had fried the wizard and the shifters working with him. And that was before they'd gotten close. So she supposed endangering her did spark his anger. Still. "Is this about me pretending to offer to find whatever it was they were looking for?"

"Of course not," he snapped, and she raised her brows at him. He let out a breath and, in a less sharp voice, said, "I know you don't work for other people. Besides, I could smell the truth."

"Okay. Then what has you all bent out of shape."

"Besides the two men trying to kill you?"

"Yes."

He let out a snort that might have been a laugh if he hadn't been so upset. Then said, "Your father put you into danger."

She dropped her chin and looked at him. "I put me into danger. And your father puts you into danger. All the time. Your father puts *me* into danger. What's your point?"

"Those men…" He sucked in air through his teeth and glanced away. "They stank of resentment. And the one in the gray coat had…unpleasant things on his mind."

"Murder or other unpleasant things?" She could guess. The type of people her dad had sometimes gotten mixed up with were not opposed to some truly horrendous acts, with murder only the tip of the horrendous iceberg. That was one of the reasons Myra didn't work for other people. She never wanted to deal with the kinds of associates her father had sometimes dealt with.

"Other unpleasant things," Christopher said with a snarl.

She nodded. Made sense why he was so upset now. "I'm a little surprised you didn't crisp them."

"Close thing."

She smiled. With obvious reluctance, his shoulders relaxed and he let out an almost smile. Not quite ready to let go of what had just happened, but willing to move on.

Or so she thought. "What if they try to find you again?" he asked. "Or do go to the police with some trumped up charges?"

"They go to the police, we'll deal with that. I'm pretty good at staying out of jail." Not out of trouble. She got into trouble all the time. But she was good at staying out of jail. "And I doubt they'll find me again. They only found me this time because they've probably been staking out Harry's place."

"For ten years?"

"I know right? I have no idea what they think my father took from their boss, but this was a long time to wait to get it back."

"Why didn't they break into Harry's to get the box?"

"Good question. No idea really. But maybe their boss knew what's in here won't mean anything to anyone but me."

"You said you didn't know what was in there."

"I don't. Not specifically. But I know what it's supposed to be. And it wouldn't do them any good." In fact, she wouldn't be surprised if they had, at some point in the last ten years, broken into Harry's place for the box. And then realized it didn't help them without her.

But that would mean they probably did know specifically what was inside when she didn't, and that was annoying as hell.

"So now what?" Christopher asked, more of the tension in his shoulders relaxing.

He still had his wings out. But as a cold breeze blew across the rooftop, she had to wonder if he wasn't a little cold without a shirt on.

"I didn't know you could partial shift with your clothes on." She gestured at his bare chest. "Will the clothes come back when you tuck your wings away?"

He gave a short nod.

"Handy. Aren't you cold?"

"Do I feel cold?" He wrapped one big hand around her waist and eased her close.

She moved the box to her hip so she could better lean into him and his heat. "No," she said quietly. "You don't feel cold at all."

He leaned down as she went up on her toes, meeting in the middle for a kiss that reignited the edgy, needy tingles that had burned through her on the train when they'd supposedly been pretending at the PDA. She couldn't have Christopher's lips on her, his breath fanning her face, his heat and scent surrounding her, and not react.

A not insignificant part of her wanted to abandon this mission of hers. It wasn't absolutely necessary. She could go home with him, take him to bed, lose herself in him without this. She could be close to him, be with him, without him having to know this.

Couldn't she?

As his mouth angled over hers, his tongue sweeping into her mouth, dancing with hers, his arms holding her tight, his scent filling her head, she almost abandoned her mission. Came within a breath of telling him to just take her back to his place and they'd forget the box.

But then, if she did that, if she didn't follow through with this, she knew she'd regret it.

This legacy first. This revelation.

And then... Well, then she had ever intention of getting Christopher out of his pants.

She eased out of the kiss, but didn't drop back to her feet, keeping her face close to his, letting his shallow breaths brush over her cheeks. Her heart was pounding harder than when they'd leapt into the air, and she could feel his heart thumping under her palm where she had her one free hand pressed to his chest.

He cleared his throat, swallowed visibly, before saying, "We need to finish whatever this is we're doing."

She raised her brows.

"With the box. With your father's…present? Legacy?"

"Both," she said. "And yes, we do."

"Okay. Then what do we do now?"

She dropped back from him, smiling when he released his hold on her only reluctantly, and then she sat down abruptly on the roof. The move so sudden, in fact, Christopher reached for her as if he thought she was falling. She grinned up at him, a long way up, the gray clouds at his back making a halo around him with the dim sunlight filtering through. She crossed her legs and settled the box into her lap.

"Now," she said, "we open this present from my dad and see what he left me."

Chapter Seven

Myra waited patiently for Christopher to settle next to her on the flat rooftop. As she waited, she took in the surroundings. A pretty ordinary rooftop—she'd been on many, enough to know the ordinary ones from the extraordinary ones, like the ones with hidden pigeon coops and really fancy water towers. This one had the usual fans and extraction ducts, glistening coldly in the gray winter light. The roof was treated with a black, weather resistance tar that was a little sticky under her. The door into the building was around the opposite side of a small raised shed to her left.

Below, traffic skuttled past. And if she turned just right, she could see the island of Manhattan and the Statue of Liberty. Probably if she stared long enough in that direction, she'd see the Staden Island ferry chugging through the bay.

The snow that was thickening in the gray clouds overhead continued to stay away. But the wind was icy. Sitting on the roof helped protect her from that wind a little. The heat pumping off Christopher warmed her even more. He was like one of those standing heat units that restaurants set up in their outdoor seating areas so they could leave those open in the winter.

He stared down at her for a long moment, his wings puffing a little behind him. She did enjoy him shirtless, but the wind fluttering the thin membranes of his sturdy wings still looked cold to her despite all that heat coming from him. The purple and yellow scales across his shoulders and chest were easier to see but more muted in the winter light. They shimmered when he moved though.

And then they flowed away when he did that partial shift that retracked his wings completely. A swirl of purple, sparkly fog wound around his upper body briefly. When it faded, he stood in his fully human form, no more wings, no more scales, and his shirt and coat back in place.

"That swirly fog stuff is the magic that enables the clothing thing, isn't it?" she asked, shading her eyes with one had so she could keep looking at him while he hovered over her.

He finally sat beside her. Dropping into a cross-legged seat with a surprising ease and grace for a man that big. "Yes." His voice was gruff.

"So, when you don't need to worry about your clothes, you can snap out your wings and put them away without all the swirling fog. But when you need to get rid of clothes or when you take your full dragon form, then swirling fog. Right?"

"Right."

"Groovy."

She'd only seen his full dragon that one time, when they were escaping a very angry female dragon. And it had been a very impressive dragon form at that. But up until then, he had only every snapped out his wings around her, and then, only when he was shirtless. He was starting to show her more and more of his shifter nature.

That was nice. Especially since she was about to show him more of her nature. Something he needed to see and understand. At least, she *wanted* him to see and understand.

She didn't know where this thing with them was going—besides eventually to bed—but she knew, for her at least, it was getting a lot more serious than a simple fling. Or even a friends-with-benefits thing. They were, and had always been, more than friends. The fact that she could call him a friend, too, only proved how much more serious this was for her.

And if she was going to get serious with a man like Christopher, he needed to see her as she was. The parts of her she'd shown him, he accepted. Even if some of her love of jumping off the side of buildings gave him heart attacks. Now it was time to show him a part of her that really only Harry and her parents knew about.

She swallowed and patted the box. "It doesn't look like much, I know. And you won't understand what's inside. I'm asking you to trust me. To trust me to show you…what all this means."

He held her gaze, and to her pleasure, didn't nod immediately. He took a moment to think, to consider what she'd just said. So that when he nodded, and said, "I trust you," she could believe him because she'd watched him come to that conclusion right in front of her.

"Okay. Here we go." She flicked the latch holding the lid down with her thumb and opened it, its plain metal hinges stiff from disuse. Once she had the lid up, it stayed raised on those old hinges, making it easier for her to study the contents of the box.

She smiled. "Thanks, dad."

Inside was a small wooden sphere, made from multicolored pieces of different wood—one strip oak, another bamboo, a third pine—all interlocked and wrapped around each other. The sphere wasn't smooth like a ball, but multifaceted, almost like a Christmas tree ornament. In fact, if she hadn't known what it really was, it could look like nothing more than a handmade ornament. That's probably even what the thugs and their boss thought it was at first. Maybe that's why it had taken them ten years to come for her and the box. Maybe they'd assumed for a long time this was all it was, a nothing. And they'd only recently learned it was more than a decoration.

"What is it?" Christopher asked, leaning forward to look at the sphere inside the box.

"It's a puzzle." Myra grinned up at him. "I love puzzles. And this one—" she looked back down into the box again, "—requires magic to figure it out."

And not just any magic. Thief magic. The kind of magic she and her father shared.

She let her fingers hover over the sphere, just above a narrow strip of oak, and smiled at the tickling feel of the magic. She could sense the spells, the power. Sense the threads of the puzzle.

It was a very nice sensation. It reminded her of her dad.

She studied the sphere both visibly and with her magic, found the places to push, to slide, to move the different little pieces of wood. The sphere looked like it would open at one point, then another piece had to be moved and it covered up the hole. More pieces slid. A click. The feel of one part of the magic snapping open.

A lock and a puzzle all clicking and dropping into place. With each move of the physical puzzle, she had to make a simultaneous move of the magical puzzle. Slowly finessing the locks that held the pieces in place in order to move them.

A particularly clever magical lock rose up at a crucial place in the physical puzzle and made her chuckle. "That one was tricky," she murmured. Her eyes were half closed as she focused on the game her father had left her. Her vision taken up by the sphere's wooden pieces and the magic she could see in her mind's eye as well as feel.

Each twist, each movement, each unclicked lock, brought the puzzle slowly, slowly to opening, to revealing what her dad had hidden.

Peripherally, she was aware of the cold air blowing across her cheeks, of the presence of Christopher, still radiating an enormous amount of heat, of the distant traffic and the sounds of seagulls screeching out over the bay. But most of her was inside the puzzle.

And when the last magical lock opened under her nudge and push, when she slid the last physical piece of the wooden sphere into the right place, she let out a triumphant laugh. As the sphere opened wide in her palm.

The clever wooden ball turned into a sort of open flower, the wooden pieces flaring like a rose, each "petal" spreading wide to reveal a hollow center. Inside was a small key, the sort of key that might open a kid's diary, just a tiny bit of tin. Next to the key a piece of paper folded small enough to fit.

She looked up at Christopher, smiling. "Brilliant, isn't it?"

Christopher had creases along his forehead and his brows were bunched. He just looked confused. "Those are the treasures? A key and a piece of paper?"

"Those are the next clues," she said. "What fun would this be if it was easy?"

"Clue? As in… Your father left you a scavenger hunt?"

"Yes." She beamed. "He told me before… Well, before he and my mother were killed, he said he intended on leaving me a scavenger hunt as his last act. That he thought I'd enjoy that better than hearing some stuffy lawyer read out what I was left with. He knew me well."

This made Christopher's scowl soften into almost a smile, but the smile couldn't hold out against his confusion.

"When he… When we talked about that," she went on, "about him dying, I figured that would be fifty years later, when he died of old age while breaking into some impossible-to-crack vault somewhere." She chuckled at the remembered image she'd had of her dad, in his nineties, breaking into a vault successfully, then laying down and dying peacefully on the floor.

She got more serious when she said, "I didn't expect to lose them so soon after that conversation. I've wondered, over the last ten years, if my dad didn't suspect something. Have some sort of premonition. If my mom maybe had some sort of flashing insight that she'd told him. I don't know. Neither of them were psychic. But the accident happened maybe six, seven months after we had that conversation about a puzzle-filled scavenger hunt. And it was more than a week after their death before I found out he'd set up the hunt. I just sort of assumed, since their deaths were sudden, that he wouldn't have gotten around to it yet."

"Why didn't you do the hunt before?"

She stood abruptly, and Christopher, looking startled, flowed up with her. He hunted the area as if looking for a threat.

"I don't want to lose the light," she said. "We should get going." She pocketed the little key and tucked the now open puzzle sphere back into the box. The little piece of paper, she opened and read. And smiled. "Very clever, dad," she murmured.

"What?"

"A riddle. But it's got a glimmer of magic over it, so what's on the page isn't the real riddle." She showed Christopher the note.

He frowned and read, "Twelve gulls and a pint of beer for Janice." His scowl deepened. "What the hell does that mean?"

"Nothing." She chuckled. "Like I said. It's a cover. You need thief magic to decipher it."

"So what's it really say?"

She appreciated that he didn't return to the question she'd not so elegantly avoided. She'd tell him why she'd been avoiding this scavenger hunt once they reached the end of it. That was half the point of bringing him along. To…explain things to him. But she wasn't ready for that part of the conversation yet. Not until she'd followed the clues to the end of her dad's game.

"What it really says is that we need to go back to Manhattan, to a building downtown not too far from the ferry station."

He narrowed his eyes. "You got all that in a few words?"

"I solved my dad's riddle. The riddle won't make sense to you." She shrugged at his frown and said, "The actual riddle is, 'Where Howard lost his shoe that one time.' And unless you know that Howard was a friend of my father's before he met my mom, and had heard the story about how my dad and Howard had tried to rob a bodega once and gotten chased out by the bodega cat, you would have no idea what that meant."

Christopher's lips twitched. "Got chased out by a bodega cat?"

"They are the best of cats, friendly to all who enter. Unless you're entering when you're not supposed to and you accidentally step on their tail."

His lip twitch turned into a grin. "Fair enough. Not much of a riddle for you, though."

"I never said my dad was good at riddles, just good at hiding things. The trick will be finding what he hid at the bodega where Howard lost his shoe that one time."

Christopher looked out over the bay. "Those men will probably be waiting for us at the ferry station. Or even on the other side in Manhattan."

"Maybe." She sighed. She loved flying with Christopher, but she'd sort of wanted to do this scavenger hunt as her dad had intended, and taken that excuse to ride the ferry back. But needs must. "Do you mind flying us back?"

"Of course not. I adore flying with you."

The expression in his eyes made her heart pound harder, reminding her why she was doing all this now. She dropped her gaze to the box, assuring everything was safely back in place and the box was latched shut. When she got home, she wanted to reassemble the sphere and set it to do what it had been originally designed to do.

Christopher lifted her chin with the side of his finger, forcing her gaze up to his. He searched her expression for a long moment and it took a lot of effort on her part not to try dropping her gaze again. Being that vulnerable, that open… That was what all this was about for her, and yet it was still incredibly difficult. She was used to hiding almost everything about her real self from everyone she knew. She didn't want to do that with Christopher. But old habits die hard.

After an intense moment, he released his hold on her chin and gave a little nod, as if he'd just decided something. Then he stepped away from her a few feet and the swirling fog circled him again, briefly. When he stepped out of the sparkling purple mist, he was shirtless again, his wings spreading out wide behind him.

She cradled the box in her arms as he stalked toward her and gasped when he swept her up and took flight in one motion. The thrill as they climbed high made her laugh. She looked up in time to catch him grinning down at her.

Even without all this, the man did know her pretty well.

Chapter Eight

Her father's clue was near the back of the bodega, and the fact that it was still in place was a testament to the sturdiness of the resident bodega cat and the consistency of the bodega itself. The cat in question was not the same one who'd chased Howard and her father out of the store, of course. Sturdy or not, that had been forty years ago and no cat that wasn't a shifter lived that long. But one of that cat's offspring had remained in residence and was just as protective of their home as their mother had been.

The bodega itself was a typical one of its kind. This particular place long and a little narrow. The shelves along one wall filled with chocolate and chips and protein bars. The opposite wall lined with glass door refrigerators filled with drinks. There was enough room at the back for two central shelves, which contained mostly food staples like cereal and pasta and soup, and one self was lined with non-edible things like paper towels and toiletries.

There was a small selection of random items like pain killers and replacement earbuds at the front next to a counter where fresh sandwiches and baked goods kept the office dwellers in fast lunches and breakfasts. This particular shop even had shelf where customers could pour themselves out a cup of ordinary coffee—no fancy flavored lattes and cappuccinos here—and tart it up with milk and sugar as they liked. When the pots were full, this place probably smelled strongly of coffee, but whether because of the waning afternoon or the proprietor's indifference, the pots were now empty.

This late in the afternoon, in the last days before Christmas, with most of the businesses in the surrounding office buildings closing for the holiday, the bodega was mostly empty but for a few people who'd come in on the last ferry and the cashier, who was sitting behind the register desk flipping through a magazine as he spoke loudly into his cellphone.

The bodega cat in residence was sleeping on an ancient cat bed near the back of the store, pushed up onto one of the shelves near cans of dog food which looked older than Myra. With Christopher acting as lookout, she knelt on the sticky floor and gently nudged the cat and its bed to one side. The cat opened its eyes briefly, gave her a teeth-revealing yawn, then proceeded to stare at her as she hunted the back of the shelf behind the bed.

It took her almost a full minute to locate the broken, wobbly piece in the shelf's wood, and to get it pulled out, all with the cat remaining stubbornly in the way. The fact that it wasn't attacking her or yowling and drawing attention was a minor miracle, so Myra was inclined not to do more than she was already doing to nudge the cat to one side. After some stretching and finagling, she removed the tiny box that had been shoved inside the secret hidey hole, and replaced the loose piece of wood to cover the hole again on the off chance that someone actually got brave enough to remove the bodega cat's bed and search back there.

She thought that was unlikely, though, given the sheer size of this cat. Not quite as big as a Maine coon, but big enough, its gray and black fur fluffy and soft. She grinned at the cat when she settled its bed back into place, gave it a scritch around its ears and head. This started it purring.

When she stood, Christopher, who was still mostly watching the front of the store to make sure they weren't disturbed, gave her a look.

She shrugged. "Payment for letting me move him around."

"Good show for the camera, too." Christopher nodded to the close circuit camera up near the ceiling, pointed at the rear of the store to discourage shoplifters.

"True, if the camera were an issue. But it's pointed far enough to the left, I wasn't being picked up."

"How did you know that?"

"Habit and a good eye for what security cameras are actually pointing at." She shrugged. "Part of the job."

She patted his chest—he was back to his shirt and coat because the wings, or even being shirtless, would have made them stand out too much as they came into the shop—then she grabbed a bottle of soda from one of the fridges and paid for it at the register. The cashier barely glanced at her, his full attention still on his phone call.

Out on the sidewalk, around the corner from the bodega, she pulled out the little box from her coat pocket, where she'd tucked it, and then handed Christopher her unopened soda bottle to hold along with the larger box he'd been carrying since they landed.

"Another box," he said.

"Another box."

A small, dark wood box with a lid that lifted completely off, the entire thing small enough to fit into the palm of her hand. She could have hidden it just by closing her fist. This one was actually locked, though, unlike the larger box Harry had been holding for her. A turning number lock, similar to the type of thing found on luggage locks, where she had to enter the right series of numbers to get it to open. There was a small spell on the lock, but it was just there to keep anyone from breaking the entire locking mechanism off. Opening the lock itself didn't require magic. Was simply a matter of entering the right code. Something anyone could do.

"Do you know the code?" Christopher asked, his gaze scanning their surroundings.

The downtown area was incredibly quiet, with a few cars passing on the main streets, but on the side street where they stood sheltered against the back of a building, there wasn't any traffic or pedestrians passing.

"That's the trick," she murmured, considering the lock and what code it might be. Not her birthday. Or her mother's. That would be too obvious. Her father hadn't known his real birthday, so he'd just celebrated on January first every year. Probably not that either. She needed six numbers, so a date of some kind seemed likely.

After a few minutes of hovering behind Christopher as he blocked her from the wind and kept her warm with all his body heat, she grinned. Ah. That had to be it. She flicked the numbers into place.

The lock clicked open.

"What was it?" Christopher asked, looking down at her and the box.

"The date of the cat incident. The date Howard lost his shoe being chased out of the bodega by a cat."

"Huh. That should have been obvious. But I'm surprised your dad remembered the date so precisely. Precisely enough to tell you."

"Well, it was the first time he met my mother, so it was a date that made an impression."

"First time?"

"That particular meeting didn't go so well." She chuckled. "He had to find her again before she'd give him the time of day."

Christopher raised a brow. "Like mother like daughter?"

Her stomach did a fluttery dance even though she wasn't entirely sure why. She hadn't made him come looking for her after their first meeting.

She'd waited until their third meeting before she'd made him come look for her.

"What's inside?" he asked. He leaned in closer, his arm resting against the wall beside her head so he could get a better look at the box in her hand. The position was a little distracting, though, because she was surrounded by his heat and his scent—his ordinary scent of musk and dragon and an earthy leather undertone, not the scent of sugar cookies that he sometimes smelled like to her—and it made concentrating on the box difficult when all she really wanted to do was pull his mouth to hers.

Later, she promised herself. Later.

She sucked in a deep breath and lifted the lid off the box.

Inside was a tiny glass Christmas ornament. Very tiny. The size of her thumb, with a little bit of silver string at the top for hanging the tiny ball on a tree. It was a soft, almost muted red color, and there was a miniature picture on it. It was so delicate, she handed Christopher the little box it had been in so she could handle the ornament carefully, one hand holding it while the other hand cupped beneath it in case it dropped.

She held it up to the light to better see the image painted on the curved glass.

"A Christmas tree on a Christmas tree ornament?" Christopher asked.

"Not just any Christmas tree." She studied the pictures. There. A tiny ice rink. That narrowed the tree down to two obvious places. But which one... She leaned in closer to see all the tiny details. "Ah! There we go." She held it so Christopher could see better. "See the tiny sitting lion under the tree like a present?"

Christopher frowned as he nodded.

"The Bryant Park Christmas tree." She grinned. When he continued to frown, she said, "Okay, see the ice rink next to the tree? That's either Bryant Park or Rockefeller Center. The lion is from in front of the New York Public Library…"

"Which is next to Bryant Park," he said as the light dawned. "So we're heading to Bryant Park."

"We are."

"It will be mobbed."

True enough. The downtown areas and office buildings might be quiet two days before Christmas, but the holiday market and ice scatting rink in Bryant Park were going to be wall-to-wall people.

"We'll have to manage," she said. "Dad's next clue is there."

"But…the tree is temporary. There's hardly a clue on the tree."

"No. It'll just be somewhere in the park. We'll need to look at some of the permanent structures." And hope, all these years later, the next clue hadn't vanished.

She pushed worry about that aside. "Subway," she said. "I don't want to make a dramatic entrance into a crowded part of town."

"I could land us on a roof and we could come down the elevator like normal people."

"First, no one is ever fooled into thinking you're a normal person. Second, that sounds like a better plan." Mostly because now that she was on the scent, she wanted to get there fast. And dragon flight was significantly faster than the subway.

She looked around their surroundings. There were a few people passing on the crosswalk, but once the lights changed, things got quiet. Only a few cars moving past. "We'd better hurry before we attract an audience."

The purple fog swirled around Christopher again, and a moment later, he was shirtless with wings.

She shook her head as she gently placed the tiny ornament back into the tiny box he handed back to her, and put the whole thing into her pocket. "Gonna have to get used to knowing you can do this partial shift even with clothes on," she murmured.

"Does it bother you?"

She blinked. "No. Of course not. Just…I'd gotten used to you needing to be shirtless. Watching clothes appear and disappear is different. That's all. But I'll adapt. It's not like I haven't seen it before."

She'd seen another shifter go from full dragon, down to a man fully clothed and then back to dragon again before she'd even seen Christopher's dragon.

She took the larger box back from him, then set her free hand to his now bare chest and grinned. "I just like when you're shirtless."

That earned her a smile that made her toes curl.

In the next moment, she was in his arms. His wings beat downward twice and they were aloft, rising up over the skyscrapers in moments. Christopher circled once and then turned north. Heading toward Midtown and Bryant Park.

And hopefully their next clue.

Chapter Nine

They found the next box hidden in the statue of William Cullen Bryant. Well, more to the point, in the base of the statue. The domed marble portico held up by columns around the bronze statue glistened in the lights from the holiday market stalls. Down a row of stalls and rising majestically above them, the brightly lit Christmas tree dominated the part of the park closest to the library. Beyond the tree, the huge, seasonal ice rink was brightly lit and busy, the music loud enough Myra could hear it over all the other people and conversations.

The area behind the booths near the statue wasn't quite as crowded as the rest of the park, but there were a couple of booths bracketing the statue, so there were still quite a lot of people pressed tightly together, trying hard to squeeze into the booths and buy last minute artisan presents. The afternoon was waning now, the lights inside the glass-covered stalls starting to glow, the lights on the giant tree brightening. The area around the statue was dark, and protected enough from the wind to be less cold than out near the rink.

Myra had Christopher sit on the steps up to the statue to keep watch—sitting because he was less obviously huge and intimidating when he was sitting—while she hunted the area around the base of the statue.

She considered searching up higher, climbing to the top of the structure surrounding the statue, but decided her father would leave his clue somewhere that didn't make finding it too obvious. A woman scaling the statue's portico would be pretty obvious. Not that that wouldn't be fun to try and get away with. But she'd need to wait until it was dark. So she searched the base of the statue first.

"You're sure it will be with this statue?" Christopher asked quietly as she moved behind him.

"It's the best spot to ensure what he hid stayed hidden for as long as necessary. Most of the other options are too exposed."

And the statue was one of the permanent fixtures in the park, here since 1911. Not likely to be moved or otherwise disturbed. Which made it ideal.

The little square cutout at the very back of the base of the statue was almost impossible to see. The lines blended in with the marble and looked like they were just joints that were part of the base's construction. Unless you were looking for it, the odd square shape just wouldn't jump out.

It took her several moments to figure out how to open the hatch, though. She pressed different sides of the square. She attempted to pry it out with one of her lock picks. She even tried a little open spell. None of it worked.

So that meant the opening latch was somewhere not on the square itself. She hunted for a button or a soft spot in the statue's base and finally found a little bump on the portico's floor, by one of the columns. Pressing it with her fingers, she realized it also needed a spell. That took another few seconds, figuring out which one triggered the locking mechanism. It turned out to be one of the more obscure spells her father had taught her when she was first learning about her magic.

That sparked a memory of sitting with him outside the apartment building they'd been living in at the time, on a low brick wall that held up a tiny patch of greenery and a single bush, and teaching her the words to this spell. She smiled at that memory, one she hadn't looked at in years.

Then she opened the secret hatch.

The square of marble popped open enough for her to get her fingers behind it and pry it out. She reached inside the little hole, pulled out a brass cylinder, and replaced the square so that the marble base looked smooth and undisturbed again.

Sitting on the step beside Christopher, she showed him the cylinder. About six inches long, decorated with a swirling pattern on the outside, topped at each end with decorative endcaps. All on its own, the cylinder was probably worth a tidy sum. It was, to Myra's trained eye, an antique, probably Egyptian, and infused with enough residual magic, she felt the tingling against her palm.

"Pretty," Christopher said. "Is it the clue or does it have something inside?"

"Haven't opened it yet so I don't know." She considered whether the scroll itself might be the clue because unlike the first box she'd gotten from Harry, which Christopher held in his lap, or the tiny box hidden in the bodega, which was tucked into her coat pocket, this was actually an objectively valuable piece. Probably part of the clue, at least. Her dad wouldn't have just tucked something like this away without a reason.

She considered the end caps, how to open the cylinder, spotted the little pressure point, and pressed it. One end cap clicked open, popping out on a hinge so suddenly, Myra thought the cap might go flying. She glanced around, making sure no one was watching—anyone who passed ignored her and Christopher—then she looked into the cylinder. Inside, she could just see a rolled-up piece of paper.

Easing the paper out, she realized it was papyrus. "Going the extra mile, huh, dad," she murmured, mostly to herself. The papyrus didn't have any words on it, not even hieroglyphs, which wouldn't have surprised her. There was just a picture of a blue hippopotamus with a flower on its side.

"Make any sense?" Christopher asked, studying the picture over her shoulder.

This one was trickier than the first message. At a glance, she could assume this led to the Met Museum because of the extensive Egyptian exhibit there. If that were the case, they were in a little trouble because without looking at a clock, she knew it was late enough that the Met was probably either closed or closing soon. Breaking into one of the major art museums in the world would be fun—she'd done it only once before—but it required time. And planning. And probably just waiting till morning and going in with all the other visitors would be easier.

But given that museum exhibits moved around a lot, sometimes went on tour to other museums, and sometimes were just tucked away in basements while other artifacts went on display, she wasn't sure her father would have chosen the Met. The little hippo and the papyrus definitely hinted that the cylinder itself was Egyptian. Where else might her dad mean for her to go besides the Met?

When her eyebrows popped up at the possibility, Christopher's gaze sharpened. "What? What's wrong?"

"Not...wrong, so much as, a little more complicated." She blinked at him. "One time, my dad was hired by a man who turned out to work for the Egyptian embassy. The job was to steal back an Egyptian artifact that had been illegally taken from the country but was in the hands of someone wealthy enough the diplomates, and even the US government, hadn't wanted to question him. It wasn't a big artifact. And there wasn't enough proof for the customs department to risk pissing this particular guy off." She shrugged. "I also think the Egyptian diplomat just didn't want to go through the hassle or paperwork and red tape that would have been required to get the artifact back and returned to Egypt. So he found and hired my dad to steal it."

"Your dad got it?"

"That. And a few more things he didn't mention to the diplomat. The extra stuff he sold and that's when we moved into our first actual house. The first of several we lived in. But that was one of his best scores, between the money the diplomat paid him and the other things he'd stolen. He'd gotten better at his craft at that point and got away with the heist. No one ever knew what happened to the artifact 'officially,' but my dad told me it made it safely back to Egypt and is in the basement of the Cairo Museum for safe keeping."

"A worthy theft."

"He thought so. He loved being able to give my mom a house, too." She rubbed a finger over the cylinder. "He and the diplomat became…friends of a sort. They worked together a few more times, successfully, and my dad was invited into the embassy a few times."

"You think the next clue is in the Egyptian embassy? That's going to be…difficult."

"Not the embassy itself. Too much risk of it being found in their regular security sweeps. But the diplomat had a nice apartment on the Upper East Side. That building had a mosaic of a hippopotamus on the lobby floor. Not a blue one, just an ordinary hippo in the middle of a jungle. You had to stand back and really look to even see it. The diplomat thought it was good luck."

"We won't be able to tear up a mosaic in a public lobby without drawing attention," Christopher pointed out.

"It won't be something that obvious. But the next clue is in that building."

"So to the Upper East Side, then." Christopher stood smoothly and held his hand out to her, still cradling the larger box in his other arm.

She took hold of his hand and let him lift her because there was something thrilling about that show of strength and she wasn't ashamed to admit it.

Rerolling the little papyrus page back up, she slipped it into the cylinder and stuck the whole thing in her coat pocket next to the tiny box from the bodega. She might need to get a bag to carry all these clues and treasures soon.

"Taxi, subway, or flight?" she asked. Flight would mean going up to the roof of one of the surrounding buildings, but it would also get them uptown in minutes, so on balance, the time was about the same for their various options.

"Flight," Christopher said. "Fewer witnesses to see where we go."

She raised her brows. "Still worried about the thugs from Staten Island?"

"I doubt they've given up this easily."

True enough. But how they'd possibly follow them when she and Christopher were flying around this city, him cloaked from observers, she wasn't sure. But as they left the park to return to the building they'd landed on getting here, she heard a few whispers in their wake, whispers about Christopher, suspicion that he was one of the dragons.

He was not an inconspicuous man. Even if the thugs from Staten Island weren't able to follow them, too many people noticed Christopher. He just couldn't blend into his surroundings very well. People noticing you meant determined people could find you by asking the right questions. She had no idea who the thugs' boss was or if that boss had extensive connections of informants. But better safe than sorry. Keeping their movements as concealed as possible seemed smart.

She just hoped her dad's scavenger hunt didn't lead them to places were being concealed or lost in a crowd would be impossible.

That was already difficult enough with a dragon shifter companion.

Chapter Ten

✦

They found the next clue in the mosaic itself. Nothing she could take with her. But some of the tiles had been replaced, a subtle change creating a subtle message. She wasn't sure how her father had even managed it. But the change, when looked at from the right angle and with a little bit of magic to see through the illusion spell, pointed the way to their next location.

"The armory?" Christopher asked as they traveled up in the elevator to the apartment building's top floor. Pretending they were here to see someone to get past the doorman might have been trickier if Christopher hadn't convinced him that his father—the dragon king—was interested in buying one of the apartments in the building, but the whole purchase and viewing process had to be kept secret.

The doorman had no problem believing Christopher was a dragon shifter. Believing he was one of the king's sons only took a few extra minutes of convincing. Since there were no photos of the royal princes anywhere, people didn't really know what Christopher or any of his brothers looked like. But it wasn't much of a stretch to see him as the son of the dragon king. People *did* know what the king looked like.

The armory was closed by the time they reached it, of course, but her father hadn't intended them to go inside. The armory was only about twenty blocks south of the hippo apartment building, so they reached it quickly. Christopher landed on the roof of the massive, block-sized, red brick structure, near the central tower of the administration building.

Myra smiled as she looked over the edge of the crenellated roof to the gray granite coat of arms in the center of the top level of the tower.

"You're sure your father would have hidden something there?" Christopher leaned over the parapet too, scowling.

"He would. He knew how much I liked scaling buildings."

She set a temporary spell on the armory security camera on the roof, to keep it from recording all this, then handed Christopher her pretty white coat which had been great for blending in with humans but would get in the way here.

"I could hover in front of that coat of arms for you to find the clue," Christopher pointed out.

"Where would be the fun in that?"

She pulled a grappling hook from her multi-pocket vest and secured it between the brick parapets, the gap between crenellations narrow enough to make a secure hold for the hook. She secured the wire to her vest, winked at Christopher, and rolled over the side of the building, letting the wire catch her after a ten second free fall.

Christopher watched her every move as she scaled down the wall, her booted feet on the bricks, her gloved hands holding the repelling wire. She walked down until she was level with the coat of arms plaque, then hunted around the smooth gray granite until she found her father's next clue.

When she got back up to the roof, Christopher helped her over the edge. "What was it this time?"

She showed him the crystal bobble that had been imbedded inside one of the nooks in the carved coat of arms and then disguised with an illusion spell.

"A bell?" Christopher raised his brows at her.

"A very specific kind of bell," she said.

"And it means?"

"Saint Patrick's Cathedral."

HER DAD HAD LEFT HER A TOUR OF THE CITY. A TOUR OF MEMORIES. From Howard's shoe, to the Egyptian diplomat, to the priest at St. Patrick's who'd caught her father trying to steal a candle when he was a teenager and proceeded to teach him about forgiveness. For years, until the priest was transferred to another parish, her father had come to visit him at St. Patrick's, and they had sat up in the northern tower near the bells to talk because her father had felt safest up high.

She'd inherited that from him. She felt safer the higher up she was. At the top of buildings, on roofs, the place she ended up a lot with Christopher...

There was probably a point to be made about that.

The next clue was tapped inside one of the nineteen bells and it required a little more maneuvering to get at. If she'd been alone, she'd have had to use a rope and lower herself to the appropriate bell from above, or used some of her magical suction grips to hold onto the outside of the bell while she pulled the piece of paper out.

But Christopher just reached across the giant gap of open space, grabbed the end of the bell, and pulled the eight-hundred-pound monster close to the circling catwalk so she could grab the note—fortunately her dad had left the note in one of the midsized bells.

Myra wasn't sure even Christopher could have dragged one of the multi-thousand-pound bells close. And if he could have… She wasn't sure what she'd have done with that information. Except the thought gave her a little thrill of excitement.

He eased the bell back into place so it didn't make noise or draw attention. The bells weren't scheduled to go off again until morning, so one of them suddenly making noise would definitely be noticeable.

The note inside the bell, led them back downtown. This time to Battery Park and the SeaGlass Carousel. A place her father had taken her only once, but she'd been enchanted by the lights and music and the way the fish "swam" behind the glass. She'd enjoyed riding the carousel, but she'd enjoyed watching the fish almost as much as the ride. And she'd loved spending that evening with her father.

The next clue was a thin brass box, shaped like an envelope, with a flap sealed by a spinning lock that had to be opened using a specific letter code this time. It only took her a few minutes thought to solve this one. It was the first letters of her name, her mom's name, and her dad's name in order.

"M. A. P." She chuckled. "Dad used to find it very funny that our initials spelled map."

"Because it was like a treasure map?" Christopher asked.

"Exactly." Her heart did a funny little flip.

"I know Myra," he said. "A and P stand for?"

"Alana and Peter."

"You haven't said either of their names before this. Harry didn't say your father's name either when talking about him."

She shrugged. "Habit. None of us used names often because we never knew who might be listening." She frowned. "I didn't even realize I was doing that. Or that Harry hadn't mentioned dad's name."

"Names for dragons…mean things. They're important. We don't take them, or the use of them, lightly either."

"That's why none of you like having your names shortened?"

Christopher growled if someone tried to call him Chris. Myra had met other dragons who had the same reaction to the mention of shortening their names. She'd suspected names were important. And she knew dragons only gave each other their names under specific circumstances, a custom that meant they often forgot to introduce themselves by name. But *why* any of that was so wasn't in any of the public information she'd found researching dragon shifters.

"When we're given a name," Christopher said quietly, the lights from the carousel reflecting behind him and giving him a bluish halo, "that name holds…weight. Power, but not the way wizards don't like their real names to be known because it can be used in spells and things. Our names are… I'm not sure how to put this. Protective. Distinct. *Us* to other dragons. Like our scent is us. Altering or changing or shortening the names feels like it… diminishes us. On an instinctive level that we don't completely control."

"Ah. I had wondered. But I couldn't find the 'why' anywhere."

"We don't talk about it to outsiders," he said. "It isn't public information."

That funny flip in her chest, her heart pounding harder again. Because he'd just implied she was not an outsider among the dragon shifters. That felt a little momentous.

Also a little terrifying.

But she enjoyed a little light terror.

Christopher's eyes glowed slightly purple in the dim park light as he held her gaze. Then he blinked and nodded to the brass envelope. "What's the next clue?"

She reached into the thin rectangle and pulled out a dog tag. The next code was written in braille.

"My dad's mom was blind and taught him braille," she told Christopher. "He taught me, but I'm rusty. It's been a few years." She closed her eyes and let her sensitive finger tips move over the raised, patterned bumps. When she finally read the message, she nodded. Of course. "We're off to Queens."

"Queens?"

"Queens."

Chapter Eleven

The cemetery had closed at sunset and had been closed for hours. It was well after midnight now, the scavenger hunt having taken them all around the city for the entire afternoon and half the night.

To finally end up here.

"You're sure this is the end of the hunt?" Christopher asked as he landed gentle in the middle of the grounds, carefully setting down on the road through the cemetery instead of on the grass and any of the graves.

Calvary Cemetery near Woodside in Queens was a wide-open patch of land with gentle hills, lots of open grassy space, and a few copses of trees. At night, the raised headstones and occasional monument loomed like watchers, waiting to see what she and Christopher would do. The wind was harsher here, colder, because of all the open space. The temperature had dropped steadily all evening. And now, out in the open like this, Myra felt the cold more than she had during the day. Even without snow.

Lights from the surrounding city, and the just visible glow of

Manhattan, turned the cloud cover orange, adding a strange sort of light to the dark graveyard.

"I'm sure this is the end of the hunt," she said. "This is where my grandmother is buried."

"Your father led you to your grandmother's grave?"

"No. Well, not technically. I mean, he didn't bury his treasures in her grave, if that's what you're worried about. I don't have to dig up her coffin or anything."

"That's a relief."

"He was a thief and a conman, but not a grave robber. He knew I loved puzzles. He wouldn't have ended all this fun with something gross."

"So…we're not going to your grandmother's grave?"

"We might swing past before leaving. But why we're here is a tomb set in a small hill not far from her grave. When I was a kid, he'd bring me here with him to pay his respects to his mother. I didn't know her well, by the way, except for visiting her here. She died when I was about two so I don't have any real memories of her alive. But I thought of this place as 'visiting grandma,' and it was a nice day out in greenery with my dad and sometimes both mom and dad. But I was a kid. So I got bored and wandered off among the stones, enjoying having so much grass and so many trees around me."

"You weren't scared? It's a graveyard."

She shrugged. "Not a scary one in the middle of the day. Pretty. And like I said, lots of grass and trees and open space. Not a normal part of my day-to-day at that time."

She adjusted her coat with one hand as she led him along one of the smaller roads winding through the place. She'd taken the larger box back from him for the flight here and carried it cradled in one arm. It now also held the Egyptian cylinder, the brass envelope, and the smaller box she'd tucked into her pocket earlier in the hunt. She never had gotten a bag to carry everything, but she wanted to keep all the little notes and treasures together because they'd been left by her father. The box was heavier now than it had been, but she didn't mind.

"Anyway," she said, "I frequently went exploring while they attended the grave, and once, I found this really nice tomb. It looked like a little house. I guess I was about seven or eight at the time, and I thought it was a house for people who'd died. I even knocked to see if I could come in."

"You wanted to visit the dead people?" He gave her an incredulous look.

"I was a kid. And we were already here visiting dead people. I thought actually seeing someone might be a nice change of pace."

The cold wind blew her hair across her face and she tucked it back behind her ears. She glanced up at the cloudy sky, lit orange from the city lights, and judged they had another half hour before more snow fell.

"The tomb's wooden door was locked of course," she continued. "There was no metal gate over it or anything. Just the wooden door and a key lock. It required one of those big keys. The old-fashioned kind. With the long neck and decorative head? Which, of course, I didn't have on me."

"But I suppose that didn't stop you."

She laughed. "It did not. I did have my new lockpicks on me—present for my last birthday—and I decided this was a great way to practice."

"You picked the lock and broke into a tomb." He shook his head, but there was a glint of humor in his eyes and that soft purple glow filled the blue now. "Grave robber child."

"I was just going to *visit* the dead people, not steal their stuff." She bumped up against his arm with her shoulder. He was too tall for her to bump his shoulder. In response, he took hold of her free hand, cradling it in his big grip as they wandered down the road. Even through her gloves she felt his warmth.

"So you broke into the tomb?"

"I broke into the tomb. And was very disappointed not to see a group of ghosts sitting around a small stone table drinking tea."

"That's what you thought ghosts did in their tombs?"

"Seven or eight remember? I was only seven, maybe eight."

He smiled down at her. "What happened after the disappointment faded."

"My parents found me reading the plaques of the dearly departed, and my mom gave me a lecture about disturbing the dead, and my dad agreed with her every word while at the same time praising my lockpicking skills and encouraging me to keep practicing. It was a lecture full of mixed messages."

"I'm sorry I didn't get to meet your parents," Christopher said. "After today, I feel like I would have liked to have known them."

"You would have. My mother would have loved you and your damsels-in-distress soft spot." She looked out over the expanse of dark headstones so he wouldn't catch the moisture gathering in her eyes or the tension in her jaw as she held back the unexpected tears.

She hadn't thought about any of this stuff in a long time. She knew, when she started this day, that she'd be opening herself to all the memories again. Letting all the good times return along with the ever-present ache of missing her parents. She'd even known what sharing this with Christopher would mean.

She just hadn't expected the tears.

They walked in silence for a few moments, the night closing in around them. In the distance, she could hear cars rumbling along Queens Boulevard, but this deep into the graveyard, everything was relatively quiet. Just the shooshing of wind through the scattered trees and a hush that felt appropriate to the setting.

When she had better control of her emotions, she said, "The

tomb is where we're headed, if you hadn't guessed. That's where my father would have stored his treasures. Someplace we'd all know and remember, but not directly associated with us in any real way. And not a place likely to be broken into or even opened."

"No new family members being interred?"

"Most of that family line is gone. It was an older tomb. We researched it when we got back from the cemetery because I wanted to know who the ghosts would have been if I'd seen them. And my parents indulged me."

It had set up a pattern for her life, too. When curious, she looked things up. She didn't always find *all* the information. Sometimes the information was hidden or not available—like pictures of Christopher and his brothers weren't available anywhere—but she'd learned how to find a lot. And she really loved the research part of her job. She liked learning things.

A habit of curiosity her parents had encouraged.

"We ended up with a whole family genealogy and history," she said with a smile. Like we were researching our own ancestors. I felt quite close to the Bravermans after all that research."

She nodded ahead. Just to the left of the road and back a row or two, the little gray stone temple-shaped tomb, with its flat roof and front columns. As an adult, she realized the "house" did look more like an ancient Greek temple with those columns and the stepped decorations around the roof, but she still thought of it as a house like she had as a kid.

It wasn't a particularly elaborate tomb, despite the temple-like construction. But it was still pretty, with a set of stone steps up to the thick, rectangular wooden door, and urns bracketing the stairs that held small, evergreen bushes. Someone had decorated the bushes for the holiday with little winking white lights powered by solar batteries. The lights were dim, but sparkly.

Myra did like sparkles.

She stood at the foot of the stairs, looking at the wooden door, memories of the last time she'd picked that lock flooding her. Christopher remained quietly at her side, a steady and warm presence on the icy cold night.

Finally, she handed him back the large box with all her treasures in it and pulled her lockpicks out of her inner vest pocket. "Time to collect dad's treasure."

Chapter Twelve

T he inside of the tomb was small, tiny really. No room for Christopher to follow her in for sure. So he waited just outside as she stepped over the threshold past the wooden door she'd opened. As she put her lockpicks back into the inner pocket in her vest, she pulled out a penlight to studied the pitch-black space.

It was a lot smaller inside than she remembered from her childhood. But then, she was a lot larger now. A series of plaques lined the walls, memorials to the Braverman ancestors who'd passed on. The air inside was cold, almost as cold as it was outside, but dry with a musty smell that was hard to describe. Christopher probably smelled the bodies. She'd never been sure if there were bodies buried beneath the stone floor of the tomb or ashes from cremation behind the plaques. That hadn't been something she'd researched when looking at the family history if this tomb. All she'd known was there were no ghosts.

There were still no ghosts. Not the Braverman ghosts anyway.

The ghost of memories did haunt the place for her, though. But they were the good kind of ghost memories. The kind that made her smile softly.

She swung the penlight around, hunting around the floor, the flat ceiling above, looking for her father's treasure. She didn't *think* he'd have hidden it behind one of the plaques, but also, if some Braverman ancestor did step forward to be buried here, he wouldn't have wanted the cemetery caretakers to find the treasure.

So where would he have left it.

There was a small cubby at the very back of the tomb, an inset in the wall with a little statue of a saint, or maybe it was the Virgin Mary. It glowed faintly white when she swung her light across it. She remembered that from her one and only other visit inside the tomb, thinking at first it was one of the ghosts and then being disappointed when it wasn't.

Ducking to keep her head from brushing the low ceiling, she went closer, studied the statue. It seemed a little crooked in its nook.

"See anything?" Christopher asked from the door.

"Not sure yet. Maybe." She gently touched the statue, pushed it a little. It moved.

She got close enough to run her light over all the details of the statue near the base of the nook, and after a moment, smiled. Then she pulled the little statue forward, opening a secret panel in the wall behind it.

Her father must have installed that somehow because she couldn't imagine why the Bravermans would include something like a secret hidden nook in their crypt. Unless they wanted to hide some sort of wealth from graverobbers. But Myra figured the other Braverman family members would be more likely to retrieve any valuables left in the tomb before strange graverobbers might come looking.

She flicked her penlight's narrow beam into the hidden cavity. It danced over a patch of dark velvet, the color impossible to really see with just the penlight. She reached in and slowly pulled out the package. A thick package, wrapped in velvet.

"Found something," she said.

She ran her light over the interior of the hidey hole again, just in case she'd missed something. It wasn't a large space and only went back about a foot. Still, she reached in a felt around. Nothing else hidden that she could detect. But then, she was pretty sure the velvet-wrapped box was all her father had left here.

Outside, Christopher stepped back to give her room, and she handed him the new box so she could relock the tomb. When she turned back, he was standing at the base of the two stairs, which brought her closer to his height. He was still a head taller her than her, but she was closer now. He was staring at her, not either of the boxes he held, and his concern was obvious in the creases between his brow.

"Why are you worried?" she asked, taking the new box back from him.

"What if it's not what you think? What if your father led you on a wild goose chase?"

"You're worried I'll be devastated and upset after everything we did tonight."

"I am."

"I won't be. The adventure of the hunt was as much the present my father left me as anything. There could be a handful of old bills in this box and I'd be okay with it. But I know what's in here. It's not old bills."

"No," said a new voice. An unfortunately remembered one. From earlier that day. "It's my boss's stolen property. And we're here to get it back."

Chapter Thirteen

Christopher stepped in front of Myra before she could stop him, blocking her almost entirely from view where she still stood on the tomb steps. She glanced around his arm to assess their situation.

Phone-Guy from the Staten Island train platform and his gray puffer jacketed friend stood about a hundred feet away, with a dozen or so headstones between them and her and Christopher. They stood right next to a large obelisk headstone that could serve as cover, but they weren't behind it at the moment. Out in the open. With their guns.

Guns again. Argh.

"Nothing that belongs to anyone but my family is in here," she said. "Nothing that's valuable to your boss is here. I don't know how many times I have to say that." She scowled. "How the hell did you find us?"

Queens was a long way from Staten Island. And she and Christopher had been flying, and been all over Manhattan all afternoon and evening. They couldn't have followed them.

Phone-Guy shrugged. "Slipped a tracker into your boyfriend's pocket."

Would that work when he shifted and did the fog thing that took his clothes with it? Except for his pants and shoes, everything else had magically disappeared when he'd shifted with that fog. She couldn't image any kind of tracking device surviving that. Or that Christopher wouldn't have noticed somehow.

"You never got close enough to me to plant anything," Christopher said, his voice very deep and low. He handed the second box with all her treasures in it back to her, but didn't take his gaze off the thugs.

Myra scrambled to take both boxes, then set them on the ground at her back, near the tomb door so she'd have her hands free for… Whatever happened next.

When she faced the thugs again, Phone-Guy was grinning at Christopher, and Puffer Jacket was smirking at her.

"Remember helping that woman carry her stroller up the stairs?" Phone-Guy said.

Myra wanted to groan. Shit. Christopher had gotten into trouble *again* trying to help someone. The poor man was going to kick himself for that.

"Not the pregnant woman herself," Phone-Guy said, probably at some look on Christopher's face hinting that more explanation might prevent a stream of fire from the dragon's mouth. "She was just the distraction. And don't worry, she got paid. Good distraction. Makes it easier to sneak up behind someone and brush past without them noticing."

Christopher patted his pants pockets and pulled out a small circular plastic tracker from one of his back pockets. Phone-Guy smirked. Christopher crushed the tracker between his fingers, the plastic and electronics crumbling to near dust as it dropped to the ground.

Phone-Guy didn't flinch. Myra did.

In front of her, she could *feel* the anger pumping off Christopher. Waves of heat washing over her, as hot as an actual furnace. He was fully dressed, having returned to his clothes after shifting his wings away once they'd landed at the cemetery. And yet she could still feel so much heat from him, she was a little afraid his clothes were going to combust.

She wanted to touch his arm, to assure him everything was okay, but she was worried she'd get burnt if she did.

Looking around his big body, she gave the Phone-Guy and Puffer Jacket a head shake. "You two have made a rather serious miscalculation here. A mistake that's gonna cost you. But if you leave now and just forget about all this, you'll probably survive. Maybe. Depends on how easy you make it for a dragon to find you."

Christopher let out that growling hiss sound that meant someone was in serious trouble. A sound that didn't bode well for Phone-Guy and Puffer Jacket's survival.

"My boss hasn't waited all these years to get his stuff back for nothing," Phone-Guy said. "We're taking that." He nodded at the ground behind Myra where both boxes sat. "We'll take them both. And you might survive the process if you cooperate."

Myra stepped back closer to the boxes and shook her head. "No. These aren't anything your boss wants. But they are important to me. You can't have either box."

She started calculating the best escape, where they could go to get cover from those guns, find a place open enough for Christopher to shift and get them airborne but not so open they'd get shot.

Normally, when Myra planned a heist, she had backup plans on her backup plans. Some of those were a little amorphous and she had to calculate contingencies and make things up as she went, but there was usually some knowledge and forethought put into even the amorphous contingency plans.

She hadn't made one here. She hadn't thought these guys could have tracked them. She hadn't even considered that they might be good enough to slip a tracker on Christopher even before she'd met with Harry. That they'd know enough about Christopher to know something like the pregnant woman needing help up slippery stairs with her stroller would attract Christopher's attention.

Whatever their boss wanted back, he was very very serious about it. But Myra *knew* what she'd recovered from the tomb had nothing to do with that. She knew what was in the new box. And it wasn't something that was valuable to anyone but her.

So she didn't have a contingency plan in place for this. She knew this cemetery from her youth but hadn't been here in more than a decade. The layout of the place scrolled across her mind as she searched for options, but the details were fuzzy after so many years, making the planning harder.

All the mental effort she put into trying to figure a way out of all this…

She should have known better.

Christopher was truly pissed. As angry as she'd ever seen him. Maybe even angrier. He might have been this angry when she'd been hit by a wizard bolt and went tumbling down an elevator shaft, but she was unconscious so she couldn't say for sure.

All she knew was that in this moment, he was angry enough that the heat coming off him felt like fire. And the scent of sulfur was getting stronger. And there was even a faint glow of purple fog swirling in the air around him that wasn't obvious in the dark but was starting to obscure his legs.

If he shifted to his full dragon form right in front of her, would any of the nearby headstones survive? Would the Braverman tomb?

She started to reach for him, but the air around him was so hot it was like holding her hand over an open flame.

Her eyes wide, she looked at Phone-Guy, at Puffer Jacket. "You have about twenty seconds to get away."

Phone-Guy laughed. "He ain't gonna crisp us. He wouldn't dare. He does, he's made an enemy of my boss. And he don't want that."

"I'll take my chances," Christopher said. His voice was so deep, so guttural, he did not sound like himself. "Back against the tomb," he said, quieter. To her.

Myra didn't hesitate. She stepped as close to the tomb as she could get, tight against the door with the two boxes just beside her.

A rush of heat and sound and fire erupted from Christopher in a stream that arrowed out over the tops of the headstones.

Chapter Fourteen

The whole thing lasted less than a second. In that second, Myra thought she might have heard gun shots, but by the time the guns went off, it would have been much too late.

The light from Christopher's stream of fire was so intensely bright, she squeezed her eyes shut. Even like that, she knew when the fire stopped. The roaring sound cut off abruptly. The heat against her skin eased slightly. The crinkling of soil turned to glass filled in the quiet. And the stench of burnt grass and…other things, wafted through the air.

In the distance, the sounds of traffic. But nothing else.

The cemetery was very quiet.

She opened her eyes and blinked away the after-image spots.

Without her penlight, with only the ambient light from the surrounding city to show her anything, the charred lumps where Phone-Guy and Puffer Jacket had been standing were hard to see in detail. That was for the best. The details were one thing Myra was not curious about.

"I did warn them," she said quietly. She'd been unconscious the last time Christopher had crisped somebody, so she hadn't been confronted by the reality of it. Knowing someone could do something, and watching them do it were two different things.

Watching fire erupt from Christopher, even for a second, had been a terrifying reality check.

Not that she forgot he was a dragon shifter. Not that she underestimated his killing ability.

She just hadn't witnessed it before.

He turned back to her slowly, carefully, and watched her through wary eyes. There was a yellow glow this time over the blue, a glow she only saw when he was angry. That glow faded, but his eyes were still lit and bright in the nighttime. He wasn't breathing hard. The heat that had been pumping off him had eased. And the smell of sulfur was gone. Replaced by…

Sugar cookies.

Not charged bodies, though if she concentrated, that smell reached her. But if she didn't, all she got was that scent of vanilla and sugar that she sometimes got from Christopher. And it was strong enough to block out everything else. Strong enough she almost smiled. It was a pleasant, yummy smell she found hard to resist.

And she realized suddenly, that was absolutely the point.

"You smell like sugar cookies again," she said.

He blinked. That probably wasn't one of the first things he'd expected her to say in this moment.

"Do you understand why yet?" he asked quietly.

"Can't find it anywhere. Been looking since the female dragon incident."

"It's not common knowledge." He nodded. "Are you hurt?"

"Of course not. Last time you did this around me, I was in your arms and unconscious and I still wasn't hurt. Why would I be hurt standing behind you?"

"Just checking." His voice was easing back to normal. Still a bit guttural, but he sounded like himself again.

"You're worried about how I feel about all this," she guessed.

His nod was jerky and quick.

"Think it'll change the way I feel about you?"

Another jerky nod.

"But you'd do it again to protect me."

That same nod. He never once broke eye contact.

"I mean… They did have guns. And we did warn them to back off. Can't blame us that they're too stupid to recognize the danger they put themselves into." She shrugged. "Not going to look at them too closely now, though."

"Don't. You won't like it." He took a step toward her, then stopped abruptly. His hands opened and closed into fists at his side.

"You still too hot to touch?" she asked.

He shook his head. "Wasn't sure you'd want me to touch you."

Oh. Well. She closed the space between them and wrapped her arms around his waist, pressing tight against him. He was still warm, but not that furnace hot anymore.

"For the record," she said, "crisping bad people with guns pointed at us is not the kind of thing that will make me want to avoid touching you."

All his muscles seemed to relax at once, like he flowed from statue stiff into a living man as he wrapped his arms around her and brought his mouth down on hers so suddenly, she gasped. Then she sank into the kiss. There was a lot of relief there. Relief that no one had been shot. Relief that the thugs hadn't taken her father's treasure. And relief that, between them at least, this hadn't changed things.

His kiss was deep, sweeping, intense. Not bruising. But the intensity, the sheer passion of it left her breathless and hungry and dizzy. Left her wanting so much more.

Finally. Soon.

She eased back, but not enough to let any cold night air sneak in between them. Blinked up at him as he stared down at her. His breathing was as ragged as hers. She reached up and touched his cheek.

"Are *you* okay?" she asked. At least one of the guns had gone off in that second as the flame swept across the tombstones.

His arms flexed around her. "Now I am."

That brought out a soft smile. "We should get out of here. The caretakers are going to have an awful surprise in the morning."

"They'll know it was a dragon."

"But not which one. Will this cause you problems, though?"

"Not with anyone who matters." Again, his arms flexed around her.

Her heartbeat pounded a little harder, and the flutter in her stomach intensified. And really all she wanted in that moment was to get him somewhere safe and alone.

"Can we go to your place?" she asked quietly, holding his gaze.

He swept her up into his arms so fast, she got dizzy. But the move made her chuckle and she was sure that was the point.

"Wait, the boxes!" He released her reluctantly, which was sweet, and she stacked the boxes, velvet-wrapped on top, in her arms.

When she turned back to him, he swept her up again before she could gasp. Then his chest and arms flexed, a shredding of clothing across his back, and his wings spread wide behind him.

She widened her eyes up at him. "Why not just do that fog thing?"

"I'd have to let you go again, and I don't want to."

"Oh." Her heart skipped giddily in her chest. "You ruined your clothes for me."

"And for me. Like I said, I don't want to let you go. Not even long enough to take the coat off. I can replace the coat."

That heart-pounding, stomach-fluttering thing got worse. Left her breathless. Left her dizzy all over again.

She cradled the two boxes tightly in her arms and leaned in to him. She wanted to wrap herself around him and never let go either. But this would do for now.

"Let's go," she said.

He dipped and then launched into the air, his wings snapping downward and catching an air current, bringing them high, circling over Queens as they turned back toward Manhattan. Back toward his apartment.

Toward something…new.

Chapter Fifteen

O n the flight, Christopher asked her about the velvet-wrapped box. What she intended on doing with it.

"Opening it. With you." Myra hugged her arms tighter around the two boxes. "That was always the plan. I want you to see what's in here. It's important."

Somehow, showing him this after the day they'd had seemed even more important now. For him to understand what all this meant to her. For her. It just felt, well, important.

Especially because she was quite certain somewhere in the last few months, she'd tumbled past desire and lust into something much more serious. She didn't just like Christopher. She didn't just want him. She wanted more from him than she'd ever wanted from a man.

And confronting that reality meant looking through her past.

As his feet settled onto the stone balcony of his apartment, he tightened his grip on her, as if he didn't want to set her down. She didn't mind. She wasn't in a hurry to get out of his arms either.

"You're sure about this?" he asked.

Myra nodded. "Never been more sure of anything."

He carried her toward the French doors that opened into his apartment. She'd been on this balcony with him several times. And fallen asleep here once, when she'd drifted off in a comfy lounger while they watched a movie—their first technical date—and she'd woken in a huge bed inside. Alone. And fully dressed.

The alone and dressed had felt a little unfortunate at the time but also a relief, because at that time, she hadn't been quite ready for where that step would take their relationship.

She was more than ready now. Beyond ready. Her body tingling and restless and eager. She had one more thing she needed to do, though, and it was show him what her father had left behind for her to find.

But instead of staying on the balcony to look through the velvet-wrapped box's contents, Christopher carried her right inside. She wasn't sure if the balcony was more comfortable for him even in the winter. She hadn't asked. But it was where they spent most of their time when they were here.

This time was different. On a lot of levels.

Inside, he nudged the door closed behind him and Myra took in the apartment at night. Recessed lights flickered on automatically when they stepped inside, but the lighting was dim and comfortable after coming in from the darkness. Only bright enough to keep from tripping on anything. Not that Christopher left much around to trip on.

The back door opened onto a large living room with a double high ceiling. The air was cool, but not cold like outside. Not overly heated like a lot of New York apartments in the winter, though. She might have even found it too cool if she wasn't cradled in his very warm arms still. The floors were black marble, the furniture minimal. Just a couch and a couple of chairs, all with metal bases and stiff looking cushions. Not the sort of couch you sank into and took a nap on. Or at least, she wouldn't. But Christopher might find that solid base comfortable for naps.

She had a hard time picturing him napping on the couch though and wondered if he ever did. That would be fun to witness for reasons she couldn't name but that made her feel a little melty inside.

There was also a wide, deep marble fireplace in front of the couch, and a huge flat-screen TV hung on the wall above the mantle-less fireplace. There wasn't a lot of art or pictures on the wall. A double-high bookshelf opposite the TV, with no ladder to reach the high shelves, and filled with mostly genre books. She'd snooped when he'd left her alone in his bed, but not too much. She'd just looked at all the obvious stuff, like his taste in fiction, which ran, somewhat ironically, to mysteries and thrillers and heist novels. Though he also had an impressive collection of Romance novels and even some literary fiction. What he didn't have, she noticed, were any fantasy books that involved dragons.

Hard to blame him for that.

A set of wide, circular metal stair near the middle back of the huge room wound up to the second floor and the huge bedroom suite. Behind the staircase, an open kitchen with shiny appliances she'd never asked if he used.

The place was spotlessly clean and pretty bare all in all. Especially for a dragon who did have a hoard somewhere around here. Or somewhere. He'd never disclosed the location of his hoard and she hadn't gone looking for it. Especially after learning that him voluntarily showing her his hoard...meant something important. It was something dragons only did with their mates. When she'd learned that, she'd tamped down her curiosity and had left that secret a secret.

She hadn't thought deeply about why until now. Now she realized it was because she wanted that voluntary tour one day. And she didn't want to spoil that or make assumptions.

The same reason she wanted to voluntarily show him *her* treasures, even if the velvet wrapped box didn't really count as a hoard. It was the closest she came to one.

"Want anything to drink?" he asked, still cradling her in his arms. It was almost like he forgot he was carrying her sometimes. Like holding her this way was so natural and easy, he forgot to set her down.

She really didn't mind and still wasn't in a hurry to leave his arms, but she patted his shoulders and he let her legs ease to the ground. "Would take a tea if it's not too much trouble."

He released her—very reluctantly, which was gratifying—and went to the kitchen while she went to the couch to sit down. He had a metal and marble-topped coffee table in front of the couch with nothing on it. No magazines or nicknacks or plants. The minimal space was nice, but she thought he needed at least one or two plants. And she wondered about the place because it felt…temporary even though this was always where they went when they needed a private place.

The bedroom hadn't felt temporary, she remembered. But those were thoughts for later.

From the kitchen, Christopher said, "Fireplace on." And a row of flames flashed up across a gas line at the base of the hearth, warming the room almost immediately.

"Fancy," she said.

"I don't use it often, but I thought it might be cold in here for you."

"Thanks." She set the velvet box on the coffee table and the box she'd gotten from Harry, which contained all their other finds from the scavenger hunt, under the table out of the way. Then she shifted on the couch so she could watch him putter in the kitchen. That felt so intimate, almost too intimate, watching him opening and closing cabinets, putting an electric kettle on to boil. All the little manual steps to making a cup of tea. Unlike his casually voice-activated fireplace, this he did by hand.

He brought her a cup of peppermint tea, which reminded her of candy canes, and that reminded her they were only two days away from Christmas, less now since it was after midnight. She took a few sips of her tea before setting the mug gently on the coffee table and picking up the velvet wrapped box, carefully unwrapping the soft material—which turned out to be a dark shade of purple that strangely reminded her of Christopher's scales.

Beneath the velvet was a brass box the size of a long, narrow mailing box, but shaped to have a flap over it that made it look like an oversized envelop or one of those file folders that people in offices used. This was all metal, though, and the tab that held the flap shut was a pretty, decorative brass rose. Her mother's favorite flower.

She set her hand on the top of the brass flap, over the small rose tab. "This was something very precious to my father, and very important. But, like I said, it wouldn't be important to anyone else. Except me and my parents. Harry might have found this important if he'd known what was really here. But as my dad's best friend, he never asked, and my dad wouldn't have told."

"You don't have to share this with me if it's too personal," he said quietly. "Even after everything today."

"No. I want to. That's the point. The reason we did this today. I want to."

He softly caressed his fingertips over the hand she had set on the box. "Only if you're sure."

She smiled, her gaze on his huge hand so gently caressing the back of hers, his thumb brushing her skin in a reassuring gesture that was both soothing and also made her stomach fluttering worse.

Giving herself a little shake, she moved her hand and he pulled his back so she could open the flap.

She considered the little rose tab, a small button that needed to be pushed to open the flap. No locks here, though. Just a gentle push and the flap sprung upward a little so she could fold it back on hinges that didn't resist the movement, even after all this time.

She said, "You know how your father won't allow pictures of any of the royal family?"

Christopher nodded, a gesture she had to look up to see.

"I sort of waved that off, thought it was a bit odd, but whatever. Except… My dad had a similar policy when I was growing up. No pictures. Not even among ourselves."

"Why?"

"He didn't want any of the people he worked with to have pictures of us. He even went so far as to buy a magical charm he would set up around wherever we lived so people couldn't take pictures of us while we were at home. He didn't want any of his enemies to figure out what we looked like, at least not in images that could be easily passed around."

"Makes a kind of sense."

"He was trying to preserve our privacy and safety. Took me a bit to realize that's what your father was doing for you and your brothers."

"That and he's a controlling bastard who wanted to ensure he kept the spotlight."

She snorted. "Yeah, that sounds right, too. Still. The ban on pictures of the royal family has helped you keep some sort of anonymity. Even if you can't hide that you're a dragon shifter."

There was a pause, and then he said, "I suppose it's helped. Did your father's dictate help you?"

"I suppose it did. Honestly, I rarely thought about it. We just didn't have pictures lying around, and it never really occurred to me that this was a thing that should occur to me. But…" She glanced down at the box. "But my mother was sentimental. And my father more so because of her. So sometimes we did take pictures. Sometimes. Sometimes, my father even kept them." She met Christopher's gaze. "I haven't seen them in ten years. I barely remember their faces because time does that. I can hear my mother's voice still sometimes. And I definitely hear my dad's voice if I'm taking too long to pick a lock."

Christopher smiled at that.

"But I haven't seen them in a long time." She patted the brass box. "This is our treasure." She laid the flap back against the couch, revealing the interior of the thin rectangular box, and the small pile of pictures inside.

Some were polaroids from way back in the day. Some were pictures from a roll of film that her dad had processed himself so no one would have access to the negatives. Some were printouts from a later digital camera only a year before they died. Pictures of them together. Pictures of her opening a present. Pictures of a sunny outing to Coney Island or the zoo. Smiling.

There were a few of just her parents, looking at each other. The love obvious even in the shot. One she even remembered taking during one of her dad's weak moments when he wanted to preserve something. There was a shot of her and mom in front of the Bryant Park Christmas tree. And another on the Staten Island Ferry. She couldn't remember why they'd been on the ferry that particular time. Probably going to see Harry.

And speaking of… There were a few photos of her dad and Harry together. A couple with her mom, dad, and Harry, all hamming it up for the camera. One with her mom holding Myra as a baby, and her dad and Harry standing on either side, looking terrified and delighted at once.

There weren't as many as she imagined other people gathered over a lifetime, but there were enough. Enough to spark memories. Enough to feel thing she hadn't allowed herself to in years.

Enough to see them again.

She touched the image of Harry standing beside her mom and dad when she was a baby. "Ten years was maybe a little too long," she murmured.

"Why did you stay away so long?" Christopher said quietly. "I mean, I get why you weren't ready for the pictures. But why did you stay away from Harry for so long?"

She shook her head, sighing. "At first… After my parents died, I got a bit…reckless in my thieving. Took the kinds of risks I wouldn't normally. I was… It was like I *wanted* to get caught. I thought, if I did, and I ended up in jail like my father used to off and on, I didn't want Harry to feel like he had to bail me out, look after me, take heat because of me. The way he'd done for my dad all those years. He'd done enough. I didn't want him taking on those same…chores with me." She shrugged. "Once the grief lifted enough to see what I was doing, I was embarrassed to go back. Then I thought I might not be welcome. And then it just became a habit. You get used to being on your own. You get used to being alone."

"So why now? As you said, ten years is a long time."

She glanced up at him from under her lashes, knowing what she was doing here and still nervous. "That thing with the female dragon, with Jasmin… That left me shaky. Left me thinking about my own mortality in a way I don't usually."

"You jump off the side of buildings regularly. Your mortality never crosses your mind?"

She grinned. "Nope. I know what I'm doing when I do that. I

have an element of control over the amount of risk I'm taking. I love risks."

He snorted, a sound half humor, half groan.

"What can I say? It comes with my innate skills, I think. My dad was the same way. But taking risks where I've calculated the odds and know what I'm getting into is one thing. That's a rush. It's fun. Having an unpredictable female dragon somewhere out there who not only knows who I am, but maybe doesn't like me so much is something else. And it's not like I haven't made some enemies over the years. But none of them quite like her. None of my enemies could lay waste to the entire island of Manhattan in a few sweeps and then go take a nap. That's next level spooky. So, yeah, I've been thinking about my life. And the possibility of my death."

"And you didn't want to die before seeing Harry again and doing…this." He gestured to the pictures spread out across the couch between them and in her lap.

But she knew that gesture took in their entire day, the last twenty-four hours of the scavenger hunt.

"Exactly. I didn't want to die with Harry thinking…thinking I didn't remember him or think about him. And I didn't want to die leaving the last thing my dad ever did for me unfinished." She glanced down at the pictures in her lap. "I didn't want to die without seeing them again." She blinked up at Christopher. "And I didn't want to die before I showed them to you. So someone else besides me and Harry could…remember them. Maybe long past when I die. Someone else will have known they existed."

Christopher reached across the space between them and cupped her cheek. "I'm honored. I'll remember them. We have an accord."

She smiled a little even as tears she *never* shed pricked at her eyes. "You said that to that dragon in Chicago, Archer. Sounds very formal."

"It is. It's a formal giving of our word. All dragons take that phrase as an unbreakable oath. We don't say it lightly."

The sentimental ache in her heart flipped over to something else, something different but just as strong.

"Thank you." She rubbed her face against his palm. "I knew you'd understand."

And wasn't that just amazing.

Chapter Sixteen

Gently, Myra put the photos back into the brass box, smiling as she got flashes of her mom or dad's smiling faces. These joined *her* "hoard" now. Not that she called her small treasure collection a hoard since she wasn't a dragon. Still, she kept a few things, special things, in a safe place. And this would be stored with them.

But in the meantime, there was something else she needed to do tonight. Or this morning since it was closer to sunrise than to midnight now.

She set the box on the marbled topped coffee table, next to her forgotten and cooling cup of peppermint tea. Christopher blinked at her when she took his mug, now empty, and set it on the coffee table, too.

He didn't say anything, but he watched her through narrow eyes.

"Why do you smell like sugar cookies to me sometimes?" she asked. "Everyone but me seems to know the significance."

She'd taken off her coat earlier, when they'd separated so he could make tea, and had draped it across the back of the couch. Christopher had dropped the last shreds of his coat and shirt somewhere near the kitchen. He'd kicked off his shoes almost the minute they stepped into his apartment. She wondered if the cool marble felt good on his feet. The heat from the gas fire washed over the couch, leaving the marble here warmer as she kicked off her own shoes, shoving them under the coffee table.

Still watching her warily, Christopher said, "Dragons can do that sometimes. Adjusted our scent. It's…biology. To put… someone at ease."

"Is it in your control?"

"Not entirely. Somewhat. But not entirely. Like I said, it's biology."

"Why sugar cookies? Does every dragon smell that way when they're trying to put someone at ease?"

"We'll smell like whatever the person we're… We'll smell like something they love."

"I do love sugar cookies." She stood and faced him.

In that moment, he looked up at her. He was so tall she rarely had this perspective, being able to look at him from this angle. She liked it, the way his expression softened, the way the angle of his mouth was just right.

He faced her more fully, and she nudged his thighs apart so she could step closer. His hand came up to her hips automatically. The same way he caught her when she jumped into his arms before a flight. Like that's where his hands were always supposed to be. His fingers flexed against her, digging into her skin as she got close enough he had to tip his head back. Not all that far. Even sitting down, he was still almost as tall as her, but she did like this unique angle.

"Thank you for showing me your family," he said quietly. "For showing me your memories."

"It was important. To me. That you…saw me. Saw where I came from." She wasn't prepared to say why yet. It was enough to even admit she wanted him to see her.

"I do." His voice was a quiet whisper in the huge room.

The fireplace at her back was a line of warmth that felt almost cool compared to Christopher's heat. But he wasn't so hot that she couldn't touch. This was the kind of warmth that made her want to get closer, want to snuggle up against him all night.

His blue eyes glittered and a faint purple glow rose from the depths, lighting his eyes. His expression, intent on her, hungry as he scanned her face, made her heart pound hard for all the right reasons.

Finally, she leaned down, leaned in, and settled her mouth over his. A kiss that started in a gentle coming together. A brush of lips. A sealing of understanding.

But before one breath and the next, that kiss erupted, intensity and need washing through her in a flash. She angled her head, deepened the kiss…or maybe he deepened it. She didn't know and didn't really care. Just needed his mouth on hers, his tongue tangled with her, his breath against her cheek, his hands tight on her body.

He moved his hands from her hips, to hug around her, banded her close, so as much of her body as they could manage pressed against him. Not quite enough, though. Not quite right.

She straddled him on the couch, climbing up and settling on his lap, her legs bracketing his thighs. Better better. She rocked against him, felt the press of his hard cock against her and moaned into his mouth.

Sensation rushed through her. The feel of his chest hard against her breasts, the muscles of his shoulder flexing under her fingers. All skin now. No scales. The feel of all that muscle, bunched and tight and hard against her was dizzying, satisfying like cracking a particularly tricky lock.

Hers.

In this moment. This night. He was hers. She felt it in his every sinew, in his every flex and groan. When she ground down against him and he growled. When he tightened the band of his arms around her back, dragging her up closer, higher against his chest so he could devour her mouth.

She wasn't sure who got her vest, shirt, and bra off. They somehow fumbled the clothing off together, but she was so high on his kiss, she barely noticed. Until her bare skin touched his. And a deep, thrilling satisfaction washed over her. Yes. She'd wanted this sensation for a long time now. Since meeting him. Since that very first kiss.

The rough scrape of his chest hair against her peaked nipples. The heat of his skin seeping directly into hers without any barrier. Her chest flattened against his. His hands splayed against her back, so large they nearly spanned the full width. His breath against her neck as he kissed along her jaw, down her throat. Her breathing heavy and deep and erratic at once.

Restlessly, she ground down against him, savoring his moan. Loving the way his fingers flexed into her skin. She felt his restraint, a tension in him that resisted release. Like he was afraid to hurt her. After watching him easily move an eight-hundred-pound bell around that night, she was grateful for the consideration. But she couldn't imagine him hurting her. Not on purpose. Not physically. She suspected he'd cut off his own arm before hurting her.

And the thought that he was so protective of her, not just any damsel in distress, but *her* in particular, seeped through her like warmed honey, leaving a deliciously deep sense of melting belonging, of delight and satisfaction and a thrilling sort of fear.

She clutched him tight as he stood abruptly, one hand wrapped under her ass to keep her in place. The change in position made her gasp, then she chuckled, because she loved that sudden, shocking move as much as she liked having her legs wrapped around his waist.

She did want to get her pants off soon, though, so there was no longer any barrier between her legs and his bare waist.

His lips still clinging to hers, or moving away only to taste more of her skin, he walked her to the wide, circular metal staircase that led up to the second level of his apartment. To his bed. She sank into his kisses, trusting him to navigate the stairs without dropping her or hurting himself, though the thought that he was going to had her heartbeat hammering. She clung tighter to him when he released the hand around her back to hold the railing, keeping one solid arm under her ass to hold her securely.

The climb was a series of rapid assents and pausing to sink into a deep kiss before he practically leapt up the next few steps. And when he finally reached the second-floor landing, she was so restless to have the rest of their close off, she was grinding against him, taking herself close to orgasm before she'd even gotten her pants off! The feel of his large hand spanning her ass didn't help.

She didn't notice them crossing the space between the bed and the stairs. Most of the second floor was his bedroom, with a huge bathroom and closet, but mostly open. That meant fewer doors in the way. That meant fewer barriers between them and the giant bed. Not that she would have noticed. He could have plowed through a solid wall and she wouldn't have noticed the dust settling on her. She was too caught up in the feel of his mouth under hers. She had her arms wrapped around his head now, kissing him so eagerly, so deeply, her world in that moment was him.

A change of position, the feel of his leg coming up under her as he climbed up onto his bed. She still clung to him, her legs firmly around his waist, and didn't relax until he'd settled them both down onto the mattress.

Almost as soon as her legs left his waist, he started kissing his way down her body, across her neck, nipping lightly at the skin between her neck and shoulder, making her arch up under him. One of his huge hands engulfed her small breast, gently cupping her in heat, her nipple rubbing against his palm. He flicked his thumb over her nipple, and she gasped, arching into his touch again.

Her entire body felt electrified, her nerves close to the surface. His lips gliding over her skin as he moved lower left a blazing trail of heated tingles in their wake. When he took one of her nipples into his mouth and sucked gently, she felt the tug all the way to her core. Already dangerously close to coming, that pressure pushed her even closer to the edge. And she still wasn't even out of her fucking pants.

Fumbling at her chunky heeled boots, she managed to kicked and wiggle them off, barely aware of the dull thud of them dropping to the rug that spread under the bed. Her pants and underwear were not so easy to wiggle out of when Christopher's big body was in the way as he continued exploring her skin with his mouth. He was taking his sweet time about the process, and that was both electrifying and frustrating.

But when his lips slid down the side of her ribs, along her waist, the combination of being overly sensitive and him hitting a lot of nerves in that pass made her thinking short circuit. She moaned and wrapped her legs around him again, desperate for some relief, pressure where she needed it most to relieve the building tension.

He trailed his lips farther down, over her belly, lower to the edge of her pants. She was wearing her usual black yoga pants, the kind of pants that didn't get in the way when she had to, say, scale a building. They were definitely in the way now, though, when she wanted to scale Christopher.

The good thing about her leggings, though, was that they were very easy to pull off. And fortunately, Christopher didn't waste time doing just that, taking her underwear with the leggings in one sweep. Though he did it slowly enough to make Myra whimper. Sliding the material down her legs in inches, kissing skin as he exposed it. Dropping licks and gentle bites along her thighs, the inside of her knees, her calves, a gentle kiss on her ankle as he tugged the rest of her clothing all the way off.

With that barrier gone, she reached for him, wanting his skin against hers again. He obliged but again slowly, sliding kisses up her legs, spreading her legs this time, and when he nibbled the inside of her thigh, licked his way higher along that sensitive skin, she bowed up, her jaw tight as the sensations made her want to scream and moan and come. And she could do none of that because it was all so much, so good, so deliciously electric. But when his mouth finally, found her slick wet heat and settled over her, licked a line over her and into her, flicked her swollen clit, Myra found her voice, moaning and panting his name.

She was so on fire, so sensitive and ready, she couldn't even open her eyes. She wanted to see him, to watch him, but her body wasn't entirely in her control in that moment. Her eyes stayed firmly shut, all her focus on that single point of building tension and sensation so perfect she couldn't even think. She bunched one hand in the sheets, another grasped his hair. He held her hips down as he pleasured her, his huge hands gentle but firm, and that only intensified the lush delight of his mouth on her clit.

Everything felt so good, so overwhelming and viciously perfect, she wanted it to last forever, and yet knew she couldn't take this level of sensation much longer. She wanted to hold back the building tide to enjoy his mouth and tongue on her as long as possible. But as long as possible wasn't very. Her body wound tight, so tight she knew she'd scream soon. Another flick of his tongue, a long firm suck...

And she fell. Tumbled completely. Free falling in an explosion of sensations that lit her body up and left her shivering and shaking. The echo of her scream filling the huge bedroom.

When she was able to finally open her eyes, finally look down at him, he was watching her, his eyes with that faint purple glow in them, and he was holding her close. Catching her as she came back down from the heights he'd taken her.

Just like she knew he always would.

That look in his eyes, the satisfaction and smugness, made her shake her head. "Get up here. I want more."

"Greedy," he said, his voice deep and graveling, rubbing over her already sensitive skin and making her shiver. "Good thing for you I like greedy and am *very* happy to follow that order."

She grinned. Then pointed at his pants. "Off."

Removing his pants went faster than hers but it still felt like too long because he wasn't touching her while he did. Then he was on the bed with her again, his warm body sliding up along hers. He was just so big he engulfed her and she loved it. She much of him to explore and wrap herself around. Which she did. Kissing every inch of his skin she could reach. His waist was surprisingly sensitive when she kissed him there. The thick muscle over his hip bones obsessed her. The thick ridge of his erection impossible to resist. And the sounds of his hissing breaths and groaning growls did make her exactly what he'd accused her of. Greedy. Greedy for more of those sounds, greedy for the taste of him on her tongue, greedy for the hard feel of his muscles under her sensitive finger tips. The textures and contrasts, smooth, hard, some roughness from the hair on his legs, at the base of his cock.

When she slipped the head of his erection between her lips and got a satisfying growl from him, she dipped lower, sliding her tongue and lips over him, savoring his taste and feel in her mouth as much as the sound of his panting pleasure. She wanted more. All. Everything that was him. And she wanted it all at once.

She was so focused on his taste, she gasped in surprise when he suddenly lifted her up over his chest, so fast she didn't even have a chance to protest until her face was in his. "I was having fun," she pouted.

"So was I," he said, his voice so rough and deep it barely sounded like him. "But I've wanted you for so long, I don't want to come in your mouth. Not this time anyway. I want to be buried in your heat, feel that tight wet pussy around my cock when I come."

She shivered at the description. "Sounds perfect. Let's do that."

His chuckle vibrated against her breasts.

He nuzzled her ear and neck, making her hum in the back of her throat, then said, "How much did you learn about dragon shifters and sex in all that research of yours?"

For reasons that seemed ridiculous at that moment, she felt a wash of heat crawling up her face. Given she was naked and sprawled on top of him and had just had his cock in her mouth, being embarrassed now felt weird.

"Enough to know condoms are unnecessary," she said.

Dragons controlled a lot of their bodily functions, including their ability to reproduce. Dragons didn't have kids on accident. They had kids because they chose to. Coming didn't release active sperm unless they wanted it to. They *did* have non-reproductive orgasms, a fact she'd be weirdly relieved to learn. And humans and dragon shifters didn't exchange STDs, so protection against those things weren't necessary either.

They were, almost, the perfect lovers in that way. Which was one of the many reasons humans tended to stand in awe of dragon shifters.

The only draw back to taking a dragon lover, so she'd read, was the possessiveness they often displayed. With a dragon, jealousy and possessiveness was fire-breathing dangerous. And a lot of humans found that possessiveness oppressive. Even scary. So it complicated taking a dragon lover. Complicated things more if you had a child with one of them.

Myra wasn't looking for kids any time soon. Maybe never, but she wasn't set on that. She was still getting used to the idea that she wanted someone in her life the way she wanted Christopher in her life. The idea of him getting jealous and possessive and losing some of what made him so attractive to her had been a little off-putting. But in the end, worth the risk.

This was Christopher after all.

She rose up enough to look him in the eyes. The purple glow covering his blue eyes was fascinating and she got caught in the bejeweled play of lights for a moment before giving herself a little shake. The gesture made him groan, and his hands on her back clenched tighter.

"Probably should have discussed this before being distracted by all the naked skin," she whispered.

"Probably." The rough sound of his voice sent another shiver through her and she slid down on him a little, nudge herself closer to the head of his erection.

He sucked in a deep breath, closed his eyes briefly. When his eyes flickered open, the purple was more intense. And the scent of sugar cookies wove through the other scents of sweat and musk and sex in the room. She smiled at that.

"I will take care of you," he said. "And I will not go anywhere you don't want to. In anything."

She wasn't sure he could control all the things enough to keep those promises. But the mere fact that he'd try burned away any residual worries that might have remained under the surface of her lust. She slid forward again to capture his mouth in a kiss she hoped conveyed all she was feeling. She didn't have words for most of this. She'd never felt like this before. But she hoped he'd understand even that with her kiss.

Then she moved down again, until his cock nudged against her heat. His sharply drawn breath filled her with satisfaction. But not nearly as much satisfaction as the slow slide down onto his cock, the way he filled her, stretched her, inch by delicious, thick inch. And he fit her perfectly. Not too big, despite their size difference—a possibility that had crossed her mind, but turned out dragons could control this to an extent too, adjusting to their partners so they were both pleased with the way everything fit together. She wasn't sure how much of that adjusting Christopher did in that moment, but she did know the way they fit was perfect for her and she wanted more. All.

She dropped her hips back hard for the last few inches and that sharp move brought a groan from both of them. A moment when she could feel all of him, felt so connected to this one man she wondered how they'd ever *not* been connected this way. Only a moment's pause though, before the restlessness, the need to move took over.

She rocked against him, rode the length of him, held his intense gaze until the sheer feel of fucking him swamped her senses and she closed her eyes. Didn't help her escape the intensity, though. The build of tension through her rose fast, surprising since she'd just had an orgasm not so long ago. Their position ensured he hit her in just the right spots, sending her spiraling upward, everything tight and desperate and urgent.

The sounds of their pants, their groans, the slap of skin against skin, the sweat that slicked between their bodies, all of the heat and friction… Myra held out for as long as possible, wanting to feel all this for as long as possible, this thrill of climbing so high, so fast, the rush of it. But then Christopher moved his hips a little, and that hit a spot inside that was like touching an electrical socket, sending so much sensation through her, she lost her bid for control.

Dropping off the side of a building was nothing to this fall, and she went with a shattered cry that echoed with his as she felt him pulse with her, in her. A moment of shivering, perfect breaking apart. Together.

Then she sank against his big chest, curled herself around him, his arms tightly banding around her waist. And she felt the security of his hold again, catching her as she sank back to earth. Just the way she knew he would.

"Worth the wait," she muttered into his neck. And grinned when his rusty chuckle bounced against her.

She wasn't exactly sure where they went from here and what this meant in the long run, but she knew she didn't want to be anywhere else but right here, right now. Nothing had ever felt quite this perfect, quite this…right.

And for now, that was all she needed. For now, this was all she wanted. The rest would work itself out.

For maybe the first time in her life, Myra was happy to go into something risky without a plan.

Freefalling.

Because Christopher was there to catch her.

Author's Note

Thank you for reading THE DRAGON THIEF SERIES, SEASON ONE, Omnibus Edition! I hope you enjoyed this season of the series.

As you can tell by my use of the term "season," I think of this series a bit like a TV show. Six "episodes" per year, though I suspect each of these novellas might make a few episodes in a regular TV show. There is a lot of influence from the TV show *Leverage* in the development of this series, and even more so in Season Two (releasing throughout 2025). But make it magic, obviously.

I also wanted the romantic storyline for my main characters to end happily (for now and ever after, eventually). This is, after all, a Romance story, with a capital R, inside a heist and urban fantasy series. Myra and Christopher's relationship will continue to develop, and I foresee some ups and downs, because that's how new relationships go, but I can also say with confidence that they're in for a happy ending. Eventually. Because Romance! (And I'm the author, so I make the decisions. LOL)

This series as an alternative history type of urban fantasy romance, different to, and therefore doesn't crossover with, any of my other urban fantasy and paranormal romance universes. In many ways, that freed me up to worldbuild in ways that I can't in most of my contemporary fantasy because a lot of those series are linked to other series. That's been a lot of fun. Though I do think Myra would get along well with some of the characters in my other series. And Christopher and Cary Redmond would definitely understand one another, what with the whole saving damsels in distress and Protector things going on.

If you explore some of my other fiction, written as Kat Simons but also some of my older work under my Isabo Kelly pseudonym, you'll see I love writing both protector characters and thieves. A lot. Strange combination, I know. But there you have it. Mostly my thieves lean toward the more Robin Hood type of character—none of them steal from people who can't afford to lose what's stolen—but something about thieves turning those skills toward the good really appeals to me. Probably because protector characters, like Christopher, also speak strongly to me.

The first story in the Dragon Thief series, and indeed the series as a whole, started from a story I wrote in a very odd and fun project called WHO STEALS A DRAGON. That book took the opening line, "Who steals a dragon?", and imagined from that line six different stories in six different genres with completely different characters and very different types of dragons. DRAGON THIEF was the paranormal romance story in that book.

Originally, I hadn't intended on ever separating those stories out and publishing them individually, or writing series with any of the characters. But I loved Myra and Christopher so much, I knew I'd write more with them. And I did.

As a side note, it seems my creative voice is wont to write series characters (as much as it loves thieves and protector characters) because at least three more of those six stories could easily turn into series for me. I can't seem to help myself. I try to write standalone things and characters turn up that I wouldn't mind spending more story time with. Ah well. It does make the writing fun.

At any rate, if you'd like to see that original fun Pick Your

Genre book, and see what I did in those other genres with that opening line, WHO STEALS A DRAGON is available everywhere in eBook and Print editions.

If you'd like to learn more about my books and other series, or just see what's new with the Dragon Thief series, you can visit my store, KatSimonsBooks.com—there's also free short stories there twice a month at The Cafe and some fun merchandise available. You can also get updated news at my author website, katsimons.com, or subscribe to my author newsletter. Subscribers to the newsletter get regular, monthly updates direct to their inboxes, and new subscribers get two exclusive, free stories, one from my Cary Redmond urban fantasy romance series, and one from my Tiger Shifters paranormal romance series. I also have occasional cover reveals, excerpts, free reads, and store discounts for my newsletter people.

Alternatively, you can follow my author page at BookBub, Facebook, or your preferred book vendor's website. I spend some time (probably too much) on social media, mostly BlueSky as I write this, where I love connecting with readers. I love hearing from readers, period, so don't be shy about emailing me either!

Thanks again for reading THE DRAGON THIEF SERIES, SEASON ONE Omnibus! I really hope you enjoyed it.

Kat Simons
May 2025

Don't miss the latest Kat Simons
news, updates, and more!
New subscribers get two newsletter exclusive stories.

Join Now!
https://bit.ly/KatSimonsNewsletter

Books by Kat Simons

Dragon Thief Series

<u>Season One</u>

Dragon Thief

The Chicago Job

The Poisons Book Job

The Vault Job

The Femme Fatale Job

The Scavenger Job

<u>Season Two</u>

The Crown of Kingship Job

The Green Scroll Job

Stories from the Café

Pick Your Genre Collections

Who Steals a Dragon

Paranormal Romance

Seven Families: Wolf Series

Tiger Shifters Series

Romancing the Leopard: A Tiger Shifters-Cary Redmond Crossover Novel

Destiny Cats Series

Urban Fantasy

The Cary Redmond Series

Cary Redmond Short Stories and Collections

Demon Witch Series

Joan of Kerry Series

Friday's Curious Shop Series

Contemporary Fantasy

Haunts and Howls Collections

*Tombstone Wizard * The Unshattered Sword * Going Out of Business: Everything's for Sale * Anger Management * Demonic Dates * The Museum of Small Art's Everyman * Burning Inside a Stone Circle * Bored Questless * I Just Ate a Bug * Ting Ling * Sophie Saves the World * Black Water Hawthorns *To Dance in Fallow Fields at Midnight *

Contemporary Romances

Designed for You

Poinsettias and Possibilities

Mystery and Thriller

Galileo's Pendulum: A Ross and O'Neill Adventure

Percy James Mysteries

Movies May Murder

Cookies Can't Crime

Diamonds Do Damage

Replicas Risk Ruin

Vacation Deadly: An Action Adventure Thriller Collection

About the Author

Kat Simons earned her Ph.D. in animal behavior, working with animals as diverse as dolphins and deer. She brought her experience and knowledge of biology to her paranormal romance and urban fantasy fiction, where she delights in taking nature and turning it on its ear. She writes urban fantasy, contemporary fantasy, and paranormal romance in series which combine action adventure, the otherworldly, and a frequent dose of sexy romance.

The newest book in her bestselling romantic urban fantasy series about Protector Cary Redmond, The Trouble with Shifters and Fae Courts, sees a new direction for the intrepid Protector, her sexy leopard shifter mate, and the entire crew. Kat also launched a new novella length Paranormal Romance series that follows the adventures of a magical thief and the dragon shifter prince she just can't seem to shake—and really doesn't want to. The first season of the Dragon Thief series released throughout 2024. Season Two begins in 2025 with The Crown of Kingship Job.

For something a little different, Kat also publishes fantasy, science fiction, and the occasional hockey romance under the name Isabo Kelly (https://www.isabokelly.com).

After traveling the world, living in places like Hawaii, Germany, and Ireland, Kat now lives in New York City with her family and a library's worth of books.

For more on Kat and her future books

Website: https://www.katsimons.com/
Newsletter: https://bit.ly/KatSimonsNewsletter

KatSimonsBooks
https://www.katsimonsbooks.com
https://www.TheCafeatKatSimonsBooks.com

Social Media
Facebook Page: https://www.facebook.com/KatSimonsAuthor
BookBub: https://www.bookbub.com/authors/kat-simons
Bluesky: https://bsky.app/profile/katsimons.bsky.social
Instagram: https://www.instagram.com/isabokelly/
Threads: https://www.threads.net/@isabokelly

KATSIMONSBOOKS

For all Kat's books and book related merchandise!
Check out the store for early releases, sales, and fun!

https://katsimonsbooks.com

www.ingramcontent.com/pod-product-compliance
Lightning Source LLC
Chambersburg PA
CBHW052014190726
48295CB00012BA/636